# Also by Robert French

The Diary of Nellie Mill

Josephine Littletree

Lynch

Sigurdsen

# Passion of Shadows

Robert French

**Passion of Shadows**

Copyright © 2016 Robert L. French

First Edition

ISBN 978-0-9952671-0-7
ISBN 978-0-9952671-2-1 (KDP MOBI)
ISBN 978-0-9952671-1-4 (EPUB)

Cover design by Caligraphics.net

Formatting by Polgarus Studio

Schloss Friedrichstein, East Prussia
Wikimedia Commons (CC-PD-Mark) (PD Old) (PD-1996)

Wikimedia Commons, File: Flag of Prussia (1466-1772) Lob.svg
Copyright © 2014 Vladimir Lobachev
(CC BY-SA 3.0) unmodified

Questions, comments, contact: afterwords@shaw.ca

# Paris 1940

In 1940 I was in love with four women. One wanted to kill me. She was a little crazy. But most of Europe had gone crazy. It was the time of the Phony War. In September 1939, the Wehrmacht had done quick business in Poland, the Russians coming in later as prearranged to carve up the country with the Germans. The British and French declared war on Germany and sent armies to the German border but nothing happened that fall or winter.

I was a foreign correspondent, had been in London for two years working for a news agency. In February 1940, I was transferred to our Paris bureau to be closer to the front. I cabled dispatches to head office in New York, stories from the front lines and press releases. Bored French soldiers wanted to go home. They griped about the weather. There were rumors about sagging morale because of low pay and anti-British feeling being fed by both communist and pro-Nazi propaganda. Nobody took the rumors seriously.

In March Harry Dunn, chief of the Paris bureau, told me Julia Fusco had arrived and New York wanted a story. I had heard of her. Classical violinist from the Midwest, she had been a child prodigy. Concert appearance in Carnegie Hall when she was fifteen, a recital there a year later. Toscanini in the audience. She had recorded with Columbia Records, appeared in London and toured the Continent and Australia. In her early twenties, she was headed for a great career. Why would she put herself in the middle of a war?

I phoned the major hotels. She was staying at the Hotel Regina, at the Place des Pyramides on the Rue de Rivoli, across from the Tuileries Gardens.

I told the desk clerk I wanted to speak with Miss Fusco. He called her room and I waited and was finally put through. A middle-aged voice with the hauteur of a bag lady wearing a tiara came on the line. She announced she was Julia Fusco's mother. And who was I? I told her and why I was calling.

"Julia can see you Wednesday afternoon for a few minutes. Submit your questions in advance and leave them at the desk in the lobby by Tuesday evening. Be here at four, Mr.—. What was your name?"

"Jim Brian. Why in advance?"

"You want the interview?"

"Asking, that's all."

I shook my head. A stage mother. I clenched my jaws, thanked her and hung up. I went back to my desk and typed out several questions, slipped the sheet into a manila envelope and wrote Julia's name and room number on it. It was Monday morning. Using the company car, Harry's old Delage saloon, I drove over to the hotel. The Hotel Regina had the usual Rue de Rivoli arcade, a Second Empire façade, including balconies, and an Empire domed roof. A statue of Joan of Arc on horseback stood in the square in front. I walked under the arcade and pushed the revolving doors of carved oak and mirrors. Inside it was Art Nouveau, with lots of smoothly rounded arches and flowing lines and enormous chandeliers. I crossed the black and white marble floor and handed the clerk the envelope.

On Wednesday I was back at four. The clerk phoned the room. I took the elevator up and tapped on the door. It opened and I met the stare of pebble-gray eyes above thin lips and a nose as sharp as a hatchet blade, a notch in the bridge. Tight coils of dark hair wound around a small head. Julia Fusco's mother was holding the sheet of paper with my questions. Handing it to me, she opened the door wider and jerked her head sideways. Her voice jabbed into my ear as I passed her.

"You can ask the ones I've put a check mark beside. Get fancy, you're out on your ear, mister."

She shut the door and I followed her through what looked like a small suite. The wallpaper and drapes were printed with designs of undulating lines of sinuous stems and luxuriant lilies. The white oak chairs had oval-shaped backs and crimson cushions. Antique vases perched on willowy-legged tables. In a sitting room with a half-moon window arch overlooking a courtyard, a woman about twenty-two sat on a divan upholstered in silk brocade. She wore a white peasant blouse, its puffy sleeves gathered at the wrist, black slacks and black shoes with silver buckles. Her straight black hair fell in a lustrous sweep to her shoulders and bangs covered the upper half of her forehead. The bangs made her look younger and her dark eyes were slyly playful. Her skin was as smooth as flawless white marble, her nose and lips chiseled by a classical sculptor in his dreams. Mrs. Fusco sat beside her and pointed to the divan opposite.

"Sit over there and let's get started. My daughter's time is valuable."

I looked at the sheet of questions. I had deliberately mixed innocuous questions with the serious ones. I wanted to distract Mrs. Fusco. She had put check marks beside only the innocuous ones. I looked at Julia Fusco. Something lurked in those eyes. I asked the first permitted question.

"What do you think of Paris?"

"It's nice."

Her voice sounded young, a little cheeky and with a touch of the flirt. Her mother waited. She glanced at Julia. I continued.

"Are you looking forward to the concerts?"

"Yes."

"How much time do you spend practicing?"

"Lots."

Her mother glared at her and pounded the seat cushion with a balled fist.

"This is ridiculous."

"I'm answering, Mother."

"Don't be impertinent. You know what I mean."

She stared at me.

"Ask what you want but don't get cute."

"This is a first for me. I don't know an arpeggio from an appoggiatura."

Julia laughed. Her laugh was soft, a giggle in it.

"You know those terms."

"That means nothing. I'm a musical ignoramus."

"What do you want to know?"

That got us nicely to the point.

"You're among the finest violinists in the world, certainly the best woman. You can only get better. People with far more musical insight than I have say that. Can you tell me why you've come here at this time? Fighting could break out at any moment. After what the Germans did in Poland, there's no guarantee the blitzkrieg won't work here."

"We've got nothing to be afraid of. We're neutrals."

The next part was tricky. Why had Mrs. Fusco been so antagonistic from the beginning? She should have been glad to have Julia interviewed for the folks back home. Coming to Europe was such a dumb move. Was it political?

"We're Americans, of course, but most of us can trace our lineage back here. Are you Italian?"

"Italian and Bohemian."

"You're part Czech?"

"Bohemian," her mother snapped.

"Where are you appearing?"

"Julia's been invited to play with Mengelberg at the Concertgebouw in Amsterdam in October. I guess you know where that is."

"Neutral Holland. Anywhere else?"

"Wherever we like. Scandinavia, Spain, Italy, Germany."

Julia glanced sideways at her mother before smiling at me. She knew I was not immune.

"I won't be in danger. Artists aren't military targets."

"I wasn't thinking of a stray bullet catching your Stradivarius."

She grinned, her teeth biting her lower lip.

"I play a Guarnerius. It was a gift from Lady Ravensdale. When I first played in London. In 1934. I had borrowed it for a concert. I hated to give it back afterwards. When we attended a dinner party at her home, she presented it to me as a surprise."

I had found what I wanted. Lady Ravensdale's sister was married to the leader of the British Union of Fascists. When I got back to the office I cabled John Grafton of our London bureau. He told me he heard that Lady

Ravensdale paid an English firm £10,000 for a Guarneri del Gesù. That could earn you a lot of gratitude. None of this got into my story. New York wouldn't want controversial suppositions about the political leanings of a concert violinist. I admit I thought later of using as a title: Julia Fusco Set to Conquer the Continent. Rejecting it was a lame way of letting the real story go. I asked Julia standard questions about concert life and trials and where she thought her career was headed. That seemed to satisfy her and her mother.

Thirty minutes of this and Mrs. Fusco stared at her wristwatch and put on a surprise act.

"You'll have to go. I've been too generous with my daughter's time."

I slipped my pencil, always a 2B for easy reading of my scrambled notes, into the coil binding of my notebook. I put the notebook into my inside jacket pocket and stood up. Julia got up and held out her hand. It looked strong, the fingers long and slender.

"Maybe we'll see you again, Mr. Brian."

"I look forward to it," I said and shook her hand.

Mrs. Fusco popped up and hurried over.

"Come, Julia, you've got to practice."

"When I'm ready."

"What did you say?"

"You heard me."

"You don't talk that way to me."

Mrs. Fusco's body stiffened. Swinging her arm, shoulder behind it, she slapped the side of Julia's face, a smack like the crack of a bullwhip. It left the imprint of a hand as red as a birthmark. Julia didn't flinch.

"You listen when I speak."

"All my life."

Mrs. Fusco's hand jerked.

"I wouldn't, Mother. I might hurt my hand slapping you. Then how could I play? How would we travel and convince everyone back home we're having so much fun?"

Julia smiled at me.

"Goodbye, Mr. Brian. It was nice meeting you."

"I'll let myself out."

I never thought I would see her again.

A week later I came in to relieve Harry and he told me a woman had phoned and asked for me.

"Said her name was Julia. Wants another interview, I guess. She gave me her number. Here."

He winked. I went over to his desk and he handed me a slip of notepaper. Underneath the phone number, "Tuesday morning, from 10 to 12." I spent an hour, feet up on my desk, debating about whether to call her, all the time knowing I would. On Tuesday morning I called at ten. It turned out to be the number of a beauty salon. In halting French I asked for Julia. The receptionist spoke as if her hair was full of frizzy curls tied with bows. I had second thoughts. They made a plaintive chorus.

*"Mademoiselle Fusco? Attendez, s'il vous plaît."*

Sounding like a teenager, Julia came on the line.

"I get my hair done every week. It's about the only time I can get away from my mother. I have a couple of hours. Want to go somewhere?"

"What about your hair?"

"A quick rinse and I'm done."

"All right, give me the address. Be there as soon as I can."

"I'll be outside. They shouldn't see."

"Suppose they peek?"

"They won't. They're French."

"They're women."

"Who cares, anyway?"

"Your mother."

"Hurry."

As I drove up to the salon I saw her standing outside in a pearl gray overcoat with the collar up. She was wearing a beret and gloves, both woolen and navy blue. It was early April and still cold. Her breath rose in plumes that vanished into the ice blue sky. I pulled up beside her and she swung in, bringing the chilly air with her, and a faraway hint of floral perfume.

"Brrrr. Don't you have a heater?"

"It's on. Standard equipment or added later. I'll have you know you're sitting in a 1930 Delage D8 N, for Normale. Let's be thankful it's not an Abnormale."

"Corny. Where'll we go?"

"I don't know Paris that well."

"You're a help. I don't either. Let's look for a bistro. I've always wanted to have a glass of wine in one. Hurry, we haven't much time."

I drove to Montparnasse and found a bistro. The proprietor was fat and bald. His wife was skinny and pale. Both wore smeared aprons. The customers were few and sullen. So much for atmosphere. Harry had told me the best time to be in Paris was the Twenties, before the Depression came along and killed the good times. We sat at a rickety table and sipped red wine from small goblets. Julia still wore her coat, beret and gloves. Some of the patrons stared at her gloved hand holding a wineglass. When they heard her young-sounding American voice they nodded at each other.

"I read somewhere that at any moment wherever you are is the absolute center of the world. So right now it's where I'm sitting on this chair on the Rue de la Something in Paris in April 1940."

She looked at her glass.

"I'm not drunk." A sip.

"If that's so, everything is related to the way I see it. It's all me. And it's always changing. By the way, I have beautiful breasts."

She drained her glass.

"So, Mr. Jim Brine, where are we going next Tuesday?"

"Nowhere, if your mother finds out I've gotten you drunk."

"I sober up quick."

"Hope it's as quick as you get pie-eyed. A walk would help."

I stood up and she tried, almost tipping over the table. I pulled her up and put her arm through mine. I got her to the street. Ten minutes holding onto me as we promenaded and she was better. I drove back to the salon. Her voice sounded stronger.

"I'll go in and call a taxi."

"Too late for that. They'll be suspicious. I'll drop you off at your hotel. You're mother in?"

"She sure is. Waiting for me."

"Can we chance the lobby?"

"The doorman will help me. Call me at the salon next week and bring a jar of peanut butter. I miss it. My mother says it's low class. She won't get me any."

"You're probably the only person who ever came to Paris looking for peanut butter. If I can find any I'll bring it."

"Thanks loads."

Half a block from the hotel I pulled over to the curb. She was humming a classical tune and her gloved hands were beating time to it.

"You've got a problem, Julia, and the problem has fangs."

"Don't talk about her that way. She's my mother."

"Is she ever. I can't play games for a couple of hours every Tuesday morning. I've got to attend press conferences and go out of town regularly. Find yourself somebody your mother would approve of. Somebody with a title and a hyphenated name. Or some rich American. You're talented and beautiful. Get yourself somebody who can afford you and can put up with your mother."

Mouth open, she leaned towards me, wine on her breath, whispers of perfume from her bare neck. She ruined everything by pulling at her beret.

"You'll do for now. See you next Tuesday, and don't forget the peanut butter."

That afternoon I asked Harry where I could get some peanut butter. He shook his head.

"The only peanuts in this city would be at the zoo, for the monkeys."

I bought a jar of chestnut spread, popular in France. On Tuesday morning I phoned the salon and the perky receptionist answered.

*"Je suis désolé. Elle est très occupée. Sa mère est ici. Vous-voulez parler avec elle plus tard? Non? Très bien. Au revoir."*

Impossible woman, impossible mother. I had called to cancel our meeting, anyway. Early that morning, April 9, the Germans had invaded Denmark and Norway. The Danes were overwhelmed and their government surrendered that day. The Norwegians continued to fight on in piecemeal actions until

June. On Wednesday I left for the front. The feeling was Scandinavia was a sideshow. The main battle here would be different. I got back to the office late Monday. Harry said there had been calls. He had told her I hadn't returned from the front. The following Monday morning I was typing at my desk and the phone rang and I answered.

"Sorry about last time. She insisted on coming. What could I do? I don't want her getting suspicious. She won't bother any more."

"Why don't you bring her along? We could have a party."

"If that's your attitude—."

"That's my attitude." I hung up.

Don't believe anyone who tells you successful relationships are based on love. Most are social bondage, long or short-term, with rings and valentines. The real stuff is chemistry, surfaces from the subconscious dripping with hormones, the verboten and a touch of the old karma. It rages in your blood, a throbbing infection. Logic, reason, even sanity go. When it finally finishes with you, you are never the same. The lucky ones die from it, but they're in operas and novels. For the rest there's no way out.

Julia knew she had me. She called an hour later. Harry answered and said I wasn't in. More calls. I grabbed the receiver, waiting for her to speak.

"I want to see you tomorrow. I'll be outside at ten."

Same coat but this time pink knitted beret and gloves. Perfume stronger, musky instead of floral. Smiling, she was going to let me in on a big secret. She shifted around in the seat to look at me.

"Let's go to a hotel."

"There's one near here. Harry said it's not expensive. No questions asked. And clean too."

"Harry?"

"He's my boss, the bureau chief here. You talked with him."

"You told him about us?"

"No, when I got here a month and a half ago I asked him where one could take a shady lady."

"A prostitute? Did you?"

"Never got around to it. Been busy, and besides, it's not my style."

"Do you love me?"

"Every square inch."

"I don't mean that way."

"In any and every way."

"Be serious."

"It takes the fun out of things. In my business there's so much crap you have to laugh or get drunk. Drinking interferes with the job. I can't see the typewriter keys or hold a pencil."

The hotel was part of a row of adjoining buildings on a shabby street. Behind a curved counter in the tiny vestibule a beaded curtain covered the entrance to another room. I banged the bell on the counter. Through the curtain emerged a man chewing on a toothpick. He wore a pinstriped shirt and black vest. The sleeves were rolled up, vest unbuttoned. He hadn't shaved recently. I told him I wanted a room for two hours. He mumbled the price and I paid. He took a key off a wallboard behind the counter and slapped it down. Turning away he mentioned the room number, pointing up a narrow flight of stairs.

I led Julia up the dim stairway. Our room was opposite the second floor landing. I unlocked it and pushed open the door. The room was dark, the curtains closed. I reached around the door molding, found a switch and turned on the light. A ceiling bulb shed a murky forty watts over a washstand, a chair and a small bed with a grey coverlet. I stepped inside, smelled dirty sheets and the stink of unwashed flesh and made a mental note to ask Harry what he meant by "clean."

I turned to Julia, still on the landing.

"Are you coming in?"

"So this is where people go."

"People in a hurry."

"Does it have to be here?"

"No. But I paid. I'll open the curtains and window, get rid of the smell and we'll sit down. You take the chair. It looks safe. I'll chance the bed. I brought you something."

She stepped into the room as if it might be contagious. I pushed aside the dusty curtains, unfastened the window latch and pulled up the window. Cold air rushed in and into the hallway, taking away some of the stench. After examining the chair, Julia let herself down onto it. I lowered the window a few inches, cutting down the draft, and shut the door. I took a jar out of my coat pocket and handed it to her. She turned it over in her hand.

"What's this stuff?"

"Peanut butter isn't available here. That's chestnut spread. Confiture de marrons. It's chestnuts, sugar and vanilla. The French like it."

"I don't want it."

"We're in France. Try something new."

"I wanted peanut butter. My mother could've gotten me this."

Holding the jar in her lap, she looked around the room.

"I didn't think it would be so low. I expected something more—."

"Romantic?"

She shrugged.

"You have to pay for romance. The gooey kind. Candlelight dinners, soft violins, expensive suite in a posh hotel, clean bed linen, room service. Everything discreet."

"That's corny."

"You wanted us to collapse in a frenzied embrace onto the wild flowers in an alpine meadow and make mad passionate love."

She blushed.

"No."

"You did. In April the grass is wet, the ground cold and sensible flowers are waiting for warmer weather."

"So we're stuck with this."

"You didn't give me enough notice for something a bit swanky."

I sat on the bed. The mattress, if there was one, was thin. I had fleeting thoughts of bedbugs. Not for a tryst.

"You've got a coat, I've got one. The floor is probably cleaner than the bed. Coats for a mat and body heat for the rest. It's romantic in a way."

"It's cold in here."

"Make up your mind, Cinderella. We're running out of time."

"All right."

She stood up, put the jar on the chair and pulled off her gloves. I got up and went to her. We embraced and kissed as if we knew this was going to happen before we ever met. Her lips were soft and slightly parted. I felt her breath, warm and rushed. I have a theory of kissing, based on pressure, from softer to harder: ignorant, innocent, practiced, seductive, routine, drunken, suicidal, homicidal. Hers was ignorant and mine had a touch of the seductive.

I unbuttoned her coat and laid it on the bed. I took off mine and my jacket, laid them on the floor, spreading her coat on top. I looked at her. She had kicked off her shoes and was standing shivering in a cotton blouse and skirt, her arms wrapped around herself. I brought her to the coats and we sank to the floor. I laid her flat, lifted her skirt and slipped off her underpants. I removed my shoes and pants and lay beside her. Arms around each other we nuzzled and kissed, slowly at first, before the kisses blurred and lost track of each other.

"This may not be a true classic but it's in the repertoire."

"Do you love me?"

"Thought I answered that."

"Do you?"

"Most emphatically."

"Yes?"

"Yes."

"I feel happy."

"I haven't done anything yet."

"That doesn't matter."

"You're easily satisfied."

"I'm an artist."

"I don't know what you mean but for the record I'd better finish up."

What with my being out of practice and the cold lumps of clothing under us, I was too quick. It was as much prestige as pleasure. But I was careful and she felt hardly any pain. There was a little blood. Afterwards I shivered with cold. We dressed without talking and I helped her put on her coat. We went downstairs and I tossed the key onto the counter. In the car she broke the silence.

"What if I get pregnant?"

"You'll have to marry your mother."

"What a thing to say. How much time do we have?"

"Fifteen minutes."

"I have a recital coming up the week after next. So I won't be able to see you next Tuesday."

She cleared her throat.

"I practice ten hours a day."

"You told me that in the serious part of the interview. I'll probably be out of town, anyway."

I could feel her staring at me as I drove. I wasn't being romantic. I wasn't upset at not seeing her for two weeks. With a woman of such talent and beauty you're lucky if what you have between you will last for a while. And with a mother like hers it would be a short while. I parked a block away from the salon. We kissed in a hurry and said goodbye. Later I remembered we had left the jar of chestnut spread at the hotel.

On Thursday of that week I left Paris for the front. Now the rumors were all about war. The British and French were waiting. The initiative was with the Germans. Informed opinion said they would attack through Belgium, as they had in 1914. The best Allied troops were massed along the French-Belgian border but there was no coordinated defense plan because the Belgians thought that it would compromise their neutrality. It was the same with the Dutch. Small-scale thinking was rife except among the Germans. Hadn't the Poles grabbed part of Czechoslovakia before their turn came to be overrun? Being a cynic was easy in Europe.

I returned to Paris the following Wednesday. As I climbed the flight of stairs to our office I could hear the phone. I knew it was Julia. I went in and Harry made a face.

"She's been calling. Tying up the line."

"Sorry, Harry. I'll deal with her."

The phone rang. I picked up the receiver and waited. She made me wait. It had become part of the relationship.

"Why haven't you called?"

"You said you had a recital and had to practice."

"You could have phoned."

"Where?"

"The salon. They would have relayed a message."

"You didn't tell me that. I can't read your mind. What about your mother? Suppose she finds out?"

"There are ways."

"Listen, Julia. There's going to be a battle. I have to cover it. I don't have time for your games."

"You said you loved me."

"Yes. I'm beginning to regret it."

"You saying you don't?"

"No. Let's meet next Tuesday and talk this whole thing out."

"All right. I've got to go and practice now."

I hung up and looked at Harry.

"Good thing I use my landlady's phone. Under no conceivable circumstances, Harry, do you give her that number or tell her where I live."

I almost managed to forget her in the next few days. Between press briefings, checking out rumors and filing dispatches time passed quickly. Paris appeared unreal, as if suspending its breath, waiting for the moment. The parks and broad avenues were quieter. Protected by sandbags, the grand public buildings and cathedrals looked grim.

On Tuesday she was standing in front of the salon. Gone were the beret and gloves. It was early May, the weather milder. She was wearing a belted gray jacket and matching slacks. Looking very young, she became more beautiful each time I saw her. Without makeup her skin glowed in the warm light, her features with an imperious innocence her own. She swung open the door and got in, wriggling her backside into the seat, her territory now. She grinned.

"I was thinking about you yesterday."

"Weren't you practicing?"

"In between."

"What was in between? The practicing or the thinking?"

"Never mind. Where are we going?

"Where we can talk."

"We haven't seen each other in two weeks. Don't you want to do anything else?"

"What, for instance?"

"Oh well, if you're not interested."

"You know I am. Don't try to sidetrack me. For one thing, you shouldn't keep calling me at the office. We need the line open. Fighting could break out at any time."

"Where then? Where you live?"

"I live in a pension, in one room with a hotplate, bed and a washstand. There's only one phone and it's for everybody, for important calls."

"I'm not important?"

"I didn't mean that."

"If that's the way you want it, let me out."

"Don't be silly."

"Let me out."

She opened the door. I swung over to the curb, shifted into neutral and pulled on the parking brake. She was halfway out of the car. I leaned over and pulled her back in. She twisted in my arms. Then we were kissing, sprawled across the seat. She was biting my face. Down came her slacks and panties. I undid my belt buckle, unzipped my pants. I was inside her before I knew. That kind of cooperation you only get from Mother Nature.

The seat was plush and wide but the steering wheel was large, the gearshift lever a prod and the dashboard too close. Afterwards a series of makeup kisses and I looked up and around. The car door was still open. We were on a side street, no vehicle or pedestrian traffic. I heard a steady rhythm. I had left the engine running. I lifted myself off her as slowly and carefully as I could. She groaned, awakened to a quick inventory and cried out as she touched one of her feet.

"I think I hurt my foot."

"Let's get dressed and we'll check."

I offered her a handkerchief. She tossed it out of the car afterwards. Her right shoe had apparently gotten caught under the dashboard in a frantic moment. She had twisted an ankle. She winced when I touched it.

"Think you can walk?"

"I don't know."

I went around to the passenger side and helped her out of the car. I held onto her as she tried a few steps. They were more like hops. She grimaced.

"It hurts. What am I going to tell her?"

"How about you twisted it admiring yourself in the full-length mirror in the salon?"

"There isn't one."

"Any mirror will do."

Embracing me, she put her cheek against mine. I felt her breath on my ear as she spoke.

"Do you love me?"

"God help me, I do. But I've got to cover a war."

"That sounds like a really corny line in a movie."

"It probably is."

She pulled her head back and looked into my eyes.

"I've got my career."

"So have I."

"You're a reporter."

"Journalist. But you're right. Journalists. Correspondents. Reporters. Small men who write about big events. We're kept on a leash. It's called a paycheck."

I kissed her cheeks and lips and she closed her eyes and I kissed each eyelid softly.

"What do you want, Julia?"

"You to love me."

"And to drive me crazy."

"That's all." She laughed.

We concocted an excuse. She tripped on the edge of the curb getting into the taxi. The hotel doorman wouldn't say anything about my car or me. I drove to the hotel and helped her out of the car and the doorman took over. As he led her away she turned and smiled at me.

"Call."

My landlady hammered on my door at six o'clock that Friday morning, May 10.

"*Le téléphone, Monsieur Brian.*"

I staggered downstairs to the phone in the hallway and picked up the receiver. It was Harry.

"It's started."

I took a taxi in the early dawn to the office. I climbed the stairs two at a time. Harry was on the phone, direct to New York. We didn't bother with cables when the news was this important. A cigar was burning in the bronze ashtray on his desk. Smoke rose into the fan of light from the silver-colored cowl of the desk lamp. Around the ashtray were sheets of paper with writing scribbled on them. Harry was leaning back in his swivel chair and reading from a sheet as he talked, glasses sitting at the tip of his nose.

"German assault along the whole line early this morning, before first light. Heaviest in the north. Reports of paratroop landings and air raids in Holland and Belgium. Bombers and dive-bombers. Air transports carrying troops. Preparation for attack by ground forces. Looks like a repeat of 1914. No statement from the French government so far. Or British Embassy. Give you more as soon as I get it from up north."

He hung up.

"I'll stay by the phone. You cover military briefings, press conferences. If there's a chance, take the car, get to the front. The tank is full."

The phone rang. He picked up the receiver, frowned and handed it to me.

"Get rid of her. We need this line."

"Hi. Can we meet?"

"I can't now. The shooting has started."

"When, then?"

"It's not Tuesday. Why do you want to see me?"

"Do I need a reason? Phone me at the salon tomorrow at ten."

"I'll try."

The big news that day was the best of the Allied forces, the British Expeditionary Force and French First, Seventh and Ninth Armies were moving into Belgium. The Allied plan was to meet the German threat head-on. The next morning I picked up Julia. I drove to the Bois de Boulogne. The big park was almost empty. As we walked along a path lined with hornbeam and horse chestnut, two gendarmes stopped us and asked to see our papers. They were looking for spies and fifth columnists. We ended up at a lake and sat on the nearby grass. We hadn't touched yet. I tore some grass and looked at her.

"You have to go back to the States. The Germans could win this."

"Would that be so bad?"

"You'd live with the Nazis?"

"They wouldn't do anything to us."

"That's not the point. They've started a war."

"Do you think it's all their fault?"

"Where have you been for the last few years, Julia? SS. Gestapo. Concentration camps. Are you going to play for Nazis as they wash the guilt off their hands between bloodfests?"

"My mother wants us to stay."

"Do your own thinking. Don't let her tell you what to do. Thousands are desperate to get out of Europe. You're an American, you don't have to stay."

"She's sacrificed everything for me. I wouldn't know what to do without her."

"You can't let her ruin your life because she's your mother."

"How ruin my life?"

"Play for Nazis and their sympathizers and who's going to want to listen to you? In the States or anywhere else? It's more than music. It's right."

"Why can't I do what I want? I'm not hurting anybody."

"How can you have a career here? Musical life in Europe is irrelevant except to opportunists. Some day you're going to be asked why you came and why you stayed. What are you going to say, you didn't understand, you were naïve?"

"You said the Germans might win the war. So what have I got to worry about?"

"If you're a Nazi, nothing. They might win short-term but my guess is long- term that gang of cutthroats is going to self-destruct."

She sighed.

"Why can't it be different? All I want to do is to play my violin."

She moved closer and leaned her head against my shoulder. I slipped my arm around her waist. The first touch after talking is always its own resolution. Arguments aren't physical. Sometimes they seem to be. A touch of the physical reassures, or at least that's the theory. The truth is somewhere in the touching. It can be a bribe.

"You'll do your reporting. I'll give concerts and recitals. You'll write and I'll practice. In between we'll meet."

"It's not a movie. There's going to be severe rationing, travel restrictions, complete blackouts, air raids. We're foreign nationals. Under suspicion."

"Not me. I'm an artist. And I'm beautiful. You said it."

"Yes, I did. As if you needed my opinion."

"If I go back, we won't be able to see each other."

"You'll have your mother."

She punched the side of my face. It was more of a knuckle rub. No trespassing. They were kin in more than skin.

"Think of your hands."

"I don't care."

"Like hell."

Another punch, harder.

"See?"

She pulled away from me.

"What time is it?"

I looked at my watch.

"Almost twelve."

"I've got to get back. When will I see you again?"

"I don't know. I'm a reporter, remember? And not only at your convenience. I should be cabling dispatches."

I got to my feet and held out my hand. She took it, pulled herself up and brushed off her slacks. Elms along the far shore of the lake were upside down reflections in the water. A squadron of ducks paddled by, chesting the silky calm, branches wavering among the ripples. Blobs and elastic lines curling and flexing reassembled into a row of dark sentinels etched on glass, illusion of an illusion. We held hands as we left the park. We were strolling through a moment belonging only to us. Julia squeezed my hand.

"We didn't make love."

"Are you sorry?"

"No. We must be in love."

"How do you figure that?"

She frowned.

"Being together is enough for people in love. The other's fine. But it's not absolutely everything. Maybe not even the most important part. For some people."

"You lost me at the last button."

"That doesn't matter. I understand me."

"A great consolation."

"Go ahead and make fun of me, but we artists understand things others don't. Our feelings are deeper."

"About your art, sure. About anything else, no. Lay down your bow and fiddle and you're only another beautiful woman in Paris. With beautiful breasts too."

"Shut up. Would you love me more if I weren't an artist?"

"Loving you wouldn't be easy under any circumstances, but with your talent and looks it's almost impossible."

"Where does that leave us?'

"Where we started. Nowhere."

"I feel miserable."

"So do I."

"Honest?"

"Yeah."

"That makes me feel better."

"What?"

"You wouldn't want me to be too depressed, would you? It would affect my playing. A certain amount and I'm a better player. More and I lose my nervous edge."

"Is that why I'm around? So you can crank up your nervous energy?"

We stopped walking and faced each other, still holding hands. Two men with white mustaches and dressed in berets and vested suits were making their way with canes along the path. They smiled and nodded at us. They looked at each other and winked.

"*L'amour.*"

"*C'est tout.*"

We started walking again. I wanted, what? I didn't know except to be with her, without that mother of hers always in the background. But I was too late by many years. Julia would always be her mother's daughter. What was happening between us would play itself out in a way I couldn't foresee. And I didn't want to know. With careful eyes Julia was guessing my thoughts.

"What are you thinking about?"

"Us and the war."

"Is that all? Oh, I forgot the time."

We hurried to the car. I dropped her off at the hotel and went to the office. Harry's ashtray was full. He was beginning to sound hoarse.

In the next few weeks events at the front tumbled chaotically over one another. Rotterdam was bombed on the 14th, the Dutch surrendered the next day, and by the 17th the Germans were in Antwerp and Brussels. The invasion of the Low Countries turned out to be a ruse. The main German attack was to the south, through the Ardennes, a forest on the French-German-Belgian border. Seven panzer divisions, strung out along four narrow routes through it, snaked their way among the trees. They struck on the 13th and in two days fought their way across the Meuse north of Sedan and burst out into the open country beyond. Subjected to carpet-bombing and dive-bombing the reservist French force in the area couldn't hold them. The bridgehead widened rapidly and by the 20th leading elements of the panzers had reached the Channel, cutting off the Allied forces to the north. The obvious tactic was to hit the flanks of the fast-moving panzers from north and south. But the French chose to dismiss the commander-in-chief, who had ordered such a counteroffensive. His replacement did nothing for days. The Belgians surrendered on the 28th without consulting their allies, leaving the BEF and the French with a dangerous gap in their lines. The Allied command structure began to unravel. Orders were delayed, coordination was poor. The British had decided by the 24th to head for the coast. That same day the panzers received the order to halt. Hitler was miffed they had disobeyed an earlier order to halt after the breakout. He thought the armored spearhead was advancing too fast and too far ahead of the support troops. Now *Der Führer* was showing the generals who was boss. It turned out to be one of his more disastrous interventions. It gave the Allies time to prepare defenses for an evacuation by sea at Dunkirk. Three days later the panzers were given the go-ahead but by then the French defenders could hold them off as British naval and civilian vessels continued the evacuation. Between May 26 and June 4, 338,000 troops were evacuated despite attacks by the Luftwaffe and German ground forces. By June 5, the defenders overrun, the massive formations of the Wehrmacht were turning south to destroy what remained of the French below the Somme.

As news got worse and the Germans closer there was disbelief in Paris, then fatalism and fear. The French cabinet moved to Tours, then Bordeaux, and on June 10 declared Paris an open city. Almost half of the population, more than one and a half million, fled south. Some of the press corps, including Harry, left. We decided he would cover the flight and I would stay. He arranged a ride with other correspondents. I went along for a day to see for myself. I strapped a bicycle to the rear bumper of their car. I saw refugees in cars, on bicycles and horse-drawn carts, all piled high with belongings. The line of traffic stretched back to the horizon, with grande dames in limousines, grandmothers in shawls, mothers holding infants, and children walking alongside the slow-moving caravan. Old men with unlit pipes in their mouths held slackened reins. Public notice boards along the way were covered with messages for friends and family that were following. Stukas dive-bombed and machine-gunned the close-packed column and everybody scrambled out of cars and off carts to take cover in roadside ditches and adjoining fields. Some were killed, many were wounded. There were cries of pain, screams of fear. Shattered vehicles and torn bodies were left beside the road. The bandaged and scared went on, the privileged to country houses and the others anywhere away from Germans.

That night I left and cycled back. I was the only one going north. The roads were quiet at night, many people sleeping in their cars or in the fields, grateful for a few hours relief from the Stukas. Some kept moving south, mostly pedestrians and cyclists. On the outskirts of Paris I hit a sharp stone and had to cycle in with one flat rim. The streets and wide boulevards were dark under the soft June night. Too tired after the trip back to go to my pension, I decided to stay at the office overnight after phoning in my story to New York. The next day the Germans came.

At noon on June 14 the German 9th Infantry Division entered Paris, followed hours later by the 18th and 28th Infantry Divisions. They were on their way south to fight what was left of the French forces. On June 16 I watched as the 30th Infantry Division marched past the Arc de Triomphe and down the Avenue Foch. Horse-drawn artillery, mounted troops and infantry in field-gray (*feldgrau*) uniforms paraded as a military band played marches. The avenue was otherwise empty. A member of the reviewing party, a staff officer, came over and I told him in German I was an American correspondent. The population that remained stayed indoors but they could hear loudspeakers announcing an 8 p.m. curfew and a complete blackout. Later the curfew was extended to 10 p.m. on weekdays and 11 on Saturdays, the last Metro trains running at 9:30 and 10:30 respectively. Machine gun posts were set up and radio stations seized. An armistice was signed on June 22. Paris was to be part of the German-occupied zone, roughly two-thirds of France, and a French government was established in the south at Vichy. The German army would run Paris. The office of the Commandant of Greater Paris was nominally at the corner of Rue du 4 septembre and the Place de l'Opera but he lived at and worked out of the Hotel Meurice, on the Rue de Rivoli. The population began to return. At cafés and restaurants Parisians and off-duty soldiers in uniform sat at adjacent tables. There was fraternization between some Frenchwomen and soldiers. Soldiers took pictures of the sights. I saw a few browsing in bookstalls on the Left Bank. Eventually thirty thousand security and administrative personnel lived in the city, commandeering five hundred hotels. There were soldiers' clubs and restaurants, cinemas and theaters and a recommended list of brothels.

Underneath was a different reality. You didn't have to look hard to know what defeat and the occupation meant.

In those final days before the armistice I had seen women weeping at the Tomb of the Unknown Soldier at the Arc de Triomphe. Passing German soldiers saluted but didn't stop. On the outskirts I saw how the French at first tried to defend the city. In village streets dead horses, cows and dogs lay among destroyed tanks and guns. As if to remind Parisians of their servitude, the German administration insisted on troops and military bands marching daily through the streets. And the Gestapo came with the occupation. Its headquarters were at 11 Rue de Saussaies. It proclaimed "Paris law." Plotting against the Reich was treasonable. Informers were recruited among waiters and concierges. At 93 Rue Lauriston were the headquarters of the French Gestapo. These French auxiliaries were mostly convicted criminals, some of them murderers, and as in Germany there was no lack of informers among the general public. This was the not-so-hidden Paris that the image of well-behaved off-duty soldiers could never dispel.

At her invitation I had tea with my landlady one evening. Mme. Journet lived at the rear of the three-story building, on the first floor. Her apartment was full of dark furniture with bulbous legs and lots of curves. Mme. Journet was a widow, her husband killed at Verdun in what used to be called before this one, the Great War. She was in her sixties, plump and with a round rosy face and fair hair and looked more English than French. I mentioned this and she told me her mother was English. We sat at her kitchen table, square and small, with a blue-and-white checked tablecloth. On it sat a teapot with a cozy, a creamer and sugar bowl, all of fine porcelain, and a tin of biscuits. I declined the offer of a biscuit or any cream or sugar in my tea. She took both, glanced at the tin but decided not to indulge. Something was puzzling her.

"Why are they so courteous, these Germans?"

"They've been told to be, and German soldiers obey."

"I have heard many bad things about them."

"If you're Jewish or believe in free speech, they're not so nice. You are or will be on a list. That list belongs to the Gestapo. They do not come as tourists."

"Some Germans I think are not like that."

"Enough are."

"The ones that are not are not so easy to hate. I am a Parisienne. Do you know what that means? Paris is my soul. I spit on these invaders. I want to hate them all. But I cannot."

What could I say to her? Half English and so French. It was patriotism. And something more. Outrage balked by humanity. That saved her. I couldn't have explained why.

As I was leaving she remembered.

*"Mon Dieu,* I forgot. A young lady telephoned this morning. Her name was Julia and you were to phone her. She said you would know."

"I would. Thank you, Mme. Journet."

I hadn't seen Julia in over a month. I hadn't had time to miss her. She had gotten lost among the defeats, debacles and dispatches. I phoned the salon from the pension the next morning, Tuesday. I didn't say anything about her calling me at the pension. It wouldn't have done any good. She obviously had pestered Harry until he had given her the number. She sounded fresh, oblivious to events.

"I was thinking about you. You didn't call."

"I've been busy covering things. Your pals are here, including the third-degree gang."

"Do we have to talk about that?"

"It's going to put a crimp in our clandestine meanderings. We've got another secret police."

"Leave her out of this. Don't you want to see me?"

"Of course. Self-inflicted punishment."

"Nothing else?"

"You have—."

"Shut up."

"And—."

"Shut up. I have an hour. Pick me up. In twenty minutes."

When I saw her waiting outside the salon everything jumped inside of me. It was like seeing her for the first time, without the guessing. She threw the car door open, dismissing it. With the sullen groan of rusted metal, it tore at its hinges. She entered headfirst. We kissed before she sat down, the kind of automatic stuff that happens before you know it. Her backside was sticking out of the car and I pulled her in without missing a kiss. Her face was flushed.

"Where can we go?"

"I'll find a place."

I found a side street a few blocks away, maybe the one we used before. There was a parked car. No pedestrians, no road traffic. We kissed as we undressed. Same confined space but we were getting used to it. Exigencies of the moment. Her jacket off, blouse buttons unfastened and brassiere undone, my mouth went to work. She squirmed and I got busier but nothing could make her forget her schedule.

"Hurry up. You're a pervert."

"Yeah, and I don't care what any clown of a psychiatrist thinks."

"Are you going to use up the whole hour slobbering over them?"

"Don't you like it?"

"I don't mind. But we haven't got time."

"All right. Lie back and we'll get to the main item on the program."

I wriggled and she wiggled and I was inside, that moment when destiny seems to call with the loudest voice in the universe, at least for lovers.

A loud tap on the driver's side window startled me and I turned my head and saw a man in a German officer's uniform and peaked cap. His right-hand collar patch was plain black, no insignia, and there were SS runes on the left-breast pocket of his tunic. On his left cuff "SD" was in a trapezium outlined in silver thread. That meant he was a member of the SS and its counterintelligence section, the SD, and was a Gestapo officer. His face was a mealy gray, his eyes the same color. Lines like gouges ran down either side of his cheeks to his chin, his lips identical rectangles and white as lard. He jerked his hand at me. I pushed myself up, tucked my shirt inside my pants and fumbled with the zipper, trying to hide Julia as she grabbed at her panties and slacks. I pushed the door open and stumbled out. A low-slung black Mercedes roadster was parked, engine running, on the other side of the street, a man at the wheel. We had been followed. The officer held out his hand but before he spoke, I did.

"I'm an American correspondent."

There was no reaction. It was like speaking to a turnip.

"I'm with my girlfriend. There was a wasp in the car. I was trying to get rid of it. That's why I parked here."

I made a waving motion at a threatening invisible wasp. He pursed his lips, two slugs slithering over each other. With the required sneer, he spoke English and French like a Nazi in a Hollywood B picture. Probably chewed barbed wire in his spare time.

"Your papers. *Les votres aussi, Mademoiselle.*"

He jerked his hand at Julia.

"My girlfriend is American too. My papers are in my jacket, on the seat of the car."

I reached in, took out my passport and handed it to him. Julia got out and came over and stood beside me and gave him hers. He looked them over, taking his time. He glanced at us occasionally, watching for signs of nervous collapse. Finally he nodded at Julia.

"You are staying in Paris, Miss—Mademoiselle Fusco?"

"For now. I'll be giving concerts and recitals in several cities in Europe."

"In Germany?"

"Yes."

There was a slight tremor in her voice, or was it pride? He handed Julia her passport, bowing slightly.

"*Trés bien. Enchanté.*"

He stared at me.

"This is your car?"

"It belongs to my boss. He's chief of our Paris bureau."

"I will see the papers."

I got the registration out of the glove compartment and handed it to him and again the slow perusal, making you wait. I wondered if they taught them that or whether the sadistic trimmings came from predisposition. When he decided it was time he looked at me. I got the specimen-under-the-microscope squint.

"Where were you going?"

"I was showing Miss Fusco the city. She's new here."

"You are aware petrol is rationed?"

"That's something my boss takes care of. I use the car on business. Otherwise I use the Metro. Or take a taxi."

"This is business?"

I smiled weakly. Deliberately. I thought of shrugging. That would have been too much.

"Miss Fusco and I are good friends. She's a musician. Enjoys beautiful things. I suggested showing her the sights because she would appreciate them. She won't be in Paris that long."

You know he knows what you're going to say and you say it anyway because he wants to hear you say it. It's his game and you have to play it and show him you will obey the rules. He despises weakness, tears, groveling. He inflicts physical and psychological pain, a doctor who tortures and kills his patients. Above all, he loves his game and how he plays it. No matter how innocent you are he must know you fear him. He must believe he can hurt you without touching you.

He handed me my passport and the vehicle registration. I kept my hand steady as I reached out and took them.

"Private transportation is to be used only when absolutely necessary. We must save petrol."

He nodded at Julia again before turning and walking to the Mercedes. With a low popping exhaust note, it raced down the street and we were alone. I reminded myself I was an American. Julia took a deep breath.

"What a creepy guy. I thought I was going to wet myself."

"They make a profession of being creepy. It goes with the uniform."

"I thought they wore black leather trench coats."

"They do in Germany. In the occupied territories they wear a uniform because some of them were mistakenly shot as suspicious-looking civilians by the army."

Julia suddenly looked scared. I put my arm around her shoulders.

"He won't come back. Besides, he likes you."

"I'm late. My mother will kill me."

"Give her a call. Tell her you were stopped by the Gestapo."

She gave me a dig in the ribs with her elbow.

"Hurry up, think of something."

"Say you fell asleep in the chair at the salon."

"That'll do. Kiss me."

Harry returned to Paris the next morning, coming straight to the office. He hadn't shaved in days and his suit was wrinkled. He had slept in it. After using the office basin to wash and shave, he told me what happened after I left.

"The Stukas kept coming back and strafing us. Everybody was hungry and thirsty. Every city we got to was already packed with refugees. Especially Tours and Bordeaux. They were bombed. Those fascist bastards in Spain wouldn't let refugees over the border. The Portuguese Embassy in Bordeaux took some, mostly rich Jews offering money. Larry knows a woman who lives outside Bordeaux. She's from Boston and she's rich. Married a title and lives in a chateau. They gave Larry, Phil and me a dinner and some good wine. They're out-and-out fascists but I couldn't argue with their wine. I managed to get a free line in Bordeaux and file a few dispatches. After the armistice we made our way back. I saw the bodies of peasant women in fields beside the road. They'd been strafed. Only a Kraut would do that."

He took a cigar out of the humidor on his desk, sniffed it and lit it before leaning back in his chair.

"Between the fascists at the top and the communists at the bottom, this country has fallen apart. When I came here in the Twenties Paris was different. I wanted to be a writer. I didn't know a soul. I went to Montparnasse and sat at a café and within hours I met painters and sculptors, writers, playwrights and poets. They came over and introduced themselves. In the next few months I met most of the big ones. Ernie, Scott, Jimmy Joyce, Picasso. I lived in an attic. There was no heat and rain dripped through the roof. There were rats and bedbugs. But I didn't care. There were the cafés and jazz clubs, lots of cheap wine and good company. Somebody would always stand you to a meal. The walls of the cafés were plastered with art that paid for a dinner. I met a woman, Colette. She was an artist's model. She was from

Lyons. Her family owned a hotel. We were together five years, had great times. One day she told me she was in love with a painter. She took off with him to Nice. By then it was the Depression and Paris had changed, lots of neon signs and movie theaters. Everybody I knew had gone and I needed a job if I wanted to stay. Albert Tickner was head of the bureau. I'd written him some stuff on life on the Left Bank. He hired me as his assistant and when he left in '33 he recommended me."

He took a few puffs and laughed.

"I'm at the chateau, listening to our hosts, Gladys and Jules. I'm pissed and pissed off. Her face is looking like a fat pear. His a horse with a pencil mustache. Their voices are coming at me out of a fog. Maréchal Pétain and Laval are the saviors of France, de Gaulle is an upstart, a nonentity, Churchill is a warmonger, Roosevelt is a fellow traveler. He wants to bring America into the war. We should all join in the fight against the Bolsheviks. They're to blame for everything. Threatening our Christian civilization. After that, I don't remember, except the fog got so I couldn't see through it. Was a blessing. Excellent vintages, though."

I filled Harry in on what had been happening in Paris. I told him about the Gestapo agent. I didn't mention Julia. When I brought up gas rationing, he grinned.

"I've been here since '24 and I've made a few friends, including guys who know how to get you what you need. Since the war started I've had no trouble getting gas and don't expect any."

He looked up at the faded cream ceiling, the color of an old manuscript.

"You know what I believe in? A good bottle of wine, an excellent cigar and the right woman. When the wine's sour, get another bottle and when the cigar tastes like hemp, reach for another. If a woman goes bad on you, that's another story. That's why you need the wine and cigars."

He took his eyes off the ceiling and looked at me.

"You like her, Jim?"

"Yeah, guess I do."

"I know how you feel."

Harry stubbed out the cigar in his ashtray, leaned back and put his feet on the desk. He closed his eyes and fell asleep. A rising column of smoke from the butt was blown into lazy wisps by the warm current of air drifting in from the half-open window behind him. Ten minutes later the phone rang. We were back in the war.

I next heard about Julia from reviews in Paris newspapers about a concert and a recital she had given at the Théâtre des Champs-Élysées, both great successes. As best I could translate the critics praised her beautiful tone, faultless intonation, admirably accomplished technique—octave leaps, double-stop scales—and defended her vibrato. It was somewhat prominent but not out of place in the romantic repertoire she played. The recital encores were showstoppers and performed with zing—my word. Apparently the audiences were thrilled. The accounts mentioned some of the more notable members, including senior representatives of the occupying forces, undoubtedly in dress uniform too. Reading between my translated lines, I got the idea the audiences were mostly German. The rest were probably sympathizers. Mrs. Fusco was getting her own way. Julia would be excited, and not too bothered about the Nazis among her fans. If she could please herself by pleasing her mother, she wasn't going to think about much else. I crumpled up the newspapers and tossed them into the office wastebasket.

That was in September. Paris had settled into the conqueror's rhythm. Daily military parades, lots of saluting at various headquarters, staff cars dropping off and picking up senior officers carrying briefcases, Wehrmacht personnel on leave, including women auxiliaries. Parisians adapted to the strict rationing of petrol. There were lots of bicycles, bicycle-taxis and battery-powered ones, and cars burning wood gas. There was always the Metro. I noticed that the parades were slowly drawing larger crowds as some became obvious in their sympathies. There was no shortage of smiles and amicable conversations between French and Germans at cafés and restaurants. That could be misleading. There were many like Mme. Journet, waiting for the day of revenge.

"I will live to see it," she said, her lips trembling, "when Paris will be free again."

Near the end of September Harry told me New York was transferring me to Berlin. I was shutting the office door. I hadn't taken off my coat. I left it on and sat on the edge of my desk.

"Bill Beckmann is getting the boot. You're being sent because you know some German. They're sending me our stringer in Marseilles. His wife types."

"Who's chief in Berlin?"

"Sophie Henser. I've never met her. Heard she knows her stuff. She's German, born in Berlin. Grew up in the States, came back a few years ago."

"When do I leave?"

"Soon as you get an entry visa. The authorities in Berlin have been notified you're the replacement."

A couple of days later I decided to take a last walk down the Champs-Élysées. It was an almost cloudless Sunday afternoon with a touch of summer lingering in the autumn air. Julia was sitting outside a café with her mother and two men. I walked faster but she saw me and called out my name. I wanted to keep going but I couldn't. I cursed myself for picking that avenue at that time. The three months since we had seen each other disappeared. I could try to forget her but I could never deny her. I went over, conscious of four pairs of eyes on me. Mrs. Fusco was wearing a hat that was nothing but a large pink bow. Her shaggy pink coat looked as if it were molting. That notched blade sniffed fiercely at me. I was daring to ruffle the feathers of a bad-tempered flamingo. One of the men was past middle age, bald, had a fleshy tanned face and wore a beige suit and shirt and a red tie. The other was much younger, blond, with pale eyes, wore a blue suit and the general expression of a fanatic dipped in the blood of the Führer. Julia introduced the older man as René de Castignac, a music critic, and the younger as Hans-Peter Moeller, press attaché at the German Embassy. She invited me to sit and called for the waiter to bring another chair, which a waiter brought as I was saying I had an appointment, but she insisted as I with more lame excuses sounded idiotic until finally deciding to give up and sit between her and her mother, who was glaring at her.

"Nice to see you again, Mr. Brian."

I smiled politely at Julia. I thought I could feel the hot breath of Mrs. Fusco on the back of my neck. I wondered if her teeth were sharp. Julia was happy, too happy. Was it success in Paris or champagne from the bottle nestled in a silver ice bucket in the middle of the table?

"You must have a drink, Mr. Brian."

"Thanks, but I have to leave shortly."

"You have to."

"All right."

"There, you see? That wasn't hard."

"Mother?"

Mrs. Fusco didn't answer.

"Mother?" Louder.

"Oh, have it your way."

"Monsieur de Castignac, Herr Moeller? You're not going to refuse me?"

Julia waved at a waiter and ordered another bottle of champagne. When he returned she put a hand over her glass.

*"Pour moi, non.* We shouldn't get drunk should we, Mr. Brian? Things happen when you're drunk. Pop and pour, garçon."

After filling the glasses, the waiter took the empty bottle out of the ice bucket, embedding its replacement with a quick twist. A nod and he was gone. Four of us imbibed, from sips to swallows. The champagne was dry and crisp. Julia looked across the table.

"You were saying, Monsieur de Castignac, before Mr. Brian joined us?"

De Castignac put down his glass. He spoke with aplomb in his mouth.

"I was saying, my dear, that you must add to your repertoire. Paganini, Bruch, Sibelius, Dvorak—each good in his own way. But you were meant to perform the best. I want to hear you play the Brahms, the Beethoven. And the Bach sonatas and partitas. Are they not the summit for solo violin? You deprive the musical world of a very great pleasure."

"Isn't Mendelssohn somewhere in there?" I said.

"Mendelssohn?"

It was the first word from Moeller since I had arrived and it sounded like a curse. Sneering he put down his glass, ready to perform as a defender of Aryan culture.

"You cannot be serious."

"He's not Bach, but who is?"

"Not of the first rank," de Castignac said. "Queen Victoria's favorite composer. Very facile. Like Rossini."

"Worse, a Jew, a cultural parasite," Moeller said. "Not to be mentioned in the same breath with our great German and Austrian composers."

"I thought he was melodious, not mal-odious," I said, draining my glass.

"Your cleverness is beside the point. But I am not surprised. America is a musical joke. Folk songs, dance bands, jungle music. The sublime magic of Wagner is beyond you."

I raised my glass.

"Distilled from an infinite complexity, Bach's music exalts the spirit. Wagner wrote for the tuba."

Julia laughed. Moeller's face stiffened. His eyes focused into the knowing stare of a predator. He grinned, the benign look of a lizard before seizing its prey.

"Julia introduced you as a friend. I did not recognize your name. I remember now. You work as a correspondent for an American news agency. As press attaché at the embassy, I know many correspondents in Paris. It is part of my job. I met your superior, Mr. Dunn. About three months ago the Gestapo sent me a report. An agent saw you parked on a street and he questioned you. He did not believe your story. But your papers were in order. There was a lady with you. What do the French say? *Cherchez la femme.* Otherwise you would have been interrogated further. Because the lady's name is not in the report, I assume the agent did not record it. You see, we Germans can be chivalrous about a woman's reputation."

"That agent should have taken her name," Mrs. Fusco said. "Obviously a tramp."

Sometimes you have to be grateful for the hopelessly stupid. Julia kicked me under the table.

Moeller's grin faded and he became one more swine shoving his snout into the Nazi bureaucratic trough. An embassy mouthpiece. A rubber stamp, like the ambassador. The Führer's boys. Guarantee your neutrality today, Stukas tomorrow. All the nonaggression you can handle. Peace offer wrapped around a grenade.

De Castignac cleared his throat.

"As I was saying, Julia, you are ready to perform the best. When shall we have the pleasure?"

Julia leaned forward and put her elbows on the table.

"I don't want to embarrass myself. Midwestern princess flat on her ass."

"Julia."

"What, Mom?"

"Watch your language."

Julia held out her glass, two fingers holding the stem.

"Fill it, Mr. Brian."

I hesitated. One escape was enough. But I didn't want to provoke her. She waved her glass. I stood up and pulled the chilled bottle out of the ice bucket and poured too quickly, so much of the wine would be froth. I returned the bottle to the bucket and when I glanced at her glass it was empty. She was looking at de Castignac.

"You know, Renny, I'm gonna agree with you. I'm prima donna of the violin, so why am I playing second-raters?"

I think she mispronounced his name deliberately. You never knew with Julia.

"I'm showing off, that's all. That I can do the tricky bits. Violinists like to show off. Public seems to like it."

De Castignac shook his head.

"You are not a technician. You have a romantic soul, one that yearns toward the profundities."

Julia cupped her face in her hands.

"I know."

"A virtuoso like you would be appreciated in my country," Moeller said. "The German soul is profound and ever-questing for its ideal home."

Reminding myself where I was being transferred, I kept quiet. Mrs. Fusco smiled at the press attaché.

"I've been telling Julia that's where she'd be most appreciated. That's where all the great music comes from and that's where you've got to go to hear it played the right way. And that's where she's going. It's her true destiny."

Julia put her hands together.

"For what we are about to receive, may we be truly grateful."

Mrs. Fusco scowled at her.

"Behave yourself."

"My self? What's that?"

"You listen to me. I taught you everything you know."

"You taught me everything I don't know."

Mrs. Fusco stood up, face engorged with indignant hauteur, as pink as her bow hat. Flamingo rampant.

"You're making a fool of yourself."

"It's my right, I'm an artist. They said so. Whatever their names. Why do I feel sick?"

Mrs. Fusco remembered the rest of us. She turned to de Castignac and Moeller.

"It's the wine. She's not like this."

Face twisted into a pink knot, she rounded on me.

"It's your fault. You've ruined my daughter."

Julia laughed, shaking her head.

"It was me, I wanted it."

"He shouldn't have listened."

"I made him."

Mrs. Fusco went to her and put a hand on her shoulder. She wrenched her shoulder away.

"Come, Julia. We're going to the hotel. You've got to practice. This'll pass."

Julia grinned at me and stood up.

"She takes good care of me."

Mrs. Fusco went to touch her but didn't.

"Why are you talking to him?"

Julia pulled the champagne bottle out of the ice bucket. She put a finger on the mouth and shook the bottle, took her finger away and flicked the contents in the general direction of the press attaché. He ducked but his face and suit caught enough to be dripping. Mrs. Fusco snatched the bottle from Julia, who smiled at Moeller.

"I wanted to see if there was any fizz left."

The press attaché got up and wiped his face with a handkerchief. Mrs. Fusco hurried to him.

"She's been under a terrible strain because of the concerts. She'd apologize but she's not feeling well."

"Artists don't waste time apologizing," Julia said. "Somebody will do it for them."

Moeller waved Mrs. Fusco away as he stared at Julia.

"I understand perfectly well that the artistic temperament needs release. I only wish to have had a bottle. We would see who would be the wetter. Might prove to be amusing."

I looked up at Julia and spoke in a low voice.

"Nazis will turn anything into a war. With sexual undertones, no less."

Julia smiled at me and I stood up, followed by de Castignac.

"Goodbye, Monsieur de Castignac, Herr Moeller. Mr. Brian. I hope we meet again. I'm ready, Mother."

She strolled away, almost strutting in her black jacket and slacks and white lacy blouse. Mrs. Fusco followed in her wake, hat and feathers flapping.

The next day I went to get my entry visa at the German Embassy. It was in the Hotel Beauharnais, on the Rue de Lille. It was an embassy in name only. Strictly speaking, there could be no ambassador because the French and Germans had signed an armistice, not a formal peace treaty. The head of the embassy could make all the ambassadorial and Foreign Office noises he wanted but the Wehrmacht, SS, SD and Gestapo ignored him. The embassy was a propaganda tool and promoted cultural relations between France and Germany. A number of writers and artists had gone south to Vichy but were beginning to return and meet in cafés and apartments. Some collaborated with the Germans, some went underground. Most settled into tacit accommodation, adhering to the principle that if everyone is guilty no one is. Most of this happened after I left Paris.

Like all the public buildings and the rest of the hotels the Germans had taken over, the embassy flew a swastika flag over the entrance. There were sentries outside. Inside the reception desk had been converted into an information center. I was directed to an office upstairs. The office was a converted hotel suite with a desk, some extra chairs and several filing cabinets. Ceiling-to-floor swastika flags were hung on either side of the wall behind the desk, with a picture of Hitler in between. The functionary behind the desk was a small man with round spectacles. He looked like a librarian. As he examined my passport he spoke in a flat voice.

"You wish to leave Paris."

"My wish would be to stay. Head office is transferring me."

"*Ja*. Why would one wish to leave Paris?"

In English I said, "As the hens in a factory farm would say, egg-xactly."

"I do not understand."

"My idiosyncratic sense of humor."

"*Ja*. American."

As if that explained everything. He stamped and signed the entry visa and handed my papers back. He took off his glasses. When they take off their glasses people with bad eyesight look vulnerable for a moment. He blinked a couple of times.

"I am enjoying myself here. There is so much to see."

"You have a camera."

He grinned and shook his head.

"I was a philosophy student at Jena University before I joined the Foreign Office."

That should explain everything too.

"We must think in European terms."

"Your leader is."

He looked uncomfortable.

"I mean culturally. We have much in common. We Europeans can learn from each other. I admire French art."

"What about National Socialist art?"

"The heroic is fine for the common man but not for connoisseurs. You are doubtless familiar with what in the Soviet Union is called social realism. Those idealized profiles of workers and peasants. It is propaganda poster art, nothing more. Simple outlines, simple colors. For the German masses somewhat better. Classical nudes, medieval knights and *Mädchen*. But my eyes take delight in Impressionism, Post-Impressionism and Expressionism."

He stood up and held out his hand.

"My name is Karl Thielmann. Have a pleasant trip."

On my way back to the office I drove through the center of Paris, noticing how many direction posts were in German. There weren't many cars or pedestrians and on the Left Bank a lot of shops were closed. Most of the people I saw were riding bicycles or in bicycle-taxis. Paris had gone quiet. At the office that night I said goodbye to Harry and went to my pension to pack. Early the next morning I said farewell to Mme. Journet. She embraced me, kissing me on both cheeks.

"Come back when Paris is Paris again."

I was pedaled in a bicycle-taxi to the Gare du Nord. I bought a ticket and carried my valises to the waiting train. It was full of soldiers returning from leave. They told stories of prostitutes and of bargains in stores. The Reichsmark had been set artificially high, so Paris was cheap for military personnel. Local merchants got even by setting high prices. Some soldiers in the day coach passed around bottles of wine and others slept. I got stares because of my civilian clothes. "American press" I said finally to some soldiers who were sitting opposite. They didn't answer but after a while there weren't any more stares.

As the train pulled out of Paris I thought of Julia. When, if ever, would I see her again? The grand exit she made on Sunday, was it out of my life too? Even without her mother she was high-strung, unpredictable. Mrs. Fusco had curbed but not helped her understand herself. Nervous high spirits and petulance made her dependent on her mother's control. And that suited Mrs. Fusco, who had become a lifelong habit her daughter couldn't break.

The train traveled through northeastern France, stopping first at Rheims, in the champagne country. Rheims had been shelled and much of it destroyed during the 1914-18 war. From what I could see from the station the city had been rebuilt, including the thirteenth-century cathedral, its towers rising above the surrounding rooftops. After a stop at Metz, in Lorraine, we crossed the German border and changed trains at Saarbrücken. As I waited on the station platform, two members of the Geheime Feldpolizei in plainclothes came up and checked my entry visa. Thielmann had mentioned the Wehrmacht secret police and said they could be in or out of uniform. Among their duties were checking travel documents and keeping an eye on neutrals, including diplomats and correspondents. The Saarbrücken train went to Mainz, on the west bank of the Rhine, and north to Frankfurt. I had a long wait there for the next train to Berlin. It was late afternoon. In the station restaurant I ordered a cup of coffee. What I got was a pale brown liquid that looked like dirty tap water and had a taste reminiscent of stale cereal. The restaurant was full of soldiers and they didn't seem to mind the delay. They were high on easy victories and thought Hitler could work miracles. I got into a conversation with a few of them.

"Why do the English keep fighting? It is over for them. They must see that. They force us to bomb them. They must accept the right of Germany to be master of Europe. They have their empire. The Führer will let them keep it."

They laughed. I raised my cup.

"How can you drink this?"

"We get better to drink as soldiers."

"You expect civilians to drink it?"

"They must sacrifice, as we do. Better that than getting shot at."

By whose guns? It was dark outside and I was tired. The station staff didn't know when the Berlin train would be ready to leave. A serving woman in the restaurant closed the heavy felt blackout curtains on the windows. The RAF flew their bombing missions at night over Germany. Some soldiers were drinking wine or schnapps and others were sleeping. I decided the ones who were sleeping had the better idea. I leaned back in my chair and promptly fell asleep.

Scuffling noises woke me. Soldiers were hurrying out onto the platform. I looked at my watch. It was after two in the morning. I stepped from the restaurant into a chaotic blackness full of noise, with soldiers tripping over baggage, bumping into pillars and swearing. As my eyes adjusted I could barely make out the dark mass of the train. I headed towards it. Shoving and pushing like everybody else, I climbed the steps of a day coach, clutching my valises against jostling elbows and knees. The seats had all been taken. I stood in the packed and dark aisle, keeping my valises between my feet. Window blinds drawn and no lights allowed, the train swayed and lurched through the night. In the blackness I could feel through my shoes the clicking of wheels riding over uneven rail joints and rumbling over crossings. At Potsdam many soldiers got off and I found a seat and fell asleep. A push against my shoulder woke me. It was dawn, the blinds were open and a soldier seated beside me was trying to get past into the aisle. I stood up and took my valises down from the luggage rack. I was in Berlin.

# Berlin

I got a taxi outside the Potsdamer Bahnhof and gave the driver the bureau address. The office was nearby, in the Hotel Excelsior. Above ground-floor rounded arches the Excelsior façade rose in bow windows and curved balconies to a classical pediment: Art Nouveau meets the Neo-Baroque and voilà, Belle Époque. I told the desk clerk who I was, left my valises at the desk and took the elevator to the office. I knocked on the door and a woman's voice answered with a businesslike "Come." I entered what must have been one of the smaller rooms in the hotel. Three filing cabinets and an oak desk with a typewriter, a telephone and cowl lamp took up much of the space. Three straight-backed wooden chairs were arranged in a semicircle around the desk and a woman sat in a swivel chair behind it. I assumed the door beside the cabinets was to a bathroom. A window with a Venetian blind looked out over the back of the hotel. The lamp was on, the blind slats were wide open but the room was dim. Beige walls and linoleum carpet the color of damp cardboard soaked up the light.

Slim and of medium height, Sophie Henser looked in her late thirties. Her sandy hair was long and gathered at the back, framing an oval face with a small nose and gray eyes. She was wearing a gray wool skirt and a lime cardigan over a white blouse. Bifocals sat perkily on her nose, looking as if she had been born wearing them. Her expression didn't change when she saw me.

"Hello, I'm Jim Brian. You must be Sophie Henser."

"Sit down, Mr. Brian."

I turned a straight-backed chair around and sat astraddle it. That didn't faze her. She had a pleasant voice. But the business-as-usual tone was obvious.

"We are the complete staff. You'll have noticed the office is not large. Other agencies here have a suite of rooms, three or more correspondents, German assistants, a teleprinter, a DNB ticker and lots of typewriters and phones. I've managed over the years and mostly on my own. I'd better fill you in. You'll have to go to the Propaganda Ministry for an identity card and permission to send cables. You can send them there or at the post office. Press conferences are held daily, two at the Propaganda Ministry, noon and 5:30, and at the Foreign Office at one. There's one tomorrow morning at ten at the Foreign Office, which could mean it's something important or they want us to think it is. There's the other stuff, attending party rallies and social events and going through newspapers and magazines and listening to radio news. I've done rallies and social events and speeches for years, the Nazis know me. I've built up an insider network of sources that give me stories, sometimes over the phone but usually in person, and that takes my time. So I'm going to delegate the press conferences, papers, magazines and radio to you and I'll help you when I can. How is your German?"

"Not nearly as good as my French, which is marginally worse than my English."

"I suggest you pick up some German soon."

"If that's the best way."

We stared at each other. Mexican standoff.

"What do I do about a desk, phone and typewriter?"

"We share."

"Fingerprints don't bother you?"

"No, but sophomoric humor does."

"The filing deadline is—?"

"For the morning papers 2 a.m. For important stuff there's radiotelephone, otherwise cable direct or relay through Berne. I should mention a couple of other things. The Foreign Office and Propaganda Ministry have foreign press chiefs and liaisons, attachés for the American press. They're pretentious party hacks. But mind your manners, they can cause trouble. Both the Propaganda Ministry and Foreign Office have restaurants for correspondents, Americans welcome. There are reading rooms, the food isn't bad, but they're full of agents, informers and Balkan rats. By the way, the phone is tapped. Your colleagues at the press conferences tomorrow will have lots more to tell you."

"I used the company car in Paris. Actually, it was Harry's."

"I have a car. The petrol allowance is forty gallons a month. There's no subway or buses after the 1 a.m. curfew, no taxis after 9 p.m. But I don't like the idea of driving in the blackout to the Rundfunkhaus. I use a bicycle instead or take the U-bahn when the weather is bad and sleep in my office there overnight."

"You broadcast?"

"I'm on the air two nights a week, occasionally more depending on the news. Transmission is between 2 and 3 a.m. I leave here earlier. They like American broadcasters to be there at least an hour before to have the script checked."

"Is there an air-raid shelter here?"

"In the basement."

"Where does the spittoon go?"

"You don't?"

"That's one habit I don't have. But I get thirsty."

"I'm not much of a drinker but I'm sure the correspondents will help you quench your thirst. Do you smoke?"

"Given it up. Chew my fingernails instead."

She glanced at the typewriter.

"I should finish this piece I'm working on, if you don't mind."

"I'd love to mind but it's against the law here."

She looked at me over her glasses for a few seconds before beginning to type.

I stood up.

"I'd better look for a place."

She kept typing.

They were waiting outside, two men in black leather trench coats who were sitting in a car. They got out in a hurry and wanted to see my papers.

They had followed me from the station, probably thinking I would incriminate myself in some way, maybe spit on the sidewalk. I told them that the Feldpolizei checked my entry visa at Saarbrücken. One of them said, "They do their business, we do ours." They handed my papers back and were gone. It was their way of welcoming me.

I went to the housing authority and found a pension that afternoon. It was four blocks from the office. My landlady, Frau Ziegenhagen, had the knitted brows and twisted lips of the permanently disappointed. I unpacked in my room and glanced around. The window provided a beautiful view of the brick wall next door. Not wanting to consider the symbolism, I lay on my bed and fell asleep. The next morning I asked Frau Ziegenhagen how the rationing system worked.

"*Ach*, you are new to Germany. You must be registered with a grocer, a butcher and a baker."

"What about a candlestick maker?"

"*Nein*, we have candles. I will register you. You will be issued with food cards. You must shop at those places where you are registered. I will buy your food if you wish. There are other cards for clothes and petrol. Those things you must buy."

Over the next few days I found out more about rationing. The cards were good for four weeks. Soap, chocolate, tobacco and coal were rationed too. For clothes and petrol you needed permission slips. Foreign correspondents were put in the same category as heavy laborers and given double rations. It was a crude ploy by the Propaganda Ministry to curry favor with the foreign press but none of us turned down the extra rations. I could also import food packages from Denmark, bringing in extra eggs and bacon. Another benefit courtesy of the Propaganda Ministry. The packages helped because there wasn't much available in the stores. Standing in long queues for herself and some of her tenants, sometimes Frau Ziegenhagen could only get me an egg, an apple and a piece of sausage. Potatoes and cabbage were plentiful unless the potato crop froze in the ground or the cabbages spoiled. Bread was usually available in quantity. Restaurant meals were scanty and expensive. Tea and coffee were ersatz.

After speaking with Frau Ziegenhagen that first morning I walked over to the Foreign Office, on Wilhelmstrasse. Press conferences took place in a nineteenth-century hall, with crystal chandeliers hanging from carved beams and painted shields lining the walls. A table ran almost the length of the hall and the foreign press chief and his assistant sat on the long side nearer the door. Secretaries taking notes sat on both sides of him, as well as various assistants plus assorted functionaries, and some stood behind. Correspondents sat everywhere else or stood across from the press chief or whoever was substituting for him. That first conference turned out to be diplomatic drivel about the Third Reich having peaceful intentions and guaranteeing the sovereignty of other peaceful nations. The press chief refused to answer questions. He left, followed by his retinue, and correspondents consulted notes, wrote stories and sent cables. I had introduced myself to the Americans. Afterwards some of us went to the Hotel Adlon, the watering hole of choice.

The hotel was on Unter den Linden, in the government district. It was beside the British Embassy, on Wilhelmstrasse, and across the way on the Pariser Platz were the French and American embassies. British and French diplomats had left in September 1939, but Americans were still open for business. Further south on Wilhelmstrasse were government ministries and the Chancellery. Its location made the Adlon a favorite with diplomats, correspondents and broadcasters. Another product of the Belle Époque, it was decorated in Late and Neo-Baroque and featured square marble columns in the lobby. Members of the American press could usually be found in the bar.

Gathered around one of the tables after the conference that morning was a small part of the American press corps in Berlin. In the fall of 1940 there were about four dozen print and broadcast journalists representing American newspapers, magazines, news agencies and radio networks. Some had been there a short time and some were veterans. I met most of them. They represented the *New York Times* and the *Herald-Tribune*, the *Chicago Tribune* and the *Daily News* and the *Christian Science Monitor*. The important magazines were *Time* and the *Saturday Evening Post*. The networks were CBS, NBC and Mutual and the news agencies were AP, UP and INS. In the bar that morning were the correspondents I came to know best. Art Neff was the bureau chief of the AP. Thin, in his sixties, he had been in Berlin for eight years. At the beginning of the war he had sent his wife back to New York. He spent what spare time he had writing letters to her. Jack Harrison, bureau chief of the INS, was beefy, a drinker, twice divorced and as loud as his sport jackets and ties. The *Times'* correspondent was Richard B. Hapgood, who used a cigarette holder and wore a tar-black toupee. Reporting for the *Chicago Tribune* was Joe Bock and for the *Herald-Tribune* Peter McNeill.

Like me the last two were newcomers. Art talked about the bureaucracy correspondents faced. Press passes were issued by the Foreign Office and the Propaganda Ministry and from the Gestapo press bureau permission slips for entry to places and to events. Jack kidded us newcomers.

"How do you guys like your monthly bar of soap? And one for laundry. Small as packs of cards. The worst stuff ever called soap."

Hapgood grinned.

"Why the sudden interest in soap, Jack?"

Jack stared at him.

"You're in luck, Dick. It's enough for a toupee. Don't use the laundry bar. The black might wash out."

I broke the silence.

"Where are the Nazis?"

Art spoke in a quiet voice.

"At the Kaiserhof, south of here, in Wilhelmplatz, near the Propaganda Ministry and Chancellery."

"No platz like home."

"They don't appreciate humor, especially if it's at their expense. They have ways of finding out things. Embassy and consular staff read papers back in the States. File anything they don't like, you're given a lecture at the Propaganda Ministry, an exit visa from the Foreign Office and told to catch the next train. If you do broadcasts, they look at your script ahead of time. Censor what they don't like. They have staff who understand American English, so you can't get away with anything over the air."

The waiter brought our drinks. Art changed the subject.

"The Adlon is building an air-raid shelter that will be the best in Berlin.

And going to put a brick wall around the lobby."

Jack raised his glass.

"To walls and to air-raid shelters, protecting us in our search for the truth."

I was back at the office when Sophie came in that evening. She was wearing a tan jacket and slacks and had a black leather handbag with a strap slung over her shoulder. There were bicycle clips around her ankles. I got up from the swivel chair and sat in one of the others. She waved her hand in protest but I waved back. No sense in wasting words on the obvious. I glanced at the bicycle clips.

"Broadcasting tonight?"

"Yes." She put her handbag on the desk and sat down.

"It's dangerous in the blackout. I've already walked into two lampposts. The military comes out of nowhere. They zip by with covered lights with a slit in them."

"I manage."

"You mind if I listen to the radio? I like to hear the BBC's version of things, find out what the Reich's Ministry of Props isn't telling the *Volk*."

"Shhhh. Keep your voice down. Go ahead. I have to go over my script."

I got up and switched on the radio. It was against the wall nearest the desk. It was a standing floor model of reddish-brown wood striped with bands of lighter wood, used vacuum tubes and could receive short, medium and long-wave transmissions. I tuned in to the BBC's European service. Correspondents were allowed to listen but Germans weren't. Many did. For those caught the penalty was imprisonment at hard labor or even the death sentence.

The news that night led off with the number of bombers and fighters shot down in the latest German raid on Britain. Each side exaggerated the other's losses and minimized its own. But the British were usually closer to the actual figures. The rest of the broadcast turned out to be unimportant. I turned the dial. A violin filled the room with a lush melody, interrupted and embellished by stabs of poignant chords. Late nineteenth-century romanticism cried out from chasms of ecstatic yearning. An orchestra joined in, adding its soaring affirmation. I remembered. It was early October. Julia was performing

Bruch's Concerto in G with Mengelberg and the Concertgebouw in Amsterdam. He was the right conductor for her. They got everything out of the score without descending to emotional mush. For a second I wished I were there. I was still standing beside the radio when it was over. As the loud applause died down an announcer began speaking in Dutch. I turned off the radio.

"I know her, the violinist. She was playing Bruch. He's not Bach, but who is? I didn't know she was that good. I've never even heard her practice."

Sophie didn't look up.

"Very romantic. I hear that Goebbels will be speaking at the noon conference tomorrow."

"The Doctor keeps doctoring, though the patient died years ago."

"Keep talking like that and you won't be in Berlin very long. People listen in hallways and outside doors."

"Don't they, though? How long are you on the air?"

"Four minutes."

"That's headline news. All news is about versions of the truth."

She raised her head.

"What do you mean?"

"There is no single unalterable absolute final truth. Not among humans."

"What is there?"

"Decency. Toleration."

I grinned.

"It must be the music."

She opened a desk drawer, took out a large brown envelope and opened the flap. She took out papers and photographs and pushed them across the desk.

"Have a look at these."

I glanced at the papers. There were two typed articles, "The Nazi Threat to America" and "America Must Fight the Third Reich." In both the byline gave credit to a George Underhill. The photographs were of plans of a light machine gun.

"How did you get these?"

She spoke barely above a whisper and I leaned towards the desk to hear.

"They were planted. I'm being set up."

"How did you find them?"

"I know where to look."

"They want you out of here?"

"They know I'm anti-Nazi. I'm supposedly George Underhill secretly cabling those stories. Bad enough. But possessing those photographs is treason. Goering and Goebbels are behind it. They've got the Gestapo after me. I've got to burn everything before we get a visit. They usually come early in the morning. There's a luncheon at the Air Ministry tomorrow. I'll tell that fatso off to his face. I'm not going to stand for this."

"May I do the honors?"

"I've got matches."

She took a box of matches out of a drawer and put it on the desk. I stood up, took out a match and scratched the head along the side of the box. It flared white-hot into scarlet flame and the smell of sulfur and burning wood filled the room. I set fire to an article, turning the pages around to burn them completely. I dropped the curling ashes into the wastebasket. She opened the window to get rid of the smell. Minutes later, everything reduced to ash, we sat in a lingering odor of smoke and stared at each other across the desk. After a while she shut the window. Because of the blackout the blinds had been kept closed. I looked at my watch.

"When do you leave for the radio station?"

"Usually one, sometimes earlier depending on the weather."

"Maybe you could answer a question. Depending on how German you are."

"I was born here, was four when we emigrated and returned ten years ago. What's your question?"

"Where does German end and Nazi begin? Bruch, whose violin concerto we heard tonight, wrote a piece based on Hebrew melodies. That has led some Nazi cultural bigwigs to suspect he may have been Jewish. There's no evidence for that. He wrote another work, which he called a Scottish Fantasy. But that didn't lead them to believe he was Scottish. Obviously because it didn't matter. Here's another example, perhaps trivial but nonetheless intriguing. In 1936 the city authorities decided to replace the mixed species on Unter den Linden with one, the silver lime. Also known of course as basswood or linden. No one had thought of doing that before. Was that a result of the German desire for order? Or was it something else, an unconscious indication of how extreme the desire for racial purity has become in the Third Reich? And if I'm not becoming completely idiotic, why the silver lime?"

"You've answered your own question. The trees weren't made uniform under the Hohenzollerns or Weimar Republic but under the Nazis."

"It's not that easy. This is the least Nazi of German cities. The Nazis are only here because it's the traditional seat of government. They may run the city now but local authorities are Berliners too. Have the Nazis released something in some, and I stress some, Germans that was always there or should we blame everything on the Third Reich?"

She looked at her watch.

"Maybe I'm not enough of a German to answer that. I should be going."

I remembered something Art had told me.

"I hear there's a restaurant open for correspondents after curfew. Do you ever go there?"

"Occasionally."

"Good luck getting to the Rundfunkhaus. I'm going to try getting back to my pension without breaking a leg or being run down."

"Good luck to you."

She hurried out after putting her rolled-up script in her handbag. I waited several minutes and then turned off the desk lamp and shut and locked the office door and took the elevator down to the lobby. I was crossing the lobby when I heard the air-raid siren. I was hustled with everyone else in the Excelsior into the cellar. There was some jostling and swearing and a few sobs but most people were quiet. Quite a few were wearing pajamas. The all-clear sounded after fifteen minutes. Most sounded confident now and a few were laughing as we filed up out of a blackness lit by a couple of flashlight beams.

Before dawn the next morning a fist banged on my door.

"You are wanted on the telephone, Herr Bine."

It was Sophie.

"I locked the office door this morning. They're outside. Get to the embassy. Hurry."

As I dressed I wondered if I had burnt everything completely. Had they planted anything else? I took a taxi. The member of the embassy staff on duty was one of those career diplomats that breathe protocol. I asked to see the chargé d'affaires, the highest-ranking official. The last American ambassador had been recalled in 1938. The official said the chargé d'affaires wasn't awake. He couldn't be disturbed. When I mentioned Sophie's name he said, "Oh, that woman." I raised my voice.

"The chargé d'affaires has got to lodge a complaint with the Foreign Office and the Propaganda Ministry."

"Don't tell us our business. Mr. Crane will handle this."

"Get him to do it before she's in a concentration camp."

"Don't be so melodramatic."

I grabbed him by his striped tie.

"Wake him up."

I shook him around. He choked out his words.

"I should flatten you. I could box your ears."

"Listen, Ivy League, you may have had bouts with pantywaists but I've scrapped with guys that could snap you in two."

"All right. Let me go."

He went to the phone and spoke in that hushed voice reserved only for doctors and diplomats. A few minutes later Crane came into the room wearing a dressing gown and slippers. He was blinking at the light and yawning. I explained the situation and he frowned.

"What's the rush? This could have waited."

"Have you ever been questioned by the Gestapo?"

His frown got deeper. He went to the phone and called the Foreign Office. You'd have thought he was talking high finance. Lots of bonhomie, doing things the diplomatic way. The Propaganda Ministry got the same backslapping chatter.

I took another taxi. As I stepped into the Excelsior lobby I saw them. There was one on either side of Sophie, escorting her out of the hotel. One carried the wastebasket. I blocked their way.

"Why waste your time? The American Embassy has been notified. An official protest has been made to the Foreign Office and to the Propaganda Ministry. Dr. Goebbels knows all about this. You hold nothing but ashes."

They seemed to know who I was. They looked at each other. The one holding the wastebasket handed it to me and without a word they left. Sophie looked upset, but more angry than nervous.

"That was stupid, coming to the office this morning. I should've gone to the embassy."

"Did they poke around in the ashes?"

"They found a couple of scraps. They made a lot out of them. I don't think there was anything. By the way, thanks."

I nodded.

"I should've flushed these down the toilet. Would you like a drink?"

"All right."

We went to the bar and sat at a corner table. I put the wastebasket at my feet and asked what she wanted. Riesling, her favorite wine, she said. I ordered bourbon for myself. We drank for a while before I mentioned the embassy.

"You're not popular there."

She grinned.

"They think I'm a troublemaker. I can be as phony as the rest at diplomatic receptions and foreign press luncheons. Flashing my pearly whites. But I write the truth, all of it."

She took a sip before leaning forward and lowering her voice.

"It's not only the Nazis who censor news. Some owners and editors for their own reasons don't want Americans to know what's going on here. They edit out the strong stuff and sometimes won't print my dispatch. I've checked papers when they arrive at the office months later. Head office doesn't care as long as subscribers pay for the service."

She whispered.

"You'd be surprised who likes Mr. Mustache."

"I was in London for two years. Bluebloods and press lords were in step with the goosesteppers."

"We have that type back home."

"Doesn't surprise me. Power admires power. Especially absolute. *Heil.*"

We were both whispering now. She shook her head.

"We're little people."

"So are they. The difference is, they've got money to spend on lawyers and politicians, goon squads and pen prostitutes."

"You're not a—?"

"I eschew all fanaticism. I actually believe in democracy for everybody, fool that I am."

She leaned closer to me.

"When I started working as a reporter Hitler was becoming a serious contender for power and I got an interview with him. I was green but my boss said it would be a good baptism of fire. It was in a hotel room and Hitler shook my hand and held it with a strong grip, staring at me, trying to mesmerize me. He repelled me, with his pasty face and that ridiculous mustache. We sat down and he ranted for an hour about the Versailles Treaty and the betrayal of Germany by the Jews. Said he had nothing against Americans but they should not get involved in European affairs. At the end of the hour he suddenly stood up and said he was busy. He left the room and an SS bodyguard showed me out.

"The next time I got close was at a press conference. He was Chancellor by then. We reporters were told he was going to make an important announcement. That was a lie. He wanted to impress us with his personality. After making some unimportant remarks he waited as his press chief arranged the reporters in a semicircle, then he shook their hands and stared into their eyes. But when he got to me he gave me a quick handshake and moved on. He knew that I couldn't be mesmerized by his look. He's clever. He knows who will fall under his spell and who won't."

She finished her drink.

"I've got to appear at that luncheon and tell fatso off, politely of course."

She hurried out. I went to the office and flushed the ashes down the toilet. As I watched the swirl of gray water disappear I thought about the planted stories. Why had the Gestapo bothered concocting them? The plans would have been enough to get rid of her. They must have had grounds for suspecting her of filing stories under a false name. She didn't trust me enough to tell me. I wondered how she managed it? Take a skiing vacation in Switzerland and file from there? I ate an overpriced meal of cabbage, potatoes and so-called fish in one of the Excelsior restaurants. I was going to the noon press conference at the Propaganda Ministry, figured the fish was appropriate.

Press conferences were held in the Theater Hall. Marble stairs led to it. It looked more theater than hall, with red cushy seats facing a stage with a long table. American correspondents tended to sit in the front row, giving us a good look at the show. Sometimes "experts" were there, usually from the Wehrmacht, to substantiate claims and announcements made by the foreign press chief or his assistant. There would be props, maps to show the latest military successes.

That afternoon we got the man himself. Short, skinny, with a noticeable limp, he made his jerky way to the table and began haranguing us on the responsible reporting of news. Like a scolding schoolteacher, he wagged his finger at us. Once he smiled, the grimacing facial muscles of a hyena. Looking around at the assembled correspondents, I knew they had heard it all before. One stifled a yawn. Most would have left but for fear of offending him. When he had finished, he rolled up the sheets of his typescript and hobbled off the stage.

Later in the Adlon bar Jack asked, "Anybody going tonight for the second dose?"

"I am," Joe said. "I need copy."

He was heavyset and spoke slowly. Jack shook his head.

"Anything important, they shoot their wad at noon. We got the big lecture. Gobbles did his star turn. The later one is never worth it. They sit there, recite stuff and refuse to answer questions."

"We're not all like you," Hapgood said. "We can't take a chance on missing anything."

"You never take a chance, do you, Dick?"

"What's that, Jack?"

"You deaf?"

"Say what you mean."

"You know what I mean. Anything for a scoop."

"Like everybody else."

"We don't kiss ass. You're not much different from those neutrals who file ministry handouts and spout propaganda over the air."

"I report the news like anybody else. Check my dispatches."

"You file what they want."

"You know, Jack, one day somebody is going to get fed up with you and take a poke at that big red nose of yours."

"Want to try?"

"I wouldn't mind."

"Let's go outside."

Art intervened.

"Nobody's going outside. There's always words between you two. What's the point of having a drink if we have to listen to this? Put an end to it."

Hapgood stood up, his cigarette holder jutting upward at a sharp angle. He left, pushing his way past some customers, and Jack laughed.

"He thinks that cigarette holder makes him look like Roosevelt. He's not kidding anybody. His wife is German. She's got him by the balls."

"He's in a tough spot," Art said.

After announcing the usual exaggerated RAF and minimized Luftwaffe losses in the air war over Britain, the evening press conference ended with a dreary recitation. The foreign press chief's assistant read a release on the supposedly robust economy of the Third Reich. Afterwards I cabled a dispatch, letting enough air out of the Propaganda Ministry balloon so it could barely float, and went to the office. As I was sharpening pencils, Sophie came in with a wisp of a grin.

"I gave him a piece of my mind. He knows about you helping me. They'll be watching you from now on. Don't commit any blackout infractions. Keep your blinds closed. When you use a flashlight, make sure it's got a blue bulb. When we use the car, it's got to be important business.

"We?"

"I didn't say you couldn't use it."

"You didn't say I could."

"It's understood."

With a groan she slipped her handbag off her shoulder, dropped it on the desk and slumped into the swivel chair.

"Another thing. They stage traffic accidents. Even during the day. There won't be any witnesses. Don't trust anyone. Your landlady or the others at your pension. Any one of them could be an informer."

"You're in danger too. Especially if they know you're filing stories under another name when you're in Switzerland."

"You guessed."

"It wasn't hard."

"I've been warned."

"Why do you stay?"

"I've asked myself that. Ten years in this place. I got out of college in 1925 and worked as a language teacher. I'm fluent in German and French. When the Depression came I lost my job and decided to tour Europe with friends. One was the niece of Walter Deering, the bureau chief then. His German was poor. He hired me as a translator. I became a cub reporter. He left in '34 and I was offered the job."

She threw up her hands.

"It's exciting, like being at the center of the world. I love it."

"Why was Bill Beckmann kicked out?"

She leaned back in the swivel chair.

"He was transferred here last September. New York sent him because women aren't allowed near the front line. The Propaganda Ministry set up trips to the battle zone and I couldn't go. He went to Poland. Later on to Belgium and northern France. He was all right at first. He'd phone in daily reports from the front when he was there and I'd cable New York. He'd get his byline. Everything was fine until a few months ago. Head office told me he went behind my back and said he could do a better job as bureau chief here. I'm the only woman correspondent in Berlin and until then I didn't realize how precarious that is."

"He should've been fired."

"Men will stick together. I've kept this job because I've spent years getting good at it. Developing contacts. Getting stories nobody else has."

"So that's why you were cool to me the first day. You didn't know."

"After this morning I think I trust you."

An air-raid siren began to wail. I looked at my watch. It was almost one. We took the fire escape stairs down to the lobby and filed with dozens of others, many in pajamas and dressing gowns, into the cellar. The only lights were flashlights. Sophie brought along hers. I could see sandbags and buckets of water along the walls, the same as in the pension cellar, except many more. After fifteen minutes there was no all-clear. The flashlights went out. We waited in the silent darkness and after a while there were dull thumps. They got closer and the walls shook. Somebody began to cry. I wondered if the hotel could take a direct hit or would everything collapse on top of us and we be buried alive under tons of rubble. I fought the claustrophobia of seemingly endless waiting in the blackness packed together with others underground. I could hear a booming sound, the flak guns trying to shoot down the bombers. A loud bang shook the building and some shouted or groaned. Silent waiting but the inevitable didn't happen.

Somebody turned on a flashlight, its faint blue circle picking out part of a shoulder or head. Voices in the darkness.

"Turn it off."

"Why? Do you think the bombers can see it down here?"

"You waste batteries. And the bulb."

"You need permission slips for them."

"There have been no flashlights for months. Even with slips."

"They were bought out early. The batteries too. I tried all the stores. Had no luck."

"We have one in my family. We share it."

"I was told there are more coming."

Somebody laughed, safe in the darkness.

I wondered if Sophie was beside me. She hadn't said anything. But nobody had until the silence began after the bombs. We stood waiting for the all-clear, fidgeting, shuffling, muttering, grumbling. Then the siren gave one wail and it died away and there was a low collective murmur. The cellar door opened a rectangle of light and we filed up into the lobby. Sophie was behind me. Everybody else scattered and we stood, an island of two.

"Are you broadcasting tonight?"

"No, I'm going back to my apartment. I'm up early."

"Please don't call my landlady before eight."

She smiled but her eyes looked tired. I glanced at my watch.

"It's half past one. I don't feel like going back to my pension right away. Think I'll try that restaurant. Why don't you come?"

"Not tonight, I'm tired. There's another flashlight in the bottom desk drawer."

She must have been one of the few people in Berlin with a spare flashlight. A resourceful woman, but I should have known that by now. I watched her cross the lobby on her way out. A no-nonsense walk, like her attitude. Why did Beckmann try to get her job? She had a decade in Berlin and a good reputation. Some guys' arrogance matches their stupidity. Or was there more to it? Why hadn't she told me earlier about that extra flashlight? Probably hadn't thought about it. She had a lot on her mind.

The Alpenhaus was near the government district. It was allowed to stay open after curfew so correspondents would have a place to go after late filing and broadcasts. Art had given me precise directions but in a blackout you're never sure of anything. There are only shapes, some darker than others. You walk into streetlights and fire hydrants, trip over curbs. Cars roar out of the blackness and you step back. Sometimes there's no sound and a shape slips past like a shadow and you wonder how you weren't knocked down or flung through the air. The dim blue beam of Sophie's flashlight was of little help. Finally, I saw a pilot light in the distance and walking towards it could make out a door and a sign. I knocked and a waiter in black pants and a white shirt opened the door wide enough that a spear of light slit the blackness. He asked to see my press pass to enter after curfew. I pulled several passes out of various pockets, found the right one and showed it to him. He opened the door wide enough for me to enter. The lights and noise were a shock after blocks of silent blackness. I looked for the large corner table reserved for correspondents. I saw Art seated beside Jack. I didn't recognize some of the others.

Art stopped tamping down the tobacco in a pipe and waved and I went over. He made room for me and I got a free chair and sat between him and Jack. He checked the draw on his pipe and took a wooden match from a box on the table and lit the tobacco. He took a couple of puffs. Smoke drifted from the briar bowl into a layer of communal tobacco smog below the timbered ceiling.

"Nice smell," I said. "What is it?"

"It's called Presbyterian. From Glasgow. No tongue bite. Stanley Baldwin smokes this, apparently. Can't get it here now but I've got tins put away."

"Trust you to smoke his mixture," Jack said.

"All we've ever had in common."

Jack took a silver case from the inside pocket of his jacket. He selected a panatela, bit off one end and spit it on the floor and scratched a match across the tabletop. Clipped rolled tobacco leaves sucked at the flame as he puffed. A red circle glowed. He raised his hand, two fingers holding his cigar forming a vee.

"Smoking a cigar may not be good for your health in Germany these days."

"The doctor?" Joe said.

"You could say that. I'm restricted to two a day."

"You can't quit?"

"Rationing."

"Where's Hapgood?" I asked.

"He never shows up here. Maybe he doesn't like Italian food. Don't let the name of the place fool you. The spaghetti is good and the Chianti the best available."

Art introduced the others around the table. Erich Burckhardt, a Swiss, represented a Zurich newspaper. He was paunchy, with a red face. Gunnar Lund, German wife beside him, reported for a Stockholm newspaper. He wore a bow tie and had a white-blond mustache. She had small eyes and large teeth. Luigi Strazza, from Rome, broadcast for Italian radio. Sleek black hair parted down the middle, lips looking swollen from bee stings, he reeked of cologne. Luis Morales, from Madrid, broadcast for Spanish radio. Small and dark, he smoked cigarillos.

At this point Peter arrived and was introduced around the table. Thin, nervous, a chain smoker, he took a cigarette from an almost empty package. He lit it with the butt in his mouth and threw the butt away. He took a deep drag.

"What am I going to do when I run out of American cigarettes? The rationed ones aren't as good, I've heard."

"Go to Switzerland," Burckhardt said. "There are good American and Turkish cigarettes."

"Chew on pencils," Jack said. "There's wood in most of the food here. A pencil will last you a month. I hear a little lead is good for the brain."

"It is not real lead," Lund's wife said. Her name was Elsa."No one is being poisoned. You spread false rumors."

"I was being facetious. Nothing like a dumb broad."

"I understand very well."

"You couldn't get through that ivory dome with a jackhammer."

"You are an insulting man."

"I try to be."

"We should leave," Lund said to his wife.

"He should leave. What is he doing in my country but telling lies about it?"

"I was merely commenting on the lack of good tobacco here."

"You have no business criticizing my country."

"Thankfully they don't try to roll cigars. Mine are Cuban. One thing you can't tell a smoker. What he's smoking."

"I do not smoke."

"Then stay out of the conversation."

"Stop speaking that way to my wife."

"A belligerent Swede. You should line up with the Italians."

"What are you talking about?" Strazza said.

"Military prowess."

"You are insulting Italians."

"You declared war on the French when they were beaten. You couldn't get past that corporal's guard they posted at your border. You needed bombs and poison gas to defeat natives fighting with spears in Ethiopia. You're a military joke."

Morales snickered and Jack looked at him.

"If Schicklgruber and Muzzi—sounds like a comedy act—hadn't backed your boys you'd have been picking Spanish Republic steel out of your guts."

Before Morales could answer, Burckhardt jumped in.

"This has gone too far. We should not be quarreling. This table is meant for pleasant company. Perhaps one of us has drunk too much good German beer."

Jack laughed.

"Always the peacemaker, huh? You guys make good business out of laundering everybody's dirty money. You park your fat asses on the biggest pile of gold in the world. I hear your chocolate is the best. Never touch the stuff."

The Europeans left and Jack smoked his cigar.

"It's been a good evening. Everybody's mad at me."

"What about the news we could've gotten from them?" Art said. "Those hints we could use."

"From that bunch? That Swede and his wife are Nazis. Burckhardt's hand in glove with them. Those other two are going to hand you nothing but shit. They're in Schicklgruber's back pocket."

"Maybe so. But socially you're making it tough on Americans. We'll be ostracized. Pretty soon we'll be the only ones at this table."

"Suits me fine. I've got no use for them."

"Speak for yourself. They're not all bad. Some diplomacy would help. You can't talk as if you're in a bar in New York."

"Did I lie about anything?"

"I'm not talking about that. Remember where we are."

"Not much chance of forgetting that."

"We've got company," Peter said sotto voce.

Two Gestapo agents had entered. They sat at a table near ours. The level of noise dropped. Most patrons were silent.

"They ratted on us," Joe said.

"I'm dying for a cigarette," Peter said.

I took a cigarette package out of my jacket pocket and handed it to him.

"Have mine. I don't smoke any more but I figure these might come in handy so I pick up my tobacco ration regardless. The Germans imitate American brands. Those are Lord Chesterfield. There's Kemals, spelt k-e-m-a-l-s. The tobacco here is mostly Balkan. No Virginia or burley."

His hands shook as he tore open the package and pulled out a cigarette. Art lit a match, leaned forward and held it for him. The tobacco lit and he took a drag, inhaling deeply and coughing. He looked at the cigarette.

"These'll have to do, I guess."

A big man with a round face went to the agents' table. I found out later he was Willi Stehr, the owner. He smiled. His voice was too low for us to hear what he said. He brought his smile to our table.

"Everything is all right with you, gentlemen?"

"Couldn't be better," Jack said. "I was telling the boys here that I have no complaints. I'll have some of your spaghetti, with a bottle of Chianti. Anybody care to join me?"

Joe said he would.

Glancing at each of us in turn, Will Stehr belabored the obvious.

"You know I keep my place open for you correspondents past curfew. I like everybody to be happy here. If there is trouble, I will lose my special license and have to close. That would help nobody."

"Well put, Willi," Jack said. "Trouble is something that's taboo with me. I'm a peaceful man. I listen to reason."

A big smile from Willi Stehr. The spaghetti came, Jack sharing it with Joe. Instead of sending a waiter, Willi brought the wine personally. Jack complimented him on the spaghetti. Another broad smile. Another at Jack's praise after sipping the wine. At one point the agents turned and stared.

*"Ich liebe Sauerkraut und Riesling und Edelweiß,"* Jack said, raising his glass of Chianti to the agents. *"Ihre Gesundheit, meine Herren."*

They nodded, leaving a few minutes later.

I told Sophie everything the next morning at the office.

"I know why Jack hasn't been kicked out. Germans are oblivious to criticism, even insults, if you do it sarcastically. Sarcasm and irony are beyond them. There's no fine edge to their humor. So when they hear anything subtle or skewed, they don't get it."

She frowned.

"They're not all that way."

"Most are. There's no such thing as tragicomedy with them. It's one or the other. They either laugh or cry. They can't do both at the same time."

"Maybe it's the Prussian influence."

"I doubt it. This goes back beyond that."

"I don't have time for a history lesson. I've got a dispatch to write."

"I've got a press conference. I didn't try the spaghetti. They thought it was excellent. Apparently it's an Alpenhaus specialty."

"It's all in the sauce."

"You cook?"

"I was once considered a gourmet chef. Does that surprise you?"

"No. What happened?"

"Rationing."

"That'll do it. But shouldn't a great chef be able to create gourmet dishes out of almost anything?"

"It's not easy with ersatz."

"Sawdust, glue, chemical dyes and grain sweepings would be hard to turn into ambrosia. I guess I've lost my chance to sample your wares."

As I spoke she looked down and began to type. My cue to leave for the Propaganda Ministry. She had to protect herself. But I wasn't a threat. Couldn't she see that?

After cabling a dispatch early on the following Sunday I stopped by the Alpenhaus. At one Sophie had gone to broadcast. It was late October and the RAF nighttime raids were occasional now. Later on she came. She hadn't said anything at the office. Art introduced her to Joe and Peter and Sophie sat between them. She ordered a glass of wine and chatted with the newcomers. When the talking became disjointed murmurs, Jack had an idea.

"Let's play the Europe game. Here are the rules for you new guys. You say something about Europe. And the first word has to be 'Europe.' If everybody thinks it's good, it makes our list of the best. We have three so far. Mine is Europe is a big museum with a lot of curators. Art?"

"Europe is a stew with too much pepper."

"Sophie?"

"Europe has a lot of Germans."

Joe raised his hand.

"Europe has more languages."

Collective head shaking at that.

Peter thought for a while before deciding.

"Europe makes the best lead soldiers."

More collective head shaking. Everyone looked at me.

"Europe is a culture dish with boundaries."

A slow nodding of heads, except for Sophie.

"It's contradictory. I understand it's one culture to a dish. Europe has too many. No."

"That's Jim's point," Art said.

"You're being picky, Sophie," Jack said.

I grinned at her.

"Europe is a small excuse for squabbles."

It made the list.

Uniformed Nazi officials and their girlfriends entered later and sat on the other side of the room. One of the officials began banging on a nearby piano and the whole group started to sing. A stocky man in a pinstriped suit came in and edged past their table and joined us. Art introduced him as Boris Petrov, press attaché at the Bulgarian Embassy. He was sweating, his bald head glistening in the light. The weather was cool but he would have sweated on an iceberg. Since Jack's fracas with the Europeans, we were being avoided. So Petrov's appearance had to be suspicious. He was there to plant a story for the Germans. Speaking in a low voice, he sounded puzzled, as if he were almost accidentally dropping a hint.

"A new and deadly gas, colorless, odorless. Death is instant. All is needed is one plane to drop it over a city like London. Even a little wind will spread it."

Jack sneered.

"Like you're spreading it. You're as full of wind as those Nazis over there."

"One hears."

"A bit of something and lots of nothing. Like press attachés."

"Yet another offended contact lost," Art said after Petrov coolly excused himself and left.

Jack went over and complained to the Nazis that the piano was too loud. They ignored him and Jack sang the Star Spangled Banner louder than I had ever heard it. It took all of Willi Stehr's diplomatic tact to keep him from being arrested. He returned with a grin.

At four we all left. Sophie told me she never took one of the taxis waiting outside. It was a special service the authorities allowed the restaurant to provide. She was heading to her apartment to get a few hours sleep before going to the office. I told her I would sleep at the office so she could get more rest. I watched her pedal away, merging with the blackness, her shoulders hunched over the handlebars. After she disappeared I stood in the silence before going back to the Excelsior. At the reception desk I asked the clerk where I could get an English-German dictionary. I wanted to improve my German. He straightened up, a uniform on a coatrack, head sticking out of the collar.

"In the library, sir."

"Library?"

He stared at me with the eyes of a constipated owl.

"Besides nine restaurants, a tailor, a shoemaker and a bakery. I will show you."

I followed him across the lobby, with its walls of marble tiles, to a hallway hung with watercolors of German landscapes. Halfway down he opened the door of a large room. Inside were leather armchairs, writing desks and bookshelves built into the walls. Most of the shelves were empty or less than half full. I asked him why.

"The owner was told that certain books were not acceptable. But we have dictionaries."

Those noncommittal eyes blinked.

"Come with me, please."

We went to the other side of the lobby and into a large hall with stained-glass windows. They portrayed religious figures and philosophers, but among them were depictions of Nazi leaders. It was mix and match icons. Christ and Hitler. Plato and Goering. Aristotle and Goebbels. The Buddha and Himmler. The desk clerk coughed politely before he spoke.

"This is Der Saal des Freien Denkens. The Hall of Free Thought."

I pointed at the Führer.

"The Nazis were not here originally, were they?"

"They replaced those the authorities said were unsuitable."

"The owner must have had something to say about that."

"He has left the country."

I raised my eyebrows. He glanced around.

"Have you heard about our underground passage to the Anhalter Bahnhof? Unique. And very convenient. You can buy your ticket in the hotel and get to your train without crossing the street."

I thanked him and he nodded and left. Informers were everywhere and he didn't know me. I found an English-German dictionary in the library and took it upstairs to the office. My feet on the desk, I fell asleep tilted back in the swivel chair and the open book in my lap. That's how Sophie found me at mid-morning. She sat in one of the other chairs. The phone rang. She grabbed the receiver after one ring but I was awake. She spoke in a low voice. I knew it was one of her contacts. She used words carefully to warn the caller indirectly that the phone was tapped. After she hung up she made some notes on a writing pad. I told her about the library shelves and the stained glass. She knew the history of the Excelsior.

"Why do you think the Nazis are at the Kaiserhof? Before they got into power, they wanted to make their headquarters here. But the owner said no. Later on, when they could make trouble for him they did. He got out when the war started."

The phone rang again. It was a secretary at the Foreign Office. A press conference would be held at eleven that morning. I left to cover it. It was the usual dung heap of lies. But the world wanted news and I had to translate crap into copy to sell enough newspapers to keep my job. Look hard enough for the truth and you find it was there all the time.

Sophie's next broadcast was the following Thursday. She left at one in the morning. I stayed at the office until dawn. I got a couple of hours sleep at the pension, went to the noon and 1 p.m. press conferences, filed dispatches and went to the office. She was sitting behind the desk, her right arm in a sling.

"I ran into a parked car. I went right over the handlebars, landing on my arm when I hit the pavement. It's not broken. I strained the tendons and pulled some muscles. The doctor said it'll be at least a month before I can write or type."

"I'll help you."

I hung my coat on the rack and sat down. She looked at the ceiling.

"Thanks. I was thinking about how I'm going to get to the Rundfunkhaus. In this condition I don't feel like taking the U-bahn that far. Seeing as you asked about my car, I thought you might like driving me there."

"Is that an order?"

"We're in the news business, Mr. Brian."

"The broadcasts are your business. I'm a news agency correspondent."

"Head office wouldn't like it if they heard you wouldn't help me."

"Which head office? The agency wouldn't give a damn. I'll take your dictation, type your dispatches and you can cable them. But driving? I'll do it on one condition."

"Yes?"

"Call me Jim. It doesn't have to mean anything. And 'you' is fine too. But Mr. Brian has left for warmer climes. Agreed, Miss Henser?"

"I only called you Mr. Brian because you were behaving like—the way you were."

"What kind of car do you have?"

"Does it matter?"

"To some guys it does."

"It's a German Ford."

"One of the Cologne Fords. How are the gears?"

"I don't know. I don't really drive."

"You don't or you can't?"

"Can't. I bought it four months ago. Cars have been cheap since petrol rationing. And when the war started driving was restricted to those with essential jobs that required a car."

"You thought you could always get a chauffeur."

"It was too cheap to turn down. The owner had to leave the country."

"Not Beckmann? Has anyone driven it since you bought it?"

"No. He said he had it checked by a mechanic."

"You took his word after what happened?"

"That had nothing to do with the car."

"When is your next broadcast?"

"Sunday morning. Direct by shortwave for the Saturday evening audience back home."

"Give me the key. I'll look at it. I've got a license but I'll have to get a permit to drive here. Where is it parked?"

"Right behind the hotel, on the street. You can't miss it."

She groped around in her handbag, right hand holding it open and left hand digging. She took out a key and handed it to me.

"You'll need a press pass for the station. Say you're my assistant. Tell them about my arm. They can phone here."

I stood up, put on my coat and walked to the door. She spoke casually as I opened it.

"Someone phoned and asked for you this morning, said you'd know. She's at the Esplanade. She sounds young. I'd have mentioned it earlier but with all this fuss about my arm I forgot. I hope the car starts."

Had she said "Jim" I would have cringed. A hint with "young" and that was all. To let me know what? To get from me what? A professional, not a confessional woman. Besides so-called hard facts, the news business is a lot of gossip, innuendo, slips of the tongue. Getting the story becomes a habit. It's nothing personal.

I walked to the back of the hotel. I tried to get Julia off my mind. I wouldn't call for a day or two. She called when she wanted. The artistic temperament must be shown consideration. Finely tuned, otherwise a squawk. Either you want the usual or you don't. She wasn't. No woman has everything. Impossible. She was impossible. I remembered her smile. Bad sign. Everything about her was beautiful. Maybe call sooner, maybe never.

Sophie was right. You couldn't miss it, a two-seater roadster, wire wheels, hood and fenders navy blue, the rest gray. The red "V" on the license plates meant the car had not been ordered off the road as most had. We were exceptions, with a car and a petrol allowance. Horse-drawn vans were common in Berlin, and of the remaining car drivers some had resorted to using motorcycle engines or burning wood or refuse gas. The registration papers were in the glove compartment. It was a 1935 Eifel. I looked under the hood. A side-valve flathead four. The top was up, no rips or tears. I got in behind the wheel and started the engine. It churned a few hesitant turns, caught and spun to life, no thumps, thuds, whine or clatter. The gears of the three-speed transmission were smooth, with synchromesh on the top two. I went to get a permit before heading to the pension for some sleep.

A few hours later I was back at the office. I had decided not to phone Julia until the next day. Sophie dictated a dispatch. I typed it for her. When I left for the early evening press conference at the Propaganda Ministry I mentioned the roadster.

"It's not a Mercedes 540K but it's cute. A nice runabout."

"It's for business, Mr.—Jim."

"Yours, not Mr. Jim's."

"We're supposed to be correspondents. Besides, cars don't excite me."

We stared at each other. She touched her glasses.

"You'd better get that press pass for Sunday."

"How are you getting home?"

"I'll try to get a taxi. If I can't I'll take the U-bahn. It's a short trip and there's a station close to my apartment, at the Fürstenhof. I'll leave early. You'd better come right back here after the Propaganda Ministry."

"Take some time off. I'll cover for you."

"I'm not that seriously injured."

"And I'm not Beckmann."

"I didn't mean that. Hurry up, you've got a job."

My resolve hemorrhaging, after the press conference I phoned the Esplanade from the lobby of the Excelsior. I was put through to Julia's suite. Mrs. Fusco answered and hung up on me. I went upstairs to the office. Sophie had gone. The phone rang. I answered. One word and she had me.

"Hi. Sorry about my mother. She blames you for what happened, says you started all the trouble at the café. I sneaked out. I'm calling from the lobby."

Young sounding and self-involved as ever, as if there was no war, only applauding audiences. In wartime Berlin she was an antidote to the machine tool conformity afflicting or inflicted upon everybody.

"What did you do, chloroform her?"

"Yawn. Your boss in Paris told me you had been transferred here."

"I heard the Bruch on the radio. You were great."

"I've never played better. Are you close by?"

"Not far. The Excelsior is southeast of the Esplanade, on Königgratzer Strasse. I've been told it's now officially Saarland Strasse. Apparently street names in this area keep changing."

"Let's meet somewhere right now. I have some time."

"There's a blackout because the British have been known to drop bombs at night. Be better to meet during the day. There's a weinhaus next to the Esplanade. Another is on a corner of Potsdamer Platz."

"Where's that?"

"You're in Potsdamer Platz."

"You pick something. I'm practicing for a concert. I can get away tomorrow at noon. Have you missed me?'

"What do you think?"

"I won't know till you tell me."

"I should keep you guessing."

"I'm guessing you did."

"Missing you is easy. Being with you is tough."

"Is it? I noticed you phoned me right away."

"And you keep giving me your spare time."

"I'm an artist."

"That's a good excuse."

"Are we going to argue?"

"No, we're going to do what Julia wants when she wants to."

"You're deciding where we'll meet."

"Weinhaus Rheingold would be easier. It has two entrances. The smaller one is next door to your hotel, on Potsdamer Strasse. I'll be waiting for you inside the entrance at noon."

"You going to be able to sleep tonight?"

"I usually work nights."

"You are really romantic."

"You're the best thing that's happened to me since I arrived in this gray city. You're springtime. You make me think of an apple orchard in blossom at the end of a country lane. How's that?"

"Better. The woman who answered when I phoned, is she your secretary?"

"My boss."

"So she's an older woman."

"I wouldn't say that."

"About your age, then."

"Is this important? She doesn't use a cane or drool and her mind doesn't wander and so far she hasn't fallen asleep in the middle of a conversation."

"Do you like her?"

"She's not an artist."

"What does she look like?"

"She wears glasses and cardigans."

"Her hair is in a bun, I guess."

"It's halfway down her back."

"You do like her."

"Because I happened to notice her hair?"

"Men don't happen to notice."

"You're right. I'm crazy about her. We're going to elope. As soon as we decide whether we should spend the honeymoon in the Gobi or the Sahara."

"She's probably more your type."

"She's a nice lady I work for and that's all."

"I wanted to know. See you."

At a quarter to twelve next morning I walked up Königggratzer Strasse to Potsdamer Platz. As I waited to cross the street I looked at the hotel. Similar in style to the Excelsior, the Esplanade shared that merging of the Neo-Baroque with Art Nouveau that produced Belle Époque. Not quite as large as the Excelsior, it looked grander, if that sort of thing is important. Huge halls, a Palm Courtyard, an inner courtyard with garden, inside and out it resembled a palace. Julia Fusco had arrived. Weinhaus Rheingold was next door, a perfect adjunct to the hotel. A huge multi-level beer palace, it featured luxurious rooms, many decorated with themes from Wagner's music dramas. For Wagner fans, they offered a winebibber's and beer quaffer's paradise. I crossed the street and saw Julia standing beside the door. No makeup, white slacks and blouse and an aquamarine jacket, blouse lapels outside. She knew the art of looking casual. That made her devastating.

"Waiting long?" I said, walking up to her. She shook her head, smiling.

We wandered upstairs and through a series of opulent dining halls. There were statues, carvings on keystones, medallions and pillars with bas-relief, some with stylized hollow-eyed Nordic faces, others with twisted torsos and martial glares. A waiter latched onto us and took us to a café near the cloakroom. Seating for two instead of those ranks of beer hall tables we had seen. I ordered two glasses of a good Bordeaux.

"You didn't tell me you were being transferred," Julia said. "I tried to get back and finally I phoned your office."

"I couldn't tell you at the café. I figured you would find me, anyway."

"The concert in Amsterdam was my big break. My agent was able to book me here with the Philharmonic. I'll be performing the Dvorak with Furtwängler. Where is the Philharmonie?"

"It's on Bernburger Strasse, not far from here. I dropped in one day. The interior looks like a cross between a provincial opera house shoebox and a Late Baroque church. Stalls around the sides, too much Rococo stuccowork. One of the janitors told me there used to be a skating rink there."

"It's famous."

"Anything can become famous if you talk about it enough."

"I'm lucky to get Furtwängler."

I didn't say anything.

"What's wrong?"

"The same thing since you came to Europe."

"He isn't a Nazi."

"Like Karajan and others he's made peace with the Nazis so he can conduct. They're public figures lending their support to this regime by staying here. They could've gotten out years ago. They're blatant egotists who want to stay on the podium. The Propaganda Ministry controls the Berlin Philharmonic. It was going broke. Financial backing from Goebbels looked good. It's known as the *Reichsorchester*. It's on call to provide propaganda for the Third Reich. The orchestra played at the Nuremberg rallies and at the Olympics in '36. There are fringe benefits. The players get the best apartments, are the only ones exempt from military service and go on foreign tours as musical ambassadors."

She was looking down and tapping a forefinger against the rim of her wineglass. I glanced around, saw no likely informers or agents listening.

"The real men of principle were Erich Kleiber and Fritz Busch.

"Never heard of them."

"They left soon after Hitler got into power. They couldn't stand the Nazis. Both ended up in South America. Kleiber left voluntarily. Busch was booed off the podium by SA in Dresden. He's also conducted in England since. He was music director of the Glyndebourne Festival. Other musicians have left. Not many. You pay for your principles. The opportunists have managed to survive, reputations intact. The opposition Kleiber and Busch showed has been forgotten except by those who respect what they did."

We were silent for a while before I said it.

"I'll get transferred back to the States. Leave with me, Julia, and we'll get married."

"What about my mother?"

"We'll find her a Gauleiter."

"That's not fair."

"She'd never accept my taking you away from Europe or from her."

"We could keep meeting like this."

"How often do I see you?"

She raised her eyes and looked at me.

"Why can't we be happy?"

"How can we be happy living in a place like this? I'm one mistake away from getting an exit visa or worse."

She flicked a forefinger against her wineglass.

"I can't leave her. I want you too."

"It won't work."

"Do you love me?"

"Yes."

"Isn't that all that matters?"

"For a while."

"Well, let's live that way."

"You'll be leaving Berlin after your concerts. What am I supposed to do, wait for your next appearance?"

"I've got my career."

"You can have a career back home. You're staying here for your mother. You're not ready to leave her and probably never will. She controls your life and she makes you feel grateful for that."

"Same old argument."

"Same old mother."

She looked at her watch.

"I've got to go."

We held hands as we left by the Bellevue Strasse entrance, the main one. Here the building looked like the concert hall it was originally intended to be. Adaptation, making do. If the authorities decree no concerts because of traffic congestion, serve beer. If a relationship isn't working out the way you think it should, maybe it's not supposed to. In the short time we were inside the weather had turned cold. The sky was white, like a sheet without a wrinkle. She shivered and I put my arm around her shoulder and we walked slowly through a noontime crowd hurrying back to work.

"You coming to the concert?"

"Tickets are hard to get for concerts there. People want to forget the war. It'll be broadcast. I'll settle for second best, as usual."

"Find a good place for us. Not like the one in Paris."

"There's nothing like that in this neighborhood."

We stopped. We were close to the front entrance of the Esplanade. I squeezed her shoulder. She pressed against me.

"We'd better say goodbye here."

I kissed her softly and then harder and she responded pulse to answering pulse. Cool lips and warm breath. It was like diving from a mountaintop into a pool of pink rose petals. Some women's kisses are worth everything you could get from other women. She was one of them. A passing German said something in a dialect I couldn't understand. Germans don't like public displays of affection unless they look like condolences. After a while I became aware of the glances and she began to notice them.

"I'm going."

I kissed the tip of her nose. We parted and I watched her disappear into the hotel. I went to the early evening press conference at the Propaganda Ministry and listened as the foreign press chief gloated about U-boat successes in the North Atlantic. If accurate, the claimed tonnage sunk in the past two weeks was cause for gloom in Britain. I cabled a dispatch and went to the office and typed as Sophie dictated from memory a story phoned in by one of her sources. I handed her the typescript and she looked at me.

"You look happy and miserable."

"You're fishing but your bait isn't good enough."

"I was making an observation."

"It's getting colder. That's an observation. Not like yours. No hooks."

For the first time I noticed that when she became irritated or angry her head would tilt from side to side, chin like a pendulum: storm warning.

"Careful, driver correspondents are out of season."

No effect. I tried again.

"When you think about it, if anyone ever does, the 'd' in 'cold' is a frozen stutter. Otherwise we'd say 'coal' and everyone would be warm, except in Berlin, where it's rationed and we're going to freeze this winter."

Her chin stopped wagging. The phone rang. She answered it and began talking. I left.

I went to the Adlon bar and talked with Art and Jack about Sophie. Art took his pipe out of his mouth and spoke in a low voice.

"Years ago Sophie used to give what she called 'social evenings.' Anybody who wanted could go. Correspondents were welcome. This was before the Nazis took over. A lot of people had written them off as a fringe party with no chance. She knew better. She got to know Goering, and Goebbels later on, and invited them to her parties. They got her interviews with important Nazi officials. At the parties she'd pick up hints and listen for slips of the tongue. After a while they caught on and the social evenings stopped. But she still digs up stories no one else has through contacts she's made over ten years."

They knew about her arm. Word traveled fast among correspondents. They thought it was getting dangerous for her. She should leave.

At one the following morning I drove the car to the front entrance of the Excelsior. Driving in complete darkness with headlights covered except for a slit was a guessing game. There were dark shapes and darker shapes, some moving, and you guessed which was a building, a wall, a truck, a pedestrian. Sometimes a shape moved past and you were grateful for not hitting or getting hit by it. I drove as slowly as I could without stalling the engine. Sophie was waiting by the entrance. She got in and we set off for the Rundfunkhaus, five dark miles away on the Kaiserdamm.

"We'll take the easiest route because you don't know Berlin."

"I can't see Berlin."

Following her directions, at Potsdamer Platz I turned onto Bellevue Strasse and then left at Strasse Charlottenberger and drove due west through the Tiergarten. The massed trees of the park formed black ranks alongside the road. The sky was a narrow strip of indigo above us. The roadster crawled like a noisy bug along a forest floor. Out of the Tiergarten we were on Bismarck Strasse, which changed into the Kaiserdamm.

"We're getting close to Adolf Hitler Platz, which once upon a time used to be Reichskanzler Platz. The station is on the left hand side. I'll show you where you can park. Slow down for the turn."

"Slow down? At this speed I couldn't put a dent in a marshmallow."

We had arranged that I would go with her to the Kurzwellensender, the short-wave station, part of the Rundfunkhaus but in a separate building. Her script would be checked by at least one censor. Sophie told me the censors were a mixed group, some being reasonable and others officious and difficult. Censorship was a two-stage process. Once a script was passed it would be read over the phone to the Propaganda Ministry and if acceptable broadcast after copies were made. The Kurzwellensender was four stories, with secretarial help and an office for each broadcaster. We bypassed Sophie's office and went directly to the censors' room. That night there was one censor. He was a Foreign Office official. Sophie explained my presence and said I had a pass. I had already shown it to two SS guards. He read her script slowly, tapping it with his pencil. He underlined a phrase and handed the script back to her. The phrase described Hitler, before the members of the Reichstag at the Kroll Opera House, as making some remarks "off the cuff."

"What does that mean?"

"The expression refers to impromptu remarks," Sophie told him, "thinking of different words or sentences as he speaks, seeing a better way of getting his point across."

"The Führer is always prepared. He would never write on his shirt."

"Not literally, no. But as I tried to explain to you, he might think of something else as he was speaking and say it."

"Not allowed. Change the words."

"What about 'last minute remarks'?"

"Why last minute?"

"It means immediately before."

"That would mean he is uncertain."

"No, that he thought of improvements."

"You must not give the idea that he changes his mind. Or that he is not clear."

"What about 'added some remarks'?"

"No good."

"'Restated his position'?"

The censor shook his head. Sophie handed me the script.

"I give up. It was your phrase, you substitute something else."

I wrote, "re-emphasized his earlier remarks," handed the censor the script. "Passed." And the Propaganda Ministry agreed as well.

As we left the office Sophie said, "How is yours any different?"

"It isn't. It leaves the Hitler icon untouched and that's what they want."

The shortwave transmitter was in a wooden building containing studios and a control room. Reaching it meant walking down some wooden steps and crossing a courtyard in the dark. Sophie switched on her flashlight. As we crossed, stepping around dim shapes, a voice shouted, "Put out that light." Sophie turned off the flashlight. I immediately bumped into something hard, metallic. I cursed. Her voice came out of the darkness.

"Follow me if you can. I'm used to this."

I could make out Sophie's moving shape and followed her across the courtyard. The shout had come from an SS guard who stood beside the building entrance. He demanded to see our passes. I looked through several of mine, Sophie having received permission from the guard to switch on the flashlight and hold it close to them. I found the right one and showed it to him and Sophie did the same. Because of her arm, I helped search through her handbag. Inside the building she explained to the engineers who I was and why I was there and they were sympathetic about her injured arm. The studio she broadcast from was small, with a table and a couple of chairs and a microphone sitting on the table. A monitor sat in the chair in front of the microphone. He would repeat the Berlin call letters and the frequency, Sophie's name and the name of her company, the Mutual Broadcasting System. He kept giving time checks and a few seconds before she went on the air she sat in his chair and put on earphones. As she put them on I could hear feedback from New York. "We take you to Berlin, Germany, for a report by Sophie Henser. Go ahead, Berlin." "This is Berlin." I held the script in front of her, turning the pages as she read. Her voice was well modulated, her delivery unhurried. In the other chair the monitor read the copy of the script she had given him. He understood American. Nazi double-check. She finished and said, "This is Sophie Henser in Berlin, returning you to New York." In the car later she asked me what I thought.

"I think you're good, very good. You have a natural affinity for the microphone."

She didn't say anything the rest of the way to the Excelsior as the roadster with its slits of light crept through the murk.

"Herr Bine."

It was Frau Ziegenhagen at my door with my groceries the next evening. She was able to get me two apples, a piece of sausage and a pound of potatoes. I thanked her for her efforts over the past few weeks and gave her from my Danish parcel two eggs and two strips of bacon. She thanked the Danes and me before her frown returned.

"The weather is cold now, *ja*? I can smell snow. This winter I think will be cold, more than last. The coal ration will be small. What can one do?"

As she said goodbye she noticed what was spread on a slice of rye bread in a saucer on my table. She thought it was jam.

"You eat *Konfitüre*?"

"No. *Orangenmarmalade*. It fills my stomach." I made a sour face.

She nodded. "The English eat jam."

She left, satisfied I wasn't a jam eater. I had noticed there was plenty of jam and marmalade on grocery store shelves. Germans didn't like them either. Because marmalade was available and unpopular, when I had the time I could easily pick up the weekly ration myself and look around the grocer's for deals. I didn't want to bother my landlady with such forays.

The next day it snowed. Frau Ziegenhagen had been a prophet. But it was the middle of November, time for snow in Germany. I bought an electric heater to help keep my room warm. When I went to the office later, there was an electric heater beside the desk. Sophie was out. When she returned, I mentioned buying one and she grinned.

"I bought this last year. It was behind the filing cabinets."

"How cold was it in Berlin last winter?"

"Cold."

"My landlady says coal may be a problem."

"It will. I've got a heater in my apartment too.

I was sitting near the window in one of the straight-backed chairs. She looked me over from head to foot and sat down.

"Look at what you're wearing. That khaki trench coat won't be warm enough. Your tweed jacket is all right. Give me a complete list of what's in your wardrobe."

"Aren't you being personal?"

"I don't want to be asked by head office why my assistant froze to death."

"Assistant?"

"Is that impersonal enough?"

"I was kidding. Do you want the list typed?"

"Be sure to sign it, Mr. Jim."

"My complimentary close, Existentially yours. I've got the coat and jacket, two pairs of brogues, one suit, four ties, four shirts, two pairs of pants, five pairs of socks and one sweater."

"What kind of sweater?"

"Heavy wool pullover."

"Are your brogues in good condition?"

"Almost new."

"Singlets and shorts?"

"I don't wear singlets. Four pairs of shorts."

"Pajamas?"

"One pair, heavy cotton, new."

"I think I'm safe in assuming you haven't used any of your permission slip points for clothes. Get yourself a winter overcoat. If there's enough points left, a pair of fleece-lined leather gloves or some woolen ones. You'll have to look hard. Leather, cotton and wool are in short supply except for the Wehrmacht and police. Germans are law-abiding apart from some businessmen who have to grease palms to speed up Nazi bureaucracy. There are rumors about a black market. If it exists and you're caught it means prison and if the Gestapo wants you already, worse."

She switched on the heater. I went through some of the latest German newspapers, looking for stories the Nazis wouldn't want correspondents to see, like blackout fatalities and teenagers executed for theft. These stories were always hidden at the back of the papers. As I walked through falling snow back to my pension, damp cold seeped through my trench coat. Slipping and sliding in the darkness, I seemed to be alone. There were no pedestrians, cars or trucks. The hollow streets looked abandoned. The apartment blocks, the government and office buildings, department stores, hotels, the empty squares and the statues were all slowly being covered. The snow was the same that fell when Berlin was marsh and pine forest and it brought with it a ghost of the old silence before the tribes came and the only eyes were those of beasts seeking prey or hiding. What would give you away but your own breath on such a night, huddled in wool, hair, fur, skin, staring into the spokes of falling stars spinning in tumult before you and hiding the land within their one white escape. Hold your breath and wait. Time is the last revenge, a soft pounce and a sigh.

Frau Ziegenhagen was right. It was cold that winter. Snow piled in drifts in the streets and Polish prisoners of war were brought in to clear sidewalks, driveways and roads. They were lower ranks, peasants and workers with blank faces who worked at a steady unhurried pace. I would have liked to interview them but knew they would be afraid of saying anything that would anger their captors. Coal became scarce and deliveries were sporadic. Even the Excelsior was in short supply. Sophie and I huddled around the heater. I got myself a heavy overcoat, which she said was smart looking. Her next broadcast, early Thursday morning, had to be canceled because I couldn't drive through the snow. It stopped snowing by the following Sunday, the roads had been cleared and I could manage them. The roadster spun its wheels on icy asphalt and pavement and slipped and skidded but traffic was light and we only slid into snow banks. We set out early and arrived in time. There were three censors and they approved the script and we negotiated the courtyard to the studio, stumbling against each other. Arm still in a sling, she had wrapped her coat over it and put her left arm through its sleeve and I buttoned her up. I had our passes ready for the guard. The monitor this time appeared uncertain and his English wasn't good. He overcompensated by crowding Sophie and constantly staring back and forth at both scripts. Sophie's concentration wavered and she spoke too fast. I made a sign with my hand for her to slow down. She did and towards the end her delivery was fine. After the broadcast she confronted the monitor.

"Why did you keep checking my script? The scripts are the same."

The monitor smirked at her.

"I was making sure there were no words you changed."

"You could tell by listening."

"My hearing is not good. I am not here normally."

"You're telling me," I said under my breath. He caught the tone.

"Is that American?"

"I hope so."

Sophie grinned at him.

"So we may not have the pleasure of your company again."

"Unless the snow keeps everyone away."

"Pray for rain," I muttered to Sophie.

"Help me with my coat, Mr. Jim."

The monitor looked puzzled and Sophie took a deep breath.

"You'll never understand American."

On our way back through the deserted streets the only sound was the dogged churning of the engine until Sophie spoke.

"It's a lot worse than when I started. I used to slip things past them in American English. Before the war I would say, 'the official word is' and 'the lowdown from on high is.' Once I said, 'Get a load of this.' They caught on and brought in people who had lived in the United States. That guy tonight was a bad joke but you saw how careful he was. They suspect every word, listen to every pronunciation. Pretty soon I won't be able to clear my throat."

Through the Tiergarten and again her quiet voice in the dark.

"Are the broadcasts doing any good? Do you think I should quit?"

"You're a born broadcaster. You have an excellent on-air voice and presence. That doesn't mean anything here. They want you as a mouthpiece for propaganda or off the air. We're parrots and get our tail feathers plucked if we're not word-perfect. If you want to do some good, go back to the States. Let people know what's going on."

"The doctor says I won't need the sling by next week."

"You'll be able to put on your coat by yourself."

"I do already. You do the buttons. Much appreciated. And thanks for driving, especially in this weather."

"We're colleagues, aren't we? I'll spend the night at the office. You can relieve me in the morning. I'll do the noon and afternoon press conferences and get some rest at my pension and be back in the early evening. It's a no-sleep business."

Like a cautious donkey carrying lost children across a frozen stream, the roadster skidded a few times and I steered it straight.

"This buzz buggy is doing all right."

We looked for the Fürstenhof, at the entrance to Leipziger Platz, next to Potsdamer Platz. As the roadster slipped and swayed into Leipziger Platz she peered, pointing at the windshield.

"It's that corner, remember? Can you see the blue light?"

I drove towards the pilot light and slowly a dark shape began to look like a building. I parked, got out and helped Sophie out of the car. The sidewalk in front of the hotel had been cleared of snow but there had been a residue and it had melted earlier and refrozen. As I helped her to the entrance, she slipped and lost her balance and grabbed my hand.

"Your hand is freezing. I've got a pair of men's gloves that would fit you."

"They didn't belong to Beckmann?"

Her laughter echoed all over Leipziger Platz. She caught herself and lowered her voice.

"They were Walter Deering's. He left a bunch of stuff behind at the office. I gave some away and kept some. Never know when things will come in handy."

"Yours was the only laughter heard in Berlin tonight. Laughter is verboten."

"Keep your voice down. Somebody may be listening."

"In this cold?"

"You'd better get back to the car or you won't be able to steer with those hands."

The entrance door opened a crack and a beam peeked out. A sliver of blue put a line between us on the sidewalk. A shared "goodnight" and she was gone. In complete darkness again I managed to find the roadster, honing in on its still chugging engine. After rubbing some feeling back into my hands I drove over to Potsdamer Platz and down Königgratzer Strasse to the Excelsior.

The cold lobby was deserted. The only light came from a lamp on the reception desk. No agents, spies or informers seated behind potted palms and eavesdropping on fellow citizens or suspicious foreigners. The night shift was taking the night off. Inefficiency keeps the human race from extinction.

That morning the office phone woke me.

"Hi. Did you listen to my performance?"

"Sorry, Julia. I've been busy and I didn't know when it was going to be broadcast."

"You could've phoned the station and asked."

"I'll listen next time."

"I'm giving a recital. It won't be broadcast."

"You'll be giving other concerts. The radio is always playing marches or concerts between the news."

"Thanks a lot."

"I didn't mean it that way."

"Have you thought about a place?"

"I forgot. I've been—."

"I know, busy. A friend told me the Fürstenhof is good. She says it isn't a luxury hotel like the others around here and nobody would notice us. It's close by too."

"There's the Palast and the Bellevue. They're nearby and classic."

"She says the Fürstenhof is perfect. Not like that terrible place in Paris."

"There's nothing wrong with it but do you want a middle-class hotel?"

"Your boss lives there."

"How would I know?"

"Like you knew about her hair."

"All right, have it your way. It's the Fürstenhof."

"You're making all the fuss. Pick me up at twelve this afternoon."

"Couldn't you make it later? I'll miss two press conferences."

"I've got an hour. What are some old press conferences?"

"Love on demand, courtesy of your mother. I have this fantasy of spending more than an hour with you."

"I'll be waiting inside the entrance."

When Sophie came in at eight I left. I went to my pension for a few hours sleep. I was in the Esplanade lobby fifteen minutes before Julia arrived, exactly at twelve. She was wearing a black fur coat and fur hat, her only makeup crimson lipstick. The effect was startling. The Esplanade vanished. She came over to me flapping her coat lapels, exposing her throat.

"Like my perfume?"

"Cough. What's it called, Belladonna, or Julia Strikes Again?"

"Keep talking like that and you'll have to ravish me with my clothes on."

"Ravish you? You are ravishing."

"Thank you. How are we getting there?"

"I have a car."

She liked the car, at least at first.

"I could put it in my violin case. I love Mercedes."

"It's and Eifel."

"Eyeful?"

"It's a Ford."

"Oh. It's all right."

After helping her get in, I drove to the Fürstenhof. It hadn't snowed again, the roads were clear. The sky was another white sheet over Berlin. A short trip to a nondescript hotel. The clerk was one of those guys whose eyes do his thinking for him. Stare, roll, squint, blink, peer, widen. He understood, no luggage. I paid and we went up in the elevator and I unlocked the door. Room furnished from a catalog for Anonymous Traveler. We undressed each other in world record time with almost no rips or tears. Julia was wild, scratching and biting. I held her down, forcing her open, and she fought me to the end, seizing and squirming. Half an hour later I was exhausted. We lay together, she resting on her elbow. Her fingers played with my chest hair.

"What's wrong? You tired?"

"Blame it on rationing. Not getting enough meat. There are other ways. Get on top."

"No. You're the one who has to be manly and forceful."

"Who's covered in scratches? I would have to meet a woman with fingers like tool steel and a disposition to match."

"Let's kiss. I've got twenty minutes."

Everything went well, lots of unexplored territory. I was getting interested again when she bit my lower lip, her teeth going almost clean through. I could feel the swelling and taste blood. She got up and brought me a towel.

"Why did you do that, Julia? Feels like a split plum."

"It's my mark. She'll know."

"I don't think she cares. What'll I tell my friends?"

"Make up something, you're a correspondent."

"Why don't you give me a couple of black eyes and complete the job. I could say I was tortured."

"What do you think I am, crazy?"

I sat on the edge of the bed, dabbing my lip with the towel. She sat next to me. We were still naked. She rubbed her forehead against my cheek.

"You're mine."

"I'm mine."

"Kiss my breasts. I want you to."

"I'd get blood all over them."

"I don't care. Go ahead."

She grabbed the towel and smeared her breasts with blood, reddening her nipples and making concentric circles like blurred candy stripes around supple slopes and plush bottoms.

"I won't wash them for a week."

"With coal in short supply, you may not be able to."

"Don't be a party pooper."

"What do you expect? You tear my lip half off, then use my blood to decorate yourself in some weird ritual."

"I've got to go."

"Hand me the towel. It's still bleeding."

We washed in the bathroom and put on our clothes. I turned the keys in at the reception desk and the clerk's eyes focused on my lip. They switched to Julia, who looked demure in her furs, her hands beating time to a melody. Outside the cloud was gray now and lower. More snow was coming. I dropped her off. She kissed me carefully, said she would be busy for a while but would call. I didn't say anything. You didn't part with Julia. She left you waiting and wondering when. I watched her strolling away, looking so beautiful. She was my antidote to Berlin. For an hour I had forgotten the city and the barbaric orthodoxy of Nazi rule. What was a punctured lip compared with that? I parked behind the Excelsior and went to my pension to sleep.

At ten that evening I returned to the office after the second press conference at the Propaganda Ministry and some sleep. The heater was on and Sophie was typing with the fingers of her left hand. I kept my head down. It was always dim in that room. I should have realized that I was drawing attention to myself. I hung up my coat and sat in the chair furthest from the desk. Sophie stopped typing, looked up.

"Anything?"

"The usual: tonnage sunk and Churchill the criminal wants war, rejected all the Führer's generous peace offers. I see you're doing fine without me."

"I cabled New York. I'm working on another story. I'll be finished in a minute. If you don't mind."

She typed for a while, stopped and looked up again.

"Anything wrong?"

"Tired, that's all."

"I'm finished, it's yours."

"I've still got to check my notes. You staying long?"

She looked at her watch.

"It's only ten. I leave at midnight when I don't have a broadcast. Or some social function to attend. You know my routine."

She pulled the sheet of paper from the typewriter and slipped it underneath others at the side, picked up the pile and tapped it on the desk.

"Would you check this for grammar? When you read your stuff right after typing it, you can't see mistakes."

"Sure. Give me something to do later on."

"I'd like it checked now."

"Bring it over."

"You won't be able to see."

"I can see here."

"You can't. Why are you sitting there?"

"Why do you want your stuff checked now?"

"All right, don't."

We sat in silence. I had made her angry and it was my fault. And Julia had known what would happen. I was a fool. I stood up and went to the desk. She didn't look up. I picked up the sheets, sat down in a chair beside the desk and tried to read. Finally I could and made a few minor corrections with a pencil. She never moved. I tapped the sheets together on the desk and put the typescript down in front of her.

"Typing errors, that's all. Nothing wrong with the grammar."

"Thanks. Take my chair."

When she stood up she saw. Her face showed nothing. She didn't say anything. Hiding my embarrassment told her all she had to know.

She left the office and I sat in the swivel chair and turned my notes into copy. I typed my story. When she returned she was pleasant. I made a show of giving her the swivel chair. It re-established the Pax Excelsiora. An hour later I was checking some words in my English-German dictionary. I could hear her giggling behind a newspaper.

"What's so funny?"

"A silly story. I think I'll leave early."

I helped her with her coat and as I buttoned it she looked away. I could hear her giggling as she walked down the hallway. Minutes later the phone rang. I knew but I picked up the receiver.

"Tell me what she said."

"She didn't say anything. I told her I bumped into a door."

"I'll bet. I'm phoning from the lobby. My mother is taking a nap. There's a bathroom here we can use. Come on over, I've got some time."

"To fit me in?"

"Very funny. Don't you want to?"

"So you can mutilate me? It's almost midnight, the witching hour. Your mother would fly in, catch us in a stall and have at me with her broomstick. There's been enough bloodletting today."

"Do you love me?"

"I'm crazy about you. I must be."

"I'll be leaving next week. I don't know when I'll be back. I'm staying in Germany. You could find out where I am and we could get together."

"I think I hear your mother calling."

"Corny. Let's kiss our phones. It'll be our farewell. For now."

"No, Julia. I'm not deranged, not yet."

"I'll bother you all night. Come on, I want to hear your lips smacking the receiver."

"My lips are in no condition to smack anything, remember? I'll complain to the phone company."

"I wouldn't do that, because my mother knows high officials in the secret police. If she complains about you, you won't like what will happen."

"For the record, I was kidding. I'm beginning to think you and your mother belong here."

"Please. Do it for me."

"If you'll promise to hang up immediately and not phone here again."

"Promise. I've got to practice for the recital and we'll be leaving the day after."

So I did it.

At four that morning through falling snow I walked to my pension. Only days now until December. The bad weather was keeping the bombers away. The number of air raids had dwindled since the end of summer. Food and heat were on everybody's mind. There was still cabbage and potatoes, though the potatoes were small and showed signs of rot. Bread and pasta were available. Otherwise there wasn't much. My Danish eggs and bacon had become essential for protein. When Frau Ziegenhagen could get me some butter I would mix it with the spaghetti I had told her to buy along with it. I didn't like the taste but it filled my stomach. Restaurant meals were expensive guessing games about what was really what. Nobody complained publically about the food or the lack of coal. German chemists had figured out how to make petrol and artificial rubber from coal and they got top priority, as did deliveries to Nazi bigwigs. People made do with scarcity, erratic deliveries and poor quality. There was grumbling out of hearing of the Gestapo and its volunteer army of informers. Your neighbors could send you to a camp for a long rest and maybe no return ticket.

Two days later Sophie came to the office minus the sling.

"I decided to take it off without going to the doctor. I don't need it. My arm is still stiff. But better than last week."

"Do you still want me to drive you?"

"Only if you want to."

"What do you want?"

"I say yes if you say yes."

"I'll never understand the way women discuss things. If I had asked a guy, he'd have said yes or no right away."

"That's the reason the world is in such great shape, is it?"

"You have to allow for psychopaths."

"They all seem to be men."

"It's Mother Nature's fault. Like most women, she can't make up her mind about men. Either she does a great job or decides they're criminally insane. Women are standard issue, no freaks, no fame."

"Spoken like a man. Have a cigar."

"Do you want a ride?"

"Do I have to say I want one?"

"No, ma'am. Your humble servant."

"Don't forget that."

"May I die."

She took off her glasses.

"I've been thinking about doing a special broadcast for Christmas. Would you like to be on the air?"

"What are you planning?"

"I'm open to suggestions."

"As cats say to Doubting Tom-mouses, it's nine lives and nine tails."

"What does that mean?"

"I have no idea. What will those who minister to truth allow?"

"Keep your voice down."

"What about head office? Correspondents aren't supposed to be on the air."

"They let me broadcast. I can get you on for one night."

"How about getting a few American correspondents together? Impressions of a German Christmas. We could sing Nazi carols. Silent Blight. O Come All Ye Rations. God Rest Ye Merry Commandants. O Little Town of Potsdam. Hark, the Herald Stukas Sing."

"Shhhh. That's a good idea about the correspondents. With the Rundfunk's cooperation we could do a live hookup. Carolers at the harbor in Hamburg and sleigh bells in Munich. I'll get on to New York, see what the network thinks."

The network agreed to Sophie's idea of replacing her regular Saturday broadcast Christmas week with an extended one two hours earlier on Saturday evening. The transmission would be at midnight on Sunday December 22, local time. In the Adlon bar the next afternoon I mentioned the broadcast and asked who wanted to be a part of it. Hapgood said he would have to get permission from head office. This was the first I had seen of him since his argument with Jack. They ignored each other. Art said he didn't see a problem.

"I know the papers and agencies won't allow us to be part of a broadcast. But this is personal, not hard news, and it's on our time."

"I'd be glad to do it for Sophie," Jack said.

Joe and Peter said they would try to get permission.

Sophie wanted me to write a script that would fill the whole half hour, with parts for each correspondent to read.

"No script. We'll wing it."

"For half an hour? We have to have a framework to hold the program together. What about the censors? They'll want to see something."

"They're not going to mind. It's not a news broadcast. It's about Christmas in Germany. Art and Jack have been here for years. They'll have lots to say."

"I'm not so sure about the censors and I don't want to go on the air without a format."

"Must it be in writing? We'll lose spontaneity."

She lowered her voice.

"You can't be spontaneous here. Haven't you learned that?"

"If we can't be spontaneous about Christmas, what are we doing here?"

She took a pencil from behind her right ear and tapped it on the desk.

"All right. I want a script but you guys can ad lib. Not much. I want to see it in plenty of time before the program."

"Don't you trust me?"

She stopped tapping. I thought she was going to throw her pencil at me.

"How's your arm?"

"A lot better."

"Glad to hear it."

The cold weather and snow continued into December. Germans tried to forget the freezing temperatures by getting excited about Christmas. There wasn't much to buy for gifts or merrymaking. Germany was master of much of the continent but its people faced a holiday season of shortages. You could buy as many books as you wanted but most of the good ones had been banned and burnt. Halfway through the month I received a Christmas card from Julia. She sent it to the office. She was in Munich. "Do you miss me?" Her signature filled the rest of the card. I put it on a filing cabinet, together with a couple of cards from relatives back home. I bought a miniature tree with decorations and put it beside them.

Two weeks before Christmas I handed Sophie my script for the program. She read it through quickly.

"Will this fill the half hour? It looks skimpy."

"I'm not getting paid. It's a labor of love."

"If you agree to do something, you should do it well."

"Don't worry. This is foolproof."

"I've got to fill air time."

"That's what the correspondents are there for. I've given you the framework. It'll satisfy the censors. The rest is Christmas spirit. As your unpaid chauffeur and scriptwriter I think I deserve a vote of confidence."

"All right. They'll need press passes for the Kurzwellensender for that night. How are they getting there? U-bahn? It'll still be running."

"They know about the passes. Art says he'll pick up the others. He's got a company car he hardly uses. I told him he should be there no later than eleven. He says he knows where the station is. He's driven in the blackout. They're going to meet at the Adlon."

"Everything seems set. The Rundfunk said no to a live hookup with the other cities. No explanation. Americans don't rate that much bother, obviously."

"Have you anywhere to go at Christmas, Herr Bine?" Frau Ziegenhagen asked me a few days before.

"Some of the correspondents will probably get together at the Adlon."

"Such a shame. You are welcome to eat with us."

I had no idea who "us" were. Visions of an ersatz holiday dinner weren't appetizing.

"No, thanks. I have to work."

"At Christmas. Such a shame."

We were standing in the vestibule, where she was sweeping. I went upstairs and brought down the bacon I had been saving for weeks and told her it was a Christmas present. She propped her broom against the wall and with both hands took the brown paper parcel and held it against her sweater. She blinked a few times.

"Thank you, Herr Bine. I wish—."

"We all do, Frau Ziegenhagen."

It snowed again before the broadcast but the main roads had been cleared by late that Saturday. On Friday afternoon I had gone to the Adlon to do a last-minute check. Everybody had gotten a press pass for the Kurzwellensender. Art was excited. He was going to phone home later to talk with his wife. He didn't want to chance getting through on Christmas Day. He went over the route.

"We'll leave here Saturday at half past ten. I'll go by way of the Tiergarten, left at Adolf Hitler Platz. The station is on the left hand side. I should be there by eleven."

I asked if any of them had done any broadcasting or been part of a broadcast. None had.

"I've only watched Sophie. I held her script for her after she injured her arm. She sits in a chair and speaks into a microphone. I've written the script for this broadcast. Sophie will begin by explaining to the audience back home what the program is about. The room is small so we'll crowd around the table and she'll introduce us and ask us in turn for impressions of Christmas in Germany. Each of us will have three to four minutes in front of the microphone. Anybody short of material?"

None was.

On Saturday the temperature kept dropping and by evening was below freezing. I ate my last two eggs for strength. In a steady cold wind under a starlit sky I walked to the Excelsior. I went to the back and started the engine in the roadster and ran it for a while to warm it up. Sophie was already in the office when I got there, sitting near the heater. It was after ten. I left my coat on and sat down. I was wearing the gloves she gave me. They were too big but warm, made of leather and fleece-lined. She was wearing a heavy chocolate cardigan and navy blue wool pants. I told her I warmed up the engine.

"Good. How is it outside?"

"Doing an excellent limitation of the North Pole."

"Let's go before the engine gets cold, and don't forget the script. It's in the bottom desk drawer."

She stood up and wrapped a knitted wool scarf around her neck, mouth and ears and put on a duffel coat. She buttoned it, slipped her hands into a pair of fleece-lined kid gloves and looked at me.

"You don't have a scarf."

"I'll put up my collar."

I got the script, rolled it up and slipped it into my inside jacket pocket. We rode an empty elevator down to a murky lobby. The blue shaft of Sophie's flashlight led us to the roadster. Cars parked nearby were glazed with ice that sparkled in the moonlight. The car sputtered and started and we set off at crawl speed. As on our previous journeys to the Kurzwellensender traffic was almost nonexistent. Since the weather had turned cold we had only seen military vehicles on the road at night. I was used to the icy roads and the snow by now and we had no trouble. I parked and we got out. I saw the usual cars parked nearby. Art hadn't arrived yet. I looked at my watch in the blurry beam of the flashlight. It was quarter to eleven. Sophie spoke through her scarf and wisps of vapor drifted out.

"What's happened to them?"

"It's not eleven. There's time yet."

"We've got to go inside."

"You go. I'll stay out here and wait for them. We'll get together in the station. We'll all go to the studio."

"Give me the script, wait in the car. It's too cold to stand out here."

"I'll go in with you and come back with the flashlight. I should've brought the other one."

In the station I handed her the script and went back. At eleven thirty a car crept along the street and I waved the flashlight. Art parked beside the roadster. They got out and I could smell liquor. Jack lurched towards me.

"We had a few. Brought some along."

Art apologized for being late. I waved the flashlight.

"Let's get inside. We're on the air in half an hour."

I led them into the station. We met Sophie, who told us the censors had approved the script. Her smile disappeared when she saw the state of her guests. Joe looked dazed. A cigarette dangled from Peter's lower lip. Jack swayed precariously. Only Art and Hapgood, slightly inebriated, appeared capable of saying anything intelligible. We had twenty minutes before airtime. Sophie looked in shock. I told her to lead us to the studio and we would manage when we got there. I told everyone to get his press pass ready and Art said they were in his wallet. The trip across the courtyard was in a weaving single file, the darkness punctuated with drunken curses as bodies slammed into objects. Sophie's blue beam led us. There was no shout from the SS guard about the flashlight. When we got to the building there was no SS guard. We went inside and found him drinking schnapps with the engineers and monitor in the control room. Ten minutes to airtime. A hurried show of passes. Nobody cared. Smiling idiotically, an engineer led us across the hall to the studio. He broadcast the Berlin call letters and the frequency, Sophie's name and company and gave time checks. With seconds to go New York came in, Sophie grabbed the earphones from the engineer, elbowed him off the chair and sat in front of the microphone. I could hear the feedback. "We take you to Berlin, Germany, for a special Christmas broadcast by Sophie Henser. Go ahead, Berlin." "This is Berlin."

In the beginning everything went well. Sophie read the introduction in a monotone, trying to hold herself together. I took Art and Hapgood aside and said we would have to fill in for the others. Everybody had removed gloves and coats and stacked them on the table. Jack took a bottle of brandy out of his coat pocket. I herded him, Joe and Peter into the control room. I could hear Sophie's voice rise as she attempted to talk over the racket. I shut the control room and studio doors. The last thing I heard clearly was Jack saying, "I've brought reinforcements." Art, Hapgood and I gathered around the microphone. Sophie finished reading the introduction. She introduced us and began with Art, who reminisced about past Christmases in the city. Unused to speaking into a microphone, Art had to be coaxed. His disjointed comments floated over the airwaves like dead fish. Bursts of laughter mixed with loud talk came from across the hall. Ten long minutes later it was my turn. Sophie's eyes glared with righteous wrath as she turned to me and I decided to chance everything on an impromptu talk.

"Berliners are noted for high spirits. Even as we talk, you can hear them making merry. As my landlady says, 'In cold weather you need a warm heart.' At this time of year warm hearts unite us all. Today I saw children making snowmen in the Tiergarten, the large park in the center of Berlin. At the Berlin zoo the lion cubs are playing in the snow. At Awag's department store children are gazing with big eyes at dolls and toy trains. I think many of us at Christmas see once again for a moment through a child's eyes. Memories accumulate silently the way snow lands on a fir tree in a forest. More than at any other time of the year family means more to us, both those who are here and those who have left us. And to correspondents overseas covering a war, many of us alone, our families are missed more now. The knowledge that our land, with all of its imperfections, is free and at peace is more of a comfort than any of you could possibly know."

I went on for more than fifteen minutes. Hapgood looked irritated but Sophie wasn't about to cut me off. During the last ten minutes of the program

Sophie would hold up fingers to show how much time remained and motion for me to keep going. With two minutes to go, Jack staggered out of the control room and lurched across the hall. He yanked open the studio room door.

"I wanna say somethin'."

"I haven't spoken yet," Hapgood said.

"Go back to your Nazi bitch."

Jack was so drunk his speech was slurred. His sport jacket, with checks like a chessboard, was up around his buffalo shoulders. Hapgood turned to face him. I signed off quickly.

"I see some happy celebrating Berliners have joined us in the studio, so I'm going to say Merry Christmas and let Sophie take over."

I tried to intercept Jack, stumbling towards a white-faced Hapgood.

"What did you say about my wife?"

"You should be working here in the Runtfuck'shouse. You both kiss his ass."

"That's it. I've taken enough insults from you."

I could hear Sophie signing off.

"Merry Christmas and goodnight from all of us. This is Sophie Henser in Berlin returning you to New York."

I dived between Jack and Hapgood as Hapgood swung, grazing my ear and hitting Jack on the side of the jaw. Jack wavered but kept his balance. He pushed me aside and swung at Hapgood, his fist landing on Hapgood's forehead. His toupee came loose and hung at the side of his head. Getting up from the floor I caught a glimpse of Sophie. She was in the control room talking with an engineer, trying to find out what had gone out over the air. Jack and Hapgood were tangled on the floor and swinging wildly. Art came over and we pried them loose from each other, keeping them apart as they hollered.

"You dare insult my wife."

"I know what you are, you two."

Sophie came out of the control room and crossed the hall to the studio. Joe and Peter followed. Joe could hardly stand. Peter's face was green. Sophie glared at us, her head tilting from side to side.

"I hope you're all satisfied. You ruined the broadcast. It was a bad idea. I'm sorry I was talked into it."

Nobody said anything. Hapgood put on his toupee and Jack straightened his sport jacket. Art sat in the monitor's chair, exhausted from helping separate the fighters. One of the secretaries from the station came into the studio. She was carrying a flashlight and a notebook. There had been a radiotelephone call from New York and she had written it down. She took a sheet of paper out of the notebook and handed it to Sophie. The secretary went to check the comatose contents of the control room. Sophie read the message and her face flushed. After a while she raised her head and looked at us. The studio was quiet.

"They liked it. They believed the noise was Berliners celebrating. They didn't hear. Even the end."

She couldn't speak for a while. When she did, she had recovered.

"I'm still mad at all of you. It could've been a disaster."

We filed across the courtyard and out to the cars. Everybody wished everybody else Merry Christmas, Jack and Hapgood ignoring each other. We waved at Art's car as he drove away, disappearing into the darkness. On the way back through a black Tiergarten I wanted to test Sophie's mood.

"The whole thing was a bit of a miracle, wasn't it?"

"I liked what you said, especially about seeing through a child's eyes at Christmas."

"You remember that bit about memories like snow falling on trees?"

"I liked that too."

"I was thinking of this place, of all the silence on winter nights as the snow settles on everything like a dream. You don't think that's corny, do you?"

"Of course not. Why?"

"Nothing."

"I love this place. My earliest memory is of my mother pushing me in a stroller here on a spring day. It must have been spring. I remember there were flowers in bloom."

She leaned back and closed her eyes. The roadster made its cautious way under the starlit night.

The next day Sophie greeted me with a stare when I entered the office.

"I don't know whether to thank you or chew you out about last night."

"Berate me. That sounds better."

I hung up my coat, took off my gloves and sat down.

"I didn't know they were going to drink."

"I suppose not."

"Of course, you could think I deliberately tried to sabotage your broadcast except for my part so I could get you fired and me hired."

"That's a rotten thing to say."

"No worse than blaming me for their actions after I did my best to save the broadcast."

She touched her glasses.

"How would you like to go to East Prussia?"

"As punishment? It's a backwater. We have our Deep South. They have their Deep North."

She frowned and motioned for me to lean towards her. She lowered her voice.

"When I first got here, in 1930, making friends was easy. People weren't afraid of informers. At a concert I met two girls from East Prussia, Wilhelmina and Louisa von Altenburg. That was in 1932, they were teenagers. A few years ago I met them again, found we shared the same political views. We socialized in Berlin and went twice for a skiing holiday in the Alps. They live on an estate with their mother, the Countess. Their father was killed at the front in 1918. Mina was three years old and Loulou one at the time. They wanted me to visit during the last couple of years but I've been busy. They phoned last week and invited me out for the holidays. My arm still bothers me. I don't want to travel a long distance. I thought I'd send you. As a favor."

"You want to send me to a place you've never been to meet people I've never met. Who's doing whom—pardon my grammar—a favor? You're not telling me something. If I've got to spend Christmas in a forgotten corner of Germany, I want to know why."

"Don't you want a vacation?"

"Who's going to drive you to the radio station and go to press conferences?"

"Art phoned to apologize for last night. He'll drive me till you get back. I'll do the press conferences. There's no shortage of copy. You'll need a travel permit. I phoned the Propaganda Ministry. They're going to give you one. I told them you're doing a feature story. There's no Polish Corridor now. You go past Pomerania and keep heading east to Königsberg."

"I don't know Pomerania from Patagonia."

"Here's your chance to find out."

"You still haven't told me the reason."

She leaned closer. Our foreheads were almost touching.

"They're one of my sources. I need a messenger. The message will be in code. You'll repeat it to me. Nothing on paper."

"What kind of message?"

"You shouldn't know. If you're questioned, you won't know anything. That's why I didn't want to tell you. So you'd think it was meaningless gossip."

"Is it military?"

"No."

"Who's been your contact until now?"

"I've met one or both of them at restaurants but it's getting dangerous for them and me. The Gestapo wants me gone. Any German seen with me is suspect. Our phone is tapped. I may be expelled at any time. And we may be in this war sooner than most people think. I don't want to be interned. You said I should go back and tell them the truth. I'm accumulating material. You'd be helping me."

"Blame it on me. Make me feel guilty."

"Will you do it?"

"On one condition."

I waited. Our heads stayed together. I could feel her breath. She didn't move or answer.

"That's the condition. You respect my judgment."

"I trust you, you dope."

"But you had to set me up with that line about thanking me or chewing me out."

She grinned.

"You should leave during Christmas week. Pick up your travel permit today. My friends know the situation. I'll tell them when to expect you. Somebody will pick you up in Königsberg."

"It's going to be tough. There'll be few trains and they'll be packed."

She groaned and leaned back.

"My neck is stiff."

"What kind of a story am I supposed to be writing?"

"Mina and Loulou will give you all the material you need. One thing I should mention. They're not as wealthy as you may expect. Like the other Junker estates theirs received Osthilfe, government loans that were never repaid. Even with agricultural subsidies and tariff concessions, the East Prussian estates have a hard time breaking even. They supply cows, horses, timber and grain to the rest of Germany. Most Germans think they're backward and out of date, feudal aristocrats. I only know the sisters."

"I suppose you've already told them I'm coming."

"I told them I wouldn't come unless you refused. But I said you probably wouldn't."

"Suppose I was busy?"

"Doing what? You work for me, remember?"

"I could be going places, doing things. And by the way, we work for the same agency. You happen to be my boss. Don't get carried away."

"And you're a decent guy. Don't let it go to your head."

"You'll remind me if it does."

"Should we declare a truce?"

"Agreed."

She opened a desk drawer and took out a package wrapped in red gift paper and tied with a green ribbon. She handed it to me.

"It's something you need."

"Why the paper and ribbon?"

"They were handy. I was wrapping Christmas presents. Open it. See what you think."

"Seeing as it's not a genuine Christmas present, I guess I could open it now."

I unfastened the bow, opened the wrapping and took out a burgundy wool scarf. She adjusted her glasses.

"I had some leftover yarn and knitted it. It didn't take long. I couldn't send you off without a scarf. You'd have frozen before you got around to buying one."

"Protecting the courier. Always a sensible move."

"Put it on with your overcoat. See how it looks."

I swathed my neck in several turns of scarf and went to the coat rack, put on my overcoat and buttoned it. She raised her eyebrows.

"It looks good on you."

I took a bag out of my coat pocket and handed it to her.

"It's not a real Christmas gift. They're not much. I didn't know whether I should give them to you. But as long as you're giving."

She felt the bag, carefully pressing her fingers over the shapes.

"I didn't want anything. What's in here?"

"A couple of oranges. I was passing my grocery and saw them. I told the grocer I'd buy some overripe limes he was selling if he gave me a good price on the oranges. You're a gourmet. Your taste buds would appreciate them far more than mine."

"Thanks. They're almost impossible to find here. Hardly anyone can afford them. You were lucky."

"I'm a bit of a Yankee trader. Even here you can strike a deal on the sly. Despite price controls and rationing. This scarf will be keeping me warm long after they're a memory."

"Good memories last."

She began to busy herself with some papers on the desk after putting the bag, with its twin lumps, into a drawer.

"You'd better get that travel permit."

I left thinking I hadn't given so little and felt so good since grade school.

After picking up the permit I went to the Adlon. I asked about getting to Königsberg. Jack mentioned the Stettiner Bahnhof, in northeast Berlin. Art shook his head.

"You want the Schlesischer Bahnhof, the Silesian Station, for the direct train to Königsberg. My wife and I took the train there years ago. Travel time was about seven hours. It would take a lot longer now. It was a nice trip. Silesia, the Corridor, the Masuren area with all those lakes and north to the Baltic. East Prussia is like traveling back in time."

They looked at me, waiting. Sophie wanted something different, I told them. Bucolic tranquility, a change from war coverage. An underreported area.

"There's a good reason," Jack said. "Nothing happens there. Except for some disorganized Russians they beat at Tannenberg, the last foreigner they saw was Napoleon on his way to Tilsit to sign a couple of treaties. Nappy wasn't impressed except for Altenburg, reputedly a real palace."

"I've heard that name," Peter said, stubbing out a cigarette.

"No surprise, fella. It's one of the most famous in Germany. The von Altenburgs claim descent from a Teutonic Knight who went Lutheran. One ancestor led Freddy the Great's cavalry. Another rode with Blücher on that timely appearance that decided Waterloo. They're related to the Moltkes and Bismarcks. The last count was killed in 1918, a staff officer who volunteered for front line duty. The old Countess likes fine wines. Her daughters run the place now. Quite a pair, those two."

"What do you mean?"

"The Junker dolls are known, fella. Nobody tells them what to do. The only reason the Nazis turn a blind eye is their name. To Junkers the Altenburg name stands for everything they value. Honor, duty, courage, loyalty. Their father is a hero. Last of a long line. Mention Altenburg to any Wehrmacht officer of the old school and he'll stand to attention, a misty look in his eyes. They sneer at all this SS bullshit. Like they sneered at that gang of SA thugs and bullies."

"Keep your voice down, Jack," Art said. "Don't forget, there are informers here."

"Where aren't there?"

"A hell of a time to be going, with those wonky roadbeds frozen," Peter said. "I've heard the railroads are in bad need of an overhaul. The rolling stock and track need replacing. Cars and locomotives keep going off the rails. Last week a freight on a spur derailed and ended up on the main line."

I stood up to leave and everybody wished me luck. I put on my scarf.

"Where did you get that?" Joe said.

"It was a gift."

"What did you do to deserve it?"

"Nothing, yet."

Early on Christmas Eve Sophie left for a skiing holiday in the Austrian Alps. I carried her suitcase and handbag down from the office for her. We reached her train through the tunnel between the hotel and the Anhalter Bahnhof. She stopped to buy magazines in one of the stores in the tunnel as I stared at the tile lining the walls. She was in a good mood.

"I sent New York a bunch of cables with more than enough copy to tide us over till the New Year. I phoned my friends, using an outside line. They expect you by the weekend. Any questions?"

"Arm completely healed?"

"Almost."

"Not well enough for you to travel east, only south to ski."

"You don't understand. I'm not ready for a long trip. I'll be on the easy runs. Do you ski?"

"No."

"I didn't think so. It's moderate exercise for my arm."

"Is that why arms and legs get broken every skiing season?"

"I won't be taking any chances."

"No, I will. I'm not complaining. I'm not pulling out. But dammit, skiing? Couldn't you go to a health spa?"

"Don't talk so loud. Voices echo in here. There's a chance we're being followed. If it'll make you feel better I won't go, then. I'll stay here and knit."

"Don't try to make me feel obligated. You're going and I'm going, so let's get to your train."

Walking along the crowded and noisy platform we were silent. Many day coaches were crammed and the rest were filling fast. It was quarter to nine. If it could be that bad in the morning, anyone who attempted to take later trains would be facing a brawling free-for-all. I found a coach that wasn't full and helped her aboard, scuffling with other passengers. She took one of the last seats and I put her suitcase on the rack above and gave her the handbag. It was open enough that I could see the bag of oranges. She saw and smiled up at me.

"I'm saving them for energy."

We said goodbye over the racket of farewells, banging luggage and shouts and curses.

"Have a good, safe holiday, Miss Henser."

"You too, Mr. Jim."

I had to elbow my way out through a jostling mass in the aisle. On the cold platform I stood and watched the train leaving. When the rear coach was a dot among trains on sidings in the yard, I turned and went back to the office. I didn't see anybody around the station that looked as if he had followed us. In the tunnel a man in a trench coat was looking at a magazine in the store where Sophie had bought hers but that was probably coincidence.

I spent Christmas Eve at the office, thinking thoughts people have at that time. Vanished faces, faraway places. The smell of fir boughs, candlelight reflected in the eyes of angels. I stopped myself from thinking. I wanted to get out of Germany, chuck the whole thing. I put my feet on the desk and folded my arms on my chest, leaned back in the swivel chair and closed my eyes. After a while I thought of Julia and the phone rang.

"Hi. Have you missed me?"

"Yeah. Especially right now."

"Where's your boss?"

"Gone skiing. I saw her off at the train early this morning."

"Why don't you come and see me in Munich over the holidays?"

"I can't. I have to go somewhere."

"You're going to meet her."

"I'm going in the opposite direction."

"Where are you going?"

"I can't say."

"You won't because you're lying."

I remembered the phone was tapped.

"I'm going to East Prussia to do a feature story on local traditions and customs."

"Where's East Prussia?"

"At the eastern end of Germany, near Russia."

"Is she making you do this?"

"No, New York wants the story."

"She's got you running errands for her. Too lazy to do things herself. And you'd rather go freeze to death than see me. Some lover you are."

"It's my job. How am I supposed to earn money while I'm waiting for you to show up?"

"I'm an artist. I've got a career."

"So I've heard. Our relationship depends on your whims, Julia. I've asked you to marry me and go back with me to the States. You turned me down."

"I can't now. I've got concert engagements."

"When will that stop?"

"My mother says my career is taking off and I've got to take advantage."

"I wondered when you'd bring her in."

"I know you don't like her but she's my mother."

"I'll never be able to compete with her, so why don't we say goodbye?"

"On Christmas Eve?"

"You'll be upset enough to play your best for your fans. But you'll recover because you're an artist. You live on emotion. And lots of practice."

The line was silent for a while.

"I thought you loved me."

I didn't say anything.

"I guess you don't."

She hung up. I hated myself. I went to the bar downstairs and ordered a double bourbon. The bartender told me I was the only one who ever asked for bourbon. I downed two more doubles before stepping out of the Excelsior into the frozen streets. Under the star-pierced night I passed gray stone houses with tiled roofs and cupolas, cornices and friezes. Porticos with miniature colonnades and statues fronted some of the top stories. Upper-middle-class classicism in Berlin. The blocks of apartments in workers' districts plain cubes, assume no tradition. Closed ranks at attention, the cannon fodder of the social order. How much respectability do you need? Enough to maintain the respectable, thank you. Cold comfort. No night for the Gestapo and all the other police Germans seem to need. What did Sophie say? They come in the morning. Christmas Eve becoming Christmas Day, I tilt towards my pension. Frau Ziegenhagen's abode. She with my grateful bacon. How is it to be appreciated for what you aren't? Love's Yuletide ration. And we'll take that in Reichsmarks. Where are your food cards? No succor without, sucker. Everyone's inside—an aside—why am I alone out here? Steps in the snow lead nowhere. Spending the night in Germany.

Stop banging, Herr Bine. You will wake the other tenants. Have you lost your key? Are you drunk? You sad and lonely bastard. My word. You poor man—that's better. Tannenberg and all that. It's Tannenbaum. Balm for a tanner. For somewhere where I can get a tan. Let me assume an incredulity. War leaves everyone's mouth open. Why is gone already. Get to the front. Give us a good fight. Why else have a king? Or gen'rals? Hinderburg and Loosendorf. Marching around flashing medals. The same with Shitgrubber. Are you swearing, Herr Bine? Herr Bine is slurring his bourbon. Saves me from a fate worse than breath. Why a Hitlure? Do you need all that screaming? That Vers-sigh-treating me bad. All those clawses. Rage for justice. What's right can go wrong. Contagion of the soul. Such talk is no good, Herr Bine. No talk is good. Germans obey and look the other way. The vanguard for the rest of history. The little men with big ideas will kill us all. Don't bet on the human race. You'll lose. Get me into that nice bed. It happens to be mine.

In the morning I had a headache. Frau Ziegenhagen came to see how I was and to nose around. I owed her. After thanking her for helping me up the stairs to my room I invited her to sit with me as I sipped something called coffee.

"I hope that nobody heard, Herr Bine. There are people here who would report you. It does not matter that you were drunk. Saying such things is verboten."

She put a finger to her lips and pointed at the ceiling.

"I myself am very careful. The wrong word and you are in trouble. I myself know of people in trouble because their joke was heard by an informer. You must know somebody very well before you say anything, and then you don't know. Better to say nothing."

She stared directly at me.

"Were you celebrating Christmas?"

"I had an argument with a woman."

"German?"

"American."

"Your own. Tell me no more. I know about things between men and women. I had a husband who is dead now."

That permanent frown lightened. She had gotten what she wanted.

"You will not come to Christmas dinner today? I have saved food. Turnips, potatoes. I have a fat chicken. Friends are bringing cakes. There will be wine. There is plenty for everybody."

"My stomach is in no condition to digest anything today. Thanks again. I have to leave Berlin near the end of the week. Be away for a few days."

She nodded and got up to go.

"It is good, Herr Bine, that you are not a drunkard. Trouble like yours everybody has at one time. Too bad it was now. But it is never good when it happens."

In the Adlon bar that evening there was no one except a couple of sour-looking Gestapo agents keeping each other company. A sign at the Alpenhaus said it was closed for the holidays. Complaints by other restaurant owners jealous of its extended hours and taxis for correspondents and by Nazi officials who had been disgruntled customers kept it from reopening. The Excelsior lobby was deserted. I switched on the office heater, leaned back in the swivel chair and put my feet on the desk and fell asleep. The phone woke me. I wanted it to be Julia. It was Harry calling from Paris. We exchanged holiday greetings and news. I didn't mention East Prussia. I didn't want to lie. He wouldn't have believed me, anyway. After we hung up I slept until morning. The best way to pass Christmas alone without getting drunk is to sleep through it.

I stayed at the office most of Thursday, going to my pension to pack late that evening. Friday morning at seven I was at the Schlesischer Bahnhof to board the Königsberg train. I figured there would be a limited schedule, so earlier was better. Art's fast and comfortable prewar trip was a fantasy now. The platform was packed with soldiers returning from holiday leave and with families for every stop between Silesia and the Baltic. I squeezed my way onto a day coach. There were no seats left. I stood in the aisle, my valise between my legs. Somebody said, "Hitler has promised more trains after he has given everybody a Volkswagen." He must have been a Berliner. Only Berliners made jokes like that.

Half an hour later the train left with a soft jolt. The sidings and signals of the marshaling yards slipped by, then warehouses, factories and power stations and on the outskirts of the city workers' shacks. Then it was small towns and farms and railroad crossings. Fields were covered in snow that sparkled under the blue sky. The train gradually picked up speed but it wasn't going to break any records. Stops were frequent and long. I began to shift my weight from foot to foot. Despite the crammed bodies it was cold in the coach. Sophie was right about the trip being too tough for her. I lost interest in the scenery. I hoped we would lose enough passengers so I would get a seat, but as some got off more got on. We seemed to be stuck with the same number, which made sense. Because there were too many passengers for the few trains made available, every day coach would necessarily be stuffed to the vestibules. But after several hours a slow attrition showed as increased space between the bodies. I looked outside. We had passed groves of pine earlier. We were entering coniferous forest, mostly pine and red spruce. I glanced around. "Ostpreusßen?" I asked. "Masuren," a man standing next to me said. We were in southern East Prussia. Masuren was known for its forests and lakes. That December afternoon sloping boughs were sleeved with snow and white drifts framed within their soft contours ice-bound lakes, gleaming mirrors of the sun. Through this silent austerity the locomotive chuffed and chugged, enveloped in the restrained raptures of mechanical indifference. Closer to the Baltic conifers gave way to smaller forests of beech, alder and silver birch. I managed to get a seat during the last part of the journey, through farmland, meadows and pastures, flat and muted universal white. After gradually slowing through the outskirts of Königsberg the train eased to a stop in the Nordbahnhof. It was late afternoon, the sun was setting.

# Altenburg

I stood on the station platform and waited. It was colder than Berlin, the air with the sharpness of the frigid north. The other passengers hurried away, some met by friends and relatives. After a few minutes a man wearing a chauffeur's uniform approached me. He was middle-aged, with gray hair and the measured compliance of a seasoned domestic.

"Pardon me, are you Mr. Brian?"

"Yes."

"I am to take you to Altenburg, sir."

He offered to carry my valise and I thanked him and said no, I preferred doing things for myself when I could. I asked how he knew when I would be arriving.

"My instructions were to be at the station every day, beginning yesterday."

He led me to a black Mercedes limousine parked in front of the station. He put my valise in the trunk and opened a rear door but I said I would rather sit in the front.

"As you wish, sir."

I opened the passenger side front door and sat down. He looked at me before getting in behind the wheel. I didn't know what he was used to, but I could guess. I said I preferred opening doors for myself. His nod had a slight twist. An American was a new experience for him. I asked him his name. I detected a frown. A nosy stranger being informal, probably after information about the Altenburgs. He answered carefully, as if he could give something away.

"Joseph."

"This is my first trip here. I would like to see Königsberg. As much as I can before dark. Would you mind very much if we drove through the city center?"

"Not at all, sir." He relaxed. No need to be suspicious. I was a tourist.

In the twilight and snow Königsberg looked medieval. He stopped in Kaiser-Wilhelm-Platz, in front of the Castle, with its soaring square central Gothic tower of red brick, four turrets at the corners and tall spire. The tower and the west front, with rising tiers of arched windows, looked more cathedral than castle. At each end of the north wall sat a massive squat tower with a low-pitched hexagonal roof. Brick Romanesque at its burliest. The clay bricks had gone gray from pollution. Joseph supplied me with the other names on my quick tour. A bridge over the frozen Pregel River brought us to Kneighof Island. The redbrick Dom featured a west front with a round south tower with spire and a nave punctuated by narrow stained-glass windows. Had there been a north tower? Burnt in a fire and replaced by a gable, Joseph said. We had a look at the half-timbered warehouses along the Pregel and at the Börse. Brick Renaissance in four stories of faded yellow brick, each with accompanying rows of windows. Ten minutes later we were speeding through the countryside on an icy East Prussian evening.

It was dark now. The big Mercedes navigated the frozen roads with impartial ease as we headed south. Bright as flares, the headlight beams lanced the blackness, a change from the permitted slits in Berlin. Joseph was silent the whole way. I was tired and fell asleep. He woke me when we arrived. We were parked in front of the main entrance on a sand and gravel driveway that had recently been cleared of snow. I got out and looked around in the numb silence. Outbuildings bulked as dark shapes in the distance. Nearby hedges and shrubs had become snow-covered lumps. Schloss Altenburg stood framed by the blue night, a wide two-story tan stucco front on a high basement, with side projections like matching bookends. In the center, built over the entrance, was a portico of four ionic columns, the outside ones square and all topped by a pediment. The entrance was at ground level, two steps instead of a staircase, with twelve-foot high double doors set inside a rounded arch.

Among the stars the glazed-tile mansard roof featured a series of oval dormer windows and at the top a row of chimneys. The Late Baroque comes north, domestic Prussian Rococo. There were lights on inside. As Joseph took my valise out of the trunk one of the doors opened and light emblazoned a lance across the snow.

We waited, looking at the half-open door. A short man emerged dressed in servant's livery. He hurried out into the cold and took the valise from Joseph. He turned to me, nothing of the imperious butler about him.

"My name is Klaus, sir. The family is making a round of Christmas visits and will be returning tomorrow. Your room is ready. If you will come with me."

I followed him into an eighteenth-century entrance hall with ivory walls and pastel green moldings. Bas-reliefs wreathed in stucco laurel leaves featured figures from classical mythology. Sharing the historical limelight were portraits of approved ancestors, the usual dull-eyed faces fixed up with uniforms and sashes, swords, wigs and ball gowns. Our shoes echoed discreetly on the veined marble floor as I took in the grand staircase, marble with gold-and-black wrought-iron railings. Suits of armor, halberds, stag antlers, boar heads and armorial crests with heraldic bearings were probably lurking in a more appropriate location. The only seasonal note was an eight-foot Christmas tree, a dense spruce festooned with strips of colored paper and topped by a five-pointed star. On a corner table near the entrance was a pile of women's leather gloves and winter hats and on the floor underneath a crowd of women's boots. Klaus saw me looking.

"In the old days this hall would sparkle. We have a small staff now."

"I like it this way," I said. Others did too, apparently.

The lights I had seen from outside were in the hall. The rest of the house seemed to be dark and silent. I followed Klaus up the grand staircase and down hallways where he would switch on a ceiling bulb to help us find our way. My room, on the upper floor, looked comfortable, with a large bed and high mattress, a washstand, a night table, a lamp and a fireplace. Klaus put my valise beside the bed and lit a pile of small logs in the fireplace. There was a radiator below the window. I asked about it and Klaus said the radiators weren't used because the house was almost empty much of the time.

"Where am I?"

"In the north wing, sir, at the back. You have a view of the lake."

"Is there anybody else here?"

"Only the servants. We are downstairs, at the back. The south wing is empty also. When the family returns it will be different. Many guests will be coming."

"Any chance of getting something to eat tonight?"

"Certainly. I will bring it to you."

"I would rather eat downstairs."

"All the rooms are closed except the kitchen."

"Would you mind if I ate there?"

"Of course not, sir. Follow me."

I took off my gloves, scarf and overcoat and we went downstairs. I could feel the cold in the house. The kitchen was in the basement, at the back and down a small staircase. The ceiling was high and the walls whitewashed plaster, one wall hung with copper pots and pans, from smallest to largest. There were storage bins, counters, two sinks, long tables, a chopping block, a fireplace with a roasting spit and a cast-iron stove with two ovens. A middle-aged woman was sitting at a small table and knitting. Klaus introduced her as Lotte, his wife and the cook, and told her why I was there. I told her I would be grateful for anything she had. There was leftover bratwurst and sauerkraut, warm on the stove. She filled a plate for me and I thanked her. It was delicious and I told her. She nodded and smiled, unsure about me, an informal stranger with a strange accent. Klaus left and returned in his off-duty clothes and filled a pipe. He touched the coals in the fireplace with a taper and lit the pipe. He sat at the table, looked at Lotte, then at me as I was finishing.

"You are American, sir?"

"Yes. A correspondent."

"Do you think the English will surrender?"

"No."

"Our son is in the army. He was in Poland and France. He is with the engineers. He spent his Christmas leave here. Went back to his unit yesterday.

Before the war he was a machinist's apprentice in Königsberg. We hoped the war would end so he could get married. But the English will not surrender."

"The Poles surrendered. Look what happened to them. And the French, Dutch, Belgians, Danes and Norwegians. The English will keep fighting."

"We have heard nothing bad."

"I was in France. I covered the flight from Paris. Paris is a dead city except for Germans. I read reports from Warsaw and Gdynia. Talked with correspondents who were there during and after the Polish campaign. I listen to foreign broadcasts."

"You believe them?"

"Ask yourself this. Why are the British allowed to listen to German broadcasts but you are forbidden to listen to the BBC? Why do so many listen despite the penalties? Why does your government refuse to trust you enough to decide what the truth is?"

"We are servants. We must trust others to decide for us."

We were silent for a while as Klaus smoked and I wondered if I had talked myself into an exit visa. I remembered what Sophie had said about not trusting anybody. They were country folk. That could work two ways. Browbeating by the Nazis could have made them think it their duty to report me. Or they were decent Germans whose psyches hadn't been warped by the lockstep mentality. Klaus changed the subject, deciding some topics were best left alone. I was about to enter another world.

"Altenburg is different now. There are only a few maids for upstairs and kitchen, two gardeners and one groom. Joseph helps the groom. I am not a butler but a carpenter. Now I do both. Our blacksmith helps with the house repairs. We have no housekeeper any more. Miss Wilhelmina looks after everything. The tenant farmers are still here but for how long? Like the other big estates, Altenburg takes more and more money and makes less and less money. Where will it all end?"

He smoked for a while before continuing.

"When I was a boy the Kaiserin would come here. She and the Countess, who was much younger, would go out riding in our phaeton with our best pair and a coachman and footman wearing top hats. Clothes were different then. Highborn ladies wore wide-brimmed hats with flowers piled on top and long dresses to the ground, full of frills, with puffy sleeves, and fur-fringed coats. You cannot imagine what it was like to have the Kaiserin visit. Royalty here at Altenburg. The staff on its toes. Everybody nervous and alert. Uniforms spotless. All food the best, perfectly cooked. When she left there was a big sigh of relief. And no small feeling of pride.

"Back then we had a housekeeper, Frau Strittmatter. She was a big woman, with a look that froze your blood. Even the footmen and butler stayed out of her way. We young ones kept our distance. If an important visit or occasion went well, she said '*Gut.*' Nothing else. But if anything went wrong, she would go after that person without pity. If a maid dropped a plate or forgot to drop a curtsy, watch out. Once she found an upstairs maid and a footman together. '*Aus,*' she yelled at the maid and made her pack. The Count heard and took the maid into his study and wrote her a reference to a wealthy family in Berlin. He gave her double her wages, had her sleep in a guest room and told the coachman to take her to the railroad station the next morning. From her new employer's home she wrote to my mother, who was a kitchen maid, to say she would never forget the Count's kindness. The Countess sided with Frau Strittmatter but Count Wilhelm did not care. He was a good man."

"He was," Lotte said. "But nothing happened to the footman, did it?"

Klaus puffed in silence. I asked him when he thought the family would arrive tomorrow.

"Before dark, I think. I cannot be sure. Joseph will do his best. But Christmas visits go on."

I thanked them again for the food and for their hospitality, said I was tired and would go to my room. Klaus went with me, said I would get lost on my own the first night. I slept soundly, the room warmed by a low fire. By morning the fire had died and I could feel the cold air on the blankets. Between the partly open curtains I saw frost on the windowpanes. The sky was cloudy. It was going to be a gray day. A few minutes after I woke Klaus knocked on my door.

"It is eight o'clock, sir. Breakfast is ready."

I got up and opened the door. He was wearing his livery.

"Did I wait long enough to wake you?"

"Yes, thanks. Where do I eat?"

"In the dining hall. I will return after you have washed."

Klaus told me where the nearest bathroom was and disappeared. In fifteen minutes he returned and took me to the dining hall. It was on the lower floor, through the first door to the left in the entrance hall. I found the armorial crests and the stag antlers arrayed around a fireplace you could stand in. No suits of armor, halberds or boar heads in sight. Not Rococo. The main feature was an inlaid oak table with a strip of lace tablecloth, candelabra and sixteen chairs with rose-colored padded backs and seats and cabriole legs. The rest was parquet flooring, walls covered with stucco bas-reliefs and bordered by a frieze, a silver chandelier and a vaulted ceiling. The usual, if you're an aristocrat with lots of space. I brushed off my pants and sat down. A few minutes later a maid came in and set down a bowl of porridge oats, a creamer and a sugar bowl. A country girl, hair in braids, buxom, healthy and pleasant. The usual, if you're an East Prussian farmer looking for a wife. The hot oats with cool swirls of fresh cream were perfect for breakfast in a cold palace. Klaus returned a half hour later.

"You might like to look around, sir. The Gartensaal is at the back. I will show you. Come with me."

I didn't have anything to do except wait. Klaus thought he was doing me a favor. But nothing could have been more boring than the Gartensaal. It was the kind of room that draws oohs and aahs from the rubberneck crowd. The people that "do" palaces and stately homes for the same reason others read romances. An upside-down wedding cake of a chandelier hung from a stippled and swirled stucco ceiling. The walls were covered in stucco reliefs with pastoral themes, shepherds and shepherdesses being especially numerous and deeply in love, encircled by ribbons and wreaths. The fireplace looked as if it were melting, not a corner or a straight line. Shell motifs everywhere, s-curves and pastels, pink and soft green being popular, if that's the right word. The place was crammed with side tables and chairs, those cabriole legs again, and dainty buffets loaded with urns and vases. A chaise longue, room enough for two, crowded a round table draped with a silk damask tablecloth. The table rested on a Persian carpet on a floor of black and white Italian marble tiles. I made a quick escape. On the upper floor I saw a half-open door to what looked like a study.

Inside I could see the room was more office than study. Stacks of ledgers, business letters, bills and bank statements lay on a walnut rolltop desk. A floor-to-ceiling bookcase contained journals and books on animal husbandry, cereal grains, botany, hydraulic pumps, plant crossbreeding, fertilizers, crop rotation and geology. Next to the bookcase on a high-backed wicker chair were piled government papers on tariffs and subsidies. Varnished wood paneling lined the other walls. There was a fireplace, a lamp on the desk and a walnut armchair behind it. Nobody invited me so I sat down and opened some ledgers. One dealt with household accounts and the rest with estate accounts. Servants' wages, servants let go and paid off, repairs to equipment and buildings, government loans, money from the sale of horses, cows, rye, barley, wheat and oats. Marks and scribbled comments in the margins, smeared blots, lines through rows of figures and sometimes a slash of ink across an empty page. Wilhelmina von Altenburg was a frustrated woman with a temper. I put back everything and noticed a framed photograph behind a stack of letters. A beautiful girl with long blonde hair was sitting astride a black pony, her smile primly confident. She looked about ten, was holding a riding crop the way a drum majorette flourishes a baton. The pony didn't look worried.

I wandered around until lunch, which was a bowl of barley soup with rye bread and butter. The hot soup was peppery and the slick grains of barley chewy. The rye was mealy and the butter as fresh as the breakfast cream had been. I spent the afternoon in my room, wondering why I should take trips seriously when my hosts weren't bothering to show up. A round of Christmas visits? At five o'clock I decided I would leave the next morning if they hadn't returned. Sophie would have to find somebody else or wait until her arm healed completely. At seven Klaus came and asked if I would care to join him and Lotte for supper.

"Lead on, I am yours to command." Like Joseph, Klaus came to understand my American attitudes, even in German.

More bratwurst and sauerkraut awaited me. At least the food there was good. After supper Klaus changed his clothes and smoked his pipe. Lotte took out her knitting. Omitting my perusal of the ledgers, I told them I had wandered into the study and seen a photograph of a girl on a pony. Was that Wilhelmina von Altenburg? Klaus nodded.

"She is on Fritzi. She would take great care of him, grooming him with a curry comb and would give him apples and carrots as treats. Many times she would braid his mane and tail with ribbons. He could be naughty sometimes. He would bump Miss Wilhelmina against the side of his stall, reach back and nip her on the shoulder or pull at her riding tunic. She had a whip but never used it. She would only wave it in front of him when he did not behave. Once in a while he would try to buck her off but she was a good horsewoman. She would dig in her heels and pull back on the reins. He would give up and wait for another time to surprise her. It never worked except once. Miss Wilhelmina got the idea she was the Queen of Prussia. She would get the boys on the estate and drill them. They used sticks for rifles. She would have them march past when she was on Fritzi. She always sat sidesaddle for that because that is how a queen would sit. Well, there was a parade in the rain, the anniversary of some Prussian victory. Our son was always one of the recruits, so he saw everything. None of the boys were happy about getting wet but she insisted. They were gloomy as they marched, she sitting proudly on Fritzi. He bumped her off, slick as you please, and she landed plop in the mud. Everybody laughed. She was furious and got up and went over to that pony. She still had the whip but she did not trust herself. She threw it away and faced him, hands on her hips and her eyes staring. She has a look, as you will know. Fritzi could not take it, swung his head away and backed up. She got back on but this time she sat astride him. Her dignity could not take a second fall. The parade finished in good order, led by a boy carrying the flag of the old Kingdom, with the black eagle, and the Altenburg coat of arms. Miss Wilhelmina had the crest made by a local seamstress, who sewed it on the flag. Later our son saw her in the stables rubbing him down and scolding him, still wearing her muddy riding habit. Then she gave him a hug. Miss Wilhelmina sat sidesaddle the next time, after staring at him for a while before mounting him. He behaved. The only time I saw tears in her eyes was when he was put down. He had stepped into a hole in a meadow and stumbled and broken his leg. She led him back to the stables. Many came out and watched as the gamekeeper put a pistol to his head and shot him. She looked and turned and walked away, her head down.

"Do you know she wrote a piano arrangement of a march, 'The King of Prussia'? She would have Miss Huntington, her governess, play it and would dance with Miss Louisa or with boys who visited from other estates. One, Gerd von Pommer, always liked Miss Louisa and is engaged to marry her. Miss Wilhelmina would use the boys on the estate to fight all the old battles out in the pastures and meadows. She always led the Prussians and von Pommer the enemy. To get him to do it, she would put Miss Louisa on his side as a nurse. Miss Louisa would bring along a doll and bandage it. He still did not like his part and once said, 'Mina, I will fight Hohenfriedberg and Leuthen but I will not be French or Russian any more.' She went too far once, wearing a bloody bandage around her forehead. The Countess found out where the blood came from and whipped her. Little Miss, well, not so little a miss now because she had become a woman. The battles stopped and not long afterwards she began to attend parties. What an awkward beauty she was, proud and pleasing at the same time, which confused many young men who came here. The only safe things to talk about were horses and her father. He means the whole tradition to her, of being true to your past and your people. Altenburg means Germany and that is her faith."

Lotte put down her knitting and smiled.

"They were so serious about it all, young children with flags, and sticks for swords and rifles. Running back and forth across those pastures. One girl leading them all. Once after, Jena-Auerstadt I think, I saw little Miss Louisa following her sister in from the back entrance and saying, 'I am sorry we beat you, Mina,' and Miss Wilhelmina, who had smeared ashes on her face said, 'Never mind, Loulou, next week I get my revenge at Leipzig or Waterloo, I have to choose.'

"Those girls did not always get along. Marshal Hindenburg came to visit after the war. The Countess received him in the entrance hall. They spoke for hours in the Gartensaal. He was a big man and swayed stiffly from side to side as he walked. After he left Miss Louisa imitated him, putting two fingers to her face for his mustache and strutting up and down the entrance hall. She kept shouting out, '*Ich bin Hin-den-burg, Ich bin Hin-den-burg.*' Miss Wilhelmina was not pleased. 'Hindenburg is a hero, you must not make fun of him.' That little one kept on and Miss Wilhelmina chased her upstairs and down again. But Miss Louisa was faster and could outrun her sister. She was my favorite, the darling, with her curls and big eyes. Her sister meant so much to her. But she had her own ideas. And has never been afraid to speak up."

Lotte went back to knitting. Klaus got up and knocked his pipe against the fireplace and the ash fell like gray snow. I asked why the sisters hadn't returned yet. I had a job to get back to in Berlin. Klaus came over and sat down.

"They have many visits to make. It is tradition. The family is important, the most important one in Ostpreußen. If you had come at another time they would have been here."

"Maybe they would have made more of an effort to return if my boss had come instead."

"If you left before they returned they would be insulted. They would blame us for letting you go."

"We must not let that happen. My boss will have to do without me. She sent me. She went skiing."

"Your employer is a woman?"

"My bureau chief. We work for a news agency."

"So?" Lotte said, raising her head to look at Klaus, who shrugged.

I said goodnight and told Klaus I would make my way back to my room.

After looking at the blurred outline of the snow-covered lake from my bedroom window the next morning, I spent some time in the library. Next to the study, it had cedar paneling and contained several thousand volumes, many of them bound in red or brown morocco. An atlas lay on a teak table near a globe of the world in a wooden cradle. I pulled books at random off the shelves. Complete sets of Greek and Roman classics and major European works, most of them in German. I sat in one of the red leather armchairs with a bulky volume containing Shakespeare's complete works. They had gone through a meat grinder and come out wurst. "Shall I compare thee to a summer's day?" *"Soll ich vergleichen einem Sommertage?"* I could hear the beloved saying, "Don't bother." My favorite. *"Sein oder Nichtsein—das ist die Frage!"* Translators will never learn. "Where's the toilet?" comes under a different heading. The best writing can't be translated into any language, even its own.

After a couple of hours enjoying unintentional humor, among the finest of pleasures, I dozed. I was awakened by voices at the front of the house. Women's voices, happy and tired, and Klaus with short questions and answers. The voices fragmented, going in different directions, with quick explanations or excuses. The sound of heels on marble came up the staircase. Through the open doorway connecting the study with the library, I saw a woman enter the study. She wore cavalry boots, an unbuttoned coat with the collar up and a moss green velvet dress. She threw papers on the desk, opened and slammed drawers and dropped an envelope into a wire wastebasket beside the desk. She turned in one motion and caught me looking at her. For something to do I closed the book. She came to the door and openly stared at me. She was tall, eyes the gunmetal gray of a winter sea, flowing hair wheat under a burning sun, skin white rose petals with a suggestion of pink. Her lower lip was full, her nose straight and chin almost square. A born aristocrat, peasant's hut or palace, anyone's queen in spades.

I had taken a quick tour of the royal zoo of Europe: bloodlines stretched thin from petty princelings to kings and emperors, the political playthings of the power brokers, royal nitwits become icons, aristocratic mumblers, a collection of institutionalized leftovers waiting to die out after the last changing of the guard. Successfully inbred with the etiquette of a flea. The best of them well-meaning morons, the worst arrogant elitists who snidely dismiss those without all that self-certified hyperventilated genealogical claptrap. History's welfare cases who believe they represent inferiors who owe them maintenance and money so they can go on pretending for those among us who need pretense. And Wilhelmina von Altenburg, all the way from the Middle Ages, had survived them.

Her voice had a latent authority. I came to think of it as the Junker imperative. She and her sister spoke English to me at times. They would take pity on my lame German. Women of their class would have learned English as well as French from governesses.

"Mr. Brian? We will talk after dinner. It will be at seven. Comfortable here?"

"Very. Been trying to read Shakespeare in German."

"I will see you at dinner." She smiled faintly, thinking about something else.

After she left there was a whiff of pine in the cold air that came off her.

I heard boot heels often that Sunday afternoon. She didn't shout or even raise her voice. I thought it was politic to stay in the library until summoned for dinner. A maid looked in and Klaus came by to make sure where I was. Thirty minutes before dinner he returned and asked if I would like to get ready. I went to my room and washed and put on a fresh shirt and twenty minutes later headed for the dining hall. The blaze in the fireplace warmed the room. There were four place settings. Klaus, who was setting the table, pointed out my chair, two down on the left side from the head of the table. I stood up when the von Altenburgs arrived, exactly at seven. Gaunt and white-haired, the Countess entered slightly in front of her daughters. Erect, head up, she walked as if leading a procession. Wilhelmina had on a violet blouse of watered silk and tan slacks. Louisa was dressed like her sister, her blouse stonewashed gray-blue. She was slightly shorter, hair the auburn hue of mahogany, oval face, eyes blue sky above a sunset, softly contoured nose and lips and a milkmaid's complexion. Wilhelmina made the introductions and the Countess merely nodded on her way to her chair. Louisa smiled and raised her eyebrows.

"*Willkommen*. Mina says you are an American. A correspondent in Berlin. You must think Ostpreußen strange. It sometimes is strange to me."

After giving her a sharp look, the Countess sat at the head of the table. Wilhelmina sat to her right and Louisa next to her. I was across from Louisa, with a vacant chair between the Countess and me. Klaus carried in a tureen and served a creamy potato soup that tasted of dill. There was a platter of rye and a dish of butter. I made free with the butter. I needed fat for the cold weather. The matriarch said something to Wilhelmina, who grinned.

"You like butter. Bismarck liked butter."

Me and the Iron Chancellor. It was my turn to nod.

After the soup Klaus brought in a round loaf of wheat bread and served slices. The center was filled with chopped fried bacon. Louisa said it was bacon quiche.

"This is a poor meal but there will be a good one for *das Neujahr*. A full table. And every seat taken. You shall see."

Klaus had filled our glasses with Riesling. The Countess had immediately drained hers and held it out to be filled again. Louisa raised her glass. She looked at me through the golden wine.

"We have a well-stocked cellar. From the Rheingau, in Hesse. Some superb vintages. Schloss Johannisberg."

Dessert was a platter of sliced fruitcake and another of something I didn't recognize. Louisa explained.

"*Weihnachtsstollen, ja*? Full of currants and sultanas. The other is Königsberg marzipan, fired on top to caramelize it. Lotte makes it once a year, at *Weihnachten*. With rose water and honey, no powdered sugar."

She nodded knowingly. I passed up dessert and drank wine. Dry but not bone dry, and full-bodied. The Countess knew her Riesling. Table talk was limited to the food. Louisa did most of it. After an hour the Countess made a sign, Klaus came to her chair and she stood up. We did too and she left and Louisa and I said goodbye. Wilhelmina and I went upstairs to the library. The halls and floors echoed to the hammering of her heels.

She turned on a reading lamp on the table where the atlas lay open and we sat facing each other in red leather armchairs. She put her hands together in her lap.

"How much do you know?"

"That I will be given a message of some kind to memorize."

"Nothing else?"

"It must be something that the Nazis would want kept secret and Miss Henser is going to smuggle out of Germany.

"How well do you know Sophie?"

"As bureau chief and someone regarded highly by all the correspondents."

"She thinks highly of you. Otherwise we would never trust you."

She stared at me, her face serene and pale in the weak lamplight, like the face of a princess in a medieval tapestry, except for her eyes. They were in shadow, rimless lenses into a personal twilight.

"Why are you doing this?"

"Sophie injured her arm and sent me in her place."

"She told us. Is that all?"

"What do you mean?"

"Is this a favor?"

"Why question the courier?"

"If you are caught, you will be executed without a trial."

"I would be executed with a trial."

"That does not bother you?"

"Of course it does."

"Is there nothing personal in this for you?"

"I gave up my Christmas. I stood in the aisle of a coach most of the way from Berlin. This is my second day here. No message yet. And quiche is something I could do without."

Her face stiffened. Most Germans are humorless.

"I was joking. I appreciate your hospitality."

She lifted a hand. The unintended was forgotten. True aristocrats forgive easily. They feel above anyone vulgar enough to try crossing swords with them without being of their class. It's like being touched by the unclean. She was silent for a while. When she spoke, it was like listening to an oracle.

"The victory in the west was too easy. He thinks he is invincible. He is going to invade the Soviet Union. America will fight with the British and Russians and Germany will lose. Germany will be destroyed. We were punished for losing the last war. We shall be punished for starting this one."

"You sure about an invasion?"

She nodded.

"We are finished. Unless he is stopped."

"Who will do it?"

"We have friends, who have other friends. They have been meeting to decide how and when, and about a new government."

"I know there are anti-Nazis in the old officer caste and in the aristocracy. As there are pro-Nazis among some of the young aristocrats. No one has attempted a coup yet. I suppose you know what your chances are."

"I am a good horsewoman but I have not wasted my time show jumping or riding to the hounds, as they do in England. I have studied the past enough to know I have no future."

There was nothing to say. She rose to go and I stood up.

"The message for Sophie is in the book you were reading. It will mean nothing to you. After you have memorized it, burn the paper. Because of the weather and holidays, there will be almost no trains to Berlin until the weekend. You are welcome to stay as long as you wish. We will have guests for *das Neujahr*. They may be of interest to you. I have many things to do until then. Klaus will look after you. I thank you for coming."

After she left I took the huge volume of Shakespeare down from the shelf. There was a folded piece of paper tucked in among the pages of *Julius Caesar*. She knew the plays and had a grim sense of humor or more likely, fate. Had an express been waiting at the Nordbahnhof, it would have pulled out without me.

Back in my room I read the message. It was in English. "A successful evacuation, 150 waterfowl, all dazed after the ice set in." I have been known to forget. I hid the paper among the clothes in my valise.

The following morning Klaus told me that I was to eat with him and Lotte for the next couple of days because the house, and especially the dining hall, was being cleaned and prepared for the big New Year's Day dinner. There would be many guests, most of them family members. Some would be staying afterwards. The Countess and her daughters would be taking their meals in their rooms or in the Gartensaal. I told him a bowl of porridge brought to my room in the morning would do me until dinner, which I would take with him and Lotte. He looked relieved. A houseguest in the kitchen once a day would be enough. And they were short of staff. I had seen four upstairs maids and two kitchen maids. There were no footmen and he was doubling as butler. After dinner that night I tried to find out the reason for the skeleton crew. The pipe, ball of wool and knitting needles came out after the bratwurst and sauerkraut.

"You told me the staff has been sharply cut back. But tenant farmers are still working the land. There is plenty of food. Like all the others, the estate received Osthilfe. The Mercedes is top of the line. The family dresses well, is hosting a New Year's dinner. Why is this place mostly dark and empty?"

They looked at each other before Klaus' eyes shifted to me.

"We are servants. It is not for us to say."

That night I lay on my bed thinking. Before leaving Berlin I had done some research. East Prussia voted heavily for the Nazis in the last days of the Weimar Republic. The Nazis had tapped into traditional Prussian respect for order and authority. And East Prussians were bitter about the Versailles Treaty, especially the Polish Corridor, which cut them off from the rest of Germany. Backs to the Baltic, they had lost Danzig, were surrounded by Poland and Lithuania and the Bolsheviks were not far away. All of which meant what on a freezing night near the end of 1940? Junkers were reactionaries, extreme conservatives. Constituted authority might be respected, even if its officials weren't. If you were a Prussian aristocrat and part of an anti-Nazi conspiracy, could you be sure none of the Junker plotters would betray you to the Gestapo? What about those who came to find out about the plot? One aristocrat, motivated by misplaced loyalty or a personal grudge, could destroy everything. The smart thing was for the conspirators to avoid suspicion and that's why a largely empty and dark house was wrong. As I fell asleep I was sure of one thing. Something had already happened.

New Year's Eve was quiet, shoes moderating Wilhelmina's distinctive step. I only heard her twice. I spent the day and early evening in the library. Towards evening some guests arrived and were installed in rooms in the south wing. Klaus had told me all the family and guest bedrooms were on the upper floor, the smaller ones in the north and south wings. In between and at the back were two large bedrooms, one for prominent guests and the other used by the Countess. Wilhelmina and Louisa had adjoining bedrooms in the south wing. Occasionally I glanced out of the library windows. Like those in the study, it overlooked the front of the house, its expanse of lawn punctuated by trees, shrubs and hedges and navigated by the driveway. I could see tire and sleigh and horseshoe tracks further down the driveway where it had not been cleared of snow.

I sent word to the kitchen through one of the upstairs maids that I would take my dinner in my room. I didn't want to inconvenience Lotte and Klaus, busy preparing for the big dinner. Later that evening I could hear voices coming from the hallway in the south wing. The maid brought my dinner. I ate and went to the library and read until I went to bed. During the night I was awakened by noises, probably from farmers on the estate. Locals out in the cold after drinking their fill were celebrating. I thought I heard ladles banging on pots, but that could have been a sleepy childhood memory.

On New Year's Day thin cloud covered the East Prussian sky. A maid came with my breakfast oats. She told me dinner would be at eight. After breakfast I went to the library. At twelve the maid brought me barley soup. I ate as I read. In the afternoon guests arrived and some were given rooms in the north wing.

At seven I went to my room to get ready. I heard muffled conversations in nearby rooms. I deliberately left my door open but no Junkers dropped by to introduce themselves. I hadn't seen or heard the sisters or the Countess all day. Germans are punctual and expect their guests to be on time. Being early and especially being late are considered major social blunders. I went downstairs at ten to eight. The entrance hall was crowded. Some were new arrivals taking off hats, coats and overshoes, the rest milling about and chatting as they waited for eight o'clock. More than two dozen guests, I reckoned. I got a few stares but Germans are known for staring. It's not considered impolite. As I wondered where everyone would be seated, I saw Klaus coming out of the dining hall. He looked tired but pleased at what must have been the largest social gathering of the year. Dressed in his livery he stood at the door and bowed slightly as guests began in groups to enter the dining hall. Extra chairs, some undoubtedly from the Gartensaal, had been placed around the table and everybody but me knew where to sit. Klaus looked at me and stood behind a chair and I went over and he promptly left. I was seventh down from the head of the table and to the left. All stayed standing as the Countess, followed by her daughters, came into the hall. Smiles and nods and everybody sat down. Wearing a black gown and a double strand of pearls, the Countess sat at the head of the table and Wilhelmina and Louisa in the same places as three nights earlier, Mina a white satin dream and Loulou likewise in crimson. Seated to my right was an ancient relative, the kind invited to big occasions because nobody can come up with a reason not to. Mustache drooping over his chin, which hovered inches above the tablecloth, he sported a monocle in an eye that was closed. I never did see it open. To my left was a big-boned woman wearing a yellow wig who took it as her sworn duty to ignore me. Altenburg was on show, the best plate and silverware had been set out, chandelier and candelabra lit and a pile of logs was sedately incinerating in the fireplace, and I felt a vague regret, like watching something for the last time. At the opposite end of the table from the Countess a tall heavyset man rose with a wineglass in his hand.

"My dear Augusta, let me say how fortunate I feel to be here again with you and our family and friends to welcome in another new year. We are the oldest family in Ostpreußen, tracing our lineage back seven hundred years. We have never failed in our duty to our country or to God and the honorable traditions that we hold sacred. These are in our blood. Our land was won by courage and work. And that is how we have kept it. To past and present glories, and to you, dear Augusta."

Everybody stood and drank the Countess' health. A month ago I hadn't even heard of Altenburg and there I was toasting the head of the family on New Year's Day. We sat down and Klaus got busy, together with the kitchen and upstairs maids. It was a communal effort. Damn the hidebound rules about who was supposed to be upstairs or downstairs or serving. Tureens and covered silver platters began appearing. There was a creamy potato soup with bacon bits, a ragout, smoked stag, and meatballs in white sauce with capers and potatoes. These were followed by Rominter Hunt pie, consisting of layered potatoes, herring, ham and bacon topped with sour cream and baked. Somebody said it was the Kaiser's favorite. For dessert platters of Tilsit and dark rye, winter pears, Königsberg marzipan, *Weihnachtsstollen*, and *Lebkuchen*, gingerbread sprinkled with chocolate, all of which I passed up for Riesling.

I didn't want to get drunk but there didn't seem anything else to do. I was teetering on the edge of that chasm of sweet free fall when I heard the voice of an angel calling my name. I looked around at the diners. Some had moved their chairs back from the table and were talking in groups. One was looking directly at me. I focused and it was Loulou, smiling. I put down my wineglass.

"Mr. Brian. You must meet some of our guests."

She introduced me to the man sitting beside her, Gerd von Pommer, her fiancé and a Rittmeister, or Captain, in the cavalry. Hair cropped at the sides and back, he sat erect in his dress uniform. He nodded at me. The man who had proposed the toast was Berthold von Altenburg, younger brother of the dead count. I found out later he lived nearby on another estate owned by the family. He had a habit of tapping the side of his nose with his index finger. Sitting beside him was Dr. Heinrich Schliesman of Königsberg University. A professor of philosophy, he counted himself an expert on racial theory. A small man in a tight suit, head mostly eye sockets and receding chin, he looked like a species of pale monkey dressed up for the occasion. Loulou's intention wasn't entirely innocent. She knew what was coming. The professor began with a leading question.

"So you are American. What kind?"

"What do you mean?"

"The racial origins of your mother and father."

"Irish."

"Nothing else?"

"As far as I know."

"Many Americans have been tainted with the blood of inferior races. Nigger, kike and Indian."

"You forgot wop, spic, bohunk and Mick. I'm a Mick."

"I did not think you were descended from the Pilgrim Fathers."

"They hanged witches. More your style."

"A religious sect. But racially pure. We are ensuring racial purity in

Germany. The mixing of inferior blood is verboten. It taints our Aryan blood."

"Your pure German blood is partly Celtic, Frankish, Lithuanian, Polish, Bohemian, Hungarian. Who knows what else? The original Prussians were a group of Baltic tribes who were not German and were wiped out by the Teutonic Knights. As for 'Aryan' characteristics, blond hair and blue eyes are as common in Russia, the Ukraine and Poland as in Germany. Anyone can see differences between Bavarians, Rheinlanders, Hanoverians and Brandenburgers. If we apply your standards, anyone is suspect who is short, skinny, fat, stocky or has dark hair, brown eyes, a hook nose or a round face. Send them all to concentration camps and your cities and countryside would be half empty."

"You are being simplistic. Our ultimate goal is the Aryan ideal. Of necessity it must be a gradual process of selecting for the best characteristics. Based upon scientific principles."

"Nature works in its own way. A man may be small and weak and be Mozart. Can you improve on him? What are you breeding for?"

"You are a typical American of the half-educated populist sort. But others see things differently. We have learned from the eugenics movement in your country. It calls for the removal of the physically and mentally unfit and for excluding inferior racial strains."

"The other part of your breeding program, Professor? Weed out the undesirables. Cull the handicapped and the mentally ill. The privileged and their paid scientists are leading the eugenics movement in my country. They want Aryans. They call them Nordic Americans. The Pilgrim Fathers all over again. Displace the heathen, put them on reservations. Everything for the chosen few. Who decides who is unfit? But some people like to play God. Nothing like being righteous and not in danger."

His head kept nodding the same distance, as if on a hinge. The nodding stopped on my last word and he sneered.

"You are a pathetic Christian."

"I accept no false gods."

His lips twitched but he glanced at Mina and Loulou and said no more.

They had been listening intently. The Countess was talking with one of the older women, who had commandeered von Pommer's chair and moved it to the head of the table. He was off in a corner talking with another uniformed officer. Diners near me had moved their chairs away, realizing now I was more of an outsider than they had at first thought. But Berthold von Altenburg was tapping the side of his nose, anxious to jump into the conversation. I drained the Riesling in my glass, ready. No chance of getting drunk now.

"What about those gods you do accept, sir?"

I made a gesture with my hands, as if to say, do your worst.

"Let me open your eyes, Mr. Brian. Heinkels could not bomb London without tetraethyl lead, an anti-knock fuel additive in their high compression engines supplied by Standard Oil through its British subsidiary. Standard Oil and Texaco tankers sailing under Panamanian registry are helping to refuel our submarines with American diesel. Besides refueling U-boats at sea, there are shipments to Spanish ports, including bright stock for our tanks. Our best military truck is the Blitz, built wholly by Opel, German subsidiary of your General Motors. Ford has refused to make aircraft engines for the British. But it is readily producing trucks, chain-driven vehicles and eight-cylinder engines in Cologne for our military. And your IBM provides computers for data processing in the Third Reich. I could go into dealings between the Union Banking Corporation, the Chase Bank and other financial institutions in your country and the Nazi Party ever since the Twenties. But you see my point, Mr. Brian."

"Some American businessmen are shortsighted in their pursuit of profit."

"In this case the profit motive is farsighted. We are the bulwark against Bolshevism. Your democracy is all a lie. Liberty. Equality. What nonsense. Americans are fools ruled by liars controlled by big corporations."

"For those who look, the truth has never been in short supply."

"One or two here and there have never made a difference. You are a dollar bill anybody can fold and put in his hip pocket. Germany needs friends and appreciates forward-looking Americans who help us. Your shrewd businessmen see that in the long run they will need us in a world ruled by the Third Reich."

"And if you fail to rule the world?"

"In that unlikely event, your businessmen will continue in their unrestricted greed, which makes for an uncultured society governed by money. We are, as for so many, their salvation."

I let him gloat before he continued.

"Luck and failure make great leaders, sir. Reports say that Churchill likes to watch air raids from the roof of Number 10 Downing Street. Millions will die to make him a famous war leader. In 1938 he was on the verge of bankruptcy and a wealthy Jew paid his debts and saved his country house, his Chartwell. Without Hitler he would have remained a political failure known only for the Gallipoli disaster. The Norwegian landings, another of his failures, were blamed on Chamberlain. 'We shall never surrender.' Without the English Channel the British would have been overwhelmed and he would have sailed to Canada.

"Your President Roosevelt was a failed bond salesman supported by his mother's money, put down his profession as a tree farmer, sold Christmas trees grown on the family estate at Hyde Park, but that would not have bought him his cigarettes. Did he end the Depression? Hitler did, starting a war that will be fought with deficit financing. Where did he come from? From the Versailles Treaty forced on us by those vindictive political jackals, Clemenceau and Lloyd George, and your piously hypocritical President Wilson. Read the true history of how he fomented anti-German feeling to bring your country into the war. American aid won that war, not justice. To avoid the blame, our generals talked the Social Democrats into signing. Do you appreciate irony? In 1936 Lloyd George visited the Berghof, then praised Hitler in a London newspaper. Churchill once said that if the British had been forced to sign a Versailles they would have needed a Hitler to speak up for them. You cannot slice history as if it were a loaf of bread."

I didn't answer. I didn't trust Schliesman, probably a Gestapo informer. Churchill was on the other side and Roosevelt wasn't popular. Not among Nazis.

Berthold von Altenburg grinned.

"You are silent."

"What can I say? Roosevelt was what the nation needed after three years of the Depression. Except for the ultra rich he brought the country together. That more than makes up for the bonds and Christmas trees. As for Churchill, I defer to the British, who would be pleased to defend him."

It was his turn to be silent. Whether he had intended to trap me or not, I had stopped him short. Professor Schliesman turned to him and said something I couldn't hear. They began talking with each other as if I weren't there. I looked at my wineglass. I didn't need or want a drink. I had taken on two Prussians in their own bailiwick and not done badly. Almost everybody had left the table, probably wanting as much to get away from the political fusillade as socialize. Most had gathered their chairs into circles and were chatting. Others were standing around the fireplace or off in groups in corners. Loulou came over and dragged an empty chair beside mine.

"Is it what you expected?"

"No quarter given to guests. Is that a Junker custom?"

"Of course not."

"Maybe I talked myself into an exit visa."

"You are a neutral. Some allowance will be made. I liked what you said to Berthold. He thinks he is so clever. Sophie told us you were opinionated but intelligent."

"What is Professor Schliesman doing here?"

"He is a friend of my uncle. We tolerate him. The snow is beautiful but this is not the best time to see Altenburg. You must come again."

It wouldn't look good for her to be seen talking with an American who had anti-Aryan views. Schliesman was probably watching. Her invitation wasn't empty. Germans say what they mean. I thanked her and we said goodnight. I looked a moment as she walked away, more delicately made than her sister but no weakling. That feeling of regret returned. The New Year's dinner, the great dark house with its brilliantly lit dining hall, the moldy relatives, the flame-shadowed crests around the fireplace, the stag antlers like gigantic thorns, the beautiful sisters, the snowbound estate, all seemed to be passing away. Altenburg was a painting lost in an attic corner among piles of junk slowly being covered by the breath of ghosts.

It was past eleven. Some guests were leaving, lining up to say goodbye to the Countess. I left the dining hall and went back to my room. I could hear car horns and sleigh bells, shouts and farewells. I opened the door to my room and switched on the lamp. My valise had been moved slightly from where I left it at the end of the bed. I opened it and searched for the paper. It had been taken. I waited until after midnight. The guests who were staying were going to their rooms. I went to the dining hall, empty except for Mina and Klaus. The table had been cleared and the extra chairs taken away. Mina thanked Klaus for the work the staff had done. He left and I told her what happened and we went upstairs to the study. I felt like a fool. She turned on the desk lamp and shut the door. She took a deep breath.

"Sit down, Mr. Brian."

I put the papers in the wicker chair on a bookshelf and sat down. She moved a ledger on the desk and held up the paper.

"I told a maid to check because I knew you would not burn it."

"I thought Schliesman had gone through my things. I have a short-term memory because of the amount of stuff I have to read and write."

"About these things we know more than you. You must train your memory."

She handed me the paper. I read the note again, memorizing it before crumpling the paper and tossing it onto the live coals in the fireplace. She sat down at the desk and rearranged the ledgers. She must have been tired but she hid any irritation she felt with me.

"Your sister told me Schliesman is a friend of your uncle. Is he an informer?"

"Yes. It is useful to have your enemy close at hand. He can be observed. And he suspects less."

"What about your uncle?"

"He is a fool. Behind Schliesman's back he sneers at his Nazi fake science, considers him an inferior man. But he does not want to be an old-fashioned Junker, a Prussian joke, so he tries to outwit everyone he talks to. He likes to pose as one of the aristocrats who put Hitler into power. He did nothing for or against. He never did anything but talk. We tolerate him because of our mother. Most people here, including him, are monarchists."

"So unlike Munich, no wealthy hostesses in the Twenties and early Thirties were keeping Hitler in cream puffs, but the Nazis did well in elections."

"The Soviets. The Corridor. Many Poles live here. Nobody wanted the Social Democrats."

"After Osthilfe?"

"The car Joseph drove you here in was bought with Osthilfe. Back then my mother wanted a new car and said, 'If those socialists want to throw money away, we will spend it.'"

"I have to get back to Berlin. Sophie told me you would provide some material for a story as cover for my being here."

"She did not mention that. There will be something in the bookcase."

"I can write the story tomorrow, leave the day after. Take my meals in my room. Or with Lotte and Klaus if they agree. You have guests."

"You are welcome to dine with us."

"Thank you, but no."

"As you wish."

"Before you go I wonder if you could satisfy my curiosity. There are many portraits here, including those of the Countess and of your father. But none of you or your sister. Have I missed them or are they somewhere private for privileged visitors?"

She frowned and was somewhere else before her eyes focused again. She stood up.

"I must go."

I wanted to eat in the kitchen because that would give me another opportunity to pry something out of Lotte and Klaus. After putting together an article in the study, I was back with the knitting and the pipe for more bratwurst and sauerkraut next evening. Before I knew it Klaus was telling me what I wanted to know. It started with a compliment about my handling of Schliesman.

"I like the way you spoke to that professor, sir. There was someone else here who spoke as if he knew everything. Miss Wilhelmina's friend, a painter named Anton Klapperich, from Vienna. He painted her. She put them away, never showed them. He was here twice. During his first stay they would argue and sometimes we heard. The second time he was here until a year ago. After a dinner party, the only one he attended, police came and took him away. It was early morning and I heard loud voices and went upstairs and saw from an empty bedroom in the south wing. Two men were holding onto him, one on each arm, dragging him. They pushed him into the back of a car and drove away."

Klaus scraped out the bowl of his pipe with a penknife. Bits of carbon fell onto the tablecloth. He pulled the stem and bowl apart and blew hard into the stem to clean out debris. He swept the debris and carbon into his hand, got up and dropped them into the fireplace. When he sat down he put the pipe into his jacket pocket.

"That man would not have been allowed here in the old days. But the Countess, as you have seen, is not well. She began to change some years ago, became forgetful and always talked about the past. When he first came here and brought his friends, she never knew what was going on and no one was going to tell her. It all happened in the summer house, anyway. They stayed for weeks. Miss Wilhelmina finally ordered them to leave, all but him. There was that one dinner he attended, his second time here. And you can imagine how shocked the Countess was to see someone like that at her table. You cannot mix classes."

Lotte put her knitting down and took over.

"He painted her when she was not wearing any clothes, too. We heard about those pictures before Miss Wilhelmina put them away. A maid saw them in the summer house. A good thing her mother never found out. When his friends came they would have parties there. The parties would go on all night. Screaming and drinking, running around. No one has ever been able to tell Miss Wilhelmina anything. She was always wild. She would go out riding when it was raining or foggy. She would swim naked in icy water. She would climb trees and mountains and she would hit her governess. Many a governess has come through here, I can tell you. Her mother tried to discipline her but it was no use. Not having a father made her the way she is."

The knitting again and Klaus.

"I never liked that Klapperich. He was loud and a show-off and his hair was long. Miss Wilhelmina knew he was not a painter, a real one. I was near the summer house and heard her tell him he was only good enough to paint portraits for money. He became very angry. There were many fights at the end of his first time here. She would have a hard look on her face and the heels of her boots would strike the floors like a hammer on an anvil. We tried to stay out of her way. She would go out riding. She threw him out finally. He came back two years ago, then the police came for him. She stayed away from the summer house after that morning. She sat very still at dinner and would hardly speak to anybody. We expected the police to return and ask questions but they came that one time. None of us know what he did to be taken away. But you can be sure she would never betray him. She is an Altenburg."

Early the next morning Joseph drove me to the station. It wasn't until late afternoon before a train to Berlin was ready. The coach was crowded and I had to stand in the aisle. When I finally got a seat I fell asleep until the train pulled into the Schlesischer Bahnhof at noon the following day.

# The Anhalter Drop

I couldn't find a taxi outside the station and took a tram. I was hungry, decided to eat at the Excelsior but wanted to see if Sophie was back. I took my valise to the office. As I walked to the door I could hear voices inside. I opened the door and saw Peter sitting in the chair I used when Sophie was in. Heads close together, voices low, they didn't hear me enter so I dropped the valise on the floor inside the door. Their heads jerked back and she looked indignant and embarrassed. I grinned.

"I thought you worked for the *Trib.*"

He stood up and made much of buttoning his overcoat and looking for his fedora.

"I came to say goodbye. I'm being kicked out. Last week I filed a story about skimpy rations and an embassy official over there read it. He radioed the Propaganda Ministry. I'm on my way to the station."

I took two packages of cigarettes out of a filing cabinet drawer and handed them to him.

"These will help tide you over until you get American."

He thanked me, stuffed the packages into his coat pockets and we shook hands. He shook hands with Sophie and left. She sat down again and stared at me. Her look was stranded somewhere between satisfaction and irritation and I decided to ignore it.

"I'm going to get something to eat. I've been standing in the aisle of a coach since yesterday afternoon."

I lowered my voice.

"When?"

That broke her stare.

"Later."

When I returned I could hear her through the office door. She was on the phone.

"Am I the old bag who's his boss? Oh. Really? The same to you."

She hung up as I walked in.

"What did you tell her?"

"Nothing. She's mad. We broke up over Christmas. You're not an old bag."

"Thank you."

"What's wrong?"

"Nothing."

I made a sideways motion with my head and raised my eyebrows.

"Let's take a walk."

The late afternoon sky was overcast. In the Tiergarten snow-covered paths and groves of trees alternated with open white parkland. Skaters were taking advantage of frozen lakes. Kids were throwing snowballs or sliding down hills on sleds. The only vehicles passing through on the park drive were army trucks. As we walked I gave her the message. She asked me about the trip.

"I felt I was watching people turn into history right in front of my eyes. I like the sisters. I got to know the cook and butler, a married couple. I'll make a bargain with you. Tell me what the message means and I'll tell you a secret about the sisters."

"You sure you want to know?"

"I'm already a courier. I would like to know what could get me killed."

"Have you heard of Columbushaus?"

"No."

"It looks out of place in Potsdamer Platz. That ultramodern office building with the curved front and all the glass. The SS and Gestapo moved in right after the Nazis got into power. They set up prisons. The Gestapo had secret interrogation and torture rooms. They moved out later on and in 1939 most of the offices were rented for an operation that became known as T4. That refers to another address, Tiergartenstrasse 4, where the operation moved in the spring of 1940. It was set up to kill the mentally and physically handicapped and the insane. It's the Nazi euthanasia program being carried out by special military units. The message you brought back is that 150 mentally ill people in East Prussia were killed several months ago. Code words are used: 'successfully evacuated' means killed. It's always been a secret program because the victims are German. The Nazi leadership knows it would never be generally accepted. There have been protests from Catholic and Protestant clergy who found out about it. Because newspapers and radio are censored, most Germans don't know what's happening. I've heard from one of my sources that the chronically ill are to be killed as well. The idea is that care workers are wasted on them and could be better employed looking after wounded military personnel."

"How many have been killed?"

"It's hard to know. The total is 1600 in East Prussia. In Pomerania it's 1400. At least 8000 mental patients for the whole Reich. The origin goes back to 1933 with the compulsory sterilization of the handicapped, the insane and people of mixed race. With the war Nazi thinking was that sterilization wasn't enough because 'undesirables' still needed care. In 1939 they started killing children under three with disabilities. Later on they included older children and teenagers. Six psychiatric hospitals are used for the killings. There have been about 5000 children killed so far. Injections of phenol are administered by doctors. You know what's chilling? The words they use. Headquarters, that villa at Tiergartenstrasse 4, is known as The Charitable Foundation for Curative and Institutional Care. The buses transferring adults to transit centers in hospitals before shipping them to killing centers, to hide the trail, are part of the Community Patients Transport Service. The drivers are SS. They wear white coats. For the disabled adults fatal doses needed to be greater and were too costly, so Hitler recommended gassing with carbon monoxide in shower blocks. That started in January of 1940. No family visits are ever allowed, bodies are cremated and families are sent any old ashes and a phony death certificate. By the end of the year every Jewish patient had been taken away and killed. All public nursing and old-age homes, hospitals, asylums and sanitariums are targets. Private ones aren't, so families who know what's going on put their relatives in private institutions or look after them at home. I've heard that some doctors are sympathetic and diagnose patients so they won't satisfy the T4 guidelines. Staff at the killing centers have talked. People who live nearby have noticed that buses arrive full and always leave empty. There have been showers of ash mixed with human hair."

We walked for a few minutes in silence before I told her about Mina and the painter. She shook her head.

"He could be in Flossenburg. She's from a prominent family, could appeal to a high-ranking Nazi, but she'd bring suspicion on herself. They can keep people like him indefinitely. One day he'll disappear, if he hasn't already."

"Lotte and Klaus have no idea why he was taken away. Unless wild parties are against the law."

"Could be an informer heard him say something."

It was early evening and becoming colder. A haze had settled over the trees, snowy meadows and frozen ponds and lakes. We retraced our steps through a deserted park, our shoes sounding louder crunching through the crusty snow. The drive was empty. In the abandoned streets fading light merged into a petrified gray with the buildings. We were silent on the way back to the Excelsior. I picked up my valise and said I was headed for my pension to get some sleep. She motioned for me to sit down.

"Correspondents go without sleep. Who do you think informed on the painter?"

"My guess is, Professor Heinrich Schliesman, Nazi racist par excellence. Tautology acknowledged. I argued with him after dinner. Mina told me he's an informer."

"He'd be the last to find out. Mina and Loulou would be careful to keep a dangerous situation hidden from an informer. It has to be somebody they don't suspect and isn't after them. Why weren't they at least questioned? It doesn't make sense. Did she say anything else about the professor or anything out of the ordinary?"

"No. She said Hitler is going to invade Russia. That ties in with what you told me about killing the chronically ill to release health care workers to nurse wounded soldiers. The house is empty most of the time. There aren't many servants. Having even your former boyfriend sent to a concentration camp would put a damper on any festivities. But they made Christmas visits and held a New Year's Day dinner. The Altenburgs aren't easy to read, but you know them better than I do."

"I thought I did."

I opened my valise, took out a sheaf of papers and casually tossed it onto the desk.

"That's my feature story on East Prussia. It's on soil erosion. I should call it my cover story. Double entendre, anybody?"

"Soil erosion?"

"You got your message and I had to eat Rominter Hunt pie. Herring, ham and bacon with slabs of potato."

"There are people in Berlin who would be happy to eat that."

"I'm being ungrateful. Lotte no doubt was asked to make it. I overheard somebody at the table say it's traditional, named after a local former imperial hunting ground. The dinner was first-class, appropriately."

I took a package wrapped in red cellophane out of my valise and handed it to her.

"Lotte sent something. She asked me what Fräulein Henser would like and I said gingerbread. There was *Weihnachtsstollen*. And Königsberg marzipan, estate made with honey and rosewater for the holidays."

"Königsberg marzipan? And you didn't bring me any?"

"You look like a gingerbread eater. It's sprinkled with chocolate."

She took a deep breath.

"I thought it over and told her to give you everything."

"Sometimes—."

"I know what you mean. You see me for a few hours a day but I'm stuck with me."

"Get out of here. And thanks for everything."

"Nice touch. I can't be topped. You know that. But you're good."

She tilted her head from side to side.

"I'm going. I'm putting on my coat. I'm picking up my valise. I'm walking to the door. I'm almost out."

I closed the door softly. I could hear the crinkly sound of cellophane being unwrapped.

"It's all marzipan. You—."

As I walked to my pension I remembered Julia had called. She decided when to do what and how and where and left the why of it to be explained by others. She had been trained by Mrs. Fusco. Frau Ziegenhagen met me in the downstairs hallway. She smelled of vinegar.

"*Allo*, Herr Bine. There was a telephone call for you today, and yesterday. An American girl. Not haughty, like the English."

"When did she call?"

"At one this afternoon. The same time yesterday. She wants very much to speak with you. You deserve a nice girl after the trouble you were having. And she likes you, I can tell."

That was before she called the office. She wouldn't want to speak with Sophie unless she had to. How did she find the address and phone number of the pension? She told me her mother knew members of the secret police. They could get any information about me easily. I was registered with the Propaganda Ministry as a correspondent. There had been a veiled threat behind her mention of her mother's connections but I had passed it off as more of Julia's attention-getting behavior.

"You are lucky to meet somebody so nice, Herr Bine."

Julia phoned the next morning and I answered. She would have kept phoning until I did. The other tenants would have complained about the line being tied up and Frau Ziegenhagen would have asked why I wouldn't speak to such a nice girl. If I had moved, Julia would have found me the same way. Hearing the taps on my door and Frau Ziegenhagen's expectant voice, I knew I had been trapped. The phone was on a table in the downstairs hallway. She followed me down and lingered over a faded travel poster of the Bavarian Alps tacked up on the wall across from the table. I picked up the receiver and waited and she waved a handkerchief over the poster and left. I said hello and there was no answer. I knew if I hung up she would phone again. She was waiting for me to say I was sorry.

"Is that you, Julia?"

There was a slight sound at the other end of the line.

"I got back from my trip yesterday morning."

Another sound, not so soft, maybe her clearing her throat.

"Julia? Are you there?"

I had to grin but my voice didn't give anything away. There was no safety valve with her.

"Um."

Slight progress. To her probably a major concession.

"I've got to go to work. Anything you want to say?"

"Hm."

I took that as a no.

"Goodbye, then."

I hung up, waited by the phone for a while and left. I told Sophie, who put a finger to her lips and leaned across the desk.

"As long as she doesn't phone here. I'm running an office."

"She must have used her mother's Nazi connections to get my name and number. She hinted at something like that once."

"How could she use them? She's an American."

"You don't know her mother."

"What are you going to do?"

"You mean, what are we going to do? You're the other woman."

"She called me an old bag yesterday."

"That's what I led her to believe. Otherwise she'd be more jealous than she is."

"She's going to call again. How are you going to handle it?"

"So far there's nothing that she can use against me. I told her about my trip. Said I was doing a feature story. She went for it. She's tied to a concert and recital schedule and has to practice. That doesn't leave her much free time. She was in Munich at Christmas, is probably still there. I can find out her schedule from the agency that books her. Keep track of her. As long as she's not here, we're not in trouble."

Sophie touched her glasses.

"There is one thing in your favor. She's in love with you."

"That cuts both ways. Depends on what's going on in that brain of hers."

A secretary at Julia's agency told me she was scheduled to appear with the Berlin Philharmonic for two concerts at the end of April. She wouldn't come before then. I couldn't see Julia shivering in a day coach because she had to see me. A comfortable berth in a sleeping car was more her style. And she knew her priorities. I wasn't at the top of the list, not the real one. As I went over to make sure the blinds were closed on the deepening Berlin evening, Sophie said what neither of us had mentioned.

"She's not normal. We've figured everything but that."

"She can be. But she changes. I don't recognize her. All part of being Julia."

"She's going to keep doing what she wants. And she'll try to get you to go along with it."

I sat down.

"Ever find yourself falling and wondering what it would be like to hit the floor?"

"I'd make sure there's a mattress. I mean—."

She touched her glasses. I couldn't resist.

"Sometimes a mattress makes things worse."

After the press conference the following Monday evening I went to the Adlon bar. The talk was about Peter being expelled.

"The *Trib* wanted the truth and he told it," Art said.

"He didn't know how to sneak a bit of the truth in among the manicured lies they're handing out," Jack said. "How was your trip, Jim?"

"Long, cold and boring."

"What did you write about?"

"Soil erosion. Apparently it's a problem there."

"How serious?" Joe said.

"Deforestation is leaving the land open to water and wind erosion of the topsoil. It could lead to flooding in low-lying areas."

"Sounds bad."

It was hard to keep a straight face. Art and Jack exchanged looks. I hoped the Foreign Office and Propaganda Ministry were half as gullible as Joe was. Sophie had refused to file the story unless I buried the erosion angle under some harmless personal observations about the Christmas season out there. We knew an American editor wouldn't publish it otherwise and the Nazis wouldn't be happy about a story featuring a nonexistent problem.

"I revised it, made it more of a seasonal feature. It's a bit late, so I added some interesting local color."

Now all three stared at me, not knowing what to make of my story. I needed a diversion.

"Any thoughts as we head into 1941?"

Jack made a face.

"We're sliding into this despite the America Firsters and the rest of the isolationists. They tried getting rid of Roosevelt in November. He's waiting for a way in without getting the blame. Could be the North Atlantic. American destroyer escorts are going to tangle with U-boats sooner or later. There's going to be depth charges and torpedoes. The Chancellery and Kremlin still exchanging New Year's greetings, I hear. There've been rumors of an invasion this year. It's all in *Mein Kampf.* Lebensraum. *Drang nach Osten.* Aryan masters, Slav slaves. Nappy couldn't pull it off. Schicklgruber thinks he can. We're animals, boys, animals, and the wolves among us know it."

Art began opening his tobacco pouch, stopped and lowered his voice.

"I heard the date has been set for an invasion. The middle of April or maybe some time in May."

Jack called the waiter over and we ordered another round of drinks. A few minutes later a thin-faced man stopped by our table. Jack introduced him to Joe and me as Hermann Stubenrauch, a German newspaperman. He declined Jack's invitation to join us.

"You still on the crime beat?" Jack said.

"I do business affairs now."

"So you can't tell us where the bodies are buried any more."

If he caught the broad hint, Stubenrauch didn't show it. He glanced around the bar, anxious to leave. But Jack wouldn't let him go quite yet. He winked.

"How's business?"

"Good."

"Paying for all that war matériel?"

"I cannot reveal secret information. I can tell you everything is, as you say, well in hand."

"And we know whose. Where's the coal? I'm freezing my ass off in my apartment. Fingers too frozen to hit a keyboard. If I didn't know better, I'd think it was a plot."

"The problem is with the distribution. The authorities are clearing it up and the coal will be coming."

"She'll be comin' round the mountain when she comes, huh?"

"I must leave, gentlemen. Goodbye."

After Stubenrauch left Jack lit a cigar and told us about him.

"For years he was the crime reporter on the *Frankfurter Zeitung*. Works for the *Deutsche Allgemeine Zeitung* here now. They're all DNB boys. They mouth the official Propaganda Ministry line. DNB. Dumb Nazi Bullshit. Getting so it's not healthy to be seen talking to Americans."

Later on Luigi Strazza strolled past our table. He sauntered arm in arm with a dumpy woman who looked thirty years older and a good bet to be a widow with money. His patent leather hair was glued to his head with hair oil. The odor of lanolin mixed with his cologne. He smelled like the garbage at the back of a fruit and vegetable market. He bowed slightly as he gave us a condescending smile. Jack picked up his stein and made sucking noises draining it. Strazza frowned and stopped.

"You are insulting this lady."

"I'm drinking, you spaghetti prick. Besides, grandma should be in bed."

"If I hear what you say."

"Don't play deaf."

"We should settle this like gentlemen, though you are no gentleman."

"You wops are nothing but pussy when it comes to fighting. All pop and no piss."

"*Bastardo*. You insult the honor of Italy."

"What honor? As long as I don't turn my back, I'm safe."

"If this lady was not here."

"Hiding behind a woman's skirt. Pardon me while I yawn."

Strazza took his arm from inside the woman's and leaned forward.

"*Figlio di puttana.*"

"Go and fuck grandma and she'll pay you off, greaseball."

As Strazza lunged for him, Jack leaped up and caught him on the side of the head with a straight right. Strazza fell forward and his weight took them to the floor. Joe and I jumped in to separate them, their fists blind hammers as elbows jerked. It was like tangling with a crazed animal with too many arms. I got my arm around Strazza's neck and pulled him up. Joe wrapped his arms around Jack's chest and held him back. Suddenly it was over. We let them go, the woman said something into Strazza's ear and they left. Jack brushed himself off and combed his hair. The manager came over and Art said there had been a difference of opinion. The manager left and we sat down. Jack's smile was wide.

"I slugged him good."

Art lit his pipe.

"I think you like to argue and fight, Jack, and it doesn't much matter who."

"You sticking up for that wop?"

"I don't like him any more than you do but I wouldn't pick a fight with him."

"There's a real looker at the bar. Think I'll try my luck."

The woman was well dressed. She didn't seem like a pickup. Jack sat on the stool next to hers and spoke without looking at her. A brief scan of her body before he took out his wallet. A uniformed SS officer walked up to her and she spoke to him. He stared at Jack, who retreated to our table and sat down still holding onto his wallet. The officer and woman left and Art took his pipe out of his mouth.

"Here they spot the pickups and throw them out. He's her boyfriend or husband. She probably couldn't understand your fractured German. Good thing for you."

"I thought she was playing hard to get. Thought her seeing a little of the folding would do the trick."

"She didn't look hard up enough for that," Joe said. He laughed and slapped Jack on the shoulder. "That wop's got somebody at least. You got two handfuls of nothing."

A while later an obvious prostitute wearing a fake mink coat and too much makeup came in and a waiter told her to leave. As she turned to go, lingering so the patrons could see her, Jack stood up. He caught up with her and they walked out together. Art knocked the ashes out of his pipe.

"I've never been too quick to criticize anybody. Fate takes a hand sometimes to make you look small."

It was cold all through January and heat remained a problem. Frau Ziegenhagen, at the mercy of coal dealers, could do little. Most Berliners were putting up with short supplies. In my room and at the office I relied as usual on electric heaters and warm clothing. Most war news was coming from North Africa and the ongoing Atlantic battle between U-boats and convoys. The Propaganda Ministry and Foreign Office skewed the news the Axis way and that's what we correspondents were stuck with for dispatches. Among the not so incidental items was the fact that Julia didn't phone all month.

On a slow news day I fell into an intellectual morass of introspection, pondering, musing and daydreaming. I asked Sophie a question I had been asking myself.

"Do you think it's possible to love more than one woman at the same time?"

She adjusted her glasses and put her elbows on the table.

"Not if this woman is one of them."

"That's not what I'm asking. It's got nothing to do with being monogamous or polygamous. Sounds as if I'm talking about Greek philosophers. And it's not social convention. The box of chocolates, the ring and that trip to the bedroom. I mean feeling for a woman, not feeling her up her skirt. Does love mean one?"

"Yes. Otherwise it's something else. Only a man would ask that. A woman knows."

"But maybe to a man love is different."

"What do you mean by love?"

"An overwhelming feeling. Can be instant. Or can grow. Sometimes it sneaks up on you. However it happens it's that feeling, nothing else."

"It's the same for a woman. You know what I think? You're not in love. With any woman."

"Did I say I was referring specifically and categorically to myself?"

"I assumed you were."

"Perhaps indirectly. I never thought I'd meet a tragic figure."

"She's a neurotic spoiled brat."

"I don't mean her. Mina von Altenburg."

"We've been talking about her?"

"She sees her own end in the end of her class. She accepts it. She's paying for history. It was quite a trip."

I stared into space and Sophie began pounding on the typewriter.

In 1941 there were sporadic nighttime raids over Berlin by the RAF. They were to be much heavier and the damage far greater beginning in 1943. But even small numbers of bombers were enough to make people forget the victory parades of 1940. At the Excelsior Sophie and I would go to the new shelter in the Anhalter Bahnhof, one of five large shelters in the city. At the pension the tenants would hurry down to the basement. Frau Ziegenhagen would call the roll to make sure everybody who was in the building was present. I was glad I was usually elsewhere when the siren sounded. The pension would have been demolished by a direct hit, everyone in the basement killed or buried alive under the rubble. Once I was near a U-bahn station when the siren wailed and I headed towards the entrance. U-bahn stations had been converted into shelters, as the underground had been in London. In daylight I could see there hadn't been a massive amount of damage, the odd building or apartment block in heaps and sections of road torn up. Fire trucks would be nearby and rescue parties digging among the debris. I wanted the British bombers to flatten Berlin but I felt sorry for the average citizen in an exploding crashing inferno. For hours afterwards the smell of smoke and brick dust, of burnt wood and smashed plaster drifted through the gray streets. And something fainter, the private heart of a city shriveled in the charred bodies, the dust-caked faces and limp arms carried in a stagger across the ruins.

Sophie kept collecting information from her sources. Because the office phone was tapped, she met informants in public places. Her sources included officials in government ministries, journalists and Wehrmacht officers. As winter edged towards spring Sophie and I walked in the Tiergarten and discussed what to do about the accumulating information. It was still cold and shrunken crusts of snow lingered on the frozen ground.

"You should know where everything is," she said, "in case anything happens to me."

"What could happen? You're an American."

"Don't joke. If somebody under torture implicated me, I'd be arrested as a spy. There'd be a show trial if that suited them or I'd disappear. I know I'm endangering you but you're already in this. I think you're safe. You told me the Propaganda Ministry liked your feature story. You're not under suspicion. At least not as much as I am."

"That ass of a foreign press chief told me that's the kind of story we should be sending and I was a friend of Germany."

"You should thank me."

"Why? I came up with soil erosion, remember?"

"And I told you to add those touches of local color."

"If it wasn't for you I wouldn't have gone there and gotten into this mess."

"Are you sorry?"

"No."

I stopped walking and looked at her.

"We're going to be in this war. So what difference will T4 make back home? I'm not saying it shouldn't be told, but go back home and tell it. Don't put yourself at risk."

She grinned.

"Are you sensible?"

"Not when it counts."

"Neither am I. I want to gather as much information as I can before I leave or am kicked out. Are you with me? I have to know."

"I had to have the last sensible word, that's all."

We began walking again. After a while she spoke.

"I've known lots of people over the years. One was an actress. She was beautiful and could dance and sing as well as act. Her career began in the late Twenties. Some of her films were good and some were fluff. Her father was a newspaper publisher in Munich. I met her at a party he gave when I was passing through on a skiing holiday. That was in 1932. I didn't see her again until four years later, when she came to the office. She was pale, couldn't sit still. The Nazis wanted to feature her in a series of propaganda films as the perfect Aryan woman. She had light blonde hair, pretty blue eyes, a well-shaped head and delicate facial features. She'd performed in one piece of junk and told them she wouldn't do any more. Her other problem was she wouldn't get rid of her Jewish boyfriend. I told her to go to Hollywood and take him with her. She wasn't sure they'd let her go, thought they might keep her boyfriend here to make certain she would return, and she was afraid for her family. I came up with a plan. Pretend to split up. Send him to Switzerland. Do another piece of propaganda. Go to London to act in a film—she'd already starred in a musical there—then on to Hollywood, to be reunited with him. I told her no harm would come to her family and there were plenty of German expatriates in the movie industry who would help her. I said that if she went on living the way she was, she'd become a nervous wreck. She'd think over my plan, she said. I never saw her again."

Sophie stopped walking and looked up at the white sky.

"A few months later I got a call. She'd jumped from a hospital window. The Propaganda Ministry said she was an epileptic. When that didn't go over, they said she'd been admitted because of morphine addiction. One of my sources told me she jumped or was pushed from her hotel window minutes after Gestapo agents were seen entering the building. I also heard that she had drugged and drunk herself into an almost continual daze and died after a serious fall. But they killed her, one way or another. She was the Aryan ideal."

The next morning Julia phoned the pension.

"I've decided to speak to you."

"How lucky can I get?"

"I'll ignore that."

"As you do everything else you don't want to hear."

"You've got a nerve after what you said."

"Every man since we've come out of the caves has heard that. What did I say?"

"You don't even remember?"

"Between the bombs and the bull I forgot. Whatever it was, I didn't mean to hurt your feelings."

"I'm in Wiesbaden. Why don't you drop by?"

"I'd have to get a travel permit and I've got no business in Wiesbaden."

"You've got me."

"The Gestapo wouldn't go for that."

"Mention my name."

"What would I say? I've got a date with Julia."

"Corny. Say you're dying to interview me about my career in Germany."

"Dying?"

"Well, you know."

"I can't. We're stuck with the phone."

"I'll be coming to Berlin in April. Won't that be great?"

"Yeah."

"You could be more enthusiastic."

"It's not easy with a war going on."

"We're not involved."

"I'm a correspondent, remember?"

"Your boss still sending you places while she sits on her fanny or goes skiing?"

"Let's not start that. You're much too beautiful to be jealous of another woman."

"Who says I'm jealous? By the way, I met this pianist who adores me. Rudolf something. Sickert? Anyway, he sends me flowers. My mother says he walks like a girl. And I met this flyer. He's in the Luftwaffen. He's got nineteen kills, or something. His hair is almost white and my mother says he looks like a mountain goat."

"Your mother met any interesting Nazis lately?"

"If I'm not going to mention your old boss, you can't mention my mother. Do you miss me?"

"Now that you mention it I do miss—."

"Shut up. I'm more than body parts."

"You're beautiful, desirable, sexy, a great artist and seriously wacky."

"You don't understand artists. Lots of men would like to know me."

"Look at what you're missing, stuck on a beat-up old correspondent."

"Who says I'm stuck on you?"

"You're calling me."

"Someone to speak to, that's all. Anyway, I've got to practice."

"Give my regards to your mother."

"Give your boss a kick in—."

"Remember, you're a great artist."

"Um."

She hung up. I stood holding the receiver and Frau Ziegenhagen came by.

"You were speaking to that nice young girl?"

"Yes."

"Such a shame she is not in Berlin."

She gazed at the travel poster of the Bavarian Alps and as an afterthought dusted a few of the top peaks. I put down the receiver.

"Good skiing there."

When I told Sophie at the office that morning about the call, she frowned.

"What are you saying? That she's all right now because she cooed at you today? You realize there will be a next time, don't you? Go and get yourself mixed up with her again if you want. But don't involve me or this office. I've got a press bureau to run."

"I don't plan to. You're overreacting, aren't you? I thought we agreed I had to keep her from causing trouble. That's what I'm doing. What did I say that was wrong?"

"Whenever she massages your male ego, it makes you feel great. And you don't mind if she calls me old and tells you to give me a kick."

"I thought you'd laugh."

"Laugh? I do not enjoy being insulted by a neurotic bitch who's full of herself."

"The more I defend you the more jealous she'll get."

"There's another way. Stop being flattered by what she says. She's saying it to get her own way. She's in love with herself."

"I know and I forget every time I talk to her."

"I don't think you forget. That's why you give her those digs about her mother. Get over her being infatuated with you. It'll pass and she'll move on to some other sucker. Keep doing things your way and you might set something off in her you'll be sorry for."

"It'll work itself out, whichever way it goes."

"Leave me out of it. I don't want to be a casualty of your fatalism."

A week later when I arrived at the office Sophie looked pale, her lips tight, hands folded in front on the desk.

"I had a close escape. I was ready to make contact with somebody and saw an agent nearby and left."

"What about your contact?"

"I signaled her as I was leaving. We have prearranged signals. It's happened twice in the past two weeks. It can't be a coincidence."

She shivered.

"I'm shaking. Damn heater, damn cold, damn winter, damn Berlin."

I took her coat off the rack and draped it over her shoulders, with the collar up. I kept my coat on and sat down.

"Maybe it's time to leave."

"Would you?"

"Probably not."

"Neither am I."

"Want to get something to eat downstairs?"

"Can you stomach the food in those restaurants?"

"No."

"Neither can I."

"We haven't agreed like this in quite a long time."

"We could agree on one more thing."

"I drive you to the radio station, I was your courier but I'm not playing footsie with the Gestapo next door to their headquarters."

"We have a second rendezvous set up when the first is unsafe. She's a nurse. She's highly qualified. She's worked in nursing homes and psychiatric hospitals. You'd meet her in a theater."

"I'm not meeting her anywhere."

"They're killing helpless people. I'm trying to get the story out."

"You're playing savior."

"I'm not playing. I've risked my life. I won't beg you. It's not in me."

I put my hands up.

"I wouldn't want you to. It's getting so I can't say no to a woman. I thought that was a woman's problem. I'll tell you where to send the body. My folks would want my earthly remains."

She opened the bottom drawer of the desk and took out a brand new pencil and a sharpener and sharpened it. The shavings fell into an ashtray we used for that purpose.

"The theater is old. It'll probably be half empty tonight. Be there at eight. Before going in, check to see if you're being followed. If you are, walk away. She'll be in the tenth row from the front, in the second seat from the wall, to the far left as you walk down the left aisle. She'll pass you a piece of paper. Put it in the pencil. The eraser end unscrews. Leave after ten minutes."

She handed me the pencil and I unscrewed the end. The wood adjacent to it and the top of the shaft had been hollowed out enough for a tightly rolled piece of paper.

"Where did you get the pencil?"

"It was passed to me with a message in it. I don't remember when. I haven't used it. I thought tonight would be a good time."

The theater was in Wedding, a working-class district. I stood outside and pretended to look at the sign as I checked to see if anyone had been following me. The streets were deserted. A parked truck looked of pre-Weimar vintage. I bought a ticket and went inside. No chandeliers or Rococo scrolls, pilasters, frieze or gilt staircase. A rectangular box with a small balcony, hard seats and scuffed carpeting. The dream was on the screen. The feature was a musical set in an early nineteenth-century German town, complete with stout jolly burghers and a pretty Fräulein with flaxen braids. Third Reich moviemakers tended to overdo this stuff, which is why Goebbels and company imported lots of the Hollywood product, where phony adversity seems gritty and the hero—the Nazis preferred heroes to heroines—triumphed *uber alles* after a manly tussle.

Making my way down the left aisle in the semidarkness accompanied by organ-grinder operetta I reached the tenth row from the bottom. It was empty except for a figure in the second seat from the wall. I edged along the seats and sat down next to the figure. I waited, listening to off-key singing. After a couple of minutes a hand touched mine and slipped a piece of paper into it. I took out the pencil, unscrewed it, rolled the paper up tightly and slid it into the shaft and screwed on the end. I put the pencil back into my inside jacket pocket. I checked my watch and waited ten minutes before leaving.

I was walking back to the U-bahn station for the trip to the office when a car screeched to a stop at the curb. Two men in leather trench coats got out and hauled me to the open rear door and shoved me onto the seat. They got in, one on each side of me, and the driver raced through the dark streets. All without a word. The moon shone between shreds of cloud and I could recognize Unter den Linden. The driver skimmed down Wilhelmstrasse past the monolithic government buildings. He turned right on Prinz-Albrecht-Strasse for the short sprint to Gestapo headquarters at Number 8. I was hustled into the entrance hall, with its barrel-vaulted ceiling, and up a wide staircase with a squat wooden railing to the second floor. From there quick steps along a corridor to an interrogation room, where I was dumped into a chair and a door slammed behind me. I waited fifteen minutes. I thought I heard a scream but that could have been a recording to get me in the mood or a hoarse Brunnhilde practicing for the Ring. Finally a side door opened and two of Himmler's super-Aryans strolled in and sat on the opposite side of a long table from me. Not all Gestapo were former police officers in trench coats. These wore suits, looked university educated and altogether had the air of rising junior executives, but with a touch of Doberman pinscher. No preamble, a series of questions from one as the other watched me for beads of sweat.

"What were you doing in north Berlin?"

"I was watching a movie."

"Why did you leave after ten minutes?"

"The movie was boring."

"Where were you sitting?"

"Near the front."

"Where?"

"In the ninth or tenth row."

"Who was sitting next to you?"

"How would I know? It was dark."

"What was the name of the film?"

"It started before I went in."

"You must have seen the name outside."

"I glanced at it and thought I might want to see the movie."

"I want to know, what were you doing in that district?"

"I was watching a movie."

"There are many theaters in better districts but on a winter night you took the U-bahn to a small theater in Wedding."

"Illogical behavior is not illegal."

"Why did you leave after ten minutes?"

"I told you, I found the movie boring."

"You were there to meet someone."

"I was there to watch a movie."

"You went there as a spy."

"I went there to watch a movie."

"You were passed information."

"Nobody passed me anything."

"We will find it. You left after ten minutes."

"The movie bored me."

"You are a spy."

"I am a foreign correspondent."

"Empty your pockets, put everything on the table."

I thought of holding back the pencil but decided if they strip-searched me I would be finished. They went through my wallet, ration cards, permission slips, press passes, the notebook I used for press conferences and inspected my

Propaganda Ministry identity card. The talker picked up the pencil, held it between thumb and forefinger at each end.

"Everything breaks, according to how much stress it can take."

"Hey, that costs money. I write with it."

"Americans. Always thinking of commerce."

With a thumb and forefinger holding the eraser end, Aryanman made the pencil oscillate like a metronome and then tossed it on the table. His clone grabbed it and drew a line alongside my most recent press conference notes to see if the graphite was the same dark shade. Last joke, I thought, 2B or not 2B, the grade I used. It was. They weren't ready to let me go. An underling was called in and strip-searched me. As I was putting on my clothes another underling appeared and spoke to my interrogator. Among the words I heard was "*Botschaft*."

"You are free to go," my interrogator said, looking almost hurt.

Outside I breathed in the wonderfully cold air. I began to shake as my nerves gave way to the stress. I wanted to walk over to the Adlon for a drink but I knew Sophie would be waiting at the office. I recovered as I walked the few blocks to the Excelsior. Sophie was pacing up and down as I entered.

"Maria called. She left right after you and saw you being picked up. She phoned and used a code word and I went over to the embassy. I got back a few minutes ago."

I took out the pencil and handed it to her, hung up my coat and sat down.

"You'll have to change your code. I wasn't followed, they were already there, probably parked a couple of blocks away. They waited ten minutes. Knew when I would be coming out. Your Maria's been turned or is languishing in one of the ground floor cells at Number 8."

"Didn't you see her?"

"I saw a figure in the dark. Could have been a man."

"She called here."

"Maybe somebody's imitating her voice. Whoever phoned is covering her tracks. If they'd found anything, I'd have been done. But whether they did or not, she'd still look good. You obviously didn't tell her about the pencil."

Sophie sat down and unscrewed the pencil. Using the nib of a fountain ` pen, she teased out the rolled-up paper, flattened it on the desk and read it.

"There's been a public protest against T4 in Absberg. In Franconia. That's a first. Party members too. Protestant and Catholic clergy are protesting. In private though. Why did they let me have this?"

"They're arrogant. They expected to find it on me. It's genuine. Probably from Maria."

She took off her glasses, rubbed her eyes.

"Poor woman. I hate to think of what they've done to her. I've heard, though, that Number 8 is one of the best jails, prisons or camps in its treatment of the inmates. If they send her anywhere, it'll probably be to a labor camp. Nurses are needed, so hopefully they'll go easy on her."

"It doesn't look much like a police headquarters."

"It wasn't originally. It used to be the School of Industrial Arts and Crafts. The Gestapo took it over in 1933. In '39 it became the RSHA, The Reich Security Main Office, headquarters also for the SS and SD."

She put on her glasses.

"Maria was betrayed. They depend upon informers. Setting somebody up, as you were, is unusual. They come at dawn, bang on the door. They shout 'Gestapo,' put you in handcuffs, take you in for interrogation. That spreads fear, exactly what they want. Some people are informing on others before it happens to them."

"You've ruined my reputation. I'll have to write another story on the customs of East Prussia."

"You're a courier. They want me. They want to break up my network. None of my sources knows about any of the others. That way the network won't be compromised if one of them is caught and confesses. I get dozens of calls every day. They don't have the manpower or enough time to keep track of them all and figure out who's passing me stuff. That's not their way. They wait for somebody to inform, then they pick up the suspect. And that suits me."

"It doesn't have to be an informer. It could be a staged accident."

"I don't think I'll meet anybody any more. I'd better burn that message before somebody barges in here."

She took a notebook out of the lower desk drawer, wrote in it, lit a match and set fire to the message. When the paper was a blackened curl with a lip of flame, she released the edge held between her thumb and forefinger. It fluttered like a lost wing into the ashtray on the desk. She screwed the pencil together, put it into the lower desk drawer with the notebook and put her elbows on the desk. We were so used to speaking softly in the office that even when her voice became a whisper as then, I could hear her.

"Might need that pencil. I convert the messages into a code only I understand and use it in recipes in letters I send my mother in New Hampshire."

"New Englander, are you?"

"New Jersey. My mother used to live here with me but she got sick two years ago. I took her back and bought a house in New Hampshire. I stayed with her a few months. She knows people there."

We didn't speak for several minutes. It was almost midnight. Something had been bothering me. It wouldn't let go.

"If they depend upon informers, why have they started shadowing you? Why set me up? The interrogator called me a spy. I think they're expecting to be at war with the United States within a year. To them we're fifth columnists gathering intelligence for the future. They've marked us out from the other correspondents. The longer we stay, the greater the chance we never leave. All they have to do is wait for the next mistake."

She frowned.

"Maybe I was wrong getting you involved."

"I made my own choice. I'm with you until you say quit. But you may get homesick. If you ever decide to catch the night train to Basel, I'll carry your bags."

We grinned at each other through the quiet yellow cast by the cowl lamp.

After that we took extra precautions. I walked Sophie to the U-bahn at midnight. She stopped using her bicycle. It would have been easy for her to be knocked over in a fake accident. I checked the brakes and steering of the Eifel every time I drove her to the Kurzwellensender. Censorship had become so tight she was considering giving up her broadcasts. It seemed the censors had been told to object to anything to discourage her. The censors and monitors were still friendly but they were employees of the Propaganda Ministry. Her news broadcasts consisted of reading without any inflexions summaries of Propaganda Ministry and Foreign Office handouts. It was a verbal straitjacket.

Sophie had to accept the likelihood that Maria told everything she knew. Another telephone code would have taken too much time and could have been compromised by another confession. With arranged meetings ruled out, that left chance encounters and a message drop known only to some of her more important sources. Sophie spent the next couple of weeks warning callers that the code had been broken. She used a prearranged word for this at the beginning of calls from sources. In late March we received a cable from head office advising us to get out at the first sign of danger. We had already passed that point.

One afternoon near the end of March Sophie went to check the drop for messages. She didn't come back. Skipping the lies on offer at the evening press conference, I went to the embassy. Crane phoned the Propaganda Ministry and was told by the assistant foreign press chief that Sophie had been arrested by the Gestapo. When asked why, the assistant said on suspicion of spying. Where was she being held? He wouldn't say. Crane tried unsuccessfully to speak with Goebbels, lodged an official complaint and hung up. He called the Foreign Office, lodged another one. He thought American diplomacy had done enough. I didn't.

"She's at Gestapo headquarters. You're coming with me."

"That's unheard of."

"To hell with diplomatic protocol. If you don't come with me I'll cable a story that you left an American newswoman at the mercy of the Gestapo. They don't have to answer to anybody in Germany: courts, lawyers, government or press. You'll have to answer to Americans if anything happens to her. You're a career diplomat. You don't have any political clout. I have editors, newspapers and public opinion. You still want to sit there and let her go it alone when all you have to do is follow my lead?"

We took the embassy car. One of the attachés drove. He stayed in the car and Crane and I went inside. We identified ourselves and asked various functionaries about Sophie and finally were taken up to an office on the second floor. A middle-level functionary, another junior executive in a standard issue suit. A picture of the wife on the desk and the Führer on the wall. He gave us a cool greeting and said Sophie was being held as a spy. What was the evidence? He wouldn't say except that it was conclusive. Where was she being held? Downstairs in a cell. Could we talk with her? No. I decided to adopt the diplomatic approach, which means you lie with a smile.

"In view of the delicate state of German-American relations at the present time, this could be an embarrassment for both governments. Miss Henser had decided this week to apply for an exit visa. Far be it from me to make suggestions to the RSHA, but this case should be reviewed at the highest level. And as soon as possible. I think we can agree that harmonious relations are the top priority. I can safely say President Roosevelt would be greatly displeased if he came to hear of this. The quickest way of resolving the matter would be for Miss Henser to be expelled without prejudice."

The functionary stared, wondering which of us was the diplomat. He made calls and left the room. Crane and I sat silently. A half hour later the functionary returned. Miss Henser would be released. The Foreign Office would issue an exit visa. She must be on a train out of Germany that night. A few minutes later Sophie came into the room, the color drained from her face. We left without speaking and were driven to the Foreign Office for the exit visa. We changed to the Eifel at the embassy and I drove her to her apartment. She packed what she could and left instructions for shipping the rest. Then over to the office for her notebook and through the tunnel to the Anhalter Bahnhof and the train to Basel and the free air of Switzerland. We stood on the dark platform near the waiting train and talked. She was still recovering from shock and I was concerned.

"Did they do anything?"

"Some yelling. And lots of threats. The cell was a treat. I was hoping you'd get there before I was transferred to Ploetzensee."

"What did they have?"

"Message from a government official about T4. They arrested me after I picked it up. But they didn't see the drop. I'd seen them coming and walked away. I should tell you where it is because Maria was one of my sources who didn't use or know about it."

She leaned forward and whispered the location in my ear. We embraced, holding each other for a long time before she spoke.

"For most of my life I've been waiting for the right guy and when he finally shows up, it's got to be somebody like you. Look after the office and take care of yourself, Mr. Jim."

"It'll always be your office, Miss Henser."

"Come and see me in New Hampshire."

"I can hardly believe it exists."

"It does if you want it to."

The conductor shouted and coach doors began slamming. We boarded and she found a seat and I put her suitcases up on the luggage rack. On the platform I watched the blacked-out train disappear in the darkness. After staring at the empty tracks, I went to the Adlon for a drink.

I told them what I had to, leaving out much. Silence around the table. They suspected. Sophie was known for her sources, the stories only she could get. Finding out the truth was getting to be more dangerous as the war went on. We were all involved in it but she had taken more chances. Art broke the silence.

"They've been trying to get rid of her for years. I was worried about her. I thought something might happen. She's safe now."

Joe looked uncertain.

"What about us?"

"It's not like '39, with the French and British correspondents. The shooting war hadn't started in the west. If the United States gets involved, we'd be interned, like our diplomats. Who knows for how long? Maybe the Swiss could work something out."

"So we'd be prisoners."

Jack put down his stein.

"You're a correspondent. You take your chances. If you're nervous about being caught here, apply for an exit visa and hope they won't make you sweat waiting for it. If you've been a friend, like Hapgood, they'll give you one right away. But if I know that bastard, you'll never find him straying far from his Frau."

"I didn't know I was getting into this."

"You didn't know? This isn't the city hall beat, pork barrel politics or the Washington social whirl. The boys in power back home are small-timers, making news to order like your aunties make quilts. Welcome to world politics, fella, where every card is wild and only the biggest egos can play. The wops have been getting a boot in the ass in Africa and Greece. But Rommel and his Afrika Korps are starting to kick dust in British faces. A good bet would be the Greeks will be next to feel Schicklgruber's wrath. And anybody in the Balkans that stands in his way. If the Axis controls the Balkans and gets to the Suez Canal, the British will be frantic. The Empire will be cut in two and Schicklgruber will have all the oil he needs to conquer everything in sight. If Britain goes under and the Russians were to get panzered, the United States will stand alone. The isolationists would make peace with the Axis."

"Too many ifs," I said. "Nobody has conquered the world yet and I don't think we're going to see it."

"You speaking from your head or your heart?"

"My gut."

First thing next morning I cabled head office about Sophie and the return cable said I was the new bureau chief. The news in the next few weeks was mostly bad. Press chiefs at the Propaganda Ministry and Foreign Office gloated as they read military dispatches from the Balkans and North Africa. In eleven days Yugoslavia was overrun and surrendered on April 17 and Greece surrendered on April 20. The Afrika Korps was pushing the British back into Egypt. A curious item was overshadowed by the rest. An American destroyer had dropped depth charges on a U-boat and hadn't been attacked. American naval vessels were apparently off limits. Naval vessels had to be identified as British before U-boats were allowed to attack them. The Nazi leadership had no love for Americans. They wanted to avoid incidents that might provoke the U.S. government.

I had more to do after Sophie left but I was an old hand now. No more nights driving to the Rundfunkhaus. Mutual didn't hire a replacement. I wasn't interested in fighting ever tighter broadcast censorship, anyway. I wrote dispatches quickly, using a spare style and mentioning essential details. Head office cabled that my style was instantly recognizable but a little more drama wouldn't be amiss. I cabled back that the drama was in the spare prose. It wasn't much different from what I'd written previously and New York came around to my view. During April there were several office calls from Sophie's contacts. I didn't know the code and she hadn't time to explain it to me. It had been broken, anyhow. I realized there was a good chance I was being set up. For the benefit of any Gestapo agents listening in, I would only say Sophie had left Berlin and was on her way back to the United States. To any follow-up questions my answers were brief and professed complete ignorance. I felt uneasy about cutting off people who were risking torture and imprisonment to pass on information. But the network had been compromised except for the message drop. The location Sophie whispered was in a store. It was in the Anhalter Bahnhof tunnel and sold souvenirs, postcards, newspapers and magazines. Sophie had stopped there to buy magazines before her skiing holiday. I decided to look inside the next time I used the air-raid shelter at the Anhalter Bahnhof. Near the end of April there were some heavy bombing raids. On my way back from the shelter after the all-clear I peered through the almost closed slats of the window shutters. It was late in the evening and the small store was closed. It was crammed with stacks of newspapers, racks of magazines and displays of postcards of Berlin as well as the inevitable swastika flags and pictures of Hitler. I could only glance in without arousing the suspicion of passersby. The drop was a slit between two magazine racks against the back wall and couldn't be seen from outside the store. I didn't know when I would return to pick up messages.

The next day Julia phoned.

"Hi, I'm in Berlin. I called your pension but you weren't in. I thought I'd call there and give your boss a heart attack. How come you're answering the phone?"

"I've taken over from her. She's gone back home because of her health."

"I'll bet. You got rid of her. I told you she was using you. You've got to attend one of my concerts."

"Tickets are hard to get."

"Not that hard. I'm sending you one. I'm checking the audience. Better be there."

"All right."

"Don't sound so grateful. People are lining up for tickets. Come to my dressing room afterwards. Don't worry about my mother."

"You'll have her on a leash."

"Yawn. I wish we could get together before but I have to —."

"Concertrate."

"I'm holding my nose."

"There may be some noise during the concert."

"Nobody boos me."

"I was thinking of explosions. Berlin has been bombed a couple of times in the past week."

"So? They're finished, won't come back for a while."

"You've heard from RAF Bomber Command, have you?"

"The only explosion will be the applause after my performance."

"You're not nervous?"

"Of course. I have to be to be good."

"Ah, that edge. Julia Fusco, fearless of bombs and of bombing."

"You're making fun of me."

"You love it."

"Do I?"

"You need somebody who won't play second fiddle."

"That's the worst. I've got to practice."

The ticket arrived at the hotel the next morning and later Mina von Altenburg phoned. I told her about Sophie, omitting details as a precaution against eavesdroppers. She and Loulou were coming to Berlin for a concert at the Philharmonie and had wanted Sophie to attend and Mina promptly invited me in her place. I explained I already had a ticket and she said to check the date. It was the same as theirs and we agreed to meet outside the Philharmonie. I wanted to see the sisters anyway and our having tickets to Julia's first concert seemed preordained. The weather had improved, wind teasing flowers in the parks. Meeting outside wouldn't be a problem and we could talk freely. If they invited me somewhere afterwards, I would tell them I was going backstage to see Julia and congratulate her as a fellow American. I would see them the next day at their convenience.

The evening was mild on the day of the concert, a shining Venus in a green sky over a brassy horizon. Within the hour the blue descent would come with sudden stars. As I was waiting outside of the Philharmonie the black limousine came up and Joseph got out and opened the near side rear door. Mina and Loulou stepped out wearing gowns under their short coats with fur collars. Next emerged an army lieutenant in dress uniform. He was introduced and turned out to be a friend of von Pommer who was filling in at the last minute. Acknowledging my presence with a nod, he looked as if he would rather have been on maneuvers. The sisters looked up at the flush of emerald and breathed in the evening air. Mina spread out her arms. Loulou spoke quietly.

*"J'adore l'air du printemps. Mais parfois, je veux que mon coeur à geler pour que je ne sens rien."*

Mina gently mocked her.

*"Ah, ne rien sentir."*

The sisters locked arms and began goosestepping along the sidewalk.

*"Nous devons aller à Moscou, maintenant. Marchons à Moscou, Allemands."*

Their escort protested and Loulou answered him.

*"Pardonnez-nous, nous sommes seulement pauvre jeune filles. Vous êtes un bon soldat."*

Red-faced, he raised his voice and they marched back to the car and Mina grinned.

*"D'accord, mon pauvre garçon."*

She turned to me.

"Good to see you again, Mr. Brian."

We went inside, the lieutenant lingering behind and looking for an escape. I found out later he excused himself at the intermission and left. My seat was ground floor, near the center and twelve rows from the front. The sisters were dead center and two rows in front of me. I could see them whispering to each other before the concert. They were seated together and their escort next to Mina. They never looked at him.

The first half of the program featured Beethoven's Sixth Symphony, with Julia scheduled to perform the Brahms' concerto after the interval. The concert began with Hans Knappertsbusch conducting the overture to Beethoven's Creatures of Prometheus. A somnolent plodder, he made molasses seem like bubbling spring water. In the Furtwängler and Karajan mold, he was an opportunist who would cohabit with the Nazis and would later forget everything in a Germany wanting to forget. After the creatures succumbed to rigor mortis, he led the slowest performance of the Pastoral I ever heard, the players lapsing into narcolepsy under a zombie's baton. After the interval he led Julia onto the stage to polite applause. The audience wasn't going to be overly enthusiastic towards an American it hadn't heard yet. She wore a strapless black satin evening gown and her eyes were live coals. She and the orchestra tuned up, her movements assured and feline as a panther's. This was where she had to be. The opening bars of the concerto sounded arthritically ponderous and as she waited for her entry she glanced at the audience. Tensing now, eyelids lowered and bow to strings, her attack supple, fiery, she swaying, her violin weaving its warm tone above the fatuous solemnity of the accompaniment. Its voice said this is your glimpse into a world you will never forget. Some aficionados might have considered her performance romantic but never sentimental. It throbbed with its own inner strength. To this non-expert she dispatched the first movement cadenza with élan. Spontaneous applause followed and her playing was on the same level in the rest of the concerto. There was absolute silence at the end, followed in seconds by a sudden tumultuous outburst of clapping. Julia had conquered the Philharmonie. She received the customary bouquets and was called back four times by the sustained applause. I found Mina and Loulou in the lobby.

"She is a great musician," Mina said.

I said I knew Julia and was going backstage to see her.

"We would like to meet her," Loulou said.

I invited them to her dressing room. The door was open and the room crammed with flowers and fans. Julia looked excited and was sipping a glass of champagne from a bottle undoubtedly presented by the BPO management. Mrs. Fusco caught sight of me and frowned. I waited before catching Julia's attention and she smiled an I-told-you-so smile. But that disappeared when I brought Mina and Loulou through the crowd to meet her. I introduced them and she said nothing. Mrs. Fusco jumped in.

"You're vons, are you? Pleased to meet you. I have noble blood. From a Bohemian king."

Mina ignored her.

"You play beautifully, Miss Fusco. With much flair."

Julia glared at me as she spoke to Mina, each word chiseled in granite.

"You know him?"

"Mr. Brian visited our estate in East Prussia."

"I believed you."

"I wrote about soil erosion. They offered me their hospitality."

"I'll bet. What've they got to do with soil—whatever?"

"Their estate is the largest one there. I thought it would be perfect."

"You brought them to see me."

"I met them outside. They had tickets for the concert."

"You bring them to my dressing room."

"They wanted to meet you. They love—."

"Love?"

She swung around, picked up a metal serving tray and hit me over the head with it. I staggered and as I slumped to the floor, I could hear Mrs. Fusco.

"This happens every time my daughter sees you. You're nothing but a troublemaker."

In my semiconscious state I heard voices, and one above the others.

"King of Bohemia, I forget which. Julia's father is related to the Pope."

Mina got me to my feet as Loulou left the room. We went into the hallway, away from the gabble of voices. Loulou returned with Joseph and he helped me through the empty Philharmonie, the scene of Julia's triumph, and out to the limousine. Having recovered by then, I was going to walk the short distance back to the Excelsior but the sisters wouldn't let me. I sat in the back with them. They didn't mention the incident. They were too inherently patrician to draw attention to the public embarrassments of others. Mina asked why I didn't want to be driven to my pension.

"I'm the bureau chief now. I've got a few things to do at the office."

"Did Sophie tell you anything before she left?"

I told them about Sophie's hurried departure and what led up to it and what I knew.

"We suspected something and we knew you could not say anything on the telephone. Did she take the information with her?"

"She took her notebook. It's in a code only Sophie understands, so it's safe. No customs official, Feldpolizei or Gestapo agent is going to guess what it is. She's going to write about T4."

"More will be happening. Do you wish to know?"

I didn't hesitate. I couldn't. I was taking a risk, but what was it compared to theirs? They would never get out.

"Sophie's network is finished. All that's left is a message drop in Berlin and you two. Give me the code. We won't use the phone. Nobody will know except Sophie, you, me and anybody using the drop. I'll cable information to her in care of our New York office. It won't be published for a while yet and not in a newspaper, so Nazi embassy officials over there won't see it. When she's ready to publish, I should be out of here. Thanks to my article on erosion, I'm considered a friend of Germany. It might be a good idea to write something else like that as a cover."

When we reached the Excelsior I told them where the drop was. I said to be careful if they or their friends used it. The Gestapo didn't know where it was but the tunnel might be under surveillance. Mina asked for a light. Joseph took a flashlight out of the glove compartment and passed it back to her. She shone it on her concert program and wrote quickly for a couple of minutes and handed the program to me. She had written out the complete code, making changes so the Gestapo wouldn't recognize it. There would be two codes, one used by people who used the drop and didn't know about Sophie's departure, and the other for us. The third code Sophie disguised as recipes and used in her notebook. I got out and we said goodbye.

The lobby was empty and dim. I went upstairs to the office and switched on the light. Julia was sitting behind the desk. She was holding a gun and it was pointed at me. Her voice was calm.

"I turned on the heater."

"That's all right. How did you get here?"

"Got a ride from the manager. I said I needed to get out, my nerves were bad. In the car I told him to drop me off here, that I'd be fine, and not to tell my mother. How's your head?"

"Better."

"When I saw you with them I couldn't think, and when you said 'love' I hit you before I knew what I was doing."

"I was in the middle of saying they loved your performance."

"Oh. I guess you hate me."

"No."

"You don't love me though. I wanted to make passionate love after the performance and that happened. Now I don't feel anything. I thought I'd shoot us both. Sort of like a double farewell."

"Where did you get the gun?"

"The flyer I told you about. He showed me how to fire it. That was in Wiesbaden. I kept it in my dressing room at the Philharmonie. I was going to throw it away or give it to somebody."

"Why don't you give it to me."

"You want to shoot us?"

"I'll get rid of it. I don't want to shoot anybody and certainly not you."

"You're only saying that. And don't say I'm beautiful and talented. Or you feel sorry for me. I'm not stupid."

"You're mixed up. Two pulls on the trigger and we're dead. What will that solve? You're a great artist, Julia. That was the best performance of the Brahms I ever heard. The applause went on for ten minutes. When an audience is quiet for a few seconds after a performance, then erupts, that's the greatest praise a musician can receive."

"Why do I feel like crying?"

"That's a good sign."

"You're going to be funny, aren't you?"

"With you holding a gun? When people feel nothing they're not human but when they can cry, they are."

"I thought you'd be afraid when you saw the gun and you'd say you loved me so I wouldn't shoot you."

"What kind of love would that be? You can't make feelings feel what they don't. I don't say it. Because I do."

"Really?"

"Yeah."

"How could you love me?"

"Oh, Julia."

"You think I'll always be this way?"

"I don't know. Better give me the gun or you'll be wondering what adagio to play in tribute to my memory at your next recital."

"I knew you'd get funny."

I walked over to the desk and she dropped the pistol into my outstretched hand as simply as putting a coin in a parking meter. After putting on the safety catch I slipped the pistol into my coat pocket and sat down. We looked at each other. She smiled.

"I saw you in the audience, in the twelfth row. I knew where you'd be. I got excited when I saw you. I thought, I'll make him remember this night."

"You did."

"Turn on the radio so we can dance." She unbuttoned her overcoat.

I got up and switched on the radio. Across the broad rectangular dial the numbered wavelengths and bands and the names of cities were lit by an amber glow. The tuning knob slid a vertical wire along the frequencies and from the static emerged bursts of noise, voices and music. A classical piece came through clearly and she stood up.

"That's a suite. It's dance music."

She came around the desk, I unbuttoned my coat and we held each other and moved slowly to what she whispered in my ear was a sarabande. Next came something faster she called a gavotte, followed by something quick, a galliard, then a stately minuet and a country dance called an allemande. She stopped whispering after that. I put my hands inside her coat.

"This is better than the concert. I'm getting a musical education as I'm feeling you up."

"Don't spoil the romance. It's like we're meeting for the first time."

"We haven't seen each other since before Christmas. No wonder it feels like the first time."

"I went out with that flyer. After we broke up. He's a wing commander or a squadron leader or something. I can't remember what it's called in German. He's serious about me, wants me to meet his family."

"Is that why he gave you the gun?"

"I asked for it."

"Did you tell him you were going to knock somebody off?"

"I wasn't planning to. I happened to ask."

"You don't happen to ask for a gun."

"All right. He asked me to accept it as a keepsake in case anything happens to him."

"This guy ever heard of letters or photos?"

"You're the one to talk. You've never given me anything. Aren't you jealous? He's good-looking."

"Your mother will chase him away, and the others that come along. Besides, if you really liked him I wouldn't have a bump on my head."

"Maybe I'm a bitch."

"You're hot-blooded and hot-tempered and a handful but you're not a bitch. Does your mother still hit you?"

"Not since the day you interviewed me. She knows I'll hit her back."

"When did it start?"

"When I was a kid. I had to do everything she wanted when she wanted. I remember feeling ashamed going to music school with a cut lip or a bruise on my temple. She used a hair brush or her hand."

"Why did you put up with it?"

"She was my mother. You get into something, you don't know how, and you don't see any way out."

"You're out now."

"That afternoon you were interviewing me, not her, and she interfered as if I was her property. When she hit me, I thought, that's it. Next time I'll slug her. She knows it too."

"You could leave. That would be better than slugging her."

"I know but it's hard. I've been with her so long."

She pressed against me.

"Are you feeling romantic?"

"I reached that point twenty minutes ago. During the sarabande."

"I think these clothes are keeping the passion point up."

"Passion point?"

"You know, like boiling point or melting point."

"If you take down your—."

"Don't ruin things by being funny."

"I'm being realistic. The passion point will come down right away."

"Why is it we use floors and cars and cheap hotels? Why can't we have a normal relationship?"

"You're the one who comes and goes as you please. Besides, doesn't this appeal to your sense of the romantic?"

"A little comfort wouldn't hurt."

"You're not getting domestic, are you, Julia?"

"Because I don't like this crazy way of making love any more?"

"Let's review. You clobbered me. I took a gun away from you. And now we're considering how to lower the passion point."

"So it's my fault you bring two women to my dressing room. I invited you."

"They're fans. They appreciate a great artist."

"Don't flatter me."

"The truth isn't flattery."

"I was good, wasn't I?"

"You were magnificent. Incidentally, I'm feeling woolen pants and sweater and a cotton blouse under that heavy coat."

"You didn't expect me to wear my expensive gown here? Anyway, it would've seemed suspicious if I hadn't changed clothes to go for a ride."

The music faded and slowly drowned in static. I went over and shut off the radio. Julia sat on the desk and suddenly laughed. She blushed.

"How's your passion point? I got the directions backwards. I should be ashamed of myself. I'm getting like you."

I went to her and we kissed. I drew her up off the desk and glanced around and she stared at me.

"What's wrong?"

"There must be a better place."

"I get it. She worked here."

"That's not it."

"Then why?"

"It's uncomfortable."

"Everything is uncomfortable in this damn office. I'm leaving."

"Why is it so hard for you to see that I would rather not?"

"If you loved me, it wouldn't matter where."

"Your violin is number one and your mother number two and I'm number three."

"You're not even that."

"Fine. I'm fed up with your jealous tantrums. You don't want love. You want to be worshipped at your convenience."

"Go to hell, you bastard."

She swung at me and I grabbed her. Suddenly we were kissing. I don't expect anybody to understand why. I don't understand myself. We ended up on the floor. She tore at me. More swinging, scratches too. I used all my strength. It was like fighting to get somewhere you hope hasn't changed. It hadn't. Repetitive clutching at a wild sorrow. The gain, the loss, the measured release. Afterwards we lay there drained of everything. There was no use talking. It had been a long night.

I drove Julia to the Esplanade and we said goodbye with a single kiss. No promises or plans. She had a concert in two nights. When I got back to the Excelsior I went to the library. As usual it was empty. I took out the pistol. It was a Parabellum. It's called a Luger in English-speaking countries. A semiautomatic 9 mm with a narrow barrel, an angled grip with black bakelite panels and an eight-cartridge box magazine, a round in the chamber. I hid the Luger behind some volumes of Fichte and Schelling, safest place in Berlin. I couldn't go up to the office. Through midnight streets I trudged to my pension. Sleep hit like a drug. I dreamed of a violin with strings of human sinew.

Julia didn't call during the rest of her stay in Berlin. After the concerts she left the city. I had no idea if I would ever hear from or see her again. We had said enough. I put her out of my mind.

Beginning in May there were rumors of a German buildup along the borders of the Soviet Union. An attaché with the American Embassy told me that two of our legations in Eastern Europe were sources of these rumors. He had received similar information from a high government official. The exact date of the invasion and the battle plans were purported to be known. The foreign press chief at the Propaganda Ministry denied everything. The official line was the army was conducting maneuvers in the area. I said at the Adlon that I thought the Germans were going in and soon.

"I heard it's June 22," Art said.

Jack stubbed out his cigar.

"The commies are still shipping raw materials to Germany, the stupid buggers. After all the purges, there's nobody to run the Red Army. Officers are scared shitless to issue an order in case it's wrong. They'll be shot. Nobody farts without getting permission from Stalin. Whole place is fucked up. Schicklgruber's panzers will be setting new speed records."

I put down my bourbon.

"Forget the government. Russians are tough. What about the winter? I don't think the Wehrmacht is looking forward to this. You can bullshit the troops but not the high command."

Jack grinned.

"The question is, will Schicklgruber run out of bullets before Stalin runs out of bodies?"

Joe slapped the table with the flat of his hand.

"I got a good one. It's not the Soviet Union, it's the State of Paranoia."

Jack stared at him.

"Yeah, sure, Joe."

"It's getting closer for us," Art said. "That freighter sunk a couple of days ago was outside the German blockade zone."

"A long way yet," Jack said. "Roosevelt can go only so far. He can't let an overeager U-boat captain force him into more than saber rattling. The isolationists wouldn't care if the British sank like that freighter."

I drank the last of my bourbon.

"The Nazis will hold back too if an invasion is close. Quite a contrast last month. An American destroyer goes after a U-boat with depth charges. No reaction here, four days after Belgrade is bombed into rubble."

Jack took out another cigar, held it under his nose and inhaled.

"They're saving us for later."

Sophie was right about the Gestapo. They didn't engage much in surveillance. I didn't notice anyone following me or lurking in the Excelsior lobby in a black trench coat and a fedora behind a potted plant. Our arrests destroyed much of the good will I gained inadvertently with my article on East Prussia. But I was safe as long as someone didn't inform on me. At the beginning of June I decided to check the drop. I picked a Saturday, hoping to melt into the weekend crowd. The little store in the tunnel was packed with travelers. Perusing newspapers and magazines I moved slowly towards the back wall. There were people close to the slit between the magazine racks. I waited, feeling queasy. I was sure an agent was waiting for me to put my fingers into the tiny space. One of those shoppers thumbing the *Voelkischer Beobachter* was bound to have a pair of handcuffs handy. But they depended on informers, I told myself. I decided to hold a magazine close to the slit as I checked, so I could hide what I was doing. I glanced around nonchalantly, which always make you look guiltier. I didn't see anyone wearing a trench coat and a fedora. But that would give him away, so he would probably be wearing a disguise. If he was there, if they wore disguises. It was all stupid, unless you've ever been in that position. I picked up a magazine and a man stepped in front, his back to me. He slipped something in between the racks. I saw his face as he moved away. It was Hermann Stubenrauch. I dropped the magazine and followed him out of the store, catching up with him as he hurried along the tunnel.

"I met you at the Adlon. Jim Brian. American correspondent, remember? I saw you inside the store. I think we should talk."

"It is not safe for us to talk in a public place. Come and see me tonight."

He gave me an address before disappearing into the crowd. I went back into the store, browsed until I figured I was safe and then squeezed two fingers into the drop. There were two pieces of folded notepaper. I made a fist and crammed them into my coat pocket. I bought a magazine and strolled out.

I cabled a dispatch to New York. Some drivel the assistant foreign press chief at the Propaganda Ministry had spouted about the traditional friendship that existed between the Russian and German peoples. When Nazis talked like that, it was a sign the knives were being sharpened. I read the messages from the drop. Written in a woman's neat hand, one listed monthly numbers of euthanasia victims at a psychiatric hospital. The other was Stubenrauch's, contained the names of two Protestant clergymen who had protested privately to Hitler about T4 plus quotations from the letters. The night she left Sophie gave me her personal code to use for information sent to her. I put the messages into that code and cabled them to her in care of head office. I transferred all three codes to one of my coil notebooks and hid it. In transferring the second, I saw Julia's name printed in script in Mina's concert program. I burnt the program.

Stubenrauch had moved to Berlin to work for the traditional and conservative *Deutsche Allgemeine Zeitung*. He lived on the north side of the Tiergarten in a gray stone house with a portico fronting the upper story and a tiled roof. He and his wife lived downstairs. Her sister and brother-in-law, who had a baby, lived in a suite of rooms upstairs. I never met them. When I arrived it was deep twilight and all the blackout curtains were drawn. I figured coming at dusk would cut down on the chances of my being recognized. Any later would have been rude. The door opened quickly after I knocked. I followed Stubenrauch's shadowy figure to a light at the back. The light was in the kitchen, where a dull bulb hung from a ceiling cord. Stubenrauch introduced his wife, Helga, stocky and square-faced, sitting at a table. He invited me to sit down. I declined his offer of coffee, guessing it would be ersatz, or if actually genuine I would be imposing on their hospitality to accept it. After my explanation for not coming earlier, which they understood, I gave them the barest account of Sophie's arrest and departure. The less they knew the better for all of us. I told them both network and code had been compromised and the drop was safe until someone who used it was caught and confessed.

"I can warn sources who phone the office by simply telling them Sophie is no longer here. That should not arouse the suspicion of wiretappers. Sources who still use the drop will know nothing has gone wrong. If the drop is compromised, the Gestapo can pick them up one after another."

Elbows on the table, Stubenrauch nodded as he stared down at the tablecloth, lines engraved into his forehead and thinning hair receding far back from the temples.

"Always the luck. What else is there?"

He raised his head and stared at me.

"Why are you doing this?"

"Sophie got me into it. And I dislike the idea of grandmothers being expendable because they move a little slower."

"Sophie is German."

"German-American."

"What is the difference? German is German."

"If she were here she would tell you."

Helga broke the silence.

"My sister's baby has a deformed foot. He will never walk without some help. She is afraid he will be taken away. The doctor is protecting him. He lies about how bad the lameness is."

It was personal. That's why they were involved. They were all taking chances, including the doctor. How many were being hidden?

"Your sister could put the baby in a private institution. Sophie told me the T4 inspectors never visit them."

"They are expensive. We are trying to save the money. She has a job. So do I. We all help look after him. It is hard. She is afraid to hire anybody."

I looked at Stubenrauch.

"How extensive are the protests?"

"There are more and more. That will force the T4 program underground."

I felt useless. How were a few cables to New York going to help? It would take a year, probably longer, for Sophie's book to appear. In the meantime how many newspapers would carry the story? Isolationist owners and editors would say it was nothing but rumors. Germans wouldn't do that to Germans. They were civilized. The Nazis had been in power for eight years and how many Americans knew about the concentration camps or even how the Propaganda Ministry managed the news? Sophie had done what she could but her stories had been ignored or censored. Correspondents were parrots in a cage.

Helga picked at the tablecloth with hesitant fingers.

"Maybe if there are enough protests fewer would be killed, and only the severely handicapped. All we can hope for is that they pick the worst."

Stubenrauch glanced at her before speaking to me.

"They go too far. But there are some that are animals. To put them out of their misery is not bad. Those that live in their own shit and eat it."

"That makes for good propaganda," I said.

"They are not human."

"What is human? Some men treat women and children sadistically, beating and sexually abusing them. Are they being rounded up and killed? If I asked ten people who should live and who should die, I would get ten different answers. Which one would be right?"

"The doctors should choose."

"Doctors should never be allowed to choose. They know the basic functions of the body and brain. They know nothing about mind, character, temperament, spirit. All that makes us human."

"So who should choose?"

"Nobody can tell you that."

"Every society must make this decision."

"Why?"

"Because these creatures, such Untermenschen, are a drain on our resources."

"Germans are being made prisoners of priorities. The Nazis want more guns and soldiers and places for the wounded to recover. You are sacrificing for militarism. The problem is not at the bottom. The shit is at the top."

They stared at me. It was time to leave. There was a chance they would inform on me if they were caught, but I didn't care. That would get me an exit visa but I was close to one, anyway.

Four nights later, on Wednesday, a woman knocked on my door at the pension. She was young and wore a tight skirt and sweater over her sumptuous curves. She introduced herself as Gretchen Kreyling, said she had moved in down the hall and wondered if I would help her. I invited her in and asked her what she wanted. She was having trouble filling out forms for the government. Would I come to her room and look at them? She didn't look like the other women at the pension: wives, secretaries in government offices, nurses, teachers. I wondered if the Stubenrauchs had gone to the Gestapo. But they weren't known for using women as sexual bait. While I was pondering the situation and that enticingly filled sweater, Frau Ziegenhagen happened to be walking past the open doorway.

"What are you doing in Herr Bine's room, Fräulein Kreyling?"

"I came to ask him to help me."

"Help you? How?"

"I am having problems with government forms."

"There are officials for that. I do not allow a woman and man together in a room unless they are in love. I am not a narrow-minded person. I myself have known love, the flitting heart like a bird. But this cannot be it. You moved in yesterday. I will not have the other. Money and love do not mix, unless of course you are married. But as you cannot be in love and are not married, you must leave. You said you were a secretary."

"I am."

"Forms should not be a problem. Meet Herr Bine downstairs in the dining room if you want him to look at your forms. You do not have any on you I can see. Were you thinking of asking Herr Bine to search you for them?"

"They are in my room."

"Where they should be. Not Herr Bine. Please leave now. Together with me."

Fräulein Kreyling moved out the next morning. I didn't tell Frau Ziegenhagen my suspicions. She knew one already. It hadn't taken her long to spot a part-time prostitute.

Although the incident turned out to be nothing, there was the possibility the Gestapo might try to set me up the way they had Sophie. I asked Frau Ziegenhagen to phone me at the office if an envelope or package arrived for me at the pension. If she couldn't reach me, she should leave it on the mail table in the downstairs hallway. Under no circumstances was she to take it to my room.

"As you wish, Herr Bine."

"I have nothing to hide. But I must be above suspicion or the authorities will ask me to leave."

"I ask nothing."

I gave her two eggs and four slices of bacon. That meant a sizeable cut in protein. But I had started eating yogurt, which wasn't hard to get. I noticed a small drop in my energy level but it was close to summer and the weather warmer, so the effects were minimal.

I went to the drop that Saturday. There was one message. More statistics, this time how many were killed during the past month at another psychiatric hospital turned into a killing center. I encoded it that afternoon and cabled it to Sophie in care of head office. I decided I wouldn't go to the drop for a couple of weeks and the next time wouldn't be a Saturday. I didn't want to arouse suspicion in the staff by appearing regularly and not catching a train but returning to the Excelsior. And I would try to find a magazine there that wasn't sold anywhere else. If that didn't work, I would buy postcards and mail them to relatives back home.

It wasn't a surprise. There had been too many rumors. But when German radio announced the next morning that the Wehrmacht had invaded the Soviet Union in the early hours of Sunday June 22 I stared at the dial for a few moments before typing a dispatch and phoning New York. Press conferences the next few days were nonstop predictions of a quick victory, backed up by army reports of rapid advances along the fifteen hundred kilometer front. Three and a half million men in three army groups were armored spearheads plunging into the expanses of the Soviet Union. Reports of hundreds of thousands of prisoners were coming in. Ribbentrop and Goebbels and their press chiefs were liars but we in the press had come to trust army reports. They were usually accurate. It amounted to a catastrophe for the Soviets. But apart from the Nazi hierarchy and the military, Germans weren't celebrating. The ones I talked to were cautious and several actually worried. All sounded as if they had signed up for something and couldn't get out of it now. They hoped for a quick victory and peace. They had been hoping for years. Everyone expected more rationing and shortages, blackouts and air raids.

Over the next few weeks rumors began circulating about the *Einsatzgruppen*, killing squads of SS and police units shooting Jews, partisans and political commissars, and there were stories of Russian POWs being shot or starved to death because no plans had been made for such large numbers. At the Adlon we shared what we heard from various sources. We would have been thrown out if we cabled it. Jack had been told of mass murders.

"A captain in the regular army said he saw huge pits and Jewish men, women and children standing at the edge and being shot in the back of the head and falling in on top of those already dead or dying. After the pit was full of naked bodies a bulldozer pushed earth into the hole to cover the bodies, some still alive. It's worse than in Poland. I saw some of that."

He puffed on his cigar before continuing.

"I heard from a high-ranking staff officer that humane treatment of soldiers and civilians is verboten, on orders from Schicklgruber. A few of the executioners can't take it. They've become heavy drinkers. Putting a bullet into the back of a baby's head might get you thinking. Most couldn't give a shit. They've been told Slavs are subhuman and commies are worse. After a good spree they go out and grab a commie wench and fuck her to death."

Art frowned.

"There are better ways of putting things, Jack. Things are bad enough without that language."

Jack snickered.

"You're living with beasts, Art, whether you like it or not."

"You don't have to talk like one."

"There's nothing wrong with four-letter words."

"Four-letter words mean four-letter attitudes. Show some respect for those suffering at the hands of sadists."

"That's where you've got it wrong, Art. Schicklgruber's boys are the guys down the street. Grocery clerks, apprentice tradesmen, schoolteachers, bakers, postmen. The beast is within us."

There was a lull before Joe spoke.

"How about the look on the face of—what's his name—the foreign press chief at the Propaganda Ministry a couple of weeks ago? After Roosevelt announced that the U.S. was taking over the occupation of Iceland from the British."

Another puff from Jack.

"They're too busy to take on Roosevelt and he knows it. Two weeks after the invasion he announces he's protecting American interests in the North Atlantic and even the America Firsters haven't got much to say. They'll bitch but who's going to listen? I heard the Nazi brass were boiling."

Arriving at my pension the next night I saw Frau Ziegenhagen in the downstairs hallway. Her eyes were red, frown deeper than usual. She glanced at me, expecting a response. I asked. She tried to control her emotion.

"Today my sister received a letter. Her son is dead. In the next building a friend received a letter too. Her husband. I hear of all our victories but nobody speaks of the dead but us women."

She took a damp handkerchief out of her apron pocket and blew her nose.

I went up to my room. The day had been warm. I opened the window and breathed in the cool night air. The war was getting closer.

The T4 program was another casualty of the invasion. In July a pastoral letter from Catholic bishops was read out in all churches, declaring killing to be morally acceptable only in self-defense or a morally justified war. A few weeks later Bishop Galen of Münster publically denounced T4 in a sermon. I received both at the drop as illegally printed leaflets. I encoded them and cabled them to Sophie. In August there was a report that Hitler was jeered by a crowd at Hof, in Bavaria, as he sat in a railroad coach at the station. That same month T4 was canceled. I kept checking the drop every couple of weeks and found that Stubenrauch had guessed right, the killing had not stopped. I received information that individual institute directors, doctors, and Nazi party officials took it upon themselves to continue the program unofficially. Gassing stopped and lethal injection and starvation became the preferred methods again. According to the figures I received and what Sophie told me, there had been over 70,000 victims of T4 by the time of the cancellation. I cabled all this to her as well.

I only saw two of the people who left messages at the drop. Stubenrauch was one and in late August I met the other. I had edged my way through a Wednesday evening crowd at the store and saw a young woman slip something quickly into the slit. She hurried past me on her way out and I followed her along the tunnel. I caught up with her in the Excelsior lobby and introduced myself. I mentioned Sophie and she agreed to talk up in the office. I switched on the desk lamp and checked to make sure the blinds were closed. There had been light sporadic air raids by the Soviet air force since early August and I didn't want to commit an infraction of the blackout regulations. I apologized about not having a drink for her and she said that was all right, she was going on shift that night, anyway. Her name was Ulrike, she was a nurse. She agreed to my taking notes of our conversation after I told her I would be sending a summary to Sophie along with Ulrike's message.

"Where do you work, Ulrike?"

"In the psychiatric hospital at Sonnenstein Castle."

"The euthanasia center in Saxony?"

"It is an old asylum. I have been there three years. Before T4 started. I found out patients were killed with injections or starved. In June of last year walls were put around a group of four buildings. In the cellar of one, Haus C16, a gas chamber and crematorium were installed. Many of the regular staff, including me, were assigned to work there. Nurses, aides, doctors, secretaries, police. Buses came not only from Saxony but Silesia, Thuringia and East Prussia. The buses passed police at the gates and patients were brought to the cellar and the men separated from the women. Each patient was brought before two doctors for an examination but they did nothing except make up a false cause of death for the death certificate. Afterwards in another room we nurses and aides undressed them and they were told they were going to take a shower. Twenty or more at a time were put into the gas chamber. One of us locked the steel door and a doctor opened the valve on a cylinder of carbon monoxide and waited for half an hour. It took that long for all of them to die. After that time he waited another twenty minutes, the gas was extracted and the bodies taken out and burnt in the two coke ovens. The ashes were thrown on to the hospital garbage dump or into the Elbe. The same letter was sent to all families. Also the certificate with the false cause. We killed children too. In August T4 was stopped and so we are back to killing with injections and starvation.

"But already at Sonnenstein Aktion 14f13 was begun. This was in April. Now the gas chamber is used to kill people from concentration camps. Before that doctors talked about the 'elimination of life unworthy of life' [*Vernichtung lebensunwerten Lebens*] and 'deadweight existences' [*Ballastexistenzen*], but now they speak about 'special treatment' [*Sonderbehandlung*]. I was told the camps have no gas chambers so we are to kill the sick prisoners, and the old and those who cannot work. They have come from Sachsenhausen and Buchenwald. Also Auschwitz. No children, *Gott sei Dank.*"

She stopped. I looked closely at her. She had a round face with eyes that looked directly at me. Not an unusual or notable face but with something of that selfless dedication that makes a nurse.

"How does T4 proceed unofficially?"

"The same as before. When the program started three doctors were supposed to make an assessment from an examination and agree that a patient should die. That was ignored after a while. Dr. Krill is the director of the hospital. He uses the reports of T4 personnel that visited institutions and determined which patients should be sent to the euthanasia centers. The other doctors go along. He picked them because they are like him. They say Germany has no room for useless mouths, that care is wasted on them, that soldiers should not be dying to feed the unworthy."

"Who administers the injections?"

"Usually Dr. Krill or another doctor. They use phenol. Some are starved.

If a nurse tried to feed a patient who has been left to die she would be discharged and probably punished. And even when T4 was official some thought that by lying to the patients about what was going to happen they were helping them. German nurses are working class and have been taught always to obey a doctor. My father is a doctor and so I have not the same blind respect. Nurses could transfer if they did not wish to be part of the program. A few did. Those who stay believe, like the doctors, in what they are doing. I stayed because I wanted to tell what is going on. It will go on until the end of the war. I have told what I have found out. I am going to transfer.

"I have been thinking about it since T4 began. But when we began gassing patients the day they arrived and there had been no examination, I told myself, you must let Germans know. Then Aktion 14f13, and the camp prisoners were not mentally ill but sick, old or they could not work. I decided to tell about this before transferring. I remember the moment I could stand it no longer. It was something Dr. Krill said to me one day. 'These people are *asoziale*: Gypsies, vagrants, beggars, prostitutes and criminals.' I thought, no, you are the criminal, Doctor, and I am also."

"Did you have time to get to know any of the patients?"

"Those who were at Sonnenstein before T4 and were killed when it began."

"Tell me about them."

"There are so many. But some I remember well. One woman was put in the asylum by her husband because he planned to marry his mistress, a much younger woman. He said his wife was suffering from dementia. She was confused by all the lies he had told her, by his criticism and his insults. She did not know her own mind any more, but believed him. He got her to blame herself for everything and to believe she was mentally ill. She did not trust herself to have an opinion on anything. She was gassed last year. I had to lie to her about what was going to happen. That was hard.

"There was a girl committed by her family because they were embarrassed by her. They were upper class and rich. She would stutter or stumble and fall at receptions and parties. She kept to herself and loved animals. She was a dear soul. Gentle as a lamb. They said she was retarded and must be put away.

Her mind was clear. She told me about her life. And she would never believe her parents would do her any harm. She was gassed too."

She looked down at her hands, as if inspecting them.

"There was Elisabeth, who was a painter. I would bring her some paper and a pencil or sometimes a piece of charcoal and she would draw my portrait or those of the other nurses. That was done in secret. The doctors would never have permitted it. Patients were to be refused anything but food and blankets. She had been diagnosed as manic-depressive. She would become excited at times or keep to herself. Many people are like that. She told me her paintings had been condemned as degenerate by the authorities in charge of culture. She would not change. She had been classed as a social deviate. They told her there was only one place for her. She knew what would happen to her. I will always remember what she said when she left to die.

"'I must go. Think of me when spring comes.'"

In late summer and through the fall German-American relations worsened. In early September an American destroyer was the target of U-boat torpedoes and Roosevelt ordered the navy to attack Axis warships violating our defense zone. In mid-October a destroyer depth charged a U-boat and was torpedoed and another was sunk on the last day of the month. The Propaganda Ministry no longer downplayed the growing and escalating incidents. Hitler was still preoccupied with the Soviet Union, even though on October 9 his press chief, Dr. Dietrich, had announced the battle was over.

The press conference was held in a packed Theater Hall at noon. After we had cabled our dispatches we met at the Adlon. Art spoke as he filled his pipe.

"Looks bad for the Soviets. Three armies are surrounded."

"Where do they keep getting the men from?" Joe said. "They must have lost a couple of million by now."

Jack winked.

"Keep this under your hats, boys, but I heard Stalin has been trying to negotiate a peace through a third party. The French quit with less excuse."

Jack lit a cigar and tossed the match into an ashtray, the flame flickering among the ashes in feeble pulses along the charred withering stick. Cigar smoke drifted across the table, aromatic, acrid.

"Hapgood looked smug, sitting there listening to Dietrich. He asked somebody in the party of flunkies if there was going to be a big victory parade down Unter den Linden."

"It's not easy for him, his wife being German," Art said.

"Nazi, you mean. Garbles and everyone else at the Propaganda Ministry call him a friend of Germany. Stop trying to protect the bastard. He sold out to the master race."

I grinned. My turn.

"I was told I was a friend of Germany for my article on soil erosion. Not lately, though. Time for another article. Something bucolic, about the eternal verities."

They stared at me. In those days people would read almost anything into what you said. The blandest comment could be rife with innuendo, the wildest rumor true. And humor wasn't welcome unless it was too obvious to be misinterpreted.

"You going back?" Art said.

"Probably. You guys going to the front?"

Press bureau chiefs had been invited on a trip to the war zone, beginning the next day. I had already turned it down. It would be a carefully rehearsed show. We would see what the Propaganda Ministry wanted us to see.

"I'm not going," Art said. "I phoned and said I wasn't well. The action is here. We'll be briefed on everything."

"I've been on their tours," Jack said. "Constant bullshit. You have to get away from your guides to see something of the truth. All they want to show you are bomb craters, shell holes and grinning Aryan conquerors. Everything will be on the newsreels pretty quick except the executions, and we wouldn't see that stuff."

I stared at my empty glass. Jack flicked some ash off the end of his cigar. Walking to my pension I noticed the night air was getting cooler. I could feel it on my face. Touch of autumn. The dark streets were silent. Occasionally a double-decker bus passed, its white exterior glimmering, and inside a pale blue light. Dark shapes slipped by and never quite bumped into me. And always the black behemoths of military transport that lurched out of and back into the darkness. No bombers that night, the air raids sporadic. They would come in thousands later and sirens would wail their lament, the voice of the city.

At the beginning of the Russian campaign the stories were mostly factual, based on army reports of huge swathes of territory gained, enormous numbers of prisoners taken, the speed of the advancing armies and an ever-growing list of cities occupied. As fall set in facts and numbers began to disappear into repeated generalities about victories. These victories began to dwindle in number into further generalities about victory itself, which the public was assured was imminent and inevitable. Anyone who had been to the Stettiner or Schlesischer stations and seen troop trains full of wounded knew something was wrong. Deep mud combined with stubborn Russian resistance delayed the victory. Snow and subzero temperatures were to doom it. Nazi propaganda became fatalism in many Germans. A joke I heard on the U-bahn that autumn expressed it best: "Send your coat to Russia to warm a dead soldier."

By late summer for the first time there was anti-American feeling, pumped up by German propaganda because the Russian campaign had stalled and German-American relations were strained. Speaking English on trains, buses, trams or in restaurants got you dirty looks, and if you were a man, curses and challenges to fight. American broadcasters became so frustrated with censorship they stopped news transmissions for a while. The press corps felt the change too. Gestapo agents raided Jack's office at dawn, ostensibly looking for treasonous material, but the intent was to scare the staff. The following Saturday was his birthday and he brought along two other INS correspondents with him to the Adlon. Ed Rumbley, a veteran of four years in Berlin, and Norman Lanner, there two years, wanted out. Their head office agreed to take Rumbley back but Lanner had been told to stay.

"I couldn't take it any more," Rumbley said. "Too much of a strain. I'm always looking over my shoulder, thinking there's somebody following me. I was on overnight duty when they walked in, put me up against the wall and began going through the desks. They wouldn't talk, ignored me when I said I wanted to call the American Embassy. One showed me his warrant disk, that oval metal badge agents carry, eagle on one side and 'Gestapo' on the other. And when Norman, my relief, came in, up against the wall he went. They were there two hours, went through every drawer of every desk. Finally the one who showed me the disk went out and returned and said something to the others and they left. They weren't mad or mouthy, it was business."

"You can relax, you're getting out," Lanner said.

"I won't relax till I get my exit visa and I'm on the train."

"I suppose now is the time to tell you all," Art said. "New York is recalling me. They figure I've had enough. I can't say I'm not happy to leave. I'll be seeing May."

"It's October," Joe said.

"That's my wife's name."

"I phoned Chicago today and my paper told me to stay till it gets dangerous. I said I'll phone you from the morgue."

"They're keeping close tabs on us," Jack said. "The press is spooked. Every word you write can be twisted and held against you. If our numbers keep dwindling, pretty soon we'll be extinct."

"You leaving?"

"No, I'm sticking around."

On November 7 there was a big air raid on Berlin. I was in the office and heard the drone of a large number of bombers. The sound of exploding bombs was close. I hurried down to the shelter in the Anhalter Bahnhof. I had been through a number of raids by then. When I first arrived in Berlin I saw fear among some during a raid. But after two years of intermittent bombing most had learned to cope and the anxiety wore on the nerves more slowly. I controlled mine by being a reporter, observing the reactions of others. Mothers hushing crying children, people huddling together, some sleeping, brave jokes, muttering that could have been praying. Lucky Berliners were in the public shelters, the rest taking their chances in basements. The newspapers and radio condemned "English barbarity," not mentioning the bombing of British cities except as revenge. Much worse was to come but I had left by then.

In the middle of November Mina phoned, inviting me to Altenburg and telling me in code she had information about the continuation of T4. I had cabled Ulrike's information to Sophie. I didn't think anything happening out in East Prussia would add much more. There was nobody to run the office while I was away. With German-American relations deteriorating, head office wasn't likely to send help. I couldn't justify a trip. I told Mina I would try to get away in December, maybe near the holidays.

That winter turned out to be the coldest Berliners could remember. Subzero temperatures and coal in short supply made life hard. I didn't take off my overcoat except for a wash. I managed a bath once a week but heating enough water on an electric hotplate was impossible. A couple of warm panfuls into the cold water in the tub followed by a quick dip. I slept with the bedcovers over my head. Cusps of ice like frosty quarter moons lodged in corners of panes in the window. As during the previous winter, electric heaters at the pension and office made things bearable. There was no significant news from North Africa or the eastern front, both in flux, nothing decisive or likely to be in the near future. At the beginning of December I decided to accept Mina's invitation. At the Propaganda Ministry I told the foreign press chief I wanted to study crop rotation in East Prussia, mentioning the fine library at Altenburg. He was wary because of Sophie's expulsion and my being interrogated by the Gestapo. I reminded him about my article on soil erosion and he agreed to issue a travel permit. What harm could I do?

I phoned Mina and told her I would with luck be in Königsberg on Friday December 5. On Wednesday evening, after filing a handful of dispatches, I locked the office door and on my way out of the Excelsior decided to take Julia's Luger. In the empty library I reached behind the volumes and took out the pistol and put it into my overcoat pocket. There wasn't much chance of being stopped and searched by the Gestapo that freezing night. I went to the Adlon to say goodbye to Art. He had received his exit visa and was leaving Friday evening. I ordered bourbon and the waiter said there was no more. I had finished the last bottle in stock. I ordered an Irish, neat, and Jack laughed after hearing I was headed east. He was drunk.

"I'll bet there's not another bottle of bourbon in Berlin. There's no use in you coming back."

"What are you going to write about this time?" Joe asked.

"Crop rotation. There's a good library there, with books on local conditions."

All three stared and I took a sip of Irish.

"You're tired of reading Nazi papers, that's all," Jack said. "Too much *Der Angriff.* I don't blame you. Some of that shit—."

Art gave him a warning glance and he looked around.

"The place is empty except for that broad at the bar."

Art shook his head and spoke in a low voice.

"There are two guys at the end of the bar and another two coming in. And don't forget the waiters."

"Maybe we'll get lucky and they'll give us exit visas. We're pretty well fucked here now, anyway. The whole place is one big fucking keyhole with everybody lined up to peek and squeal on somebody else before he squeals on him. Heard about Himmler? Herr Supersquealer. He's breeding Aryans. He's got stud farms for the SS. With willing *Mädchen.* He's gone from breeding chickens to breeding blonds. You can get these Heinies to do anything."

The two men who had come into the bar as Jack was speaking came over to us. They were obvious Gestapo agents, stolid and stocky, former regular police officers. They looked at each of us in turn. One spoke to Jack as I swallowed the rest of my Irish.

"What did you say about Germans?"

"I was making an observation, gentlemen. You can do anything with chicken, especially good German chickens."

"You said something else."

"Ask these gentlemen here. We are correspondents. We attended press conferences today at the Propaganda Ministry and Foreign Office. We were instructed on the latest developments in the war."

The agents looked at each other and then one stared at me.

"I have seen you somewhere. I think we have met."

"Yeah, and I have a pistol in my coat pocket."

I didn't know which way he was going to jump. And I didn't care. Maybe it was the Irish. One way or another.

They glanced at each other and at us again to make sure we were suitably intimidated, all part of the role. After they left Jack grinned at me.

"Not bad. They have trouble shifting gears."

We left the hotel together. Wind scooped up snow, spinning wisps of it along the sidewalk. We huddled inside our overcoats, gloves and scarves. Art pulled down his hat brim and held onto it. Jack jammed his hat down over his eyebrows, voice booming through his scarf with blasts of vapor.

"The American press corps in Berlin, minus Dickie Hapshit and a few minor players. Let's go to Jim's, help him pack and give him a send-off at the station."

Art's car wouldn't start. I had given up driving the Eifel when the weather turned cold. We got out and I led the way in a buffeting wind to my pension. The seven blocks felt like seven miles. At the pension I pulled off a glove and with stiff fingers worked the key into the lock, turned it and opened the door. I swung around, put a finger to my lips and we stepped into the vestibule. Soles and heels scuffed against the runner as we climbed the stairs to my room. After switching on the ceiling light I shut the door and handed out bottles of beer from a crate. Art sat on the one chair. Joe and Jack sat on the bed. I took the rest of the bottles out of the wood-and-wire crate, put them on the floor and set the crate on end and sat on it. Art was sipping from his first bottle as Joe and I started on our second. Jack drained his third. He looked around.

"Where do I take a piss?"

"It's to your right, at the end of the hall."

He bumped into walls on the way back and slumped onto the bed after picking up another bottle.

"It's dark in there. I think I found the bowl. Know what I think? What I really think?"

He waited as if expecting an answer.

"Problem with my wives was they had brains. I'm on top forking them and they're figuring out how to empty my wallet and bank account. I need a retarded broad who smiles all the time and can't get enough. There's women who'res, I mean who're—still doesn't sound right—out for sex and women who aren't. I'm looking for one and getting the other. Where are all the brainless sexy broads? Schicklgruber got 'em locked up?"

Joe grinned.

"If you were SS you could get lots of blondes to breed with."

"That's where I'm not a racist. I have no preference for blondes. Redheads, brunettes are fine too. Any shade will do. Lots of blondes get dye jobs. When you look between their legs you get a surprise. First time it happened I actually pointed. Stupid prick that I was. Put the broad right off. Women get into moods."

"What gets me is too much hair down there," Joe said.

"Carry a pair of scissors around with you," I said.

"You serious?"

"It was early morning but it hadn't dawned on him yet."

"OK, I get it. Don't you think a big bush looks too hairy, sticking out everywhere? Unless it's blonde, easier on the eyes. A blonde pussy is more erectrifying. Not bad, huh?"

"Taking into account the hour, the alcohol, and the offense to the English tongue more or lèse-majesté, any reply infra dig."

"What's that supposed to mean?"

"What it does."

Jack took a swig.

"Ever seen shaved pussy? I have. On whores. Trimmed ones too. Makes everything go better."

Art put his empty bottle on the floor.

"I don't believe I'm hearing this."

"You found true love, Art. The rest of us haven't been as lucky."

"I didn't know you looked, Jack."

"Maybe when I was sixteen. Then I wised up."

"Got burnt, huh?"

"Wouldn't put it that way."

"No, you wouldn't."

"I'll tell you something, Jim. Peter was after Sophie when you were away last Christmas. She came back from skiing. He brought her to the Alpenhaus. The week before it closed for good. They left together in a taxi that night. Why didn't you go after her?"

"I don't like Sophie talked about," Art said. "She's a decent woman."

Jack raised his eyebrows.

"Did I say she wasn't? I'm having a little fun with Jim."

"Do it with one of your whores."

The sound of bottles being opened.

"I worked my way through college," Joe said after a while.

"Boola boola," Jack said. "I didn't go to college."

"That's not my fault. Anyway, what I was going to say was that I worked on the railroad during the summers to pay my way. The guys on the repair track used to change boxcar wheels. At each end of a boxcar is what's called a truck, with two pairs of steel wheels. They get flat spots and have to be turned on a lathe. A crane would lift the end of the boxcar so they could get out the flat wheel. And when they wanted it lifted a bit higher or lowered a bit they'd say, 'up a cunt hair' or 'down a cunt hair.' Never forgot that."

"You making a point?"

"I thought you guys might like to know. I have to go to the john."

I remembered I had a flashlight, took it out of the bureau and handed it to him. It was a while before he got back.

"Quite a mess in there. I mopped it up with my shoe and some newspaper."

"I didn't have a flashlight," Jack said.

"There's a light switch."

"The switch doesn't work and the bulb is burnt out," I said. "Saves the landlady money. The exciting adventurous life of a foreign correspondent in Berlin. Freezing and boozing in a tiny room between visits to the toilet. That's what I call a feature story."

"Too late to go home now," Jack said.

"You're welcome guests. Spend the night."

"When are you leaving?"

"Seven. I have to catch the early train. It won't be early. And there may not be another."

Jack looked at his watch.

"It's after three. You better get some sleep."

"I'll sleep standing up on the train."

"Impossible," Joe said.

"I was in the army," Jack said. "When you're dead tired you can sleep in any position, including vertical."

I looked over at Art. He'd fallen asleep in the chair, legs sticking out and arms folded on his chest.

"Art's beaten us to it."

Jack stood up.

"Take the bed, Jim."

"No, you guys draw lots. I'll sleep sitting on the crate, back against the wall."

"Take the bed, Jack," Joe said. "You're old and out of shape."

"Watch it, fella."

"I didn't mean anything."

"Better not."

Jack lay on the bed. Joe sat on the floor, back against the bed frame and promptly fell asleep. I moved the crate up against the wall and sat on it and stretched out my legs. I closed my eyes.

"Jim?"

"Yeah?"

"I didn't mean that about Sophie."

"I know."

"She's a good kid. Make somebody a good wife. Art was like a father to her. You can't say a word against her, even in fun. You keeping in contact?"

"Yeah."

"Good."

When I left they were still sleeping.

# The Summer House

The Schlesischer Bahnhof was already crowded at seven. There was no train. The empty tracks stretched into the yard like a forgotten journey. An hour went by and people began complaining to the station officials, who said a train was being made up and would be arriving shortly. At nine-thirty the coaches rolled along the side of the platform and the madness began. Shoving, pushing, swearing, the corner of a suitcase in your back, an elbow jabbed in your face. No concessions were made to the sick or old, women or children. I found an aisle seat, slung my valise onto the luggage rack and sat down. The aisle was jammed with passengers and I ignored them. Some jostling and I heard a baby cry, looked up and saw a girl holding an infant. Hovering over me and clutching her newborn, she didn't look at me but straight into the misery of her long trip. I got up and gave her my seat. She gave me the merest of glances, squeezed by and sat down. After a while she looked up and smiled.

I had forgotten how many stops the train made on my last trip east. How long it took to get going again. Everything came back like a dull ache. To forget, I thought about Mina and Loulou. It had been a year. I didn't plan on being a guest. I would stay no more than a day, pick up the information on T4 and leave. In my parting flurry of dispatches to head office I said I was sick and was taking a few days off at a spa. In case the Gestapo searched the office while I was away I had brought along the notebook. It was in the valise, with the Luger. The codes were disguised as recipes and travel writing and I was ready with stories if the Feldpolizei stopped me and searched the valise. I couldn't have explained the pistol. But I figured they most likely wouldn't bother with the valise because my papers were in order. I thought the risk worth it.

You can sleep standing up. The trouble was at every stop a departing passenger would push past and wake me. I didn't sit down the whole trip. The Nordbahnhof in twilight and Joseph waiting. I handed him my valise and slumped onto the front seat of the limousine.

"How have you been, Joseph?"

"Very well, sir."

"Mind if I sleep?"

"Not at all."

"Nothing like a train that is slower than an arthritic caterpillar."

"I suppose you are right."

"No supposing about it. Why am I talking like some idiotic tourist?"

"You may need sleep."

"I may."

Silence. The soft comfortable ride and the dark road pierced by the large headlight beams began to take effect and I nodded off.

"We are here, sir."

Parked in the driveway again and the house mostly dark, the estate covered in snow. One of the doors opened, Klaus came out and we exchanged greetings. He took my valise from Joseph and I followed him inside. The piled hats and boots were in the entrance hall but no Christmas tree. We went upstairs to my old room in the north wing. After putting my valise at the end of the bed Klaus lit a fire. I yawned.

"Too early for a Christmas tree?"

"There will be no celebrations this year, sir. Miss Louisa's fiancé was killed."

"Sorry to hear that."

"We received the news a short time ago. I will tell Miss Wilhelmina you are here."

I took off my coat and laid it on the bed, sat down and waited. I decided I would spend the night, get the information the next day and leave. Klaus returned and told me Mina would see me in the study. The door was open. She sat hunched over in the walnut armchair, a sweater draped over her shoulders. She heard me approach and looked up. There were bags under her eyes. I felt like an intruder.

"Klaus told me."

"Please sit down. You must excuse my appearance. One expects these things. But when they happen—."

After moving the wicker chair so I would be facing her, I sat down. I could see on the rolltop desk part of the framed photograph of her mounted on Fritzi. Stacked letters blocked my view of the rest. I wondered if they were the same letters. She gazed at me, trying to keep me in focus.

"Have you eaten?"

"Forget about that."

"I will tell Klaus to put something out for you."

"I would rather eat in the kitchen later."

"If that is your wish."

"My pleasure."

Her lips creased into a faint smile. It was enough to break her mood. I would want to hear. She sat up, her back against the chair.

"He was killed more than a month ago but his body was found only recently. His division was clearing the Pripet Marshes of Red Army units and Soviet partisans. He led a reconnaissance patrol and it did not return. Search parties went out but found nothing. Then a captured soldier said Gerd's patrol was wiped out and the bodies thrown into a swamp. He led a search party there and the bodies were recovered. Gerd's family received a letter from his commanding officer two days ago. His mother phoned Loulou."

She looked down for a moment before continuing.

"The military tradition is strong in Junker families. Gerd loved horses and joined the Reiter Regiment garrisoned at Insterburg, not far from here. In October of 1939 the regiment became part of the First Cavalry Division. It fought in Poland and France. It was sent to Russia this year. He wrote to Loulou and sometimes would add something for me. We knew each other since we were children. He had written in those earlier campaigns but this time his letters were different. 'I have seen terrible things.' 'A soldier must do his duty.' 'The Russians will never forgive us.' I know Gerd was not alone in feeling this way. His regiment is Prussian. Most of his fellow officers are Junkers. They come from an honorable tradition."

"I can accept that. But to me Germany is Bach, not Frederick the Great."

"History is more than music. Napoleon taught us a lesson. We learned it and beat him. Our nation was founded on French defeats."

"What lesson is being taught now? Sorry, that was inappropriate, I apologize."

She raised her hand in acknowledgment.

"I will try to persuade her to go away for a rest. We have friends in Austria."

She turned and looked at the cluttered top of the desk.

"I have the information for you here somewhere. You must give me time to gather it. If the Gestapo were to look they could not sort this mess. After your tiring trip you must stay at least the weekend. By early next week I shall have everything together for you. Much has come to us since Sophie left. T4 has gone underground, as you no doubt know. That reminds me, I hid some messages in the forest. There is so much, as I said. Some Germans seem to look for an excuse to kill."

"That type is everywhere. They have more opportunity here."

She grinned.

"A year ago I asked you why you were doing this. You answered with some nonsense about standing in a coach aisle all day and not liking quiche."

"It was my version of British understatement, with a touch of humor."

"But one must say what one feels, especially on important matters."

"Hitler does."

"That is an unfair argument."

"You can say what you feel and be phony because you see a false truth. I sneak up on the truth."

"You would not make a good Prussian."

"You mean Junker."

"They are the same. You are American, so it would be difficult for you to understand. When my mother first came here as a young bride she felt out of place, a foreigner. She is from Hesse. One day soon after she arrived she was walking in the gardens. The head gardener was there and she spoke with him. He was an old man and had worked on the estate his whole life. He said to her, 'You are our mother.'"

"That sounds Russian."

"At that time, in Tsarist Russia a workman would have bowed, as if she had been anointed. More religious. Here it has always been a secular bond as well, understood and honored by everyone. Duty goes both ways."

"Seems feudal to me."

"You see, you will never understand."

She looked at her watch.

"I must leave. I may not see you for a while. Klaus will take care of you. Goodnight."

We stood up and I felt tired. Mina's boots echoed along the hall, sounding further and further away. I sat down again and fell asleep in the wicker chair. When I woke I looked at my watch. It was almost midnight. I was hungry. I didn't want to bother Lotte and Klaus at that hour. But I had to get something. I would eat it in my room. I went to the kitchen and knocked on the door. Klaus opened it.

"I went to the study, sir, and you were sound asleep. I did not wish to wake you."

"Do you have something I could eat in my room?"

"We are up for a while yet. Come in, please."

As usual Lotte was knitting and the smell of cooked food was in the air. She prepared a plate of bratwurst and sauerkraut. After thanking her I began to eat so quickly I hiccuped. I slowed down and finished. I turned down Klaus' offer of a bottle of beer. He was smoking his pipe. They were part of the timeless world of Altenburg, where lifetimes meant nothing, tradition was everything, what Mina had meant by honor and duty. They were all fading into history with those sepia photographs of the landed gentry in horse-drawn carriages, fashionable women with sausage curls and dressed in ribbons and bustle gowns posing on yachts, and a house full of servants in livery and starched caps and aprons gathered on the back lawn of a stately home for a group picture. Old Europe, tight as a corset, stiff as a bodice or celluloid collar, roles in a masque, all the cinched flesh and winked at privilege. No, thanks.

Lotte was worried about Loulou.

"Poor dear. She has not eaten for two days. I made some broth. She must eat that or she will starve."

Klaus shrugged.

"No one can get her to eat."

"Oh, I will go up there myself if I have to and make her eat."

"Starving herself will change nothing. She cannot bring him back."

"Men are so stupid when it comes to understanding women."

"So, why then?"

"She wants to die too."

"To join him?"

"She thinks she cannot live without him."

"That will pass."

"And if not? She will die."

"You worry for nothing."

"I will go up there tomorrow."

"How would that look? Your place is here."

"You make her eat."

"How can I? It will pass, I tell you."

Klaus looked into the bowl of his pipe.

"What about Manfred?"

Lotte stopped knitting and looked at me.

"Sir, do you think the war with Russia will be over soon?"

"The Russians are still fighting hard."

"Our son is there, but not in the front line. We hope he is not in very much danger where he is."

"You may be right. Support troops, like engineers, usually take fewer casualties."

"Damn war," she said under her breath and went back to knitting.

I slept soundly that night and into the morning and Klaus' knock woke me at eight o'clock. I had porridge oats with him and Lotte and wandered around the rest of the day. I heard nothing, not even Mina's boots. No sign of any other guests or of the Countess. I saw one of the maids with a smile on her face as she descended the staircase carrying a platter with a bowl on it. Apparently Loulou had started eating again. I passed up lunch and had dinner in the kitchen. Afterwards I went upstairs to the library and fell asleep in my chair. I woke up at midnight and went to my room and slept until Sunday morning. Klaus told me the family would be having dinner in the dining hall at eight and I would eat with them. Porridge oats again, and barley soup with slices of buttered rye for lunch held me until dinner.

I was in the dining hall at five to eight. At eight they came in, the Countess as usual slightly in front. I stood up and Loulou nodded, the slightest tilt of her head. She looked tired, her eyes dazed. We all sat down and Klaus served the first course, a beef broth with slices of pumpernickel. As we ate Mina started a conversation.

"Do you hear from Sophie?"

"I cable her in care of our head office in New York. She lives with her mother in New Hampshire."

"And where is that?"

"New England."

"Help me."

"North of Boston."

"Cold?"

"Cold and snowy."

"She can ski. Sophie loves skiing."

Mina glanced at Klaus, who was standing in the doorway.

"What is it?"

"There is some important news. We heard it on the radio."

"Yes?"

"America has been bombed."

I put down my spoon and stared.

"The United States is too far away from German bombers," Mina said.

"No. Japanese."

"Japanese?" Four voices echoed in unison.

I stood up.

"Would you excuse me? I want to hear this."

I followed Klaus to the kitchen. The staff was gathered around a radio and listening to the BBC German language service. I pretended not to notice and told Klaus I wanted to listen to the BBC. He understood, shooing everybody out into the hallway. Fifteen minutes later I returned to the dining hall and remained standing as I spoke. The situation seemed to call for it. I felt like the voice of history.

"I tuned in the BBC English language service. A Japanese carrier task force attacked the naval base at Pearl Harbor in Hawaii on Sunday morning. The President will go before Congress tomorrow and ask for a declaration of war. Churchill will declare war on Japan. No reaction from the Wilhelmstrasse yet."

"So Germany and the United States are not at war," Mina said. "You can finish your dinner and we can talk later."

I sat down and tried to concentrate on food but a chaos of random thoughts kept me from being able to see or taste anything. Rooosevelt wouldn't declare war on Germany. There wasn't an obvious excuse and isolationists were still making speeches. Our quarrel is with Japan, they would argue. So would Hitler and Mussolini honor the Axis Pact and join Japan against the United States? It was a good bet they would. Purely as a matter of realpolitik, the Japanese had been recognized as eastern Aryans. I would be interned with the rest of the correspondents. I was glad Sophie was safe. What would Julia do? Keep stringing along? Swastikas hanging in concert halls hadn't bothered her. Not being a neutral any more wouldn't make any difference. Mrs. Fusco would continue to believe they were on the winning side. I felt sorry for Julia. It was a kind of pained love. Beauty and talent she wore like the rarest of amulets and yet they cursed her.

After dinner Mina and I talked in the library, facing each other in the red leather armchairs.

"If we get into this, I would be interned if I went back to Berlin."

"Stay here and see what happens and you can decide. We offer you sanctuary."

"Failure to report to the Propaganda Ministry for internment would make me a wanted alien and you and your sister accomplices."

"We will hide you in the summer house. There is a fireplace and lots of wood. A maid or I will bring you food. Loulou will visit when she feels better."

"I told the Propaganda Ministry I was going to study crop rotation. The Königsberg Gestapo would be notified. You would get a visit. Smoke coming from the chimney out there is going to look suspicious."

She frowned. The moment passed, her face relaxed.

"Our contacts will warn us. We shall tell the Gestapo you never arrived."

"I should try to get to Switzerland."

"The mountain passes are full of snow. Spring is better."

"Lots of firewood, lots of oats."

"We have a forest and stores of grain."

"Are you teaching me a lesson about Junkers?"

She blushed slightly for a moment, her cheeks tinting a soft pink. She stood up quickly.

"So you are staying. I will have the summer house prepared."

I didn't have long to wait. Some German correspondents were arrested in the United States and on Wednesday the German government retaliated, arresting all the American journalists and broadcasters except Hapgood and me. The Propaganda Ministry was waiting for me to return. Together with diplomats, newsmen were taken to a hotel away from Berlin and interned on December 15. I found all this out later. Hitler on December 11 in a Kroll Opera House packed with his rubber-stamp Reichstag deputies declared war on the United States. I heard the speech on the radio in the kitchen. Afterwards Mina came to me in the library with news about Berthold.

"You must stay in your room tomorrow night. Berthold phoned. He will be bringing his girlfriend to dinner. Apparently no more peasants and poor working women. She is a fervent Nazi and more than twenty years younger. A teenager. Her father, a former butcher, is a high party official. I shall tell you everything tomorrow night."

She didn't get to the library until after ten the next night.

"They were waiting in the dining hall when we entered. She was holding onto Berthold's arm. They raised their arms in the Nazi salute and shouted, 'Heil Hitler.' He introduced her as Fräulein Gubler. It was shameful to see Berthold saluting. We of course did not, which brought a frown from Fräulein Gubler. Mama stared at them. 'Keep your voices down. My daughter is not feeling well. Her fiancé was killed in Russia.' The girl, that is all she is, said, 'He gave his life for his Führer and Fatherland.' 'For the Fatherland,' Mama said. 'My sister-in-law is old-fashioned,' Berthold said. 'I am a good German,' Mama said. Smirking, Berthold looked sideways at his girlfriend, as if to say, she is a dotty old woman. 'I will bear many fine sons for the Führer,' she said. 'You are built for it,' Mama said. Berthold looked uncomfortable, probably about the many sons.

"Berthold is taking no chances this time. His Aryan ideal has platinum hair, skin as white as chalk, and colorless eyes. He is showing her off. As he caters to her vanity. 'Your eyes are the lightest blue, my darling. And your skin is exquisite.' 'I have been told it is delicate,' she said proudly.

"Loulou is feeling better. I could tell by the way she was grinning at them. My sister can be mischievous when it comes to pompous idiots. She is subtler than I could ever be. Tonight they were a tonic for her."

"'Your many fine sons will die in battle.'

"'I will be happy that they have died for their Führer.'

"'Such happiness must be hard to bear.'

"'Not for a follower of the Führer.'

"'Follower is right.'

"'A true believer. Put it like that. He shows the way. And we follow.'

"'Your trust is amazing. But why waste your time thinking?'

"'He thinks for us. That is why he is the Führer.'

"'A simple arrangement. All you have to do is obey. He has all the hard work. Thinking up wars for his soldiers.'

"'Come, come, Loulou,' Berthold said. 'You are trying to make a joke out of something that should be taken seriously.'

"'I am trying to find the source of Fräulein Gubler's adulation.'

"'You obviously do not understand.'

"'Perhaps you would enlighten me. This is the first time you have ever given the Nazi salute or favored us with their greeting in this house. A true believer should not alter his behavior to suit circumstances. What kind of Nazi are you?'

"Berthold's face went red. He put down his soup spoon.

"'I refrained before because I knew I was among the unconverted and out of respect for Augusta, who would not have wanted me to. I will not apologize for my behavior, either to my Führer or my sister-in-law.'

"'I understand your behavior, Berthold. It is your adulation I find puzzling.'

"'Because you refuse to share it. Many times over the last few years at this table I have said enough to convince all but the most stubbornly self-deluded.'

"'You certainly said enough to convince yourself.'

"'He is an old dog,' Fräulein Gubler said, 'but I am training him in the new ways.'

"If you could have seen the look on his face. A butcher's daughter speaking that way about him. She even asked for a copy of *Mein Kampf* so she could read aloud some instructive passages. Loulou told her we did not have one. Fräulein Gubler was amazed and indignant.

"'Everyone must have one. Every couple that is married is given one. It is the Führer's thoughts on the destiny of the German people. The future of our race.'

"Mama had had enough.

"'I was married long before you were born or your Führer became a German. I received a Bible as a wedding gift. We have a library. But neither the Count nor I would ever allow in this house a political diatribe.'

"I doubt if Fräulein Gubler had ever heard the word 'diatribe.' But she knew what Mama meant. She was learning about Junkers. We are not all like Berthold. Old dogs that need obedience training. Loulou and I looked at each other. We enjoyed seeing how uncomfortable he was. Fräulein Gubler was undeterred.

"'I am going to instruct all of you. Not you, Countess. You cannot be helped. But you two. You should be married. Doing your duty. Bearing sons for the Fatherland.'

"'I never thought I would have to leave my table because of somebody I would not have clean my floors,' Mama said and stood up.

"Berthold stood up. He looked at Fräulein Gubler. He sat down. Klaus came over and pulled back Mama's chair. Berthold stood up. As Mama turned to go, she made a sign for Loulou and me to stay. Otherwise we would have left with her. She made a grand exit. I think she was tired. She wanted us to stay and enjoy Berthold's discomfort and perhaps make it worse. She was disgusted at his traitorous behavior, to his class and her. Fräulein Gubler was smug.

"'The past has gone.'

"'Not for those who are able to understand it,' I said.

"Fräulein's Gubler's smirk was very much like our uncle's and probably learned from him.

"'Time is wasted on such things.'

"'It would be wasted time for you.'

"With Mama gone, Berthold sneered more arrogantly. All he can think is, this butcher's brat is much younger than his other conquests and her father could be of some use to him. Before he flew the swastika flag he was simply opinionated and conceited, guaranteed to clear a dinner table quicker than the most efficient staff. When he began bringing Professor Schliesman, those two were like a pair of wolves stalking their prey. You had a taste of that. Now this Nazi prize. But Berthold would not want to risk banishment, to which Mama has condemned those who have offended her beyond her endurance. They were not happy when they left. She will not want to come back. Loulou and I can be merciless.

"'You are pale,' I said to Fräulein Gubler. 'Do you get any fresh air and sunshine? Do you go outside? How do you expect to be a good example of German womanhood? You were a member of the Jungmädel and Bund Deutsche Mädel, I am assuming, and are old enough and doubtless have volunteered for Werke, Glaube und Schönheit.'

"'I was exempted. I cannot be out in the sun or I will get sunstroke.'

"'You are almost an albino,' Loulou said. 'Nature does not appear to be on the side of the Aryan ideal past a certain point. What is perfection in a woman, Berthold? How white? Enough so even the sun is your enemy? The blond ideal is tricky. Nurses in the Lebensborn program administer UV radiation to Aryan babies whose hair has begun to turn from blond to brown.'

"'You are being ridiculous and unfair to this poor girl.'

"'No more than Professor Schliesman when he attacks most of the world for being a different color.'

"'Be careful what you say. You tread on dangerous ground.'

"'I speak to the facts. The sun is our benefactor. Don't Nazi boys and girls wear shorts and short-sleeved shirts? The sun makes us grow and be healthy. Someone who cannot tolerate it is unusual. Being unusual in Germany is to risk being seen as counterproductive to the welfare of the state. We know where that leads.'

"'You exaggerate.'

"'Exaggeration is part of life in Germany now. A virtue today may be a crime tomorrow.'

"'I should not have imagined that you two would behave so badly,' Berthold said, coming to the rescue of his beloved. 'How can you be so cruel? Is Ilse to blame because she cannot be out in the sun? How is that her fault? In every other way she is perfect. Kind and generous and thoughtful. A very loving person.'

"Loulou looked at me.

"'I hear the price of women's underwear has gone up.'

"Fräulein Gubler recovered her arrogance. She and Berthold do belong together. Nazi girl and Junker traitor. Her tirade was appalling.

"'You think because you are aristocrats you can say whatever you want? Even treason. I am going to tell my father. We will see. You are not the kind of people we want in Germany. You should be exterminated. You are the past, like your mother. We have our Führer. Why do we need you? You stand in our way with your stupid old ideas. You think you are safe out here, can say anything you want? You are not part of Germany? Your Altenburg, what does it mean any more? It will not protect you. You think I am less than you? I will breed sons for our Führer. For the greater glory of the Third Reich. I will give my life for it. You are useless mouths. Spreading your filthy lies. The poison of dirty minds. I am the future, not you Junkers.'

"Berthold was looking uncomfortable now. It had been a mistake to bring her but he could not leave without his dignity intact or with an empty stomach.

"'Calm yourself, Ilse. You are unused to dinner table conversation of this kind. Useless aristocrats have nothing better to do. I speak as a reformed Junker. My nieces are beyond help. You would be wasting your time attempting to bring them into the twentieth century. They find it more comfortable to live in a medieval fantasy. They labor under certain delusions, one of which is everybody else is a peasant.'

"'I am not a peasant.'

"'Of course not, my dear.'

"'They insult me.'

"'I know, my pet, but sometimes it is better to let insults die from their own poison. Answering them is a waste of time.'

"He was holding her by the hand. He had turned and leaned towards her, his bald spot, which he tries to cover with his remaining hair, clearly visible.

"'Lotte is a wonderful cook,' I said. 'That soup is days old. With a bit of fresh dill added. You did not even notice. If you are expecting her chicken in wine sauce, you are going to be disappointed. Dinner tonight is poor fare. No proper meat dish. Leftover stew. Dessert is week-old cake. Not too stale, we hope. And Mama has decided to close the cellar. The bottle on the table will be our only wine.'

"'That is insulting. Unheard of. You knew we were coming to dinner. You are doing this deliberately.'

"'There is a war. We must economize. It would not do for us to be gluttons while the rest of Germany is on rations. Surely you agree.'

"Loulou finished him off.

"'Nothing gourmet for the gourmand tonight. You have enjoyed yourself countless times over the years at our table. No one ate more than you. No one drank more. One skimpy dinner should not discourage you. We are falling into line. Not beyond hope at all.'

"'Giving us this swill,' Berthold sneered, pushing his soup plate away. 'You think I could not tell the difference because I said nothing? Of course I knew. I did not want Ilse to know how base you can be.'

"'You were enjoying it up until now. Can it be you are not the gourmand you say you are? You have more appetite than discernment? Your taste lacks a certain refinement. Perhaps there are degrees of taste, like aristocracy, and some find it easier to abandon the traditional well-laden table for the glories of rationing. That being so, you should be the first to praise dinner tonight. It meets the strictest ration standards. No coffee with our cake.'

"'This is an insult meant for me and for Ilse. I will not forget it.'

"'You will, enough to pester Mama with your politics and your flattery.'

"Loulou is right, of course. He will be back. But next time he will not dare to bring her because Mama would not stand for it. They stayed for the stew. You have tasted Lotte's cooking and know how good it is. She can turn anything into a tasty meal. The stew was delicious. Berthold had three helpings and took the cubes of meat from his beloved's plate. Immediately afterwards, they stood up and left without saying goodbye. She turned her broad back to us. He bowed toward Mama's chair."

I didn't take any more meals in the dining hall. I figured the Countess and Loulou needed a break after Berthold and his Nazi teen. For the next few days I skipped breakfast, took lunch in my room and had a late dinner in the kitchen. I spent a lot of time in my room because of the chance of visitors seeing me. Lotte's leftovers beat anything available in Berlin. We didn't talk much. Lotte worried about her son on the eastern front and Klaus smoked, resting after his long hours. He saw Loulou every day. One night I asked him if she was much better. He began to talk about the von Pommers.

"They have not been here nearly as long as the Altenburgs. The family came to Ostpreusßen late in the last century. From Schleswig-Holstein. They are relatives of an old Junker family and inherited the estate after the Count, who had no children, died insane. Their manor is not a schloss like Altenburg. The only son, Miss Louisa's fiancé, was not worthy of her. All he knew or cared about were horses and his regiment. They played together as children and the Countess thought he would be a suitable match. But Miss Louisa was too lively for him, much smarter. She put off the wedding many times. The

Countess never made a fuss about that. She was after Miss Louisa's uncle, a professor, and his fiancée to become engaged and get married but for some reason ignored her daughter's delays. The von Pommer family became upset but Miss Louisa did not care and neither did the Countess. The only von Pommer daughter, Constanze, was a big tall young lady who loved horses as much as her brother did. She would visit on horseback instead of in a car. Nobody in the family liked her. She was loud and rude. She would tell crude jokes about animals and make noises that were not polite. At the dinner table, mind you. The Countess was not amused. Once after Constanze had left the Countess said she had inherited her relative's insanity. That could be the reason she did not push for the marriage.

"When that painter was here the first time, Constanze found out that Miss Wilhelmina was having her portrait painted and Constanze wanted him to paint her, too. She blackmailed Miss Wilhelmina, saying if she did not get Klapperich to paint her she would tell the Countess about him. One of the upstairs maids heard the two of them arguing in Miss Wilhelmina's bedroom. They had known each other since they were little girls or else Constanze would never have dared go into that bedroom. What could Miss Wilhelmina do? They made up a story that would satisfy the Countess and the von Pommer family. They would be told an artist in Königsberg had painted her. Klapperich painted her in the summer house and we saw the portrait. It was shown in the entrance hall for a day before it was taken to be hung in the von Pommer house. That painter did everything he could to make something out of Constanze. Her body was like a sack of potatoes. She had a big face with tiny eyes. Miss Wilhelmina was not friendly after that happened and she did not come here much. Two years ago, after she got married, she visited with her husband a few times. They were invited for *das Neujahr* last year, but you probably did not notice them because there were so many guests.

"I think you saw the last big dinner. There will be more dinners but they will not be the same. In the old days we needed two tables for the guests. There were the von Tiefenthalers and von Gieseckes. Besides the von Pommers and others. It was a tradition to invite the leading Junker families in Ostpreußen. The kitchen was full of trays and platters going and returning, course after course, and wine corks being popped and somebody almost bumping into somebody every second. So many visitors would come during the holidays. We servants cooked, cleaned, made beds, did laundry, polished furniture and floors. It was hard work for us but we knew nothing else. When you are raised a certain way, that is what you know and believe. I can honestly say that we came to feel a part of this family, but who will know what I mean? Who will not smile sadly and think, poor man, he is a drudge and has fooled himself his whole life into believing he was more than that. We had almost nothing, so what they had became ours. There are fewer and fewer guests and visitors. It is all passing away. It was our life too."

The following week the summer house was ready. It was on the far side of the lake at the back of the main house and connected to it by a gravel path. The path went around the lake and the section between the houses had been cleared of snow. Snow lay on the roof like icing on a gingerbread house. There was a pile of sawn logs in a nearby shed. The one story was the same tan stucco as the main house, topped by a glazed tile roof, with a tall chimney at the north end. On either side of the front entrance was a multi-paneled window. Two stone steps led to a wooden door set within a rounded shallow archway. Inside were four rooms, all with pine floors covered with rugs. At the front the largest room took up half the interior from side to side. The decoration was rustic rather than Late Baroque, with boar and stag heads on wood paneling, and in the north wall a stone fireplace. The other rooms, at the back, were small, one with a bed and one empty and the other a pantry with an enameled sink. The tables and chairs were plain beechwood. There were windows in the bedroom and empty room and the back door was in the pantry.

Mina and I stood in the short hallway connecting the front room with the others. There was the smell of fresh paint. She told me the walls of the bedroom and empty room had been whitewashed. She said a servant couldn't be spared to look after the fire. I told her I was capable of setting and tending a fire. We grinned at each other. She quickly mentioned the rest. At noon a maid would bring me my food for the day. I should stay away from the main house to avoid any visitors. The fewer who knew about me the better. If I wanted books from the library a maid would bring them. Loulou wouldn't be visiting for a while but Mina would when she could. There was no radio in the summer house. She would listen to the BBC German language news, again when she could. As she left she paused at the front door.

"I have had a maid put out a book that you may find interesting. It is in the bedroom. They are writings by my uncle Friedrich. Unlike Berthold and my father, he was a university scholar. There is a tradition at Altenburg that a family member may stay as long as he wishes. He came to live here, later resigned his professorship at Heidelberg and moved into the summer house. He spent his time writing, riding round the estate, visiting the university in Königsberg and attending dinner parties in the main house. He was engaged to a distant cousin of ours, Viktoria von Giesecke. She came here and stayed with him. In 1937 she was killed, thrown from her horse. He was never the same and did not finish the book. Early in 1938 he walked into a winter storm one night and days later his body was found in the snow by one of the farmers."

With that enticing preview she walked back out into the winter morning. I remembered what Lotte and Klaus told me about Anton Klapperich, the painter from Vienna. So two others before me had lived in the summer house. I wouldn't have known about the painter except for backstairs gossip. The bigger the house the bigger the leaks are among the servants. My predecessors, one a suicide and the other betrayed. I had interned myself, and I wondered for how long?

A maid appeared at noon. In a galvanized pail she carried a bowl of porridge oats with cream, a pot of stew, a plate of buttered rye and a bottle of beer. The oats were my late breakfast, the stew to be heated later. After eating the porridge I lit a fire and went to get the book. It was on the bed. I took it into the front room, pulled a chair next to the fireplace and sat down to look at it.

It was a small volume, somewhat larger than a pocket book, hardbound in buff leather, with approximately two hundred unlined pages of linen bond. Half had writing on them, some on one side, some both. The writing was in a precise, spare hand and there were breaks forming sections of varying lengths, apparently written at different times. Following the last section were two blank pages. Then came an uneven scribble of broken words. Much of it was hard to make out. Did Mina know about these later writings? Why was the book left lying around? One thing was certain. There were two writers.

I went outside, could feel the sharp bite of the air as twilight came on. The main house looked dark and far away and behind along the western horizon a bleached lemon sky was fading up into cloud streaks pale as ashes. In back of the summer house the pine forest was filling with shadow, green dissolving to black, and treetops formed a palisade against deepening shades of blue. I brought in two small logs and put them on the fire. I read until dinner. Because the pages had not been numbered, I used a piece of folded notepaper as a marker. After dinner I read until well past midnight. The writings by Mina's uncle are a mixture of reminiscence and social and political commentary, with some of the commentary allegorical. A sense of loss, both personal and national, dominates everything. I recognized some names in this relic of a sad man's life. The later writings are by the painter. His thinking is like his writing, an emotive scrawl of arrogance, bluster and self-justification. But underlying this is the feeling he has lost control. I reprint both parts, complete and unedited.

# The Professor's Book

The world is foreign to me. I am a stranger to myself. What do I care if others think I am neurotic and full of self-pity? I never cared what others thought. It was part of being a Junker, but something else. Not wanting to accept what I was told. It was stubbornness to gain time to consider. I was stubborn about everything. It became a trait. I remember Berthold saying to me once I was born to doubt. Willi had come back from the front and I said nothing about the war. Berthold was full of patriotism and waiting to be of age to join up. Willi said, Fritz lives quietly with his doubts, leave him alone. Willi was much older than us, we were his little brothers, and Berthold idolized him. At least on that occasion Willi could shut Berthold up.

Only once did I never doubt, and that was when I saw you for the first time. It was in July 1931, at a garden party at Altenburg. I was on vacation from university and you were visiting Augusta. You were introduced to me as a distant cousin and I remember saying, I think all Junkers are more or less distant cousins. How distant are you? you asked. Too distant from you, I am afraid, I said. We laughed and that was how it started. You were so beautiful, Viktoria, and there I was with you on the lawn in the back garden, a stiff awkward show-off. I was so nervous my teacup rattled in its saucer. I mentioned the rattling to you months later and asked if you noticed and you said no.

The teacup was the beginning. Everything I did was wrong. Love is more important than what you do or how you do it but you are desperate to do everything right. Our first kiss and I missed your lips and kissed your chin. You smiled. We will have lots of time together, Fritz, for you to practice. The first time I held you and too soon I would touch you in the wrong place. You will ruin my reputation, you said, and again that smile. I thought we were too perfect together and I did not deserve such happiness. Doubt again, the old habit. Even love could not keep it away.

I would not like you to be too smooth, you said. There is no practice for love. It merely happens and you fall. There should be something awkward about it.

We were lying under a pine in a meadow in the woods behind the lake, leaving the horses to graze on the wild grass. Afternoon shadows swept across your face as a breeze moved the branches.

What have you ever done wrong? I said. You behave impeccably.

No. But you are too busy watching and criticizing yourself to notice that I am far from perfect.

You are perfect.

You force me to confess. You remember the ball at the von Pommers? It was our first appearance in society together, if that means anything any more even among Junkers. I promised a dance to Gerd and I completely forgot. He came up to me and I said, Sorry, I am waiting for Fritz. He turned and walked away without a word. Augusta took me aside later and said, Gerd is such a proper young man and he cannot figure out why you refused him after promising a dance. Did I? I said. I must have forgotten. Augusta went over and spoke to him. But he never looked at me the rest of the evening. He has not asked me since.

You wilful woman.

Because of you.

My fault.

No, Fritz, nobody's. You can blame it on love if you wish, but you may as well blame it on the stars or moon.

I would never blame you.

I would never blame you.

Anyone hearing us would think we were the most ridiculous couple in the world. But all we have to say is we are in love. Like being crazy, you are excused and not even put away. Why are lovers laughed at? Nobody laughs about sex. Those who do laugh wish to be bawdy or cruel. They hide embarrassment or jealousy.

Most love is infatuation, Fritz, and people laugh at that. The lovers get tired of each other after undressing a few times. They become friends or strangers. They feel cheated and look for somebody else. They never find anybody.

Why?

Because you never find love, it finds you. Sometimes even if you are deserving, it will not happen.

Are we talking too much, Viktoria?

Not for lovers. The unlucky others will never understand, will laugh or snicker. Why should we care what they think? It has been a year since we met. Do you feel any different?

Even more in love, if that is possible.

It is the same with me.

Why did you ask?

You question so many things. Sometimes I think you believe in very little, if anything.

I believe in you. I always will.

Nothing else?

Nothing and no one else is worth it. Our world is vanishing, Viktoria. Taking part of us with it. We should let it go. We are much more.

But our past is part of us.

It is being rejected by history. I am not a fool who thinks Junkers are a bad joke, but the landed aristocracy is a doomed species that we can survive. Altenburg has been losing money for years. How long can this continue before bankruptcy?

Is any of it worth saving?

I value our traditions of duty and, strangely enough, piety. I admit the land itself has a hold on me. I have no blind belief in modern industry. I abominate industrial magnates who dictate ruinous foreign and domestic policies and conspire to foment profitable wars. But we cannot live in castles forever.

Do you believe in castles in the air?

You are in all of them.

When you speak that way, Fritz, I believe we will always be in love. I want our love to be so pure it is almost too much, like breathing pure oxygen. Does that worry you? Are you afraid?

Not a bit.

We lay in the wild grass in each other's arms as twilight covered us. Our breathing quickened, filling a silent world. I felt the beating of your heart, faster and faster, the rising and falling of your breasts. We went far away wrapped in a blanket of stars.

It has been a year, Augusta said to me at dinner one night in July 1932. When are you going to announce your engagement?

We feel engaged already.

Are you certain Viktoria feels that way?

Ask her.

You are my brother-in-law, I am asking you. I thought you were serious.

We are.

A modern couple.

Old-fashioned, truly.

You and Viktoria seem very modern, Mina said.

Augusta looked down the table.

It is not your place to speak on such matters, Wilhelmina.

Yes, Mama. But you never ask Uncle Berthold if he is getting married to Madame Lupinski.

That is quite different. She is not our kind. I have asked him not to bring that woman here again. Once was quite enough.

She looks like a cow, Mina said.

Her hat was full of flowers like a garden, Loulou said.

They laughed.

Be quiet or you will have to leave the table.

Yes, Mama, in chorus.

Have you asked her, Fritz?

No.

Please do.

We became engaged and Augusta was happy but Mina was not. She was seventeen and full of self-styled rebellion.

This wedding nonsense is a farce, she told me on a rainy afternoon in the study as she watched me going over the household and estate accounts. I will choose a man and we shall live together. Or even in different places. Meet when we so wish. Every married person I know is miserable.

Viktoria and I will be happy after marriage.

For how long?

For ever and ever.

You dreamers.

Marriage will make no difference to us.

So why would you dreamers be happier than anybody else? Marriage is a business, the same as running an estate.

There are two kinds of marriage, the practical and the happy. The practical is arranged, a business as you said. The best you can be is satisfied. Many are not. When the couple has chosen each other it is often infatuation, not love. Infatuation leads to disillusion and misery. Love, if it be the true and rare thing, does not.

Is there one person you can love or many?

For some there may be more than one. For me there is one.

That sounds so romantic and silly.

I know.

Why do you believe it?

Viktoria and I think each other the most wonderful part of our lives and so we love, not as two but one.

You are both lucky to have met someone as silly as yourselves.

But who is to say any are happier than us? You should not judge others if you have no idea what they feel or think.

Wait until you are married. Mama had to force you to become engaged.

I told her we were engaged already. She wants the formalities as a kind of social sanction, and I agree as long as we leave it at that.

I shall ignore them completely.

Do as you please but find love first, unless you want to end up as unhappy as most married people are.

The Republic died. The Depression killed it, along with extremists of the right and left. How could Germany repay the loans that paid the reparations? How could millions find work? Ostpreußen was quiet but when I went to Berlin I saw marches and street battles. And finally something worse, the silence of empty streets, as if the strain of hunger, unemployment and despair was about to burst. I despised the Communists and Nazis, felt contempt for the Social Democrats, could barely tolerate the Catholic and centrist parties, felt ashamed of the nationalists and monarchists. I had no political home. My political philosophy was not to trust any political philosophy. Where could I turn?

Not to our thinkers. German philosophers and professors have been the footmen of its rulers and the ruin of its people. We have been told by Fichte, Hegel and Treitschke the state is everything and the individual nothing, and by Nietzsche that we are the true masters of the world and are entitled to enforce our will upon all other peoples. These men of ideas have helped our rulers lock us in a Prussian prison of unquestioning obedience. Frederick the Great, Bismarck, the Kaiser and Hindenburg have been our jailors. We suffer so they can be our heroes. We lick the boot that kicks us. Hohenzollerns and Junkers have told us that we cannot do without them. Is this not the worst trickery ever inflicted upon a people? They have told Germans who their enemies are, but there has only been one enemy, my own class, the enslavers of Germany.

Germans have never felt comfortable being rebels. Their orderliness has a conformist side, which hesitates to take disagreements to the next level. This allows them to be bullied by the powerful and the fanatical. Their response is to accept their fate. The rebels are always glancing wistfully towards reconciliation. The handful who don't are brothers of the fanatics they fight. A society at the mercy of rival gangs of fanatics will be shown mercy by neither.

You do not know the German unless you know the forest. With the Romans it was the fasces, the bundle of sticks, strength through unity in cut and trimmed wood become a club, within and without enforcing order. With the German tribes strength lay in the living trees, each tribe standing in a green silence. Each was nourished by and flourished in its own land, deep and dark within itself. In the Teutoburg Forest they wiped out three Imperial Roman legions. The Romans returned for their captured eagles and beat the Germans at the Weser River but gave up trying to conquer them. And what of Hermann, victor of Teutoburg? He was assassinated by his own people because he wanted to be their emperor. He ignored the lesson he taught Rome. His victory is celebrated, his assassination passed over, and there is a lesson in that.

Rome came again, this time with a church, and drained the tribes of obeisance and gold until Luther, the princes' man, said, No more. Luther's was half a victory but German Catholics are German unto themselves. Rome has been shrewd enough to accept that. The British were crafty too, taking a petty German elector as monarch, and have been content with the dull-witted descendants ever since. Let us not forget Bismarck who, instead of forcing a king on the German tribes, gave them an emperor. But the chalice of unity contained poison. Prussian militarism was Roman by another name. The Roman eagle had become the Prussian eagle. Caesar had become Kaiser. The tribes had become a nation, had become an empire. Our forests became standing armies, then marching armies. The green silence had gone forever and from the mouths of new leaders came the old ideas of swagger and conquer and superiority, of robbery in uniform.

We lost, the Kaiser fled, and the war-crazed fanatics fought each other, making up in ferocity what they lacked in reason. From the stumbling generals, the red-bannered working-class zealots, the racists, the paranoid pan-Germans came cacophonies of hate and finally intrigues of power. We were given another Kaiser, the Nazi demagogue. I would declare him a travesty of the Kaiser if the Kaiser were not a travesty himself. This Nazi, a virulent neurotic inspired by Wagner, believes he has an ordained mission. Wagner is ludicrous enough, but at least his nonsense is mercifully confined to the stage.

His heldentenors and heavy sopranos can bellow at each other, hoisting their spears and shields amid a fake forest in a parody of Nordic lust and greed. This is the forest we will be offered, stage scenery full of false gods and hysterical rants passed off as profundities. When music becomes politics and politics music, fantasy is a drug and anybody can hum the tunes. The truth will be no exit at the final curtain as the theatre burns.

In the old forest where the sun penetrates to the floor, shadows move with the passing day. They trace it, leaving no trace of themselves and merge with twilight. Lengthening, shortening and lengthening again, they mark time. From west to east, grey fading out to grey flowing in, they emerge and then are reabsorbed. At noon, with the sun at its highest, they are the measure of all things. Behold stem and bloom, bud and bough, moss and rock. In that moment is the passion of shadows.


Berthold became a Nazi sympathizer and a friend of Dr. Schliesman, who promotes the party line in Königsberg at the university. Before the Nazis came to power, he spoke out against his Jewish and liberal colleagues. He called for their dismissal but the university authorities would not respond. When the Nazis took over, those professors were dismissed and so was anybody in the administration who spoke in their favour. All German universities have been infected, including Heidelberg. The student unions are Nazi as well. So far I have said nothing about this infringement of our liberties. What good would it do? That mob in Berlin decides for us now. It has come down to a case of martyrdom or silence.

Dr. Schliesman, Professor of Philosophy, is among the most noxious fellows I have ever met. An intellectual criminal, he twists everything to suit his own views. I can almost see foam coming out of his mouth when he condemns Jews, Gypsies, Slavs, Negroes and others he believes to be inferior. Berthold has invited him to Altenburg. To spare poor Augusta and to avoid quarrelling with Berthold I have maintained silence at the dinner table, though provoked by this moral dervish. I have had several jousts with him in clubs at the university. He is impervious to logic.

Your racial ideas are illogical, I said to him last week. How can every last member of one race be inferior to every last member of another race? The same applies to superiority. Can you believe all members of a race share the same character traits, when often members of the same family do not? Among Germans in any village you care to name there are different levels of intelligence, different talents and differences of character. Yet you make generalizations involving tens of millions of people.

It is a verifiable scientific fact, he said, that Germans and Europeans in general are more intelligent than Africans or Asians.

Verifiable fact? What kind of verification? I like your phrase, Europeans in general. Is that a grudging nod at the supposedly lesser races round us? In the streets of Königsberg I can find you people as stupid as any in the world. And I can find you Germans as intelligent as anybody anywhere round the globe. Spare me your specious generalizations, Herr Professor.

Such thinking is not in tune with the times, Professor Altenburg.

Does that make it wrong?

And impolitic.

Do we have to choose between being right and being safe?

It is possible to be both, if you think clearly.

Joseph had taken Augusta to visit the von Pommers, so Berthold had driven me to the university. On the way back to Altenburg we argued.

Are you trying to make trouble for the family, Fritz? Why did you have to provoke him?

Was the fool angry?

Can you blame him? He is a National Socialist. The Nazis rule Germany. A word from him to Heidelberg, then what?

*Ja*, then what?

You will be dismissed. No professorship, no salary. What about Viktoria? Have you thought about her?

How can we live in a Germany ruled by his like?

If not, you will have to leave.

Why do you associate with that man?

There is no alternative for us now.

You accuse me of compromising the family. Yet you associate our name with such trash.

I accept the inevitable. What are you doing?

I stand for what I am. Do I have to do something?

In these times, yes.

You sound like him.

I will not say I disagree with what he says.

*Ach*, a nice way of putting it. Why not admit you are a Nazi? If I say nothing, less trouble for you, no shadow cast on your name. You think only of yourself, not the family. Willi would never associate with such scum.

He is not here to make that choice. I am and must.

And I make mine.

I am trying to warn you, Fritz.

Warn me about something I can plainly see? Somebody like you has no right to lecture me on behaviour. I had two brothers once. One died honourably. The other died a traitor.

Berthold's Mercedes roadster sped faster and faster. We parted without a word. Now the backstairs manoeuvrers who made Hitler Chancellor must watch their marionette pull his own strings in this absurd Third Reich. On his next few visits Berthold and I did not speak to each other. Augusta noticed but said nothing. Months after the argument he came to dinner with Madame Lupinski. It was Easter Sunday. As usual, the whole family was present, as well as other Junkers. Sitting across from Madame Lupinski, a broad-faced stocky woman in her forties, Mina and Loulou teased her. She told them she was from Krakau and had married a Pole in Masuren and after he died moved to Königsberg. Annoyed at her presence, Augusta did nothing to stop the teasing.

What do Catholics do at Easter, pray to the Pope? Mina said.

We decorate eggs, take eggs to church, Madame Lupinski said with a heavy accent.

For the priest to eat? Loulou said.

Not for eating, as offering.

What a waste of eggs, Mina said.

I did my best to blunt the teasing.

Eggs are a fertility symbol, appropriate for spring, and also symbolic of Christ's resurrection.

It makes more sense to read the Bible and eat the eggs, Mina said.

Religion is about worship, not logic. Would you melt all the metal crosses for coins and use the wooden ones all for firewood?

If necessary, yes.

Would you do it if there were lots of firewood and plenty of coinage?

No, but people would be put on notice, the minute they are needed, give up your crosses.

Do you think they would?

They would have to.

You are beginning to sound intolerant. That comes from making fun of another's beliefs.

It was harmless.

To you, yes. But your beliefs may seem ridiculous to some.

They would not.

Because they are yours?

Shut up, Fritz. You are becoming a bore. We are going to make Madame Lupinski an honorary Junker for Easter. Stay out of this.

Perhaps she does not want to be a Junker, even honorary.

I do not mind, Madame Lupinski said.

They are mischievous girls.

Go away, Fritz, Loulou said.

I feel full, Viktoria whispered in my ear. I would like to go for a walk.

Listen to the siren's call, Mina said.

We left the table and walked down to the Gartensaal. Viktoria mentioned that Augusta was drinking too much. She noticed her having her glass refilled every few minutes and hardly touching her food. I had been too busy defending Madame Lupinski to see anything else.

What can anyone do? I said. Her drinking has been getting worse lately. She becomes angry at the mention of it and says she is a moderate drinker and people should mind their own business. Mina and Loulou must notice.

Viktoria mentioned Berthold was ignoring Madame Lupinski. I nodded.

He will leave her. He uses peasant women and those of the working class. Treats them as servants. Discards them like dirty laundry. Makes him feel the complete aristocrat. What do the English say? Lord of the manor. He must show off his conquests. But a Polish woman would be an embarrassment for a Nazi sympathizer. In future his women will be Aryan.

He looks at me as if I would swoon if he crooked his finger.

He has an endless faith in the power of his charm over all women. But not one of his own class has succumbed to him. He talks so much about himself that he bores them. Better to pay a peasant woman to listen. She stays for the money.

You and he ignore each other.

I refused to stop arguing with Dr. Schliesman.

That horrible little man. He said I was the ideal Aryan woman. He got quite close. I thought he was going to touch me.

I think he believes Berthold will give him one of his castoffs.

Poor Madame Lupinski.

We should get back and see what they are doing to her.

We could hear laughter as we entered the dining hall. Madame Lupinski was wearing a paper crown on her head, a coil of sausage round her neck and holding a dill pickle in each hand. Mina and Loulou were smearing rouge and lipstick round her eyes and over her lips. Sitting near the head of the table, Berhold was laughing. I spoke to the girls.

You should be ashamed of yourselves. This woman is a guest. Have you no compassion? This is not the behaviour of an Altenburg.

They stepped back from Madame Lupinski and lowered their eyes. She looked at me.

Please, I want to leave.

I looked at Augusta. She nodded. I could use the limousine. Viktoria appeared at my side.

I am coming with you.

You are a chauffeur, and such a passenger, Berthold said.

I went over to him.

Get up.

You would fight with me over that woman? Take her, I am done with her.

He picked up his wineglass. I swung my hand and knocked the glass away. It smashed on the floor. He tried to smile.

*Für eine Hure? Nie.*

*Du bist die Hure.*

We left, Viktoria arm in arm with the unfortunate woman. Various relatives shook their heads. As I drove to Königsberg the women talked beside me in the front seat. Viktoria found out that Madame Lupinski's name was Wanda and she had family in Krakau. She had been a seamstress before she married. I asked if she could find work in Krakau. Yes. Did she have any money? Very little. I said I would pay her train ticket. We went to her room in a working-class tenement, she cleaned her face and packed her few belongings and I drove to the Nordbahnhof. It was almost dawn. I bought her ticket and gave her some extra Reichsmarks. We waited an hour, drinking coffee in the station restaurant. When the train was ready to board we said goodbye. She thanked me shyly. She pressed Viktoria's hand.

On the way back Viktoria leaned her head against my shoulder and fell asleep. When we returned the house was quiet, the dining hall empty. We went to the summer house and spent the night there. At dinner that evening Augusta, Mina and Loulou were present besides Viktoria and me. For a long time no one spoke except for an occasional word to a servant. Mina began exchanging glances with Loulou. She looked at me.

What did you do with Madame Lupinski?

Paid her train fare back to Krakau.

You did that?

I could do no less. She deserved something after the treatment she received.

We were curious. Not that you did anything wrong.

I was speaking of Berthold's treatment of her. I criticized but never blamed you.

Are we friends again?

Did we stop?

The girls smiled at each other and began singing a song they had written and would subject dinner guests to on occasion.

*Altenburg, O Altenburg, wie wir lieben dich,*

*Deines Felder und Wände, deinem heiligen Hallen,*

*Deines Seen und Bäche, die unsere Träume zu halten,*
*Deines Wälder und Wege, die zu uns sprechen täglich.*
Please, Augusta said. I have a headache.

Berthold did not visit often after that night. He kept to his own estate, Schlieferstein, which he had never tired of complaining was no more than a country house and a few fields. He made frequent trips to Königsberg and Berlin. Family members kept us informed. Frau Strittmatter retired and went to live with her sister. I helped Augusta with the household and estate accounts and taught Mina, who was eager to learn. Viktoria and I kept postponing our wedding until it became something of a family joke. But we were happy and the worsening economy was a good excuse. Grain and livestock sales brought in less money, the staff had to be cut back severely and Altenburg came a little closer to bankruptcy. The holiday season ended a dark year.

At Heidelberg I taught my classes and stayed away from politics. Altenburg was a relief from the Nazi fanaticism on campus. Book burning took place in Königsberg and two long-established newspapers were banned. Only professors considered racially and politically acceptable by the Nazi regime had been kept on or were hired at the university. I wondered when my turn was coming. Viktoria and I spent time walking and riding round the estate. We took trips to the Baltic, where we swam and sailed. We avoided talking about what was happening.

Mina and Loulou had been to see American "talkies" in Königsberg and had picked up the slang. Mina's English sentences became sprinkled with it. She teased me about Viktoria. I hid my grin.

Why ain't you two hitched yet? Level with me, Fritz. You don't believe in this phony marriage business. You and that Giesecke dame are plain yellow, scared your love can't take it. Why don't you spill your guts? I'm gonna scram, blow this burg for Berlin. A moll like me has got what it takes to make the big time. Do I sound American?

Absolutely.

I wanted her to go to university. I tried to interest her in academic studies.

They bored her, were the fossilized remains of the past, irrelevant in modern society. Who cared about old books and old ideas? She became fascinated by theatre and the arts. She began going to Berlin to attend plays and concerts and visit art galleries. In the beginning she would take Loulou and some of their Junker girlfriends, along with a chaperone. But they did not share her fascination and gradually it was Mina alone, without her mother's knowledge, slipping off to the Nordbahnhof. I did not want her to fall into the wrong hands at such a young age, so I would travel with her on my way to Heidelberg and pick her up on the way back, having her stay a week or two with a woman friend of Viktoria's. Sometimes Viktoria would go to Berlin with her. Augusta would be told Mina was with friends on a neighbouring estate. Occasionally there would be an embarrassing situation when the neighbours came to dinner and said they had no knowledge of Mina's whereabouts. Depending on which of us happened to be present, Viktoria, Loulou or I would have to come up with a story. This went on for several months and during that time no noticeable change occurred in Mina's outlook. She held to the values she grew up with as she tested them against the ones she encountered and found them true. She remained tied to her class in some fundamental way, unwilling to or incapable of rejecting it. She wanted to see if the intellectual class could satisfy her as a Junker or a German and it did not.

She had met her painter. She told Viktoria they met at a small private gallery where he along with several other artists was given a showing. She took her there to meet him. Viktoria came away with a low opinion.

He is vulgar and an egotist. He cannot stop talking about himself. What she finds attractive about someone like that, I fail to see. I said nothing to her. She never asked my opinion, probably guessing it. They insult each other. He calls her a spoiled aristocrat and she him a pretentious mediocrity. He is very short, has long hair, does not shave regularly or wash, judging by his smell. Mina may be satisfying some urge in herself. What is between them will not last.

Viktoria was right ultimately but for three years Mina lived mostly in Berlin and she had me tell Augusta she was enrolled in university there. I was not happy with the lie but she had the right to do what she wanted. I did not want her bound by the strictures of Junker morality any more than I was. We were outmoded and passing into history and had to change. Mina never said anything about her life in Berlin and none of us asked. Augusta was happier with Loulou, who was more the dutiful daughter. She was very popular at balls and other events in the social calendar and approached by all the eligible Junker bachelors. One glance from Mina and they scattered. Life with the avant-garde, pretentious or not, must have made Junkers seem intolerably provincial. Yet she did not sever the link or even repudiate it. Mina was a perfect example of someone caught between two worlds, but I always knew the one she would inevitably pick.

In 1934, her first year living in Berlin, the Nazis shoved aside the cabal of aristocrats that had given them power. The so-called best, including many Junkers, had chosen the worst. They hoped to use them. That became a futile hope as the country was turned into a one-man dictatorship in short order. In June the elimination of the SA leadership by the SS was used as a convenient excuse to murder many past and present enemies, including here the President of Ostpreußen, a Königsberg town councillor and a newspaper editor. A blindness, deafness and dumbness have been imposed upon us. We can only see, hear and speak what is allowed. We are told this is for our benefit and for the future of Germany. That future will also be determined for us. Our role is to obey authority, question nothing. It is as if a whole nation has been turned into automatons. We have been robbed of our humanity, our individuality and become mindless parts of a military-industrial machine. There is no room for the one, only for the many become the one called the state, whose collective brain knows a single response, obedience. Who would knowingly accept such a fate? Too many.

Churchill is one of the few among us who understand Hitler. He is a war lover like Hitler. He understands that military force, not diplomacy, is the way to deal with him. Hitler is a dissatisfied man whose dissatisfaction resolves itself in conflict. He must blame someone for his dissatisfaction: Communists, Jews, liberals, foreigners. He plays with toy soldiers but they bleed and die. To him that is nothing. They are part of his war fantasies. To him war is what matters and conquest is the object. He would dominate the world.

Imperialism or insanity, call it what you wish. All propaganda is equal. In Churchill we have an imperialist, in Hitler a megalomaniac. They share a truth, that war is a pleasure with the highest of stakes, death and fame. They are the same species. We must use one to get rid of the other. The guard dog must kill the mad dog.

My strategy has been to ignore slavery while seeming to accept it. Anticipating my dismissal, I resigned from the university, citing ill health. I wonder if I deprived Dr. Schliesman of some twisted pleasure in doing so. I can say what I want as long as I say it in private and not in front of an informer. They are everywhere, so one must be careful. Viktoria became my primary confidante, the summer house and the woods the safest places. An easy privacy is one of the benefits of living at Altenburg. I feel guilty about all those who are without such a safeguard. But I can do nothing about that. It is one of the ironies of my situation that my sanctuary derives from feudal privilege, which once severely limited freedom and now protects it.

We saw Mina rarely but when we did there was much to talk about. In the privacy of the summer house she showed Viktoria, Loulou and me a sketchbook filled with pen-and-ink and chalk drawings. She said they were preliminary studies for oils. She asked our opinion. Viktoria responded first.

You are beautiful, Mina, clothed and nude. It would take an absolutely incompetent artist to convey nothing of that. Does he do you justice? There is something lacking.

I know he is not a great artist. I want a good likeness, not immortality.

Is there even that? What do you think, Fritz?

You have the better aesthetic eye, Viktoria. I would say, too generic, not enough Mina.

Yes. Loulou?

Was the studio warm enough? I see goosebumps on your arms and legs.

Go ahead and be silly. Those are spots of ink and chalk marks.

How was I to know?

You did.

I did not.

You did so. You are jealous.

I am not.

Please, no quarrelling, Viktoria said. Perhaps he is better with oil paints. Or watercolours, Loulou said.

We were sitting round the beechwood table in the front room. It was late summer and a chilly evening and logs were burning in the fireplace. Mina talked about Berlin. What it was like since the change.

More and more Nazi uniforms. SA, SS. Long swastika banners are hung on the front of public buildings and others, reaching almost to the pavement, in places whole streets of them. You see them in Königsberg, all over Germany. But Berlin must be the worst for uniforms and flags. Many of our friends have been taken in and questioned and some have been put in camps. Modern art is seen as degenerate and dangerous. They want to use art only for propaganda.

Is your friend in danger? Viktoria asked.

He is Viennese. But his artist friends are anti-Nazi, so he must be careful. And Anton did something that could put him in danger. I may bring him out here and he can stay in the summer house so Mama will not know about him.

What will he think of not being invited to dinner?

His friends can come and keep him company.

All the way from Berlin?

If that is necessary.

You do love him? Loulou said.

We are passionate friends. But he would not expect me to hold his hand.

Does he eat with his fingers and smell of paint?

He is an artist.

And you are passionate friends.

Be careful or you will not meet him.

We will. You want to show him off.

Is there anybody waiting to paint you?

I feel no need to be painted. Especially without clothes.

Mama's little girl.

So you are the brave one? Take him to meet her. I dare you. No answer?

Can you tell us what he did that could put him in danger? Viktoria said.

He drew caricatures of Hitler that were published in an anti-Nazi magazine. Before Hitler became Chancellor. The Gestapo has not found out yet who did them. When it does, through interrogation or an informer, he will be in great danger. It was unintentional. They were meant as a private joke. A friend of his told me Anton was drunk and drew them at a party and the magazine editor took them without telling him. Anton was angry when he learned they had been published.

Anti-Nazi by default, is he?

He has no political convictions except for condemning politicians as philistines who hate art.

Artists are poor, Loulou said. Do you give him money?

No. And he would be too proud to accept it, anyway.

How do you like living as a bohemian?

What an old-fashioned word. I am a modern woman. This is something I want to do. For how long, who knows?

Why not pick a handsome man with talent?

Mina looked at Viktoria.

Have you been talking?

I said he was unworthy of you. Sorry if I have said too much but that is my opinion.

I wish everyone would please stay out of my business.

You mean your affair, Loulou said.

Button up, my prudish little sister.

Prudish because I have not undressed and lain naked in front of a dwarf?

Enough, I said. We are relations and friends and there are enough enemies.

You sound pompous, Viktoria said. Time for coffee.

By 1936 the Gestapo had learned Mina's painter was the creator of the caricatures. She convinced him he should hide at Altenburg. He was put in the summer house. The servants brought him his meals. Viktoria, Loulou and I knew he was there. All was quiet for a time. But when Mina allowed him to bring out his friends, there were noisy parties lasting for days. I would make excuses to Augusta. Some tenants were celebrating and mistakenly wandered near the house. The painter and his friends became more unruly and in a drunken state would wander round the lake, fighting and yelling. One of them drowned. The body was taken to Königsberg. I told the authorities the man was a lone trespasser who had gotten lost at night and fallen into the lake. Mina quarrelled with the painter earlier that evening and told him his friends were no longer welcome. Their relationship was apparently over by then and she rarely saw him. A few months and he was gone. Mina told me she helped him cross the border into Poland. He would make his way back to Vienna. Using a false name, his friends shipped his paintings there from Berlin. Mina learned those at Altenburg were shipped secretly under another false name. She was upset because she had been promised her portraits. The summer house suffered extensive damage. Smashed windows and doors needed to be replaced, garbage removed and filth cleaned from walls and floors. We all helped.

By now our lives had become more circumscribed. There was a sense of time closing in on us. We avoided thinking by working on the estate. The outbuildings needed repairs, the fences and stone walls replacing or rebuilding. The weed-choked lake, the brush-filled windbreaks and hedges, the clogged irrigation ditches all had to be cleaned. There were plans to clear the streams feeding and draining the lake, rebuild the dam and mill and improve the irrigation system. We laboured together with the tenant families and the estate workmen in a quiet communal effort that is unending and satisfying because it is so. Loulou and Gerd von Pommer drew closer together, which pleased Augusta. Viktoria and I moved into the summer house permanently and planned to be married within a year. The not-so-little things in little lives were moving on like water in a stream.

We were not entirely insulated from outside events. Berthold's occasional visits brought with them news of a changing Germany. We exchanged the stiffest of greetings at dinner. He never let that bother him. One night I could hear no more and excused myself and left before dessert. Viktoria followed but insisted next time I remain until she had eaten her cake. His droning got to everybody at these dinners. The other diners began to follow our example, until he would be left with Augusta as the sole audience for his harangues. She was so tipsy she understood nothing. But all he wanted was a sounding board.

The new Reich, my dear Augusta, will be a model for all progressive nations. Outmoded and set ideas must give way to futuristic thinking. Encrusted traditions must be ruthlessly swept away. We have no room for fossils, for the unproductive privileged.

On her way out of the dining hall Mina said, You are finally making yourself useful, Berthold, as a propagandist for the destruction of your own class.

Viktoria and I had a conversation one evening early in 1937. It was one of the last important conversations we had. We had pulled the beechwood chairs close to the fireplace and were looking into the fire as we drank our coffee. She asked me why I thought Berthold and I were so different. To me the answer was obvious.

Berthold is a little Führer. Germany is full of them. All of them together form a pyramid and at the top is Adolf I. It is the Kaiser and his nobles again. I am an aristocrat and I reject it all, the parading of one's forebears like some tribal chieftain's necklace of sacred charms. What makes this reincarnation ludicrous is that our ordained leader is a petit bourgeois.

But Berthold is not stupid. Can he be blind to the arrests, the concentration camps, the informers?

He must believe he stands for something important and his Führer gives him that. He has transformed himself into a snobbish aristocratic Aryan, courtesy of his Führer, who is the master of the master race. He gives you what you want to get what he wants and when you finally realize what he wants, too late. In this bestiary of a single exalted species, he is the manic deity who will lead the *Totentanz* to ultimate oblivion. Berthold is too egotistical to see that.

You cannot compare Berthold to the worst of the Nazi racists.

There are grades and degrees of little Führers. But all shit smells the same.

She laughed.

There is no answer to that. But as political theory, Fritz, really.

Sometimes the truth stinks. Is it wrong to use the worst when describing the worst?

He is your brother.

It makes me angry that an Altenburg has betrayed our traditions.

You said you reject aristocracy.

Of the blood, not of the spirit.

How can you separate them?

As easily as separating him and me.

I accept that, but not that Germany is full of little Führers. Many of our people are decent, trapped in a situation they did not create.

I have a potato analogy that will help.

Make me laugh, Fritz.

It is obviously wrong that all the members of a nationality or race are the same and yet racist propagandists say that. How do they get people to believe this? No potato looks like any other but if you peel them they appear similar. This is not enough. You must boil them, taking away every last trace of individuality. Into the pot, the scalding water they go. Drain the lifeless, amorphous mass, mash it, add a little butter or cream, a sprinkle of black pepper to taste and they are ready. The enemy to be consumed or a promoted self-image swallowed with delight. They taste the same. The difference is propaganda.

You have satirical taste buds.

Late one night we were lying in bed, unable to get back to sleep. I awoke first and watched her. When she woke up, I put my arms round her. We settled against each other, naked as we always slept regardless of the weather. Each time touching her was discovering her once more. I could feel her warm breath. I could smell her. Like freshly baked bread. Moonlight from the window shone on her hair, silvering the tops of the waves. I wanted to talk.

We cannot sleep because we fell asleep by the fire earlier. I woke and watched you breathing. It was so shallow I was afraid you had stopped breathing. As usual I tortured myself for a while. Then I remembered you never breathe deeply. I immediately felt better. I began to think as I watched you.

Do I snore?

Never.

That would be a real test of love.

Not of mine. You inspire me. Like tonight. Listen.

Do I have a choice? Why are you pulling away? I was joking. Really, Fritz. Do you understand me yet?

Do we ever understand anybody else?

Stop looking for a way out. Your not knowing when I joke makes me wonder how much attention you pay me.

Does love mean paying attention?

To a woman it does. How else is she to know?

Some men pay too much attention.

Of the wrong kind. So you watched me sleeping and it has inspired you? I care what happens when I am awake. Your instinct is to pull away.

Is that why I kissed and embraced you a while ago?

That is your pleasure. I refer to your reactions.

Have you always known this about me?

I love you despite it.

It has taken you a long time to say this.

I would have said it sooner or later.

Sooner would have been better, but I should know myself. I behave this way because I feel unworthy of you.

I know, but listen to me. We deserve each other. You must not be so serious with me all the time. I like to play too. Now tell me what I have inspired.

You said something more important. What I was so eager to tell you seems trivial now.

Tell me.

We have one breath. Most inhale quickly and begin a slow release until nothing is left. Some never stop inhaling and take in more and more until they feel the universe expanding inside. That is the lesson of time.

And you thought up that rubbish while watching me sleep? We laughed.

It was the spring of 1937. More repairs to the estate were done that spring and summer. Becoming withdrawn from events, we looked for diversions. We cycled into the woods with Mina and Loulou and our friends and had picnics. Summer slid into autumn, we were alone again, but the soggy landscape was an invitation. The horses found the going hard and had to be walked through more difficult terrain or be left in the stables. At night we wandered across the moonlit fields, our boots sinking into muddy turf. We held hands and would stop to gaze at the fields of stars, pinpricks of light in the lapis lazuli of arching stained glass.

God has never needed us, Viktoria said one frosty night.

I agree. All philosophers seem to do is try to make room for us in the universe. Scientists explain us, historians excuse us and politicians use us. We make ourselves the focus of everything, the children of fate.

Stop thinking, Viktoria said. Be overwhelmed.

Impossible for me. I have to analyze.

A waste of time. We are all we have. And God. Does that sound egotistical? I believe what I feel most deeply, despite what the rationalists say.

Human life is a series of accidents. We add the reasons.

That sounds too severe. I must and I do believe in something beyond what we are. And in the love between us. That too, dear Fritz.

She kissed my nose, said it was freezing. We hurried to the summer house and a warm fire.

We knew a war was coming and yet we never talked about leaving Germany because neither of us wanted to leave Augusta, Mina and Loulou. It was a point of honour to stay. There was a growing coolness between Berthold and the rest of the family and I wanted to give them my support. Mina was her own person now. She would never back down to anybody. But I knew it would be easier for the others if I stayed, especially when war came. Germany was slipping into mad militarism and only the wilfully blind could not see it.

Winter brought icy rain, sleet and snow and Viktoria and I were on horseback, riding into the wind along slippery trails and across snowy fields. I blame myself for what happened. I should have been more cautious. We dared too much, as if willing disaster to come. Concern for the horses held us back. But gradually the worse the weather, the fiercer the storm, the more we wanted to brave it. It was a kind of madness, like that of those who were leading us. We were the bankrupt Junkers battling the ancient storm gods.

We would dare each other. Who would be first to reach the woods or cross a stream or get to the other side of a field? It had to end the way it did. I see that now. I wish I had died but I would not want her to undergo my punishment. I would not want her to know the emptiness I feel. I deserve all of it. But what is the point when suffering has no end, no purpose? I will see it every day for the rest of my life.

I remember her last words. Whoever reaches the forest first must shout for the other. She galloped into the blizzard. The white distance blotted them up, gathered and hurling ahead. I followed, the snow blinding me. A cry, too soon. Silent blurs, her mount on its back, legs in the air. She lay twisted, flung like a mannequin, her pale hair smeared ochre with slush. The snow was burying her, filling her eyes, dropping a cape over her face. I knelt, knees on the frozen ground, and picked her up. She felt warm and heavy and I thought, she must be alive, she must. I stood, the storm draping our statue. Flakes melted down my cheeks. I carried her with invisible steps through sightless air. I brought her into the house. Her face was unmarked. She looked as if she were sleeping. One of her earrings was missing. I went back the next day, looking for it along the trails, over the fields. I will keep looking. Time means nothing now.

Her parents took her. She was buried with her ancestors. I told her mother and father it was an unforeseen accident. Who would understand if I tried to explain what happened? Who could but us? So much has vanished with her. I have no desire to do anything. She comes to me in dreams but is always silent. I go to her and the dream ends. When I wake the disappointment aches for hours. I had to bear her funeral.

It snowed during the church service and at the cemetery. Low clouds hovered over the largest gathering of Junkers I had seen in years. Every family was represented. Viktoria was loved by many. I sat and stood stiff and silent throughout or I would have broken down. Returning to Altenburg in the limousine, the family was silent. I had dinner with them that night. Augusta mentioned that Berthold did not attend the funeral and nobody answered. I said I would stay in the summer house instead of live with them. I needed solitude and time. The shock would wear off, I would decide.

Repairs begin in a few months, Mina said to cheer me up. That will take your mind off of it. Go into Königsberg. See your friends at the university.

*Ja*, there may be one that has not been dismissed yet.

Grim humour was better than nothing. Augusta had not touched her wine during dinner and now she looked down the table at me.

You must not brood over it. Thinking will not change anything.

Thinking does not bother me as much as feeling, I said. You can play with thoughts but not feelings.

Men are afraid of feelings, Mina said. They are quicksand for them. They say women are nothing but feelings. They excuse themselves by changing a minus into a plus. Men say they are the rational sex. Woman is a poor squishy sack of feelings. She cries and wails and moans and is full of sorrow. But who charges across a battlefield, screaming and killing like a maniac? Who cries singing patriotic songs? Who marches round dressed up like a bunch of prancing peacocks? Who swears allegiance to things you cannot see or touch?

You had all of us children march and fight battles, Loulou said. We became part of your Prussian fantasy. I never understood why. I did it to please you.

That military history was in my blood. We were the children of soldiers. I learned better later. But I am still a Junker.

Your father died in battle, Augusta said. He was a brave and decent man.

I know, Mama. I am not disparaging his memory or courage. I honour him. He honours us. But men excuse their selfish, murderous passions by pretending they are rational.

Not all men, I said.

I was generalizing, Fritz.

The only true generalization is that no generalization is true in the real world.

Whose real world?

Exactly, Mina. I have lost the only woman I will ever love. Nobody else can understand or feel that. I do.


Germany has become a circus with performing animals. Politicians, bureaucrats, lawyers, judges, doctors, musicians, professors, philosophers.

There are almost no exceptions. The ringmaster is the messiah with a mustache. He struts in front of them shooting blanks and cracking his whip. They cower and cringe. The crowd roars its approval. Round the outside of the ring are the clowns in uniform, strutting with rubber truncheons, their fake grins painted, their dead eyes watching the crowd. Every so often they see somebody they want. A police van, with buckets and ladders and painted red to look like a fire engine, siren moaning, rushes to the edge of the crowd. The clowns in their oversize floppy shoes pull somebody out and he disappears into the back of the van and it races away, klaxon honking. The crowd laughs until the ringmaster shouts at the caged beasts and they stand up on their hind legs in a circle, surrounding him with adoring homage. The crowd screams in paroxysms of adulation. The clowns run back, their eyes searching. They carry fire buckets holding a handful of excelsior and fling it into the crowd and see who does not flinch.

When belief becomes accepted truth, truth has become a devil. Belief needs a devil to be true. The believer does not want facts, information, logic or reason. The believer needs to believe. This need becomes more important than truth. It becomes truth and everything else becomes a lie, becomes the devil. The devil is by definition evil and to the believer must expect no mercy. Mercy becomes a sign of complicity, an evil in itself. Any argument or statement that examines belief becomes a threat to belief and invites repression. The mind that needs belief needs repression like a disease that feeds on corruption. The more corruption the greater will be the disease and the stronger the belief. Nothing is true unless it can be verified, and even verification may be faulty. We must live with truth as it is and never believe it to be true. Truth must never become belief or belief will twist it into something different and call that true. Ultimately, truth is a series of impossibilities, the mask of God. We can never remove that mask. We can only gaze upon it. That makes us human. When we say we know the truth we wear a mask. It is a fake. It sears and burns itself on to our face and we scream that we see the devil. The mask cannot be removed, we cannot stop screaming and must die with it. There will be many to kill before we finally die but we will never kill the devil. The devil dies with us.

I see them round us. They wear the chains of silence. They are the justification for their own repression. The state serves itself in serving them. And the more they are told what to do, the less they can do. Where is the truth in ideas but in their power? They give you your destiny. Conquer your inferiors. History has given you the grievance and biology the right. Your race speaks with one voice through your one leader. One brain for so many millions. One conscience. One is enough if you are right. What are you building? Labour camps, prisons, concentration camps, torture chambers. For enemies, of course, who are everywhere. There are never too many cells or guards or barracks or soldiers or campaigns or victory parades. In whose mind is all this happening? In the mind of your deliverer, come to save you. He will give you the world. He can do no less. He looks the same wherever he appears. The man with the smug look lost in the crowd. The old photograph with party members, the mug shot in police files, a poorly retouched newspaper likeness. Not in short supply and quite ordinary except for that look. Presumptuous and possessed but not to be quickly dismissed, the man who wears the mask of God. Grass outlives the conqueror's tread but not our love of conquerors, which will outlive us.

He who rejects mankind must go insane. He who can accept it must hold onto his sanity. Where are our decent people, the ones afraid to be anything else? They hide among the masses, pretending to be as fervent. They become tainted by osmosis, until it is hard to tell which is which. Always reasonable, they whisper in dark corners about how awful things are, but of course something had to be done, but it has gotten out of hand. They wait for another of history's men to change things. They wait for somebody better. Nobody comes except more of the same. And the great ones, history's heroes, have haloes made of iron. Through justifying them we justify ourselves. One man cannot enslave a nation. There has never been a shortage of executioners. We lock the doors of our prisons behind us and then await our deliverer. We, not he, hold the key. Disappointment is the one free offer the world makes. But time will calmly collect us in that endless moment when everything lives and dies.

We live in a framework of approximations, knowing events and intervals.

And philosophers go on playing with ideas the way monkeys swing by their tails. It may be an agreeable sensation but it is not the most important thing about being a monkey. To be lost in specifics is the work of an artist. Leaders use details to free themselves of responsibility for their own freedom. Their distortions they call reality, ideas with blood on them. Every age is the prisoner of its ideas. The way out leads to the next prison.

Time is a poor way of measuring life, the ticks and tocks of impoverished souls. Mine is over. Why be a whining regret to the family? They will have burdens enough. I cannot help them in what they face. I will not bury life in life. I will not pronounce death. No universal notice. It has come. We will share as we always have. Nothing between us. Who cares if anyone understands? Understanding is the shortest way to ignorance, an endless peeling of layers. I would be wasting time. I know the end of this age. Smoke and rubble. I leave early. Not quite bored. She left in winter. So will I. We opened a door together at the beginning of our lives. It shut behind her and I will open it now, alone, and go to wherever she is. I vanished once in her to come alive. I will vanish again.

Hope is a bird flying into the wind. It flies until exhausted and plummets to earth. It lies in the dirt, head on its side, its feathers ruffled by the passing wind, as if encouraging or taunting. An eye stares at the sky. The last wish is the wish to die.

# The Painter's Story

I am stuck here, having to read this man's ravings. I am not surprised he is your uncle. You are making me pay for the past, you bitch. I did not touch Loulou. I swear she will be pure when von Pommer takes her in their wedding bed. Constanze? What was I to do? She came to me, so sweet and fresh, so young and eager. I am flesh and blood, a painter and a lover of the female form. She wanted me to paint her portrait. Of course I said yes, not knowing where it would lead. I had a vague idea. I left it all up to her. She is one of your Junkers, von Pommer's sister, and knows her own mind. She was the betrayer, not me. Your quarrel is with her. And yet you leave me in this damn place with no company but flies.

I am tired of pumpernickel and oats and those so-called stews by your so-called cook. I have eaten in Parisian and Viennese restaurants. I am sorry I ever met you. I curse the day in that Berlin gallery when you asked, Did you paint these? Yes, this is a showing of my recent work, I said. Do all your paintings look like copies of van Gogh? you said. I would have strangled you but I could not stop staring at your breasts and your legs. That dress, the colour of molten cobalt. I swear no painter could capture your flesh tones, such cream, such delicate pinks. They drove me crazy. They still do when I think of them. Infidelity? We were not even married, you bourgeoisie. Is a man like me to be condemned for accepting the attentions of an enticing young woman? It is a matter between you and her, nothing at all to do with me. Your childhood friend—what do I care? One day I will walk into

Altenburg and throw you on the floor and take you the way you liked it. You would not use your father's gun, an empty threat. Though you might, you Junker bitch, and get away with it. You would get a medal from these yokels for bagging a Viennese painter. Why am I here again? Why do I put up with this? You will not allow me in the house. Your mother would not approve of me. Back then I painted you out here and we made love on the floor among the stacked canvases and smell of oil paint. It was better I never saw the old dragon. I would have told her, I am fucking your high and mighty Mina and she loves it. Why did you go on about my ego being taller than my talent? A genius is entitled to be short. You share me with my work. You were one of the lucky women I allowed close to me. Into my bed and my thoughts. But you always had to judge, presuming to know more. The insults I took from you. A failed expressionist seeking another ism—Antonism. There was no life in my portraits. I did not know how to use colour. How did I put up with you? You are too Prussian to suit me, in bed and out. I could not leave, that is how you fixed me.

Those drawings in Reimann's magazine put in without my knowledge. How did I know that gang would get into power? Reimann went into hiding. They tracked him down in '35. He was on a Gestapo list. They have endless lists. I heard about Reimann from Groh. I dropped out of sight, waiting for a safe way to get back to Vienna. Come to Altenburg, you said. You will be safe there. From you? In '36 that was, three years ago. For half a year I stood the isolation, your coldness, damned hauteur. It was your idea I paint Loulou's portrait. She told you I was adjusting her dress when you came in. I think you wanted an excuse to hit me that day, all that week. Calling me an evil dwarf. In bed all men are the same height. Saying I was a failure as a man, and in front of your sister. But you two stick together, like all you damn aristocrats. Your turn is coming, every one of you inbred parasites. Your Prussian piety sickens me. Holding hands *mit Gott*. Patting your tenants and servants on the head. They sweat to put bread in your mouth. That damn pumpernickel makes me fart and shit all day. You send it out deliberately, wanting me to be miserable.

Back in Vienna after this prison. Women who appreciated me. A studio full of models. How could you stay in that place? my friends said. It's still in the Dark Ages. I showed them the paintings I brought back with me. She is beautiful. Who is she? A Prussian, a Junker. No talent needed to paint somebody like her, Rudolph said. A monkey could do it. He has always been jealous. A monkey with talent, Liselotte said, and kissed the bald spot at the back of my head. She knows I hate that. She is too old and fat to be a model any more except for washtubs. The last I heard she was whoring round with some Nazi officials and passing herself off as the illegitimate daughter of a crown prince. You wrote and said I should not have taken your paintings away. They belong to me but you can buy them, I said. Paints are expensive. Brushes, easels, canvases. Spend some of your sweated riches to keep a genius supplied. You came and I was cool to you. I had beautiful women at my feet. The money you offered not nearly enough, not even for one of those canvases. I watched you leave with nothing but your sad face.

Anschluss. I should have gone to America. All the money I wanted lay waiting in piles for me. And no Gestapo to chase me. Too late. I had to find a refuge somewhere. I thought of Paris. I could support myself selling any old canvases to stupid Americans and their arrogantly beautiful wives snaked in furs, lathered with lipsticks and reeking of musky perfume. I had met them there when I was a student. Oh, I go for all that modern art. I love Manny, Moany, Pigasso, Cees-an, De-gass, Gogan and specially van Gawk. In a bistro in '25 I saw a fat middle-aged American woman sitting alone. I sat down and said I needed money to buy paints. Would she like to sleep with a real Parisian artist?

You don't sound French and you're awfully short.

Painters are born short. The best stay that way and the rest lose talent as they get taller.

You must be a genius, I guess.

I keep telling people that. There is a hotel around the corner.

I don't know. My husband will be along in a minute.

Forget the sex. Give me some money and I will do a sketch of you in charcoal.

How much?

A few francs. Or come to my studio and I will do your portrait in oils for a few hundred.

That's cheap. How come good paintings are so expensive?

The old ones are. New ones are cheap.

Why is that?

The paint ages, looks better. I am telling you this as a painter but keep it to yourself because if the truth gets out there will be trouble in the art world.

Don't worry. I won't say anything.

This man bothering you, honey?

A man with the face of a banker appeared at her elbow. His vested belly stuck out over the table.

No, dear. He was explaining about art.

What does he know? He looks like a tramp. You got to go to museums and galleries. There's experts who know what they're talking about.

He's a painter, dear.

They're all painters in Paris.

I'd like to have my portrait painted. He's cheap.

We'll get Josiah Fenimore when we get back.

He's old-fashioned. I want something in a newer style.

I speak their French. *Combien, gar-kon, pour chaque temps de faire Madame?*

Keep your damned money.

I stood up and walked out. Some things an artist cannot tolerate. The world is divided into those who see and those who count. Great artists refuse to be counted.

Paris. Poor but carefree days.

It is hard to believe I was challenged to a duel because of a woman. Why should it be? Adèle, the model of models. The most perfect firm little tits I have ever seen, so soft pink silken nipples barely buds, arse like petite pear halves, and so tight a cunt.

Am I your first?

*Non, Monsieur Anton.*

I pressed no further. Quantity is a peasant measure. Quality an aristocratic one. Aristocracy of talent, *natürlich*.

You stole her from me—that oaf Claude.

She is a model, free to choose.

She has broken my heart and you are to blame.

A Frenchman talking about his heart when it comes to sex. He wanted to keep fucking her. Hypocrite. A duel? With what?

Pistols.

Are you serious?

You are a coward.

How dare you? I am a Viennese and a genius. You are a peasant. I will not soil my hands. Find another peasant to shoot.

Coward. She goes with you because you don't stretch her. She will be like a virgin when she meets her businessman who will keep her. She told me, you monkey's prick.

Liar. I give her more pleasure than you ever did, you ox.

Pleasure? She would like to read a fashion magazine but it would hurt your feelings.

She starved with you. I feed her.

A stale crust. Coffee from dregs. She faints. She is too weak to leave you.

We fought with palette knives right there in his studio. I had a bad moment when I saw red on his knife. Then I remembered he had been painting a pot of scarlet geraniums. What a bourgeois. Beret and smock and he thought he was an artist. A couple of feints with my knife and he was backing away. So he must kick me in the shin. So much for honour. If it had not been for Adèle screaming, I would have finished him off. Beneath my dignity, but some insults must be avenged with blood. A woman's cries have always melted my heart.

The bitch went back. He pleaded. I was through with her, anyway. She was beginning to bore me. I could have kept her. But I have never begged a woman. If she is too stupid to see me for what I am, I give up on her.

Paris was stale by then. Too many tourists. Weekend painters, poseurs on the Left Bank. Stockbrokers, bond salesmen, bank tellers, government clerks, cufflinks sticking out from the sleeves of their starched smocks. Not a drop of paint on them. Artists in their spare time. Amateurs. Groh told me about Berlin.

Berlin is the place now for the avant-garde of the avant-garde. Filmmakers, writers, musicians, painters.

Germany is not for artists. I am going back to Vienna.

Vienna is conservative. Neurotic. A Hapsburg leftover. Nobody with any talent works there. Berlin is different. Not like the rest of Germany. You will not be sorry. The nightclubs are fantastic.

What are the women like?

Sweet young *Mädchen* with bobbed hair. Very serious about modern art. They fall into your lap. They gather in cafés and restaurants. They believe anything you tell them. You will have to outtalk the writers, with their anarchist free love. That should not be a problem for you. You were always good at talking about yourself. There will be less competition for you in Berlin, for work as well as women. This attic is damp and cold, the roof leaks. If you get arthritis in your hands, how will you paint?

An artist does not live well. He suffers because no one wants to buy his work.

You will suffer less in Berlin. Paint portraits, make money. A friend of mine, Obermeyer, has a studio. You can share with him. He knows many art dealers. He will get you showings.

What is this Obermeyer like? I do not share well.

A sculptor and very sentimental. Tell him you are in love with a whore and he will start crying.

He sounds out of his mind.

He is, a little. All sculptors are. Painters too, I hear. What do you say, Anton?

How much rent?

I told you, he is sentimental. Tell him you are penniless and he will let you pay him when you get some money.

How does he live?

His people are rich. They give him money to stay away.

Lucky man.

Share in his luck.

It was March 1929. I moved to Berlin that summer and into Obermeyer's studio. It was the top floor of a warehouse and was heated. The thing about Max Obermeyer was he never did any sculpting. His chisels and mallets had no stone dust on them. The blocks of marble and granite in the studio were untouched. He said they were too perfect to ruin. He would run his hand up and down the sides of the blocks and say it was like touching a woman. How can I improve on perfection? What kind of women have you known? I said but low so he could not hear me. I did not want to be thrown out. He was not concerned about money or how much food I ate. He was quietly drunk most of the time. He would bring in models, have them strip naked and say he would phone them when he was ready to start working.

Obviously he was no artist. I asked about dealers and showings. Who told you? he said. Groh said you knew. Yes, I know about such things. You want dealers to see your work? You want showings? Why do you think I paint? Why not live for the pure experience of your art? I would like to show the public that experience, I said. I see what you mean. But he did nothing.

I told you sculptors are odd, Groh said when I told him. Groh talked with Obermeyer. But the stock market crashed in New York. Dealers did not want to take a chance on an unknown, even a genius. For a pittance they offered to take my paintings off my hands. No thank you, you vultures, I said. I had showings with other unknown artists, none of them geniuses. That was not altogether bad, because my work outshone theirs. But as usual the public was blind. I suffered years of showings with mediocrities in small galleries in déclassé districts of Berlin. And you showed up one day, you bitch, offering me my first commission as a portrait painter. A comedown for a great artist but how could I rely on Obermeyer's generosity forever? Suppose he was committed? Besides, I was drunk on your beauty and wanted to rip your clothes off. You got me excited making me wait, as you are making me wait now for another reason. You have not changed. Self-centred, cruel.

Where was I to go in 1938? Not to the Soviet Union. I would be rounded up by another secret police. Czechoslovakia looked to be next on Hitler's list. The rest of eastern Europe was nothing but pro-fascist regimes. A stay would be temporary. Switzerland to France and then America was best but I had to leave Vienna in hours and I had no money. Nobody could or would lend me any. My friends were broke or said they were. I was sitting in my studio contemplating the best form of suicide for a great artist when there was a knock on the door. The Gestapo. No, your chauffeur saying his Miss Wilhelmina sent him to take me to your estate. I was to bring all of my paintings, including those of you. So that was it. What could I do?

You sent a small van with the car. I was told to hide in the back. Your chauffeur had travel documents for himself and the other driver, the vehicles and the art but it was not possible to get me one. I was a fugitive in my own country. All of my paintings made the journey. I was jammed together with them in the back of the van. All of us were kidnapped. I drank half a bottle of brandy. I slept most of the way troubled by dreams of a woman with a whip riding me, both of us naked. It was the bumpy roads.

Junkers are insufferable when they gloat. They do not smile or grin. They are busy being serious. Moral superiority only feels good if it hurts you almost as much as your victim. The rear door of the van opened and I stepped on to the gravel of the driveway and there you were in your riding habit. A whip would have given you away. Two of the estate workmen transferred my paintings into the main house and you supervised as if I had nothing to do with it. After the workmen had finished, you came over to me.

I will keep my portraits. When you painted them, you said they were works of love. Your gift to me. I am taking you at your word, Anton. If that is possible. The rest are yours. As soon as feasible they will be put in the summer house with you. Stay as long as you wish. Whenever you decide to leave, we will forget your presence here, for everybody's safety. If you leave your paintings, they will be stored on the estate and kept safe for you.

You turned and strolled away. Cold woman. I was at your mercy and you knew I must accept anything. It amazes me now to think we were lovers for more than three years. The longest I have spent with any woman. It must be my artist's sensibilities but I do not understand how anybody can be so unfeeling without a good reason. Constanze? That is no reason. An artist is brimming over with feelings. Sometimes they are distracted momentarily. He may be criticized for this perhaps by people ignorant of great talents, but scorned and rejected? You wanted to get rid of me and Constanze was the excuse.

So here I have been for a year and a half, rotting away in this corner of Prussia, this medieval relic. My artist's soul is tortured. I draw with the burnt ends of firewood grotesque shapes. I don't know what they mean. In the writing desk are bottles of ink and some pens and a box of paper but charcoal suits my mood. I draw the shapes on the walls of the empty room. Lizard beasts feeding on each other, their jaws agape, shark teeth bloody and eyes bulging. At night in the candlelight their scaly bodies writhe and tighten round each other, throats locked in a death grip of crunching jaws, frantic claws scraping at them. Slashing teeth, lashing tails, their screams in black streaks and smears the squeaks and squeals of burnt wood rubbing across the plaster. I smell them in the air, spurts of blood, tatters of flesh. That room is all I have now.

The bitch has told the maids to stay away from me. They put my food down and leave. Not even a smile. I have to ask questions. I asked the one who came yesterday what month it was. September, she said. What is happening out in the world? There is war between Germany and Poland. Poland has surrendered. I moved towards her and she backed away. I will not harm you, I said. I am a painter. Would you like to see my work? I will draw you, make you immortal, the servant girl of Altenburg. You will be famous. *Nein, danke*, and she left. She will warn the others. They will keep their distance. When I think of Viennese women, of my models, I could weep. The bitch means to drive me mad. Put me away in some dungeon. My work would be hers. She must suspect. I am never given a knife. Not that I would harm her. I am an artist, not a murderer. But she could drive me to it. She could drive any man mad. With her body or her schemes. She was the best. I must admit. Her taut skin, like warm silk. She smelled of apples, of freshly squeezed cider. Her ooze, her tightness. A connoisseur's dream, and I am a connoisseur. A bit too long in the shanks I said once playfully. She was cold for a month. I was not serious, I said. I had to beg her before she opened her legs again. Never made that mistake again. She accused me of others to spite me, to make me grovel. She enjoyed that. There was no satisfying her. I was too this or too that. It was like living with a witch. I told her once. You are speaking to an Altenburg, she said, as if that justified her cruelty.

Yesterday I went for a walk round the far side of the lake and in the gardens behind and the woods beyond. The gardeners are peasants, like the rest, and incapable of much more than a nod. They speak the worst German, a dialect impossible to understand. Prussians must be the dullest of Germans. Which is saying something. What is there to say to such idiots? One stared at me and to say something I said I was from Vienna. He kept staring. I might as well have said the moon. I should have. A good joke. I need one.

The bitch came out today and asked if I needed paints or other supplies.

I need my freedom.

Take it any time you want, Anton. Believe me, I have no wish to stop you from leaving.

How can I? I have no car.

Where would you go if you had one? There is a war.

The maid told me. Because I asked. No one tells me anything. I am isolated.

You would be in danger anywhere else.

Not in Switzerland or France. I need money and your Mercedes, Mina.

Our car is known. I can give you money and the name of an underground contact in Königsberg. One of the farmers will take you in his waggon. The underground will give you fake identity papers. You can make your way to the Swiss border through contacts.

Hide me in your car. Drive me there. It will be like before. We will be lovers escaping to our freedom.

We were standing close to each other. I tried to kiss her but she turned her face away.

No, Anton. That is over.

As friends?

We are not friends.

You are still the same, you bitch.

So are you.

Go. Leave me alone.

I can see the trap. The waggon will deliver me to Gestapo headquarters. Or to some squalid basement or attic where I will be conveniently disposed of. I am too smart for you, Mina. I will stay here until I can find another way. I will accept my kennel, where charcoal streaks screech in spasms of ancient forest demons.

Why should I have expected her to change after she stole my paintings and put me away in a hovel alone? I glorified her with my brush. Gave her immortality. And what happens? I am treated as a pariah. Inventory: four canvases, all oils, one in ball gown, one in riding habit, and two nudes, one reclining on a couch and one rising from the lake. All the best Louvre quality, easily National Gallery, Rijksmuseum, Prado, Uffizi, Hermitage, etc., etc. When I think of the time I put in on her breasts, the pearly pink and dappled creamy flesh tones on those pear-shaped, musk-rose-nippled perfections. Name your painter, I outdid him. How I handled her thighs, too long but tapered to a pear shape between hip and knee, and those silken twists of flaxen hair, pouch line divining. No coy turns, shadowy smut or eye contact for a calculated shock. Everything in pure raw colour, the elemental woman.

I cannot believe it. A knock on the door and I waited for the maid to enter with my daily rations. Instead, Constanze. How many years? She is fatter. She is married. Still the same woman, a faint smell of horse liniment about her. These Junkers. But big laugh and generous body, far from an Altenburg. I wanted to tear off her clothes but she said her husband was waiting in the car. She could only stay a few minutes. She had told him it was I who painted the full-length portrait of her in a ball gown hanging in the entrance hall of her family home. Nothing else. There will be a dinner party next week. Her first here in years. She had been living in France but had to return because of the war. She cannot believe I have never been invited to any function since coming back to this dungeon.

Has Mina not forgiven you? I denied everything.

She will never forgive me. I am hiding from the Gestapo because of those drawings. She brought me here so she could steal my paintings as payment. I have been in this prison for more than a year. This is cruel, Constanze.

She never allowed you in the house before. She is being consistent, Anton. You are safer out here from sudden visits by the police. But you should be allowed to attend a dinner, at least.

You are as reasonable and beautiful as ever.

You are a shameless flatterer, but I always liked it.

There was so much we liked together. Do you remember those summer days in the woods in our own private spot? Sometimes I could not wait. Your protests were in vain.

Now I am an old married woman. I must go, my hoppy flea.

Until when then, my wood nymph.

I never liked that hoppy flea business. Damn husbands. I wanted to throw her down and have her there but the size difference was greater now. Even feigned resistance and I would have pulled a muscle. A maid brought the invitation five days later. I recognized Mina's writing, the capitals with trailing lines like streamers, as if the letters are about to fly off the page. I am to be introduced at the party as an ethnic German from Lithuania, an art teacher whose name is Albrecht Munchinger. The last line is an insult. Be sure to shave and wash. Never mind, I am going.

Constanze will be there. It will be a simple matter getting her away from her husband. Back then she threw herself at me. After the first sitting she took off her clothes, walked over to me and put my hand on the swollen nipple of her right breast. An artist remembers details.

How do I compare with Mina?

You are a woman and that is where it ends. I thought that but of course said she was more beautiful. We ended up on my bed. With a beautiful woman I could not have waited, it would have been the floor. I told her she was the earth goddess, the divine woman. She smelled of horse liniment. That first whiff almost finished me. She wanted to know why I stopped. I want to gaze on your many beauties, I said. It took all of my concentration to finish. How to suggest perfume? Scented soap. Staying away from the stable before she came to me. I said I was allergic to horses. I found out they were her religion.

Allergic to horses? *Mein Gott!* No. Surely you like them despite that.

*Natürlich.* I think it was because I was conceived in a stable. My father was an Austrian nobleman related to the Hapsburgs. My mother was a Tyrolean peasant girl of mythic beauty and proportion. He paid for my upbringing, but being illegitimate I could not inherit the family fortune. Or I would be the wealthiest man in Austria today. Instead I toil with my brush to bring beauty like yours to the world. Of course there are compensations. I squeezed her rump. She neighed like a horse. I sneezed. Even the sound of them? she said. Yes, unfortunately. Stay away from them for twenty-four hours before your next sitting. I have recovered, I said, and threw myself on her again and she began her high-pitched screaming, alternating with deep grunts. I have no allergy to pigs. She was dressing later and I was cleaning my best brush and she surprised me.

Did you paint Mina naked?

I lied. It would have been a disaster. Even I have my limits. She was a fuck, not for the canvas. For my art I have standards.

The next time she smelled of laundry soap. Two brushstrokes and we were at it, this time on the floor. The door was open. Anybody passing could have seen us. Heard her screaming and grunting. She was so excited she bucked me off and I knocked over my easel. The corner of the framed canvas hit me on the back of the head. I passed out for a few moments. When I came to I saw three white balloons, one above the others, with a crease like a dimple in a navel. I thought I was having a nightmare and started hollering. The balloon with the crease in it spoke.

Are you hurt?

She began to pick me up but I pushed her hands away.

I can get up myself.

I was going to put you on your bed so you could get some rest.

Why should I rest? I feel fine. Next time wear some perfume. That laundry soap makes me sick.

When she arrived for the third sitting I could taste the stink.

I bought it in Königsberg. *Eine Nacht in Paris.*

It smells as if you spent a year in a whorehouse.

I feel like a whore with you.

No need to smell like one.

There is no pleasing you.

Listen, my dumpling. As a painter who has lived in Paris I tell you I never smelled anything like that. It was made in Berlin from coal tar. You are wearing Prussian perfume. If you wore that in Paris you would be detained as a German spy.

What should I wear?

Scented soap made anywhere but in Germany. Take a bath and come to me smelling sweet, my dumpling.

You stink, Anton. You never wash. Why should I smell nice to please you? You are being unfair.

A great artist must live in his own smell to protect himself from the world. Infections, poisons, public toilets, industrial filth, marsh gas. If I take a bath I wash away my natural protection. You are a woman, not an artist, so it does not matter. You want to please me, so you must smell beautiful.

The fourth sitting went well. A few strokes, and many more strokes in the bedroom. People who need love bore me. Sex is the answer to love. A good fuck clears the mind. Leaves an artist free to do his work. I have never loved anybody. Women want to be lied to. Eternal this and that. I met one in Paris, an American, who never pretended. Marion Smith. I could never pronounce her name. Call me Smitty, she said. Sure, I said. She was from New York. Her father owned a company that sold breakfast cereals in boxes. Eat the boxes, she said. Better for you than what's inside. I've had a string of lovers since I turned sweet sixteen. Dad paid for the abortions. I'm more careful now. Sex is strictly business with me. You got something I want and I got something you want. Don't bother with perfume or flowers. I can buy my own. No contracts, licences or promises. When I move on, no hard feelings.

Perfect mistress, except she chewed gum and smoked cigarettes at the same time and left lumps of old gum and butts all over my studio. Place is a dump anyway, she said. How do you live in this hole? You have a hotel suite, I said. I could move in. Nix on that. Strictly business, remember? You're a cock. I'm a cunt. I don't wear panties and I don't keep a man.

I am an artist.

You call this art? Notice I never asked you to paint me. It's enough putting up with your stink. It's getting on my nerves. Take a bath, for Christ's sake, or I'm taking off. Little guys are a bore. Like fucking a monkey. I'll be sailing to New York in a month, anyway. Dad's squawking about bankrolling me. Mom wants me to get married, picked out a Yale grad who's a stockbroker. It's either that or a Harvard grad who's a lawyer. Sweet little old me going to be properly hitched to respectability. Fuck. If you had a big cock and a deluxe studio, I might stay here. For a while, anyway.

She was gone a week later and I never missed her. Too skinny for my taste.

The fifth sitting was the same as the fourth and I was not getting enough work done. Constanze was a few strokes of hair and a piece of gown. The weather was hot. We would run naked among the trees in the back. She would slow down so I could catch her and throw her to the ground. She got twigs and dirt on her back. I was on top. What did she care? But the painting was on her mind all the time. She was anxious. Her father and mother were asking when it would be finished.

Less pleasure and more work and in a few more sittings you will be able to see yourself immortalized on canvas. How are we going to meet after it is finished, my dumpling?

In the woods here. I will ride over. If the weather is bad, I will come here and tether my horse in the shed where the logs are piled. I will dry him off. A blanket will keep him warm enough. Or you can walk over to our estate, only ten miles away. We have a woodshed. Perfect for us.

Walk ten miles? I would be exhausted, in no condition to satisfy you. And I would be attacked by wild animals and peasants. No, come here. More comfortable. Get more logs. The fire is dying.

Why do I always get the logs, Anton?

I could injure my hand carrying them. How would I finish your portrait? They are your vital parts. Like a horse's hooves.

*Natürlich,* dumpling.

Who brings in the logs when I am not here?

I get the maid to do it when she brings my food.

I was suspicious when you said you were related to the Hapsburgs. Now I know you are an aristocrat, Anton.

I am a noble in all but title, an artistic genius and a man. What more could you ask?

In the remaining sittings I worked. I sympathize with court painters, who have had to turn donkeys into unicorns and turtles into swans. With Mina—the bitch—all I had to do was put her on canvas. With Constanze I had to create a substitute, somebody who looked enough like her to pass for a dumpy horsewoman but without the pig's jowls and arse. I trimmed her body and face, enlarged her eyes to ten times the size, gave her lips a sexy pout and put cascading waves in her hair. After ten sittings it was done. She stared.

Is that me?

About a quarter. I could not say that, *natürlich*.

It will hang in our entrance hall.

Why not the stable? I thought. The horses can admire it.

She told me not to sign the painting. I could sign it in front of everybody in the main house. She wanted to show it off to Mina and Loulou before it was moved to her estate. The next day workmen came to move it. She never came back. Not even a note.

Two weeks later Mina came.

Did you think she loved you, Anton? She got what she wanted. She is a trickster. She used you. She whined, threatened she would tell Mama about you if I did not let you paint her. She will deny knowing you. She has a story to explain the painting. The painter's studio is in Königsberg. An old man, an undiscovered genius. She will play the virgin now to catch a husband. You are a buried page in her past. She will never acknowledge that you painted her. The painting is not signed. It never will be. The old painter in Königsberg will suddenly die. All trace of him gone. You are a fool.

We were lovers.

Knowing you, I had guessed that. I have not let you touch me for months. It was over before Constanze. Was over before I knew it.

I miss you.

You can go on missing me.

At least let me bring my friends out here from Berlin. I need company.

I offered you sanctuary. I will honour my word. Having your friends with you will keep you from bothering me. But if you or they bother us in the main house you will all be sent away.

Thank you, Mina, my love. I want to kiss you.

Why does the thought of kissing you make me ill?

Bitch. You loved me. It was love. Admit it.

Whatever it was, love is not the right word, Anton. I knew you for what you were. I could see from one look at your paintings you were not a great artist. You are competent. That is all you will ever be. You strut around as if you mean something. You mean nothing. Your life is a bunch of lies. Did you tell her you were related to the Hapsburgs? Your birth was not illegitimate, your pretense is.

If I am merely competent, why get me to paint you?

Because I have never known a great artist. I was stuck with you.

She got up and left. I could have killed her. I swear I could. I put everything I had into those paintings of her. And what do I get in return? Insults. She made love to me, shared my bed for more than three years and now has turned away from me as if I was shit.

Three years and Constanze back now. A marriage of convenience. She misses me or she would never have come out here. She regrets abandoning me. I can see it in her eyes. Her family found out and talked her out of seeing me. Reminded her of her duty to her class, that she should marry the proper man. She was never proper. She will get me out of here, and my paintings, everything done at night. We will leave together. I can put up with a fat woman. She must have money. She can get some from her husband. We will go to Switzerland, France or England next, and then America. A studio in New York. Society women. They have lots of money. They all want their portraits painted. Their bodies will be a bonus. Constanze will simply have to realize that a great artist is a magnet to women. She is already married. We want no bourgeois conventions. I will get a postcard with a picture of New York and mail it here. Sign the back, "Anton." Let the bitch know.

As soon as Obermeyer and the others came out you began. Too loud. Mama will hear. How? We are a kilometre away. You are breaking the furniture. Furniture? A few chairs and an old table. My friends are sleeping on the floor. They need more blankets. You saw a bottle of pills and a bloody syringe. Are they taking drugs? Medicine. Some of them are ill. Do you think

I am naïve, Anton? I saw drugs in Berlin. Leave us alone. We are artists. We bother nobody. Endless questions. Why is that block of marble in the middle of the floor? Obermeyer may have an idea for it. An idea? He has never sculpted anything in his life. He thinks one will come to him away from Berlin. I want that out of here by tomorrow. He can take it to Königsberg and wait for an idea there.

You interfered in everything. You had the maids and the gardeners spy on us. The maids have been complaining, Anton. You and your friends are too familiar. No more maids. Clean up after yourselves. Get your own food. Obermeyer is rich. He drives a Maybach. You will be well fed, as you were in Berlin. You brought a woman here the other night. I gave you permission to bring your friends. Nobody else. Keep your whores in Königsberg. Do that again and I will throw you and your friends out. You Junker bitch. It was like an army camp. You grinned when I said it. In the army they shoot deserters, Anton. I would give you a medal. To which Gestapo headquarters would I mail it?

Now I have my way out, finally. I must take all of my paintings, including those of you. You lie. I promised you nothing. Gift of love to you? I would sooner burn them. And cut my throat into the bargain. I must talk with Constanze at the dinner. We will plan in some quiet corner. Her husband must be an oaf. Some decayed aristocrat who takes snuff and is soused all the time. Who thinks it is 1912 and has trouble remembering exactly when the regatta is being held. Useful though, with money and connections to move those paintings and keep them out of the hands of the Altenburgs once I have left here. How to explain me? I am a distant relative. Very distant. Constanze's family must not ruin things. Of noble blood, *natürlich*. I paint as a hobby and am an amateur art dealer. I have discovered the work of an eccentric genius whose paintings will be worth millions. The best market is America, so we must get them there, the sooner the better. Who knows what may happen in this war? Art treasures, especially valuable ones as yet undiscovered, must be protected from military outrages. War is bad only when it threatens art. Otherwise it keeps down the population by having the uncultured masses murder each other. They are blind to beauty and the fewer of them there are the better. They are a danger and prove it every time the lunatics among them enter a gallery with a vial of acid, a chisel or a butcher knife.

You were right for once, you bitch. I shall not forget to wash and shave. I must look presentable to scheme right under your nose. I wonder if Constanze will take as much pleasure in the evening as I will. She must hate you and your sister. Homely women hate the beautiful ones or fate or they nurse cripples, wipe the faces of imbeciles or become classroom dictators. They marry and help fill the world with more homely women. They see nothing but what they don't have. They don't want art, they want cosmetics. The artist has a bitter time making such a world see better. He must sacrifice himself in this great task. I must sleep well tonight to enjoy my first dinner at Altenburg.


Inside Altenburg looks like an art gallery with all the paintings removed except for the bad ones. I did not see mine of Mina. They are too good for that place and those unseeing eyes, anyway. The butler showed me to my place in the dining hall. I was late, as I meant to be. Everybody stared except Constanze, who was busy talking to her husband, an obese dullard. The Countess sat at the head of the table, scrawny, tall, with the beak of a stork. I was seated at the other end, near a small professor and Mina's uncle. The wine was good. There was roast goose. I ate and drank as much as I could get down. Near the end, between my belches and farts and the annoyed glances of my neighbours, I could hear the professor addressing me.

As a teacher of art you must have an opinion on National Socialist art.

Must I?

You do, surely.

Nude marble women. No pubic hair.

Should there be? An aesthetic experience.

There must be pubic hair. Never hairy, but in delicate scrolls round the mound, defining it. That swelling, that full, soft fuzzy apricot. Succulent, moistened with liquid pearl. The aroma of cunt must be palpable.

The uncle spoke up.

You are speaking improperly at the dinner table of a great house. Mind your manners, sir, if you have any.

A great artist says what he feels.

Great artist? You were introduced as some kind of teacher, a Balt from Lithuania.

The professor studied me through his glasses. I felt like a specimen in a laboratory. I maintained my dignity. He could stare all he wanted. I was not bothered in the least.

Pardon me, Herr Munchinger, but you resemble that moral degenerate, Anton Klapperich. The one who drew those disgusting caricatures of the Führer. Published in Reimann's magazine. Remember, Berthold?

*Ach*, Reimann.

*Ja*, Reimann. They fixed him. Klapperich had to scurry like a rat back to Vienna. But he must have left before Anschluss.

Silence at the table. The professor questioned me like a pedant.

So you live in Lithuania. Where, may I ask?

Vilnius proper.

Where do you teach?

The Academy of Fine Arts and Humble Crafts.

Never heard of it. But I do not pay much attention to these Baltic countries. What do you teach? What courses?

The female nude, in the bath, on the couch, in bed, on the floor, the toilet, in the hayloft, wherever and whenever I want her. Sometimes lingerie in the way.

A clothed nude? Surely a contradiction.

You surprise me, professor. Least is the most. Brassiere, décolletage, nipples straining against satin, lace petticoat, fluid shock of white thigh, a silk vee stretched tight, plump and cleft. Scrambled in the brain, pricks of hot wire.

That is degenerate art.

All true art is degenerate. The rest belongs on a postcard.

You could not teach that in Germany.

Why would I want to? What kind of a *Dummkopf* do you think I am?

That is treasonous talk, even for an ethnic German, or whatever kind of German you really are.

I am a great artist, you pedantic piece of shit.

I think we know what you are and who you are.

Your kind know me? Art is dead here, you killed it. You are maggots swarming over festering meat. You will leave nothing but a pile of bones as your monument.

Silence around the table, everybody staring at me. Time to leave. I stood up and bowed to the Countess. I wanted to make a grand exit but I was so drunk I stumbled over my feet on my way out. There were snickers.

The night air helped clear my head. I fell twice on the gravel path. I vomited the goose and wine at the edge of the lake. My knees sank into the marshy soil and tufts of grass and I looked up. The sky was reeling, the stars turning in a great circle like a roulette wheel. How much time do I have? Minutes, hours, a day or two? Who will help me now?

I am writing this the next morning. I slept for two hours, drunken groggy sleep. Nightmares of pounding on doors and dark shapes, lizard shapes screaming at me, pointed teeth dripping blood. All I wanted was company and some good food and drink after more than a year alone. Why was I seated between those two? The jaws of a trap. They knew who I was. I saw one trap. There were two. No escape now.

You are cunning.

Footsteps on the gravel.

I was a great—.

# Nuremberg

I finished reading the book late one night and put it aside. Mina came out to the summer house a few days later carrying the pail with my daily rations, spelling the maids. A nice take on noblesse oblige. I told her about my discovery. She had brought a bottle of Riesling and we were sitting at the beechwood table and drinking.

"So you know all about me."

"I agree with Viktoria's assessment of him. His writing only proves it."

"You will recall from my uncle's writings that I told Loulou Anton and I were passionate friends. We were passionate but never friends. It was a hopeless relationship. I was young and headstrong. His being a painter had a lot to do with it. The arts fascinated me then. In the staid world in which I grew up the closest you got to art was to sit for your portrait. You see them on our walls. All painted in the same way. They seem done by the same hand.

"You are not German. It is difficult to explain to you. In the early Thirties there was chaos. Many unemployed and hungry people, elections no party won, riots, demonstrations, shootings. No leaders of principle. I had no political belief except contempt for all politicians. Many writers and painters felt they had to take sides, be anti-Nazi and vaguely or strongly leftist. Anton felt the way I did. Politics be damned. As you know, he did not mean for his Hitler caricatures to be published. Years later I came to know my country and heritage had been given by my class and the industrialists to criminals. Anton still did not care. That was the end between us but it was over, anyway. I hid him in

1936, when we broke up, and then after Anschluss. He misunderstood, as in so many things."

"He knew who betrayed him. Do you?"

"Yes. There was nothing I could do."

"Does your sister know?"

"I told her. She had guessed."

I nodded. She stood up.

"Loulou is feeling better. She may visit in the next few weeks."

"I get to see a maid a day."

"This is not easy for any of us. The war, I mean."

"I appreciate the company and the food."

"The food is good?"

"Better than Berlin by far."

"We at least have that. I forgot to tell you the war news."

"Tell me next time."

She wasn't going to tell me who the betrayer was. I didn't expect her to. It wasn't hard to figure. Was it a surprise to her? Or did the Junker crust have as many cracks as the rest of society?

Christmas and New Year's Day passed quietly. Besides food, the maids brought me books from the library. They would relay my requests to Mina and she would give them the books. She visited twice in January, bringing war news along with the pail. At the beginning of February Loulou visited. Her face was drawn and thin but her eyes were lively again. I told her she shouldn't have carried the pail but she shook her head.

"You are both part of my recovery."

She brought a bottle of Riesling and we drank at the beechwood table and I mentioned Klapperich's version of what happened when she sat for her portrait.

"The truth is a little different. When he was hiding here the first time he asked if I wanted my portrait painted. I had seen his paintings of Mina. I knew he was not a great artist, even Mina admitted that. But he was competent, so I said yes. At the first sitting, in this room, he said he wanted to rearrange my dress. He began to stroke my knees and thighs. He said, 'I can teach you the depths of carnal desire.' It sounded so ridiculous I giggled. He believed I was succumbing to him. He threw himself on top of me and I fell off my chair and landed on the floor with him tearing at my dress. I thought, Oh my God, not him, never. I shouted, 'Behave yourself.' It sounds silly but I said that. It had no effect, so I began pulling his hair. It was greasy and he smelled so bad I felt sick. I thought, How could you, Mina? He called me a Junker—, a word I will not repeat. It was like wrestling with a hairy dog that has gone mad. I was punching him hard and he was cursing me when Mina came in. 'You pig,' she said and pulled him off. He ran at her and pushed her and she slapped him, knocking him down. He crawled and literally at her feet begged her to forgive him, saying he adored her and to give him another chance. She kicked him away and came to me. 'Are you all right?' I told her my hands were sore from punching him. 'Stay out of here,' she said.

"Mina picked up a knife from the table and pushed the point against his throat and drew blood and he fell over in a faint. 'You might have killed him,' I said. 'Who cares?' she said. Later on he found a more obliging woman here and they had an affair."

She obviously hadn't read the manuscript. Like Mina she wasn't going to name names. Bad form. Two weeks later she visited. She told me she saw Klapperich once more in the summer house. The occasion was a showing in 1936 of his latest paintings, including Mina nude at the lake on the estate. Mina's presence reassured her.

"There is something of the lion tamer about my sister. She wore Anton on a bracelet. She would despise him one minute and tolerate him the next. But by then she had resolved to be rid of him. After he had been here a few weeks she would not sleep in the summer house. She allowed him to invite his Berlin friends to stay here for a while. It turned out to be four long weeks. They would have wild drinking parties, bringing prostitutes from Königsberg. They went after our maids. They would mimic our tenants' speech and laugh at their wooden shoes to their faces. This is not a prosperous area. Country folk in Ostpreußen are frugal. Good shoes are for Sunday. Mina saw their treatment of our farmers. She told them she would take care of the matter. The showing was coming up. That would be Anton's last party."

Loulou took a sip of wine. Unlike their mother, the sisters only sipped wine but they loved coffee.

"The night was warm, it was July. The showing was to begin when we arrived. We went at eight and saw the door was open. We walked in and this room was empty. We saw no paintings. Anton and his friends had gone to Königsberg in Max Obermeyer's Maybach. Obermeyer had driven them here from Berlin a month earlier. He was a sculptor and had a head like a bald eagle. We went back to the main house and waited and at nine heard the car drive round on the gravel path to the lake. The path was not for cars but Mina let Obermeyer use it because she did not want our family and friends to see the car. We heard a crash and yelling and laughing and women's voices. We went outside and along the path and saw that the car had crashed into the woodshed. We could see, the car lights were on, and so were the lights in the summer house. There were people getting out of the limousine, some on the path and some inside the house. Chairs were being thrown around and a bottle smashed through a window. A drunken woman screamed. 'Wait here,' Mina said. 'I will get Father's pistol.' 'Wait until Fritz gets back,' I said. Fritz had gone with Viktoria to visit friends.

"She went inside the main house and returned a few minutes later with the pistol. Everybody was in the summer house. Through the open door I could see a naked man and woman making love on the floor. A man ran out and jumped into the lake, hollering. I could barely hear him because there was so much noise. Mina went to the door and I followed. I was scared but I could not let her go alone. Anton was on the table making love to a woman at least twice his size. Drinking from a bottle of schnapps, Obermeyer was sitting on the floor and staring at a large rock he was holding. There was a painter called Kretschmer who was injecting himself. Two men were sharing a woman. Two others were trying to break chairs over each other's head. Mina went inside and shouted but nobody would pay attention. She fired the pistol into the air and that brought silence. 'Come on, Blondie, join in,' one of the men said. She pointed the pistol directly at him and her voice was calm. 'The next shot will hit one of you. Get out.' 'We will rush you, you bitch,' Anton said. 'Please do,' Mina said. 'It would be a test of my marksmanship to hit such a tiny target.' 'Him or his sausage?' Obermeyer said and everybody laughed and then we heard hollering from the lake. 'Franz must be drowning,' one of them said. 'Get him and go,' Mina said, stepping aside.

"Obermeyer staggered out to the lake. The women and the rest of the men began to leave. All of them went to the lake except Anton who, on his knees and clutching at Mina's legs, pleaded with her to let him stay. Going back to Berlin meant death, he said. One of his friends might turn him in. He would go to Vienna but later. She told him he could stay until she could guarantee him safe passage there. He tried to kiss her but she pushed him away. She and I went to see what had happened to the man. We saw a body lying among the rushes along the shore. He had drowned and been pulled out of the water. Within the hour Anton's friends had collected their belongings and were gone, taking the women with them. When Fritz returned he contacted the authorities and made up a story about the man being a trespasser who had wandered in the dark into the water. His papers were burnt and Anton was kept hidden while the police were here."

She took another sip of wine. Her glass was almost empty. I picked up the bottle of Riesling but she waved a hand over her glass. I poured a civilized amount into mine.

"Anton stayed another two months. Mina would have nothing to do with him. He was left alone in the summer house except for the maids who brought him his meals. Late one night she drove him to the Polish border and gave him money to make his way back to Vienna. He had told her where the paintings he did here were hidden. When she looked they were not there. She contacted Obermeyer in Berlin and he told her they had been shipped from Königsberg to Vienna. On that very day there was to have been a showing for us later. And those in Berlin had been sent there as well. He kept those of Mina, and he had promised them to her. I had to wait until 1938, when he came here again, to see the one of her by the lake."

I asked why Klapperich stayed so long the second time.

She drained her glass and grinned.

"That takes some explaining. We did not know what to do except get him to France or Switzerland. That would not have been hard but what about the paintings? Smuggling all those canvases would have been impossible. Besides, Mina said he had told her the paintings of her were a gift. He denied having said that, so there was an impasse. He sulked in the summer house for months as Mina's prisoner. Finally he broke down, accepted her terms, which were she would keep the paintings of her and store the others until they could be sent to him. She wanted him to sign a paper declaring which paintings were hers. After what happened, she did not trust him. Months passed and he would not sign it. If he had settled the matter quickly he would have been gone before the Gestapo came to know where he was."

"Why all the fuss about the work of a mediocre painter? Being a rank egotist, he would overrate himself. Is this female vanity? Or am I missing something?"

"He is not a terrible artist and my sister is beautiful. He knew those paintings were the best he had ever done. I think she inspired him, as much as anyone like Anton could be inspired. His reputation, never high, would rise. Those canvases would fetch a good price, especially the nudes."

"So it came down to money. Are the paintings still here?"

"Mina, Joseph and I moved them to a safe place."

"Would I be allowed to see them?"

"Ask Mina, they are hers. The ones you would be interested in viewing."

"I may be interested in art. But I will say that if you had been painted, portrait or in the nude, I would have asked to see them."

"How gallant."

"If I say any more I shall be trespassing, like that guy who drowned in the lake. Men who are alone begin to hallucinate about women, painted or real."

"I must go." She stood up.

Abrupt exits. They ran in the family.

"Thanks for the visit."

She nodded and left.

I didn't see either sister for several weeks. The maids were friendly and kept bringing pails and books. But I had the impression I was an alien species to them, a strange creature that had to be hidden away. I asked them about the war but their replies left me more ignorant than I already was. Mina had forgotten her promise.

In March she came to see me with a request. She wanted to use the summer house for a meeting the following Sunday at two. I was invited, would be the only outsider. The purpose? Conspiracy. Why else would an American be at Altenburg? That Sunday I was introduced to everybody. There were a dozen altogether, but five stood out from the rest. Elisabeth von Busse, originally from Berlin, was headmistress of a private girls' school in Königsberg. Quiet and sharply attentive, she wore her hair in a ring-shaped bun, had thin features and skin the color of parchment. General Erich von Scharfenberg was Prussian-officer lean, balding and wore a monocle. Paul von Meltzer, a Kemals cigarette chewer, worked somewhere in the upper echelons of the East Prussian bureaucracy. Wolfgang von Ploetz was a lawyer who specialized in constitutional law. Ludwig von Schreck, formerly in the diplomatic service, was retired and living on his estate. The rest were military officers and government officials, all part of the same privileged caste.

Within five minutes the front room was full of conspiratorial smoke and the sound of corks being pulled and coffee being poured. The extra chairs brought over by Klaus and Joseph to accommodate the number of guests were placed in a large circle around the table. The group behaved more like a constitutional congress than nervous plotters in a dictatorship. They were the privileged and they weren't going to let the Nazis deny them their patriotic duty to set history right. It was near spring, 1942. The situation for Germany hadn't become hopeless yet. The conspirators felt they were dealing from a position of strength with the Allies. But no matter how bad the situation became, they would have had a hard time accepting reality. They believed the Allies would bargain with Germany. They were members of an exclusive club and they didn't see anything wrong with that.

"Have you made any contacts with the working class, the traditional labor unions?" I asked von Meltzer.

"We have nothing to do with the Socialists or Communists."

"What about farmers and the middle class?"

He shook his head.

"You represent a minority, the old elite. How can you form a government?"

"We represent the best interests of Germany."

"How can a small fraction of the population assume that?"

"You are not German."

They spent half an hour arguing about which one of the Hohenzollerns would make the best Kaiser, and General von Scharfenberg proposed that in peace negotiations with the Allies Germany insist on the restoration of its 1914 borders as well as the retention of the Sudetenland, Austria and the Nazi chunk of Poland. His attitude reminded me of Dr. Schliesman.

"Poles are an uncivilized people who need to be governed. They are naturally dirty. During the Polish campaign we could see in the Corridor the difference between their farms and ours. Ours were clean, well run, productive. Theirs were filthy and most of the Poles wore no shoes."

It was agreed one of the peace terms would be that the Wehrmacht retain its present size and be under the command of the traditional officer corps. No Allied troops would be stationed on German soil and there would be no reparations. The Nazis would be tried by Germans. Some dared hope there would be a split between the Allies and Germans would fight alongside Americans and British against the Russians.

I could see Mina frowning at a lot of this. She broke into the discussion and asked me to give my opinion.

"Your terms will be rejected."

"They are reasonable and honorable," General von Scharfenberg said, peering at me through his monocle.

"The Allies no longer care what you want. That ended with Munich. What they want is important now. They think every German is a Nazi. The best you can do is get rid of Hitler and end the fighting."

They ignored what I said. The next order of business was compiling a list of those who would fill positions in a new government in East Prussia. Some of those put on the list weren't present and some of them didn't know about the meeting or even the conspiracy. Mina asked to be left off because she was busy looking after the estate. At precisely four everybody left and Mina and I sat looking at a table crowded with wineglasses, wine bottles, coffee cups and overflowing ashtrays. The air smelled of cigar and cigarette smoke. A blue-gray haze hung over our heads. I had left the door open to clear the air.

"That was a good example of German thinking," Mina said, "to fill positions in an imaginary government."

Loulou appeared in the doorway.

"I heard the cars leave. Have they finished saving Germany?"

"They are putting themselves at risk for nothing. There is no point in making lists now."

"Lists?"

"Of people to serve in a new government. If the Gestapo finds it, everybody is lost."

"Are you on it?"

"Do you think I would be that stupid? Besides, I am busy, as I told them."

Loulou sat down and I found a clean glass and poured her some wine. She took a sip and looked at me.

"What did you think?"

"Amateurs facing professional killers. They have no chance."

"Some of them are officers."

"They fight by the rules. The Nazis have their own rules. And they talk about peace terms before getting rid of Hitler. Hopeless."

"No matter how big or evil a monster is," Mina said, "if you cut off its head you will kill it."

"Who will do it?" Loulou said and took another sip. After a prolonged silence she picked up an empty coffee cup.

"You had coffee, and none left for me. Who brought it?"

"Elisabeth," Mina said. "She told me she began hoarding it two years ago."

I laughed. Mina looked at me.

"Why are you laughing?"

"From conspiracy to coffee. From the slime to the conspicuous."

"Sophie told us you had an odd sense of humor."

"In revolutionary France and Russia they wanted bread. Now we expect luxuries as we plot."

Loulou shook her head.

"You have been alone too long. We should invite you to dinner."

"Will I get a cup of coffee?"

They looked at each other and decided I was joking.

I never did get that dinner. I saw the inside of the main house once more. Loulou's invitation seemed to mix sympathy with hauteur. Was I overstepping the boundaries? A correspondent, and American too, who joked with them and politely told them off. More pails and books for me. March slipped into April, the weather warmer. The wind changed that slight bit from cold to bracing. It was time to go. I told Mina when she came out near the end of the month and she reacted strangely.

"Is there something wrong?"

"I should be on my way. We talked in December about my leaving in spring, remember?"

"There is another meeting and we thought you might like to attend. You could offer your opinions again."

"My opinions are of no interest to them."

"Elisabeth will be bringing coffee."

"Thanks, I have other priorities, one of which is not being awakened at dawn by the Gestapo."

"You are safe here."

"For how long?"

"Until the meeting, anyway."

She grinned. What was going on? It's easy to become paranoid in a situation like that. I remembered my predecessors. They never did get out except to die. But I wasn't a guilt-ridden relative and I had no paintings. Was it time to start writing my last thoughts in the book? The third prisoner's narrative. I could have tried to get to Switzerland on my own. It was a long way without any kind of help.

"You are going to help me?"

"After the meeting we will make plans. I must go."

She told me the meeting was to be on the coming Sunday. After she had gone I brooded over the fact that insanity was not unknown among inbred aristocrats, and Junkers were as inbred as any. I decided to stay for the meeting and see if they were serious about helping afterwards. If not, I would go on my own. It was a free country.

On the Friday of that week Loulou came to see me.

"Mina says you wish to leave us. We will miss you."

"You hardly see me."

"We have grown quite fond of you."

"Fond? Yes, uh, let me look that up in my dictionary of human affection and treachery."

"You misunderstand. We like you."

"Your fine aristocratic distinctions are lost on me. You said the last time you were here that I had been alone too long. I agree. To be on my way I need a map and a bag of oats."

"What about the meeting?"

"Your friends have no coherent plan of action, no broad basis of support among the German people and are hopelessly deluded about the Allies. Nothing I could say is going to change their thinking and you and your sister know that."

"Mina said it was good having you there."

"You still have the coffee lady."

"Elisabeth? She is quiet."

"Will you be there?"

"This time, yes."

"Better odds, anyway. Then I go."

"Switzerland?"

I nodded.

"We used to go skiing there years ago. I miss that."

"Speaking of missing, the wine is unopened."

"I brought it for you."

"A bribe."

"I must go." She smiled and got up and I grinned

"Stone gods are worn down by what they never see."

"What does that mean?"

"I have no idea."

It was the same gang of merrymakers on Sunday, with the addition of a bristling major and a Nazi functionary who had gone over to the plotters. The major, Gerhard von Trexler, demanded to know why I was there. Mina said she would vouch for me. Her glare silenced him. The functionary, Herbert von Schmitt, put my name in his invisible notebook. Loulou sat beside me and Mina sat next to Elisabeth von Busse. I had wine and the women coffee. The smoke was like fog. Various military officers and government officials were mentioned. They were Prussians who might be persuaded to join the conspiracy.

"They are none of them from the aristocracy," von Meltzer said, glancing in my direction, "and we have made contact with a trades union official. We are open to everyone who may be of help to us."

"Contact?" I said. "He should be here."

"We have had preliminary discussions. He will quite likely be invited to our next meeting if those discussions prove fruitful."

"Are we open to everybody, regardless of importance?" the bristling major said. And looking at me, "Stay out of this. You are not German. Your opinion can mean nothing."

"Not only mine, obviously."

"What can one expect from an American?"

"Support for any attempt to overthrow the Nazis."

"We are saving Germany from those who would harm us.

"That could be a long list, especially from your point of view."

General von Scharfenberg intervened.

"We should put aside street sweepers and garbage collectors for the moment. They can be asked for their opinion after we have given them a new government."

Sneers around the table. I was the odd democrat out.

There was more tinkering with the list of replacements for Nazi officials. Names were added or deleted, then discussed and added or deleted again. As before, some of those on the list weren't present. Mina frowned but kept quiet.

The main order of business was how to get rid of the Nazi leadership. The debate was about whether to wait until the leading figures were gathered together or kill Hitler at the earliest opportunity. There had been contacts with other anti-Nazis, in Pomerania, Silesia and Brandenburg. The consensus was, and the general and major agreed, that it would be better to wait for an opportunity to kill off the entire leadership at one time. Mina disagreed.

"Such a chance may never arise and good opportunities will be lost. With him gone, the rest will tear each other apart. No one can replace him. Each of the others sees himself as the true successor. In the power struggle after his death the entire Wehrmacht will be with us. The pragmatists as well as the patriots. The SS will be alone and outnumbered. Only the fanatics will fight. Most Germans are sick of this war. Any chance to end it must be taken."

"Try to understand," the major said, smiling.

"Your insulting attitude bores me. Address my points."

A long silence as tendrils of smoke from cigars and cigarettes joined the fog hanging over us. Finally General von Scharfenberg spoke.

"There is the possibility of civil war if one or more of them is alive. No one knows how much of a possibility."

"We must risk that or Germany is lost," Mina said.

"Why must we behave like American gangsters, driving by restaurants and shooting submachine guns?" von Ploetz, said. "An attempt should be made to arrest them."

Out of the corner of my eye I could see Loulou grinning at me.

"They should be subjected to the judicial system," von Schreck said.

A groan from Mina.

"They got into power by taking advantage of people who underestimated them. You exterminate gutter rats, not try them."

"You become like them," von Ploetz said.

"Or you can watch Germany bleed to death at a megalomaniac's whims."

"We must have laws."

"That is my point. There are none now, and before we can have them we must rid ourselves of those who took them away from us."

There was another long silence. The Nazi functionary hadn't said a word. I wondered if he was a spy. How much was a "von" really worth? Berthold would know that. Being there was treason and some had said enough for a string of death sentences. The conspiracy was as frail as cigarette ash in a draft. Yet it was real, and the courage too.

"The coffee was good," Loulou said after they had gone.

Mina stood up.

"I am going riding."

Loulou nodded. Mina's boots punished the gravel on the path.

"She always goes riding when she is very happy or very upset. Stürm, her stallion, is a dapple gray. No one else has ever ridden him. Or could, I think."

"Do you ride?"

"I have a mare, Johanna. She is an ambler."

"Gentle horse, gentle rider."

"Not always. I love horses. But I am not in the least athletic. I like dancing."

"Not much opportunity for it now. You told me you miss skiing."

"I miss the travel, social life and scenery. Mina is the skier."

"Those bicycles in the woodshed. I assume one is yours."

"We used to go cycling on Sunday afternoons. In the spring and summer of 1937. We were attempting to forget, pretending it was another time. Gerd and I, Viktoria, Fritz, Mina and some of our friends would cycle to a meadow a few kilometers from here. It bordered the widest section of the stream that feeds the lake. We would take picnic baskets. The ladies would wear straw hats with ribbons and wide brims. Silk scarves too. There is a boathouse with a canoe and a rowboat. You could lie back and close your eyes and feel the sun touch your face as you floated under the openings between alder branches along the bank. Gerd or Fritz would row. Mina usually took the canoe. She would toss her hat among the picnic things and head for the bank. She used the paddle so well."

"Big sister does everything better?"

"I am the better dancer."

"As someone who has stepped on more than his share of women's toes, I scrupulously avoid dancing. But I could be persuaded if we ever meet again."

"You have a way of putting things. Sometimes funny, sometimes sad."

"Words are my business."

"Are they only words?"

"No. Sometimes I get hit over the head."

She smiled.

"At least we have forgotten the meeting for a while."

"Schmitt gave me too long a look."

"He told Elisabeth he does not like Americans."

"Is that all?"

"He said you are a nation of mongrels with no culture."

"Another Schliesman. I could be excused for thinking that most Germans were racists and cultural snobs."

"Most?"

"In the heart of Junkerdom I feel like an equal, almost. What can I expect as a crummy scruffy down-at-heels busted-up reporter who calls himself a foreign correspondent to boost his morale?"

"We went to American talkies when they first came to Germany or else I would not have had any idea what you were saying."

"The self-indulgence and self-pity were obvious."

"I know. But I like the sound of those words."

"A fellow traveler in philology."

She looked at her watch.

"I have to help the maids set the table for our guests. Klaus injured his foot yesterday."

We heard the sound of horseshoes grinding against the gravel. Seated on an enormous gray stallion, Mina peered through the open doorway. She was leaning over to see us. Her tousled hair fell across her face.

"I will see you in a few days."

The gray trotted off, champing at the bit and neck arched. We stood up.

"I will see you before you leave."

She moved with a ballerina's grace along the path towards the main house, her loose hair in the slanting afternoon light flickering to blazing red. She raised her hand at one point to block the glare reflected off the lake. Then the path curved and the rushes came between and I couldn't see her. I cleared the table and left for a walk in the woods. When I returned I saw the extra chairs had been taken away. As I ate my dinner I watched the main house fade into the twilight. The oval length of the lake was a black mirror.

Mina came by a week later, bringing the information on T4. The escape plan had been worked out.

"One of the farmers will take you to Königsberg in the back of his wagon this Saturday. A car, a gray Horch, will be waiting behind the Castle. You will be hidden. The driver will take you to Breslau and you will stay overnight and another driver will take you to the Swiss border. Under another name send us a letter from Switzerland and write, 'I am having a good time.' No return address. Will you be staying there?"

"In Berne. Working for my press bureau."

"We have a friend in Zurich. I will give you her name, address and telephone number. Memorize them and destroy the paper. You could stay, work with us."

"Your friends have little regard for my opinions."

"I can deal with them."

"Thanks, but as an outsider whose German should be a lot better I might make a mistake that would jeopardize everybody."

Early Saturday morning the three of us stood outside the summer house as a wagon approached, its iron-rimmed wooden wheels stutter-skidding against the gravel. The back was piled high with hay. The driver, face lined and weathered from working out in the fields, climbed down from the seat and bowed slightly to Mina and Loulou. I handed him my valise and he made a place for it and me among the hay. Mina shook my hand.

"Goodbye. Write when you arrive."

Loulou handed me a package wrapped in brown paper and tied with butcher's twine.

"Something for you to eat. Take care of yourself."

We shook hands.

"Thank you both for everything. I never thought I would be reluctant to leave the Third Reich."

"We shall miss you."

We were still holding hands.

After helping me into the wagon, the farmer hid me under the hay and in the darkness I could feel a jolt as we began to move. It seemed I lay there for hours on that bumpy ride. When we stopped and I was told I could get out I brushed the hay aside and looked at my watch. We had been traveling for an hour and a half. The farmer said we were in a suburb of Königsberg. I asked how far the city center was and he said a twenty-minute walk. I let myself down from the wagon and began walking. It was the beginning of May and still cool, cooler than Berlin. The wide streets and comfortable houses of the middle-class suburb were quiet. Watching for police and military, I noticed the city didn't have the oppressive atmosphere of the capital. The spire of the central tower was visible long before I got to the Castle. I walked past the bulky towers at the ends of the north wall to the back and saw the Horch parked alone. A man was sitting behind the wheel. When he saw me he started the engine. He motioned with his hand for me to get in the rear. I opened the passenger side door, threw in my valise and in a clipped upper-class accent he told me to hide under the blankets on the floor. Another blacked-out ride as I felt the car gradually speed up after ten minutes. Five minutes later he pulled over and stopped. He told me it was safe to sit in front. We were in the countryside and I could see him clearly. His hair was cut close at the sides and back. I guessed he was or had recently been in the military.

"Were you in the army?"

"I was an Oberst, a colonel, and was relieved of my command. I refused to have prisoners shot."

"Were they commissars?"

Hitler had ordered that all political commissars taken prisoner be shot. The order wasn't popular with the high command.

"Ordinary prisoners. I made no distinction. No provision had been made to feed or guard such great numbers. It was decided to get rid of them. I ignored the order."

"What are you doing besides helping fugitives escape?"

"I manage my estate. But I think we must leave. The Russians will win now that America is against us. They will not forget our treatment of them. We will feel their hatred first. I must get my family and the servants and tenant farmers out. It will be hard because the Nazis want us to stay. They feed us propaganda about new offensives and imaginary victories. It would look bad if two million Prussians began to move west. They will refuse to let us go until it is too late. You saw today everything is calm, no shells or bombs. People have no idea what is coming."

"How well do you know the Altenburgs?"

"I see them at Christmas and Easter. They usually visit us but sometimes in past years my family and I have been invited there."

"Mina told me more than a year ago that Hitler would invade the Soviet Union. She predicted a German defeat."

"We lost when we did not take Moscow last October. Or Stalingrad or the Caucasus oil fields. He is a hopeless bungler who wants to out-general the generals. Every chance was lost."

"Were you hoping for success?"

"As a soldier, yes. As a German, no."

"I fail to see the distinction."

A short explosive laugh as the car raced along the open road, the only other traffic military transport and staff cars.

"It is not easy for me to understand."

"Last year the Propaganda Ministry invited press bureau chiefs on a guided tour of the eastern front. All of us turned it down. We knew what was really happening would be kept hidden from us. What was it like out there?"

He took a while to answer.

"In the first week we knew we were fighting a different kind of enemy. The Russians fought hard, harder than anybody we had encountered. If they had prepared a defensive strategy and had competent field commanders, we would not have made much progress after the first few days. Their high command was incompetent. They kept throwing armies at us to slow us down and took enormous casualties. We took tens of thousands of prisoners in our sector alone. The lines stretched for many kilometers. You could not see where they ended. They went back beyond the horizon, that endless plain stretching before us. Dusty miserable-looking fellows plodded along bareheaded, hungry, thirsty, tired, hiding their fear. They could only guess what they faced, and it was worse than any thought.

"Our troops were happy. But it seemed too easy, despite Russian resistance. Later the rains came and our trucks were axle-deep in mud. We used half-tracks and tanks to pull them and even horses. Before our men had to eat them. Soon the snow came and everything froze. Our motors would not start. We had no winter lubricants or oils. Our men were exhausted, near to collapse. They huddled in summer uniforms around fires, flapping their arms against themselves to keep warm. The Russians had winter uniforms. Our soldiers would strip overcoats off their dead, even cut off a leg and thaw it over a fire to get off the boot.

"To a Prussian officer his men come first. That is our tradition. It goes back to Frederick the Great. Officers ate what their men ate and slept in the same kind of tent. One day during a lull I was passing a field gun and the men did not salute. This was such a breach of conduct I knew something had to be wrong. I went over and saw the gun crew were all in position and frozen solid, as if carved out of ice. Icicles hung from their noses. You can imagine my feelings. Days later the Russians counterattacked. That was the turning point. We began to retreat. I spent Christmas of 1941 in a command post that was nothing more than a tarpaulin over a hole in the frozen earth. The retreat has stopped since. A new offensive will be launched this year but the one chance we had has been lost forever.

"This spring I was relieved of my command. I told you why. I did not want to leave. I felt I should share the fate of the others. But I was happy I was going to see my family again. And I wanted nothing more to do with the whole bungled business. We officers had become slaves. Generals were accused of cowardice and of incompetence to cover up his idiotic blunders. He issued but one command that made sense, in 1941 after the Russian counterattack. Stand fast, no retreat. That prevented a complete rout. Otherwise he has been a disaster.

"You have no idea of cold if you have not spent a winter on the Russian steppes in a dugout with the wind shrieking above your head. I wake up at night thinking I am back there. When I come to my senses, I feel guilty about not being with my men. What they must be enduring, and will endure."

There was no point in reminding him of what the Russians were suffering and why. He was a professional soldier, part of a long tradition, and a decent man. I wondered if he would ever sort out the difference between soldier and citizen. I changed the subject.

"Have you told Mina and Loulou about your plans to leave?"

"There is little time for such talk. It would have to be private because someone at the table might inform on us and we would be condemned as defeatists. Not all Junkers can be trusted. Even if nobody informs, talk like that spreads fast and the authorities would find out. If Mina can see defeat coming, she does not need me to tell her what to do."

The countryside had changed. Gone were the neat, pleasant-looking farms of East Prussia, replaced by wrecked and abandoned barns and farmhouses. Emaciated, hollow-eyed people walked at the side of the road. In tattered clothes, many wore rags for shoes. Because of the scarcity of leather in Germany, many working-class and poor people there wore rope-soled shoes but this was a different order of poverty. Some glanced at the car as we passed. Despite our speed, I could see the hatred in Polish eyes.

"We must be in Poland."

"What was not destroyed by the war has been stolen. Healthy Poles are being used as workers and the rest survive on what they scavenge."

I thought of the sisters and their as yet safe life. I felt drawn back to them as the car increased the distance between us. How much time was left? Would they react before it was too late? I fought off the urge to return by telling myself I would be writing to them and could warn them in time. The miserable people walking along the side of the road faced daily a slow death from starvation. They expected a bullet from any soldier who cared to kill them for whatever reason suited him. I couldn't do anything about that. They had been betrayed, would be betrayed again. All I could do was watch and testify. And get away from them as if they had a disease. I had that disease too. We all have and we deny it as we get in or out of each other's way towards a private destiny. No place is better than any other. Long or short steps take us there. We make chance companions. I could still feel Loulou's firm handshake.

By late afternoon we reached the German border. I hid under the blankets in the rear. We were coming from another part of the Greater Reich, so the guards were perfunctory. After a while I sat in the front again and we belatedly introduced ourselves. His name was Hans von Tiefenthaler. I remembered Klaus had mentioned the von Tiefenthalers. The family had been regular visitors to Altenburg in the past. We rode through the Silesian Lowlands to the River Oder and Breslau. Built on the river, the city looked medieval, with canals, winding cobblestone alleys and gabled merchants' houses. The town hall was gingerbread Gothic, avalanche-angled roof, spires, gargoyles, busy decoration. Tiefenthaler parked on a street near the market square. He looked around.

"He should be here. There are no police. Something is wrong. I will phone."

He got out and walked towards the square. My eyes kept checking every shape and movement. Housewives with almost empty shopping bags hurried along. Some boys were taking turns kicking a ball against a wall. A window above opened and a man stuck out his head and hollered and they ran away. He stared down at me and then closed the window. The Horch had the whole street to itself. Tiefenthaler returned after fifteen minutes.

"The driver was possibly afraid. It was maybe his first time. Better to have one driver. The more drivers there are the more chance of something going wrong. But you are traveling a long way. The plan has been changed. I will drive you to Nuremberg. I have cans of petrol in my trunk to get there. You are to stay overnight. Another driver has been found to take you to the border tomorrow."

"Let me pay for your gas," I said, handing him some Reichsmarks.

Heading west, we skirted the mountains of Moravia and Bohemia to the south, entering a valley on the River Elbe and Dresden, a stately baroque showpiece, with the Frauenkirche and Hofkirche near the river, along with the neo-Renaissance opera house. We drove through in the fading light. On the outskirts Tiefenthaler filled the tank. We made good time on the autobahn south to Nuremberg. It was after ten when we arrived and Tiefenthaler took almost an hour in the blackout to find the right house. The front door opened quickly to his knock. Quiet words and we were inside. In the dim entrance I was introduced to Albrecht, a stocky man carrying a flashlight. He told us we would be sleeping on cots in the spare room upstairs. We climbed the narrow stairs, led by Albrecht's flashlight beam. The spare room was tiny, with space enough for the cots only because a battered chest of drawers and steamer trunk had been shoved into a corner. Albrecht left and Tiefenthaler said he would be leaving at dawn. I put down my valise and thanked him for his help and we shook hands. He wished me luck. I dropped onto a cot, using my overcoat as a blanket. The last thing I remember was Tiefenthaler saying I would be taken to the Swiss border west of Lake Constance, near the town of Schaffhausen. Which side is it on? I thought before falling asleep in an Alpine meadow.

"The Swiss side," Albrecht told me in the kitchen the next morning. I was eating a pretzel. His wife had made some. She left for church before I came downstairs. I had slept late.

"I have never been there, but to the lake, the Bodensee, yes. The land at that end is mostly fields and meadows."

In the morning I saw Albrecht had a round face with jowls. He smoked a clay pipe and was wearing a blue serge suit. His Sunday best? I asked him when the driver would arrive. He shrugged his shoulders and I wondered what he did know.

"Have you worked with him?"

He shook his head.

"This was arranged late yesterday."

"Have you done this before?"

"Once. I think he got through."

I changed the subject.

"What part of Nuremberg is this?"

"Altstadt."

"The Old Town."

"The Kaiserburg is above us, at the top of the hill. You can see the whole city."

I waited much of the day, mostly in the kitchen. Albrecht's wife, Eva, returned and offered me an apple strudel. She apologized for not having any coffee to go with it. The strudel was more than enough and delicious, I told her. Not the best, she said. Not like before the war. Nothing ever is, I said. She was plump, with a rosy complexion and taller than her husband.

In the late afternoon husband and wife began looking at each other. They weren't going to get stuck with me? From a fugitive I was turning into an undeserved burden. They were a way station, not a home for the unwanted wanted. We all began secretly cursing the unknown driver.

At four there was a series of taps on the front door. I went upstairs to get my valise. When I came down Albrecht was holding the door ajar. The driver was back in the car. I looked around for Eva and Albrecht said she wasn't feeling well. I was the hunted. They were still good Germans in the eyes of the Gestapo. And no eyes counted more or more often. Out the door to the car, noting the house was timber-framed, white plaster with carnation red trim. Nearby houses were similar, with different color trim, or were sandstone, all with steep roofs. What you notice when trying to get out of the Third Reich.

My new driver was nervous, obviously dragooned at the last minute. He lit one cigarette with the butt of the last, sometimes taking his eye off the road. He didn't say anything except swear once when he burnt his fingers trying to light a cigarette. His driving was uneven, either too fast or too slow. The boxy two-door sedan was a dozen years past its prime. The differential clunked and the transmission chattered with every shift. The loose tappets sounded like a demonic sewing machine when the engine was under load. I counted myself lucky I hadn't looked at the tires. The roads became narrower and empty of traffic. I was preoccupied with possible what-ifs but noticed that Bavaria, like East Prussia, wasn't choked with the uniforms, staff cars, swastika flags and banners everywhere in Berlin. It was almost possible to forget there were people waiting for you to make that one mistake that ensured their jobs.

It was early evening. The engine sounded ready to blow a gasket or throw a piston as it took yet another curve or incline. The driver stopped on a dirt road beside the steep bank of a hill. He spoke quickly.

"At the top is a field. The border."

"Is there a fence? Guards?"

"I told you what I know."

He kept glancing around. I got out.

The car lurched away, rattling down the road. The noise faded and I stood in the silent twilight. I looked at my valise and had one of those moments of enlightenment that let you know how stupid you really are. Hauling it up the hill would slow me down, and suppose I had to run? I opened it and took out my money, documents, the T4 codes and information and Loulou's package. I stuffed everything into my coat and jacket pockets and hid the valise under a clump of yellow broom on the bank. I scrambled up the bank. I could hear the soles of my brogues scraping against loose pebbles. At the top I had a clearer view. The hill was covered in heather and clusters of wild grass with leaves like dusty green spearheads. I checked my coat pockets for my flashlight and the pistol. I knew they were there but it was comforting to feel them. I thought about the Luger. The only gun I had ever fired was my cousin's .22 rifle when I was a kid. Maybe there was no fence and no guards. He said a field. Walk across and that's it. My throat felt dry, I was thirsty. I was tense, wanting to get it done. I began to climb, not looking up for a long time, feeling as if the longer I didn't look the faster I would get to the crest. When I looked the crest was near. I hurried the rest of the way.

At the top there was no field. A subalpine meadow sloped away, with gentian and heather between tufts of grass, and an occasional sycamore. There were strands of barbed wire stretched along the ground at the height of about a foot. I didn't count the strands. The driver had dropped me off in the wrong spot. I considered my options. Look for the field. Hide and wait for the guard and time the interval. Start crawling. I opted for crawling. I could get under the wire if I wrapped my coat tightly around me. I pulled out the Luger and took off the safety catch.

"Halt."

I froze for a second before whirling around to see where the voice came from and seeing a shape running alongside the wire in the fading light. I knelt, holding the Luger in front of me with both hands. The shape stopped running. I heard the crack of a rifle shot and a bullet whizzed over my head. I got off four rounds blindly and heard a yell and started crawling under the wire, holding onto the Luger. The yelling continued and I knew other guards would come. The barbs tore at my coat as I pulled myself along. I smelled dirt and grass and maybe the wild flowers on the other side. I cursed the guard for yelling, cursed the wire, cursed my luck and cursed to keep going. I heard voices over my hoarse breathing and broken curses. I thought this is it, a bullet in the back. They don't like it if you shoot one of them. Crawl, crawl, crawl, crawl. One strand after another. How many could there be? Who thought of barbed wire? Who thought of borders? What was I doing there? Why? Gossamer twilight to cover me. Ovals of light swept along the ground and over the wires. Rifle fire, bullets tearing at the wire and kicking up turf. The last wire and I tore my fingers getting under it. I kept crawling, mad elbows and knees across the lumpy ground, grass and heather in my mouth. I crawled to a sycamore, got behind the trunk, lungs heaving and sucking air.

No more rifle fire. The voices sounded far away. I was in Switzerland. I took out the flashlight and looked. My hands were cut and bleeding, the Luger smeared with dirt and bits of grass. I thought of Julia. I owed her one. A German shot with a German gun by an American who took it off an American who had received it as a gift from a Luftwaffe ace. Figure that one out. I couldn't figure anything. I listened as my breath rasped my throat like a file.

After resting for ten minutes I began walking down the slope. It was dark and I needed the flashlight. The sky was clear, there were stars and a quarter moon. I hid the Luger under a rock. I kept walking until I saw the lights of a town hovering like fireflies in the night. I knocked on the door of the largest house and a man smoking a meerschaum opened it. I said in German that I was American and wanted to turn myself in to the authorities. He said he was the mayor of Schaffhausen and would get somebody to drive me to Zurich.

# Berne

Two and a half hours later I was in Zurich, sitting in front of a desk and talking to a police official. On the desk were my passport, travel permit to East Prussia, news agency accreditation, Propaganda Ministry identity card, various press passes and a folded wad of Reichsmarks. The official, a German Swiss, was observing my dirty face, torn coat and cut hands. I fought off fatigue by trying to decide if he had a mustache or that was dried cocoa on his upper lip.

"Early this evening there was a disturbance at the border. A fugitive wounded one of their guards."

"Everyone is considered a fugitive when he wishes to leave Germany. I came here to work. Phone my bureau in Berne. Ask for Thad Wegener."

He didn't look bothered about the German guard. I found out later there were occasional skirmishes between Swiss and German border guards. He phoned the number I gave him. Thad was in his office working late and to the official's questions gave loud affirmatives I heard. I was handed the phone.

"Jim? Great to hear from you."

"What you feel I feel to the power of ten."

"Rough, huh?"

"I had to turn down an invitation. Use an extra hand?"

"You bet. I'll get on to the legation, fix things up for you."

"I'll be there tomorrow. After I get some sleep."

We said goodbye. I handed the receiver back and the official, still looking at my clothes, allowed himself a smirk.

"Your appearance is unusual for a correspondent."

"Soap is rationed in Germany."

I stayed overnight in a small hotel. I was asleep when I hit the mattress. After a shower the next morning I ate a big meal of ham and eggs with a double order of sauerkraut in the hotel restaurant. A local laundry did a good job cleaning my coat. My hands were healing. Thad went to the American Legation, which contacted the Zurich police, and that afternoon I was on a train to Berne. I was granted permission to work in Switzerland. It felt strange to live again in a free country, no lockstep idolatry and lies, no green Gestapo vans speeding with suspects through hunted streets. No blackouts or air raids, no propaganda posters or swastika flags. But Swiss neutrality wasn't a simple matter. Behind the yodeling and alpenhorns lurked foreign agents and their dirty deals.

The relationship between the Swiss and Nazis was cozy but uneasy. German trains were allowed to pass through to Italy with food and other non-military items. But the boxcars were sealed. That was part of the agreement. The Swiss relied on German coal and steel, and Swiss exports passed through Axis territory. Some of these exports, such as timing devices for bombs, were destined for the Wehrmacht. A number of high-ranking Swiss military and government officials were pro-Nazi. But fighters would attack Luftwaffe planes violating Swiss air space and some were shot down. There were aerial confrontations with the Allies, and bombers were forced to land in Switzerland. Others landed because they were out of fuel or badly shot up. The Swiss National Bank exchanged Swiss francs for Reichsbank gold and the Third Reich used the francs to buy raw materials, including minerals, from neutrals. Much of the gold had been looted from conquered nations. The neutrals knew what was going on. It was the worlds of business and statecraft winking at each other. For the ordinary Swiss there was food rationing, though not as severe as in Germany. Additional land was cultivated and there was enough for farmers to give extra to relatives and friends. I was to receive a few surprises but that was after I had settled in.

My first days in Berne were spent looking for a pension. I found one with a large comfortable room and I could leave the drapes open all night. I cabled the T4 information for Sophie to New York. I wrote Mina and Loulou, adding a postscript. The message read: "I am having a good time. Bratwurst and pumpernickel were *wunderbar.*" Loulou's package contained chunks of bratwurst between slices of buttered pumpernickel. It was worth its trip under the wire. I called the number in Zurich and identified myself to the woman who answered. I said to tell Mina and Loulou that I would send and receive messages through that address. The family name was Gottschalk. Frieda, the woman I spoke with, said they used a code for secret information. She would give it to me when I came to Zurich. It would be too risky to send through the mail.

Thad Wegener was easygoing. He knew Europe well enough to know he shouldn't let it get to him. Europe could go any way it wanted, its nationalities connive against and betray one another, but as long as he could go trout fishing he was happy. The other correspondent in that bureau was Dillard Saltonstall, who wore bow ties, suspenders and straw hats. His wife Barbara came to the office regularly. They were, one of the secretaries told me, "very much in love and almost ten years married." The two secretaries were middle-aged French Swiss and doubled as assistants. They loved chocolate and coffee, dipping the one into the other. The Saltonstalls would share a cup of coffee and a single piece of chocolate. When he wore his polka-dot bow tie she wore her polka-dot blouse. She called him "Dilly."

Thad had been asking for help when I showed up. We shared the workload. Thad preferred the diplomatic stuff, attending legation parties and receptions, picking up information and sifting through rumors. Dillard covered the war news. I went through newspapers and magazines and listened to radio broadcasts and also did feature stories on the POWs, refugees and the Swiss internment camps. For Allied POWs conditions weren't too bad as long as they didn't try to escape. They were kept in hotels initially but those who were caught escaping were transferred to prison camps, some of them run by Nazi sympathizers. I was not allowed to visit prison camps but got the truth from an escapee.

Early one evening two months after I arrived I got a call from Frank

297

Ambrose, the military attaché at the American Legation. They were hiding an American pilot who had escaped from one of the prison camps. I drove over and interviewed him. In his early twenties, Bill Carrothers looked well below draft age, as if he should have been pitching hay and slopping the hogs back on the farm. His B17, hit by flak and slowed down, ran low on fuel and he had been forced to land at a Swiss airfield. He told his story quickly and offhandedly. The Swiss had put him and his crew in a hotel.

"The hotel was OK. Food was all right. One of the guys said, nice way to sit out the war. I didn't say anything. We'd taken enough chances. You can only fly so many missions before the odds get you. But I didn't want to hang around. I'm no hero but I figured a lot of other guys were still taking chances. Well, to make a long story short, I tried to escape and was caught and they sent me to a camp. The commandant was a real bastard, a Nazi-lover. I heard he had a picture of Hitler in his office. They kept me and the others in cold barracks and we were half-starved. I knew if I didn't escape I'd come down with something serious or even die. I had to do it before I lost more of my strength. It was raining pretty hard one night and I slipped out of the barracks. I didn't see any guards. I crawled under the wire and headed for a road. I found one and walked at night and slept during the day until I reached the city and turned up here."

I typed out his story from my notes. I took it to Thad, who read it and shook his head.

"We have a ticklish problem here, Jim. If we tell the whole story, or even a substantial part of it, we're personae non gratae with the Swiss authorities. We need their cooperation. I'm as news-hungry as the next reporter but I think we have to let this one go. What the hell, he can write a book about it after the war is over."

Ambrose drove Carrothers to the French border, where the Maquis met them. They got him back to England. A year later we heard that his B17 was shot down over Berlin. The crew was lost.

After Berlin Berne was a sedative. That was until Julia found me. I should have guessed she would come to play in Switzerland. No phone call. She came to the office. It was a sunny day near the end of July. The office windows were open, a soft breeze floating in with the smell of roses. It was the kind of day when you can't imagine anything ever going wrong with the world. I was alone, working the Saturday shift. The secretaries didn't work weekends. Julia walked in and sat down in front of my desk. I had my feet up and promptly took them down. I hadn't forgotten how beautiful she was. It was being reminded that did the trick. She was all in white, sweater, skirt, jacket, shoes, dinky purse. Still the bangs, the slyly playful eyes. And no preliminaries.

"I'm getting married."

It shouldn't have meant that much. But I had to respond in kind.

"I hope your mother is happy."

She didn't skip a beat.

"In two months. I thought I'd tell you, seeing as how we know each other so well."

"We do, don't we?"

She crossed her legs. I had to look.

"Don't you want to know who he is?"

"Not really."

"Don't tell me you're jealous?"

"I know why you've come. But what are you doing in Berne?"

"I'm giving a recital."

"You need that edge to your performance."

"Something like that."

"You're still Mamma's little girl, one hand holding hers, the other free to play."

Nothing was going to stop her saying what she came to say.

"He's a friend of the flyer I told you about. They came to a concert. He's a genuine ace. His father is an industrialist. We have to get permission to marry because he's an Aryan but I'm not. It's a formality. My mother and I are considered friends of Germany. She said his family has money but I'm an artist."

"That you are."

We stared at each other. She uncrossed her legs.

"Guess I'll be going. I've got to practice."

"I thought you were."

"That's done. I needed some experience. You were it. It was nice."

She stood up.

"Goodbye."

"You forgot to tell me how handsome your flyer is."

"Is that necessary?"

Turning her head, she gave me a three quarter shot of her staring out of the window. She thought she would finish me off by taking a deep breath in that so tight sweater.

"Guess not. Those roses you smell are going to remind me of you."

That got her. She was stranded for a moment. She could never be a real bitch. There was too much of the mixed-up girl about her. Spoiled, bullied, unsure, lovely. There was no more to say. She turned and left. I was looking at an empty chair. I got up and shut the windows. I couldn't stand the smell of roses.

In August I went to Zurich to meet Frieda Gottschalk. The Gottschalks were a prominent family of bankers living in a nineteenth-century mansion in Hottingen, a wealthy district of the city. Frieda worked for the Red Cross and various Swiss charities. She was plain and used no makeup but would wear small earrings of black onyx, usually set with a single pearl. She would invariably have a loosely tied silk scarf around her neck. She had lived in England and spoke with a posh British accent. The first time I showed up the butler gave me a once-over and frowned. But I was expected, like bad weather. With a pout he opened the door enough for me to enter. Frieda was waiting in a reception room, where she was writing letters at an escritoire. She stood up and came over and we shook hands. With a wave of her hand she pointed to a couch that was the equal of any piece of furniture at Altenburg. Several feet away was its companion and she lowered herself onto a cushion as if it had been made with her backside in mind. In demeanor and behavior she was the closest the Swiss Confederation ever gets to producing an aristocrat. No danger, though, of cross contamination. It would interfere with making money. Frieda was the kind of woman who could make you forget that she was plain, but not enough for permanent amnesia unless you were into high finance.

"Did you have a pleasant trip, Mr. Brian?"

"The train wasn't attacked and I wasn't arrested."

"You're a little different."

"From what?"

"The usual American reporter doggedly in search of a scoop."

"I'm a foreign correspondent. The reality isn't glamorous. The people are as varied as in any other trade. It's the news business, guaranteed to destroy illusions."

"And yet you stay in it."

"I don't have a house like this."

"I don't feel I have to apologize."

"Neither do I."

"Perhaps we should get to the business you're here for. I've made a copy of the code Mina, Loulou and I use. It's in an envelope I'll give you when you leave. The plan is for you to correspond through this address. Any letters I get for you I will forward to your office. All letters will be addressed to me, as usual, but there will be a mark on the ones meant for you. A nom de plume would be advisable. Any questions?"

"What kind of mark?"

"A small cross. Almost invisible."

"Not an x?"

"No, a cross."

"If you don't mind my asking, how did you meet the sisters?"

"We have friends in common."

I was tempted but held back. She was doing this for Mina and Loulou and a not-so-perfect stranger. There was no sense in making an enemy. She smiled her all-purpose society smile, the one you get whether you deserve to be on the guest list or not.

"Would you like a cup of coffee? Or a drink?"

"Do you have any bourbon?"

"As a matter of fact we do."

She stood up, pulled a cord next to the window drapes and the butler came. Bourbon for me and coffee for her. The butler left, curling his lips at me in a sneer hidden from his boss. She put a finger to her chin.

"Is this acceptable? Mixing alcoholic and non-alcoholic beverages. It's not, strictly considered, a social occasion. But I'm certain it's a faux pas in somebody's etiquette book."

"Take a day off. Put your feet up."

The butler did one exemplary thing in service in that house. He brought the bottle. After a few good shots Frieda looked not half bad. And she was getting perky. Coffee was doing to her what bourbon was doing to me.

"If you Swiss were as free with your money as you are with democracy, you'd be better."

"We are. Look at the Red Cross. If people want to put their money in Swiss banks, are we to blame? We have to make a profit, or are you a Red?"

"Nope, I'm a gray."

"What's that?"

"The color of damp newsprint."

"Did you say damn?"

"No, but I'll take it."

An hour later we had lapsed into silence, having solved none of the world's problems. I had one of my own when I stood up to go. She poured me a cup of coffee. I said a walk in the fresh air would sober me up. How to get outside? She steered me into the garden. A few minutes navigating between her rose bushes and I was ready. We said goodbye at the front door.

"Please come again, Mr. Brian. I enjoyed our chat."

"I think you mean it."

"Are you quite sober?"

"I'm never quite anything. Sober people never tell the real truth behind the truth."

"Nevertheless, please do."

"I always do."

"I mean come."

"That I will. Have you heard about the mouse who lives on the holes in Swiss cheese?"

"How does he do that?"

"He makes them himself."

She handed me an envelope.

"Don't lose it."

"Or I'll catch it."

"You mean trouble?"

"No, a code."

"Oh, that's clever."

"Trying to cut me with British sarcasm. My cue to exit."

"No, I assure you—."

"Don't assure me. My jokes are bad enough."

I went fishing with Thad a few times but I wasn't devout in my observance of the rites of the angler. I was more interested in scenery than trout. And it was a good time to catch up on my sleep. Thad was too busy being absorbed in his own pleasure to spend time indoctrinating me. Once I awoke from a dream and rocked the boat and he told me he lost the biggest fish he had seen in years. The dream was about Julia. Mrs. Fusco had a hand in it too. When I explained the dream was about a woman, he nodded. Bound to rock the boat, he said. But that fish haunted him for days.

In September Thad called me into his office.

"You're going to receive an invitation to Dillard and Barbara's party this weekend celebrating their tenth anniversary. I haven't seen you at any of their get-togethers that I've managed to attend. I know they would appreciate your going to this one. For the sake of office harmony I'm asking you to go. You can do what you want after this."

Thad drove me there. He didn't want to risk my backing out at the last minute. Long-established connections with high-ranking officials meant he never had any trouble getting petrol for essential purposes and to him the distance and occasion qualified. He picked up our secretaries, Jeanne and Marie, as well. Both unmarried, they spoke of our hosts as an idyllically happy couple. The Saltonstalls lived in a chalet on the outskirts of Berne. Very Alpine chalets, with overhanging eaves looking like a wooden snowbonnet. It stood on a hill among a grove of silver fir. We arrived at eight. It was the last Saturday in September. The evening air was crisp and tangy with the smells of autumn. The other guests were already there. As we walked up the gravel path towards the front door I could hear muffled party noises coming from inside the house. The hubbub was broken by a high-pitched woman's voice, closely followed by a man's loud one, both too surprised by something to be surprised. It was going to be a long evening.

The brass knocker had been molded to look like edelweiss. Thad touched the Swiss national flower gingerly and gave the front door two light taps that were lost among the gabble going on inside. The door opened much too quickly. Our host stood there in an Alpine getup complete with lederhosen, H-shaped suspenders, knee-high white stockings and a feather in his hat.

"Come in, folks. Everybody else is already here. I'll help you with your coats, Mademoiselle Jeanne, Mademoiselle Marie. You guys can hang up your own. The cloakroom is over there."

He nodded to our left. A couple of minutes later we were ready to be led up a narrow wooden staircase built against the right wall.

"Follow me, folks. You haven't been here before, have you, Jim? I know you like to knock it back. Remember, you're among moderate drinkers tonight."

I glanced at Thad, who was rolling his tongue around his teeth. We climbed in single file. There were two large rooms upstairs. The one closer to the stairs looked like an anteroom, with chairs and a sofa against wood-paneled walls hung with prints of mountain landscapes. Through an archway leading off it to the right was a dining room with table and chairs and leaded glass windows looking out on the fir grove. Most of the dozen guests were in the anteroom and chatting in informal groups. Dillard introduced Jeanne, Marie and Thad to the other guests. He didn't bother introducing me. That suited me. Thad would understand when I left early. I wondered about Dillard's studied insolence since he had opened the door, put it down to petty resentment at my turning down previous invitations. My time in Berlin and my escape from Germany had interested the secretaries and Thad but Dillard hadn't said a word. Thad never invited him to go fishing, but he probably wouldn't have gone without Barbara. Thad's reluctance stemmed from an angler's instinct. All that billing and cooing among the polka dots would have scared off the fish.

I resolved not to touch a drop and to phone for a taxi as soon as possible. There was a cuckoo clock on the wall near the archway to the dining room. I went over and leaned against the wall. I felt some sympathy for that poor bird, going through an act on cue. Minutes later Dillard brought some guests over to stand in front of the clock.

"We decided to go Swiss when we got here three years ago. This wonderful timepiece is part of that. It's the whimsical part of the Swiss craft that goes into the world's finest watches. It touches your heart with the sound of spring, doesn't it?"

I grinned. He frowned.

"Something funny, Jim?"

"You sound like a bad commercial. The cuckoo clock originated in the Black Forest, not here."

"Don't be a wet blanket. It's one big world, isn't it?"

"You asked, I answered."

"Have you been drinking?"

"Do you see a glass?"

"You could have sneaked some."

"I don't sneak."

One of the women in the group, a middle-aged American, upbraided me.

"You've ruined our enjoyment. It's a Nazi clock."

"I don't think clocks have political opinions. But on its next appearance that bird might be commenting on yours."

She glared. Dillard led the group to the landscape prints. Thad came over. He was munching a gherkin on a toothpick and holding a bottle of beer.

"Sparks flying, huh? What's going on with Dillard tonight, anyway?"

"The same as any time, not much."

Thad finished his gherkin and took a swig of beer.

"He introduced the secretaries and me to the other guests. A dull bunch. To tell you the truth I've only been to one of these. I asked you to come tonight because I couldn't face this alone."

"What about Jeanne and Marie?"

"They're here for the coffee and cake."

"I thought they adored the loving couple."

"That's for you to hear. I went out and bought an anniversary gift from all of us. It's in the car. I better go get it."

I looked at my watch. Half past eight and the minute hand crawling like a grasshopper on one leg. Barbara came from downstairs looking for help bringing up plates and silverware. I ducked into a small room at the back of the anteroom. There was an upright piano, a stool and some sheet music on the top of the piano. I turned on a table lamp, shut the door and picked up some of the sheet music. After seeing "Home on the Range," "Get Along Little Dogie" and "In the Good Old Summertime" I put the pile down. Dillard made an announcement in the anteroom.

"Could I have your attention, please, everybody? Barb, as some of you may know, has been taking yodeling lessons for the past few months. We thought it would be rather fun if she entertained us with a sample of her singing. I think you're going to be pleasantly surprised. If you're ready, Barb, I'll put on the record now."

The sound of a wheezy wind band came through the crackling and thumps of an old recording. Barbara's shrieking soprano joined in. It wasn't singing, it was crying for help. She was lost in the Alps and slowly losing strength. The St. Bernard wasn't anywhere close by. The needle got stuck in a groove and the same few bars kept repeating themselves. Barbara was on her own and getting more frantic until Dillard moved the needle. The music finished first, Barbara came a distant second and the applause a tired third. I opened the door and saw Dillard kissing Barbara's bowed head. Thad went searching for, I presume, another gherkin. Jeanne and Marie were sneaking peeks into the dining room. I looked at my watch.

Barb's garb. She had gone Swiss too. White peasant blouse, embroidered laced bodice, black full dirndl skirt, bleached and braided hair, sturdy clop-clop shoes. Yodeling accessories.

It was time for presents. The faces of our hosts present tense. Expectant eyes. Thou hast something? Thad was first up. "From all of us at the office." They unwrapped a fondue pot. Barbara gave him the proverbial peck on the cheek. Dutiful gratitude. Thad was lucky. There were two more fondue pots.

As well as a cuckoo clock, gift-wrapped cheeses, French and German wines and cartons of cigarettes. "We don't smoke," Dillard doing the Puritan. "Maybe Jim can use these." Thad jumped in. "Jim stopped smoking." The last gift was two bottles of blackberry cordial, brought by the woman who had objected to my unmasking of Nazi clocks. Dillard glanced at me. My look said, there's twenty feet between us and it'll be the shortest distance in your life if you open your yap. "What a surprise. Wherever did you find these, Madge?"

A sudden singing of "Happy Anniversary," the tune "Happy Birthday." Two of the women carried in a large cake on a platter. On the cake were ten lit candles. The smells of flaky French pastry, butter icing and vanilla extract filled the anteroom. The cake was carried into the dining room. Barbara and Dillard blew out the candles together. Palms clapped in time to each other and the usual encouraging remarks. I stayed by the archway. Speech obligatory. Dillard obliged.

"A big thanks to all of you. I want to say that without Barb's love and support I wouldn't be where I am today. From pumping gas in Oshkosh to foreign correspondent is a long way. It's been rocky at times but together we got through. The little woman—."

Voice wobbled. He blinked. Two fat tears slid down his cheeks. He lowered his head. Barbara's arm around his shoulder now. Thad uncomfortable. "Let's have a piece of that cake." Jeanne and Marie perked up. The best French pastry. They bought it in Geneva. Barbara did the honors. A few minutes later Thad said with his mouth full, "Aren't you having any?" I grinned. "The working press needs bread. Don't tell it to eat cake." Dillard said, "Didn't—?" I shook my head.

Fifteen minutes of clinking coffee spoons and dessert forks later Dillard said the obvious to the guests, standing or sitting around the dining room.

"We've eaten our dessert before our dinner."

Barbara came up to him and kissed him on the cheek. She kissed him the way a busy nurse puts a bandage on a longtime patient.

"It's a special occasion, Dilly. We're breaking the rules this one time."

They were the only two in costume but Dillard's hat was on the table and

Barbara had taken off her clodhoppers and was going barefoot. Alpine retreat. Whispering between our hosts led to a last-minute change in menu. They announced that the food downstairs was too overcooked to eat and so they would be serving up the presents instead. Some cheese would be melted in a fondue pot and the bottles of wine would be opened. As many as needed. In announcing the change Dillard overdid it.

"Too bad about that roast. We're going to be denied Barb's great gravy. No use crying over it. Why be greedy and keep all this good stuff you've given us? Besides, it would take us months to go through it all."

Two of the guests exchanged a what-cheap-bastards look. The faces of others showed curiosity as to the exact state of the roast. Jeanne and Marie finished off the cake. Dillard hurried over, arriving in time to see an empty platter. Thad didn't make him feel any better. He could have approached him later in private. He spoke in front of everybody.

"Since you're using up all this stuff and you two don't smoke, you may as well hand over those cigarettes to me. I can use them at the office to give smokers."

"I was—," Dillard said, ready to dig himself a hole. Offering me the cigarettes had been an empty gesture as well as a gratuitous dig. The whole office knew I had stopped smoking. Dillard wanted to sell the cigarettes for a good price. Thad figured that too. Barbara, smarter, knew they were done for.

"We were going to suggest exactly that, weren't we, Dilly?"

Enough cheese was melted in one of the pots and Dillard uncorked the wine. Announcing stale bread was better for a fondue, Barbara brought up a loaf and cut it into cubes and handed out forks. I maintained my vow of abstinence from food and drink. I was sitting with Jeanne and Marie at the other end of the table from the pots. Disdaining to nibble on their cheese-covered cubes, they let them coagulate into rubbery blobs. Barbara brought a fork to me.

"Don't be hanging back there, Jim."

"I'm feeling a little sick to my stomach."

"It's not contagious, is it?"

"Strictly personal."

She stiffened and walked away. Jeanne smiled and nodded and Marie gave me a thumbs up. Their low voices on the repast. "Insulting. Disgraceful. Their anniversary too. How cheap." Jeanne nodded at Marie. "Our cake was good." They grinned.

"I feel like a cannibal eating my own gift" from a guest staring down at her cube.

"I can smell the meat," a heavyset man sniffed.

His wife shook her head at him.

Thad turned down the wine and asked for blackberry cordial. "Wine would be easier on your stomach," Dillard said, looking at the wine already open. "Open the cordial," Barbara snapped. After pouring a good shot and downing it, Thad smacked his lips. "If I'd known you two were that hard up, I'd have brought some trout."

The heavyset man alert, "Did somebody mention trout?"

Wife pulling at his sleeve, "You're hearing things."

"Cuckoo." Ten, repeating the obvious to the oblivious. By the last everyone was filing out of the dining room. "You're not leaving already?" Dillard was corking the bottles that weren't empty. Barbara eyed the remaining cheese in the pot. Thad wasn't a drinker. Two good shots and he was merry, too merry to drive. I drove, dropping off Jeanne and Marie. After dropping Thad off, I headed for the office to put in the overnight shift. The last thing he said was, "Dillard didn't give me the cigarettes."

In October I met Frieda in Berne at a reception given by the Swedish Legation. The minister's daughter was having a birthday party. Thad had received an invitation but he was busy getting ready for an upcoming fishing trip, so I got to sample the free food. There she was, earrings and scarf, and at her side a wet-looking specimen of Aryan officerhood whose blond waves were receding with the Nazi tide. She glanced at me through the crowd of munchers, sippers and tongue-waggers. It was meant to be brutally brief, though I kept eating my something on a rye cracker. Food before intrigue, at least with Frieda. She wound her way over, as women will do, and cornered me between a pair of diplomats in matching cummerbunds.

"I believe we've met."

"Probably in my dreams."

Cruel. A plain woman knows she's plain but that glance couldn't go unpunished. Frieda took it well, eyebrows dismissing me as an uncultured American. Europeans have the exclusive rights to Western culture. That's why they're arguing with each other all the time, divvying up the credit.

"You are Mr. Brian, aren't you?"

"The last time I checked."

Too flippant. What was on that cracker?

"I must speak to you later."

Intrigue wrapped in its sticky tape. Her escort decided it was time. He had to say the obvious. Nazis were good at that.

"We are officially enemies now."

"That's what I've heard."

"You will be sorry. You were warned by the more farsighted among your own people to stay out."

"Didn't Hitler declare war on us?"

"After being provoked so many times. He has only so much patience."

"He seems to have run out of patience with everybody."

"The Führer cannot be expected to be bound by the limitations of lesser men."

"It must be terrible knowing that you should be ruling the world and a few blind fools refuse to let you."

"You will find out."

"You never will."

Frieda intervened.

"Come, Gunter. I must introduce you to some people."

A man with a slight limp came over to me. He held out his hand.

"Couldn't help overhearing. Mr. Brian, isn't it? Name's Clive Taunton. British military attaché. Royal Navy. Retired from active duty. Gimpy leg. I liked how you put Herr Deinhard in his place. He's my opposite number at the German Legation. Cross paths with the enemy at these things. I came for the smorgasbord."

"I'm used to his kind. I was a correspondent in Berlin until we got into the war."

"Run to type, don't they? You weren't interned, then?"

"I came here instead."

"Not allowed, of course."

"I had help."

"Makes a difference, doesn't it? Working here, are you?"

"With Thad Wegener."

"Good man. Talked with him. Does take angling seriously. Can't say I do."

"Neither do I."

He lowered his voice, glancing around to see if anybody was close enough to eavesdrop.

"One makes friends. During the Munich thing I met some Czechs. Kept in contact. You sound as if you're not averse to traveling at times. If you ever—."

"I'll remember that."

"Must circulate, earn my keep. Never know what you may find between a slice of Gruyère and a cracker. Somebody said there are sardines. Hope it's not another one of those damn unfounded rumors."

Wandering among the diplomatic set, I was approached by Harlow Knorr, commercial attaché at the American Legation. A backslapper and glad-hander, he was a big loud guy who had been head of sales for a manufacturer of farm machinery. He originally had been posted to London in the spring of 1939 but his wife wanted to get away when the war began. He used political connections to wangle a safe diplomatic post in Switzerland. He was shepherding around a thin white-haired man with a pale, almost translucent face. His eyes weren't quite any color. The closest would be the pale tan of paper when it's beginning to age. Those eyes had the steadiest gaze I have ever seen. They were the watchful eyes of a shark swimming in familiar, always hungry waters. Knorr caught a glimpse of me and brought the eyes over. I didn't know why, because he and I disliked each other from the moment we had met. The form was in good form.

"Hey there, Jim, enjoying the shindig? Want you to meet somebody important for once. This is Alois Furst, the international banker. They don't come any more international. Thought maybe he could teach you something about high finance. Stretch your mind a bit. I'll leave you two together. Got to see what Bernice is up to."

Furst dumped on me, he sauntered off.

"Obnoxious man," Furst said. "He sweats on one."

I grinned.

"Isn't he one of yours? The buy and sell gang."

"That man understands as much about finance as a donkey does about quantum mechanics. You seem out of place here."

"I'm substituting for my boss. He enjoys these things."

"Diplomacy must have its day. The word 'protocol' makes me smile. Diplomats make good accomplices. They know how to lie and take themselves seriously enough to believe they are important. They are always after the fact."

"That's their job, isn't it? To sharpen the blade and mop up afterwards."

"Exactly. A cover, as you would say, for reality."

"And what is reality?"

"Money, and those who have it and know how to use it to get what they want."

His lips twitched. He would have called it a grin. He glanced around. Nobody was near enough to overhear.

"Take the idea of neutrality. Staying out of it, as you would say. The reality is quite different. The current activity at the Ford and General Motors works in Berne? Repairing Wehrmacht trucks and converting their engines to burn wood gas. Ford is, I am told, repairing and converting two thousand. You will as an American appreciate the irony. As a Swiss banker I am not surprised. It is business. The business of being a neutral in a dangerous position."

"What about the people who are killed in this war?"

"They die sooner and sometimes more violently but that is a result of the conditions of war, nothing to do with finance. Contrary to what you may think, bankers do not stir up wars. We do what is right for us. We make money. When men become bellicose, why should we not make a profit?"

"Don't tell me you don't have a favorite in this one?"

Another grin.

"Whoever wins, we will not lose."

Another glance around.

"I assume you know about the Bank for International Settlements that meets in Basel? Of late I have represented Switzerland. The war has made no difference to us. We meet as usual. Representatives of the eight member nations, including the belligerents, deal with problems in international finance."

"With a view to improving the world of banks and corporations."

"It is the only world on offer unless you believe in communism. We make money, you make money."

"You make lots."

"Are you against profit?"

"I'm against gouging."

"A contentious word. We live well. We think we deserve to in view of our responsibility. There is nothing shameful in that. The common man is more generous to beggars and to the poor in general than we are. The common man has been and always will be intellectually and aesthetically incapable of appreciating the arts. We have always supported the arts and have encouraged science. Without these there would be nothing."

"There would be money."

His lips fidgeted with each other.

"Without science not as much. Without art not as enjoyable. Pleading for humanity is a waste of time. Most men enjoy violence, like being stupid and need to be told what to do. They look out at the world from the entrance of a cave. That is why we have laws, prisons, police and armies. That will not change. When the common man attempts to govern himself, he produces the Jacobin Reign of Terror, the Bolsheviks. We are not on an upward path toward more liberty, equality, and certainly not fraternity. We would need a different brain. One would have to be a blind dreamer to hope for that."

"You're undoubtedly a churchgoer and know your Bible. Christ threw the moneychangers out of the temple. They got rid of him. Or thought they did. I wonder if his anti-banking attitude had something to do with that. None of the great religious leaders had much to say about finance. They didn't seem to rank it highly. One of the lesser human activities, like going to the bathroom. I'm afraid the rest, Herr Furst, is abracadabra. Banking ethics is a contradiction in terms. Otherwise you wouldn't be a conduit for gold and the other loot the Nazis stole from conquered countries or have recognized the puppet regimes they've set up. No doubt when the Nazis Götterdämmerung themselves, you and your fraternity will be there to supervise the next order of business. You'll be there when our species destroys itself, not entirely uninvolved in our demise. The only things surviving you will be various bacteria, viruses and spores."

That was the last I saw of Furst.

At the unofficial official end, when the important people leave, Frieda returned and we talked in a corner of the reception room.

"I have a letter. I was going to mail it but since I was coming to Berne I thought I would bring it to your office. Tomorrow? If you aren't there I will leave it with somebody."

I noticed her escort lingering on the far side of the room.

"Your prime Aryan is staring this way."

"Being Swiss isn't easy. We must please everybody. It doesn't mean we like them all. It's business."

I wasn't in the office when Frieda dropped off the letter. One of the secretaries gave it to me. The elegant sweep of the evenly spaced letters of the address on the envelope meant the handwriting had to be Loulou's. The cross was on the back, in the center of the flap. It was two tiny scratches. If I hadn't been told I wouldn't have seen it. I read the letter in my office, the code handy. It was easier than any of those I had to use for T4. The first letter didn't contain anything that had to be in code. I didn't have to think up a nom de plume. Loulou had already picked one for me.

October 2, 1942

Dear Mr. Scriber:

We are happy to hear you are enjoying Switzerland. You must be a man of simple tastes indeed to praise bratwurst and pumpernickel. Perhaps it was the butter. Your travels doubtless increased your appetite.

Looking forward to hearing from you. Spare us a thought.

*Mit besten Grüßen,*

Loulou

The rest of Loulou's letters follow. Some parts had to be in code. For example, in references to the anti-Nazi conspiracy and the July 1944 bomb plot, "Altenburg" means "Germany" and "dinner party" refers to a meeting. The remainder may be inferred from their context or from details in the preceding narrative. Occasionally I have added a word or explanation in brackets.

In the beginning the postal services were sufficient. Frieda Gottschalk received and sent everything from and to Altenburg and later on to Königsberg. Loulou's letters were mailed or delivered personally to my office and mine were mailed to Frieda, inside another envelope, and she forwarded them to Loulou. Loulou sent the last two via the underground. Obviously the code was unnecessary.

February 16, 1943

Dear Mr. Scriber:

The news has come about Stalingrad. Dare anybody now doubt our inevitable victory? I have seen troop trains full of wounded in the Nordbahnhof. They are unannounced and the first time I saw one I did not know what it was. I went along the platform and looked. I saw bandaged heads and eyes, arms and legs in plaster casts and a forest of crutches. There were bodies wrapped like mummies, blood-soaked bandages, soiled uniforms and wrappings, disfigured faces. Any guards or officials were busy or I think I would have been ordered away. Medical personnel aid the soldiers. But the ones who can help each other off the train and they limp along the platform. Some are carried on stretchers to ambulances. The trains slide in silently, the medical staff is quietly efficient and the soldiers' eyes are vacant.

What right have I to say anything? I was raised with the ideals of duty and honour and have done nothing.

*Mit besten Grüßen,*

Loulou

March 20, 1943

Dear Mr. Scriber:

I have become a volunteer nurse in Königsberg. When I saw the suffering of our soldiers I knew I could not hide any longer at Altenburg, feeling sorry for myself. My training has made me helpful, I believe. Hours are long and the work is tiring. What others endure makes me go on. I am used to the blood, the terrible wounds, the screams of pain, and operations that look like a butcher's work. I have carried severed arms and legs in buckets like slop. I have administered morphine to make a last few hours bearable. The soldiers are brave lads. I look at them and think of Gerd and the others dead out there. And there will be many more before it is over. Sleepy old Königsberg, how long before your time will come?

I apologize for burdening you with this. But you are a correspondent and it is surely news.

*Mit besten Grüßen,*

Loulou

July 30, 1943

Dear Mr. Scriber:

Our mother has died. It was not a surprise. She was ill for months. I went home for the funeral and stayed as long as I could with Mina. I talked with Lotte and Klaus, who reminisced about the old days. I can see everything slipping away and something inside feels like a pain. I know it must go but I feel the dull knife of the parting. Pity the poor Junker, you may be thinking. But we are all prisoners of history. No class is exempt from good or evil. We must be accountable as individuals after all.

Write and tell me about jolly little Switzerland. I need to hear from another world.

*Mit besten Grüßen,*

Loulou

October 15, 1943

Dear Mr. Scriber:

Mina is busy with improvements to Altenburg. They involve a lot of planning and work. I worry about her health. She may be taking on too much, even for her. From what she tells me the few times I see her, the workers are too full of their own opinions by far.

The dinner parties go on. She is a good hostess, like our mother. There is still wine. Our cellar is well stocked. Apparently the conversation is lively, as you can well imagine, having attended a couple. There are enquiries about me. I am busy with bandages and bedpans and the more gruesome realities, they are told. Mina remains modest about herself [she continued refusing to be put on a list of officials in a post-Nazi government].

From your account of trout fishing with your bureau chief, you seem to have spent more time sleeping than trolling your line. Do Barbara and Dillard really share a piece of chocolate and one cup of coffee? How romantic. "Till germs do us part" was unkind, but I know you meant that humorously.

I had to laugh at your account of their anniversary party. Are you certain the roast was not burnt? I may be naïve but I cannot imagine they would do such a thing. Such behaviour is unheard of here. All the same I must admit I agree with you. It was "all of a piece," if I understand that phrase correctly. I am learning more American through these letters.

*Mit besten Grüßen,*

Loulou

January 7, 1944

Dear Mr. Scriber:

What a wonderful account of Frieda's Christmas party. She is known to be a man chaser. Are you really Frieda-proof? If she has not got you yet, you undoubtedly are. If that man is a baron and deep in debt, perhaps she has finally "landed a catch," as you put it. You are not "demeaning" yourself in relaying such "stupid gossip." I find it entertaining. Those onyx and pearl earrings were a gift from Mina and me when we stayed at her house one beautiful summer. She has been a guest at Altenburg. I find it amusing you escaped from Gustav after only half an hour listening to him expounding on international high finance. We had to endure that. How many times did we hear, "I make money and my daughter gives it away"? The best bourbon in Switzerland and you did not get drunk. Writing such a letter immediately after the party would clear you of that charge.

I had to spend Christmas at the hospital but did get home for *das Neujahr*. We had a few guests. Mina and I sat in our accustomed places. It was difficult for us to look at our mother's empty chair at the head of the table after so many years. Mina presided, delivering a tribute to her.

What will the new year bring?

*Mit besten Grüßen,*

Loulou

March 26, 1944

Dear Mr. Scriber:

I have had a most disturbing encounter with a certain Professor Dr. Lincke [Schliesman]. He is an ugly shrunken creature who fancies himself a ladies' man. He is full of opinions and considers himself an authority on everything. I think you know the type of man. He came to the hospital to talk with the administration concerning a doctor here. Apparently the doctor made some remarks in a lecture to medical students about all varieties of potato being essentially the same. The remarks got back to Dr. Lincke, who holds the opinion that white potatoes are the best and yellow, red and russet are inferior. Dr. Lincke is an influential man and the doctor has been dismissed. The doctor has been ordered to appear before the board of the Institute for the Cultivation of White Potatoes and will certainly be disciplined. Dr. Lincke demanded that the whole staff be questioned about its views on potatoes. He interviewed the nurses. At my interrogation I mentioned blue potatoes. Quite impossible, he said. They are sort of a dull purple blue, I said. Are their eyes blue? he said. No, like all other potatoes, I said. I knew it, mongrels, he said. You should not mention this to anybody. The less people know about those blue things the better. Have a glass of white wine, a great vintage, with me. Why not red? I said. Treasonable talk, he said, but if you take down your panties and sit in my lap I will not report you. Glaring at him I said, your blood is red, or more likely white, but mine is blue. I will report you if you ever speak to me again. An altogether distressing experience.

*Mit besten Grüßen,*

Loulou


June 11, 1944

Dear Mr. Scriber:

Great hope for Altenburg. We have heard that new workers are coming [D-Day]. Even if they do not arrive here, they will help others. When some are helped all are. I have spoken to Mina over the telephone. One must observe the pleasantries [wiretaps] in these conversations. She is very busy. I told her not to overextend herself. But she has only ever heard one voice, her own. Time seems short these summer days.

*Mit besten Grüßen,*

Loulou

August 1, 1944

Dear Mr. Scriber:

A calamity. The crops have failed. The harvest will be a misery for Altenburg. We must rely on our stores now. Many farmers and their families will go hungry this year [after the failed assassination attempt on Hitler in July many of the plotters were arrested]. We are in no immediate danger but this is small comfort. We must share with [help] those less fortunate to the extent we are able. What each day will bring no one knows. I am in regular contact with Mina. She rides Stürm daily, she tells me. There are no dinner parties any longer but the odd guest shows up unannounced on Mina's doorstep. The rumours of begging [torture] and starvation [execution] spread and we don't know what we should believe. Our people are decent and honourable. God protect them in their peril.

The talk among some is when, not if the Russians are coming. More defeats and Ostpreußen will be on the front line. Many in Königsberg condemn such talk as false and those who spread it as rumour-mongers who don't listen to or read the truth [censored radio and press]. But the rumours persist.

My work at the hospital keeps me from thinking about much else. Staff shortages are critical and I am sometimes needed as a nurse in surgery. My first time in surgery I thought I would faint. We all feel that way the first time, one of the regular surgery nurses said. The doctors call me the Countess of Mercy. They have names for many on the staff and have a bawdy sense of humour. It is their way of dealing with the strain of taking care of so many. The surgeons look dazed from fatigue.

All of the nurses except me have received proposals of marriage. None are taken seriously, though evidently two years ago a soldier in a wheelchair married a nurse. She has transferred to another hospital, so I have not met her. A nurse said the soldiers are in awe of me. It seems I am known as the Countess. I am the worst of the nurses, I told her. They are not in awe, they are afraid of me.

*Mit besten Grüßen,*

Loulou

November 28, 1944

Dear Mr. Scriber:

There is a folk tale about a wolf that, when his own pack seemed doomed, joined another. His new pack turned out to be sheep in wolf's clothing. When they failed to kill the wolf pack's leader the turncoat betrayed them to his old comrades. He led them in their desire for revenge, sniffing out the sheep for slaughter. He tried to prove his renewed loyalty by being more vengeful than his comrades. Victims were horribly mutilated. Their cries of agony were lost among the woods in which they were trapped and torn apart.

This folk tale has become a powerful legend. Many here believe that the pack roams the woods and fields hunting down defenceless victims, animal and human, killing them barbarously. Those who must go out alone in the blinding snow and freezing wind dread these winter nights. Even daylight offers little comfort to those who are by themselves, as so many are. The wolves are said to be especially hungry this winter. Their howls are heard across the frozen land, their thrusting muzzles within the circle of the moon. The turncoat is still leading the pack, selecting helpless victims for slaughter. I am told that at night you can see his hungry eyes reflecting the hoary moon as he slinks between the trees.

*Mit besten Grüßen,*

Loulou

[Frieda delivered the last letters personally to my office on January 4, 1945.]

321

December 18, 1944

Dear Scriber:

Mina *ist tot*—killed tonight. She was hiding in the woodcutter's hut on the estate. She had our father's pistol and the gamekeeper's rifle. I brought out her dinner, which I did whenever I came home in the last few weeks. After dinner we talked, huddled around the stove.

"They will find you here. We must go west to the Americans or south to Switzerland."

"I will not leave. This is my home."

"Do you want them to find you?"

"They are trespassers and I will kill them."

"Are you going to kill the Russians too?"

"You go. Save yourself."

"I will not leave you."

"Take the pistol then. I will use the rifle."

"I cannot shoot. I would be wasting ammunition. They could come at any time. How do you stand it, hiding out here and waiting?"

"It is my duty. I will not abandon Altenburg to a traitor. He has brought shame on us all. I will redeem the family honour."

"Nobody cares about such things any more."

"I do."

Through the four-pane window beside the door I could see the night sky was clear. Shadowy light from a lantern on the nearby table where Mina ate her meals made a pale mask of her face. The hut smelled of pine and sawdust. The handles of single and double-bladed axes, mattocks and picks leaned against walls and one and two-handed saws hung on brackets. The pistol and the rifle and boxes of ammunition were on planks across a pair of sawhorses. Nearby was the cot on which she slept. We were sitting on chairs we had pulled over to the stove. We talked of the past and she remembered an incident.

"When I first became a woman I brought a boy in here. He was one of the farm lads. I knew nothing about anything. I told him to do something. He began to bump against me. 'Stupid boy, what are you doing?' I said. 'You know nothing.' He began groaning, 'Miss Wilhelmina, Miss Wilhelmina.' His jaw dropped, his eyes widened and he slumped on to me. 'You stink of manure, get out,' I said. Frau Strittmatter, always spying on me, must have seen us leave. She told Mama, who had me called to the Gartensaal and told me to lift my skirt and bend over the table. She whipped me with a birch rod. 'I am sending for Dr. Schwerin. If you are not virgo intacta, you will be packed off. You are a young woman now and must never associate with those that are not of our class, you wilful daughter.' The doctor, with his big bald head, came to my room and examined me. Mama sent for me again. 'It is a good thing for you you are still a virgin. If you ever dare do anything like that again, I will whip you in front of the servants and disown you. You are a Junker. You must stay with your own class. Now come and kiss Mama.' 'Yes, Mama.'

"Mama told me I would become engaged to Gerd as soon as it was appropriate."

"Being engaged to someone of your own class will teach you how to behave."

"He is like a younger brother to me. I cannot love him."

"Very well. We will find someone else who is suitable. Louisa and the von Pommer boy will become engaged when she comes of age. She is a dutiful daughter and does what she is told."

"So I got Gerd because you rejected him?"

"You never loved him?"

"In a way I suppose I did. I never could say no to Mama. I found out he loved another woman. That was partly the reason I kept postponing our marriage."

"Who was the woman?"

"Viktoria."

"Fritz's Viktoria?"

"She did not take him seriously and she was so in love with Fritz. When she came to dinners and parties Gerd could not stop looking at her. He asked her to dance once and she turned him down. I knew he would have had an affair with her had she wanted one. She could never be unfaithful to Fritz. She knew I knew and she disliked Gerd for how he was making me feel. I think she felt sorry for me."

I thought I should tell Mina the rest. I had kept everything inside for so long. I knew I might never get another chance. And she had always been my confidante.

"Gerd had a mistress in Insterburg."

"How did you find out?"

"I was attending my first party there, in the house of his regimental commander. He was as stiff as a plank. Gerd introduced me to him. I forgot his name immediately. He bowed and left and Gerd went off to talk with a fellow officer. One of the senior officers came over and looked at my body as if I were a horse he was judging. He enjoyed a good mount, he said. Did I go riding? I said I needed some air and went outside on the balcony. Two officers came out to smoke and talk. It was dark and I had my back to them. I could hear them. 'Did you see Gerd's fiancée? What does he see in Warmuth's wife?' 'He gets nothing from the pretty filly. So he enjoys the old mare. He is not her first. Good old Warmuth is more interested in horses. He has no idea what has been going on with his wife.' 'Better for him if he never finds out. Better for all concerned.' 'Could be awkward, something like that going on in the regiment.' 'Not done, is it? Mistresses should be kept well away.' 'Lore is not the usual, is she?' 'Sexy woman. I need a drink.'

"They went inside and I stood and looked at the stars and felt like crying. I had grown up with Gerd and now he was like a stranger to me. We were engaged and I meant nothing to him except a respectable future wife. All arranged by Mama. Our bloodlines were all that mattered. I always wanted to be more than a Junker brood mare. My love for him, what I thought was love, became something else. I asked myself, had I ever been in love with him? What had I felt? A friendship. And that was gone now. If I had felt anything more, I could not have returned to the party. I saw them together, behaving very properly. Too properly, so I knew who she was. At least he did not have the effrontery to introduce her to me. He went to get her a drink. He bowed ever so slightly to her when they parted. You may think my noticing these things meant I was jealous. I wanted to see everything with clear eyes. I wanted to see what I had been blind to. First I found out he loved Viktoria. Then I discovered he was bedding a slut. If he does not love me, I thought, he is not worthy of me. I will never marry him.

"In the car after the party he whistled as he drove. He said we should get married soon. 'Why are you in a hurry?' I asked. 'No reason, but we should. What will people think?' 'Who cares what anyone thinks?' 'You seem upset, Louisa.' 'Things are not always what they seem.' He was too stupid to take my hint. He began whistling again. How could I have become engaged to a man who whistled instead of thought? When his mother phoned to tell me he had been killed my first thought was, it is finally over, a Russian bullet has done it."

"You would not eat for days after you got the news."

"That was as much for the wasted past we shared as it was for him."

"You never broke off the engagement."

"I hesitated because of Mama. I never wanted to disappoint her. I think she suspected the reason. She never asked why I would keep postponing my marriage."

"I disappointed her, rejecting all those suitors and sneaking off to Berlin."

"Did you ever love Anton?"

"It was pure sexual attraction between us. Neither of us could love and we both knew it. He loved his work. I love who I am."

"Does that mean you would never get married?"

"You can get married without being in love."

"You sound very much the Junker."

"I am a Junker. Duty first, as Mama used to say."

Through the silence of the cold night came the faint hum of a car a kilometre away, near the summer house. Mina stood up, put the lantern on the floor and went to the window.

"Within the half hour they will be here. I will show you how to reload the pistol and rifle. Hand me a gun when I ask. Stay close to the floor. Lie flat when not reloading. The outside light is good. I will get as many as I can. If an Altenburg dies well, the spirit never."

She took the stock of the rifle and began gently knocking the glass out of the panes. Cold air entered the hut. I began to tremble, more from my nerves than the cold. She showed me how to reload the guns. My shaking fingers made it difficult but after a few times I could manage. She blew out the flame in the lantern and we waited. It seemed so long but I kept checking my watch and a half hour later we heard the voices of men approaching. I recognized Berthold's voice, close and clear.

"She is certain to be in one of these places, I am telling you. That is the woodcutter's hut."

"Quiet," a harsh voice said. "You want to warn her?"

The voice dropped to a whisper. Mina was beside the window. She was holding the rifle. I held my breath. She put the barrel through the lower left corner of the window. I dropped to the floor and could hear several shots and a moan of pain and a quick cry like surprise. Other guns fired and bullets came through the window and door, splintering the wood and bouncing off the saws and axes. More shots, too many to count, and Mina yelled for the pistol. I crawled over and passed it to her. I pulled the rifle back with me and reloaded it, my fingers working automatically. More shooting, quiet periods, sometimes a single shot. A bullet glanced off a saw and passed close to my head. Lucky, I thought, without thinking about the danger. Nothing mattered except where the bullets went. Some time later Mina had the rifle again and must have hit a third man because only one gun was firing at us now. He seemed the best shot. I heard several shots together and Mina slumped to the floor and something cried out inside of me and I crawled over to her. She handed me the rifle and in a voice I could barely hear asked for the pistol. When the man fired again she made a loud groan, pretending to be dead, and crawled to the side of the door. Many minutes later, too many to count, there was a noise near the door. I could see the toe of a shoe or boot push the door slightly open. Mina shot up through the opening a few times and a body fell against the door, pushing it wide open, and landed beside her. The silence afterwards was louder than any shot. In a crouch I went to the window and peeked and saw bodies lying on the ground. I went outside, stepping over the man in the doorway. Two bodies were lying near the hut, a Gestapo agent and Berthold, and sprawled behind a pile of wood was another agent. Berthold had been shot through the mouth.

I remembered Mina and ran back inside. Stumbling over spent cartridges, I knelt beside her. Her chest had been torn open and she could hardly speak. I realized she was dying when she shot the last man. Her head in my lap, I cried as I spoke.

"You got them all, Mina. Him too, that *Schwein*."

"*Gut.*"

She never spoke again. Minutes later she died in my arms. I went to get Joseph and Klaus, who used planks from the stockpile beside the hut to make a pine box. We buried her deep in the woods where no one would find the grave. Digging the hard ground was difficult, though there had been a recent thaw and they brought a pick as well as shovels. Klaus made a small cross from sticks. They collected the other bodies and put them in the car. Joseph drove it to the main road and set fire to it, making it look like the work of Polish partisans.

I have not been able to sleep, though I am exhausted. I have written as much as I can. The pen moved automatically. I can write no more.

L

December 22, 1944

Dear Scriber:

I will stay at Altenburg. Whoever finds me, whether Gestapo, partisan or Russian, will kill me. I should have died with my sister. I have sent the servants and tenant families away to save them from the Russians. They have taken the carts, waggons and horses, including Stürm and Johanna. I said goodbye to everybody. Poor Lotte cried when I said I would be with Mina soon enough. She wanted to stay but I said no. When they left I could see their carts and waggons stretching to the horizon like a dark line in the snow. I instructed them to take the least amount possible or they would never escape. All the farms are empty as well as the outbuildings and the main house. I am sitting in the study as I write to you. There are so many memories of my father here, though I never knew him. Joseph is waiting for the letter and will be last to leave. He will give my last letters to an underground contact in Königsberg. I will have *Weihnachtsstollen* and Riesling Christmas Day and for *das Neujahr*. Remember? My last weeks or days will be spent listening to the echoes of my ancestors. They will be good company for me in this empty house. I have looked forward to your letters and writing to you helped me through these terrible times. I must say goodbye. Remember the first time we met, at dinner, when I said Ostpreußen was sometimes strange to me? I know why now. I could not see the end awaiting me.

Louisa

# Twelve Days

I phoned Clive Taunton at the British Legation and he gave me the name of his Czech contact in Pilsen and another contact in Bregenz in Austria. I dodged Dillard in the main office and went to see Thad.

"I've got to get out of Switzerland tonight. Give me a lift to the border?"

"Sure. Mind my asking why?"

"There's somebody in trouble."

"When do you want to leave?"

"As soon as possible. I've paid off my room at the pension and brought my stuff over here. I'm leaving it with you and I'll pick it up when I get back. I'll contact you when and if I can. Sorry to leave you in the lurch."

"Forget it. Barbara worked for *Life*. She'll fill in for you. If there's a story in this, this office gets it first."

"And all my gratitude if everything works out."

Still hanging around the main office, Dillard was eyeing the boxes of clothes, manuscripts and notebooks I had dumped on my desk. His voice followed me as I left.

"Going somewhere?"

"For a while."

"Special assignment?"

"In a way."

"Thad sending you?"

"I'm sending me."

Dip that in your coffee.

"Too bad. We're having a fondue dip this weekend and you're invited. Hard cheeses too. It promises to be quite a bash. All our friends are coming."

Standing room only.

"Guess you won't be able to make it."

One of life's cruel disappointments.

Thad gave me a pair of hiking boots and a fleece-lined leather jacket, both from earlier days when he roamed the Alps. Two pairs of socks made the boots snug. Taunton had said the man in Pilsen could get me to Prague and perhaps to Silesia, as far as Breslau. After that I would be on my own. The Soviet armies were advancing into Poland. The Germans were pulling back. Maybe the man in Pilsen would know somebody who could help me. How to get to Pilsen? Thad and I looked at a map. He would drive me to St. Gallen, at the eastern end of Lake Constance, a three-hour trip. From there it was twenty-seven miles to Bregenz, on the Austrian side. He would drive close to the border to cut down the distance. There was an innkeeper in Bregenz, an anti-Nazi who would help me. From there the best route was north to Munich and Regensburg and then east over the old Czech border to Pilsen.

"You're facing a couple of big maybes, Jim."

"I don't want to think about that. I want to get going."

We left Berne at four that afternoon, drove through Zurich and St. Gallen and were at the Austrian border at seven-thirty. We shook hands and Thad wished me luck. It was cold, the ground deep in snow. The border was hilly and low cloud made the night dark and if there were guards they probably were in a hut warming themselves. Regardless of Anschluss and the Greater Reich, Austrians weren't Germans unless it was painless. I was headed for the Bodensee, an inn near the center of Bregenz, to see Franz Kinkel. The walk from the border took more than two hours. Finding the inn took another in that small blacked–out town. Peering at street signs, I followed Taunton's directions and finally saw a blue pilot light. I hadn't seen any police and it was undoubtedly past curfew. It was an inn and an inn meant public service, didn't it? I knocked softly on the door and kept knocking until a man's voice asked what I wanted. I mentioned Taunton's name, said I needed help. The door opened and I slipped into a warm dark room. From the huge shape of a man came a basso profundo.

"What do you want?"

"I have to get to Pilsen."

"You are crazy."

"Let me worry about that. I have to get there."

"Perhaps I can get you a ride to Regensburg tomorrow. You can stay here tonight."

The shape moved away and I heard a match striking wood. The match flared, I smelled sulfur fumes and saw the glow of a candle in a saucer held by a thick-fingered hand.

"Come with me. I have a bed for you."

I followed him to the upstairs hallway, wide enough for one person. The candlelight reflected off the walls and ceiling ahead of him. At the end was a room, four walls around a bed and no window. He shut the door and I lay on the bed in darkness. I was tired and fell asleep immediately. Some hours later the door opened and a woman's voice said to come downstairs. I felt my way out of the blackness and along the hallway. Downstairs everything was still dark except for a light in the dining room, where two men sat at one of several round wooden tables. A man in overalls and workshirt was eating. A cap and woolen jacket lay on an empty chair beside him. The other man was Franz Kinkel, even bigger in the light. I asked for the bathroom and he told me. When I returned there was a plate of warmed-up vegetable stew waiting for me. I ate the stew and two slices of rye bread quickly, surprised at how hungry I was.

"He will take you," Kinkel said, nodding at the other man. The man had finished eating, had a lined face and tired eyes.

I offered to pay for the room and food and Kinkel shook his head. He nodded at the man again.

"Give him something later."

It was almost dawn when we left Bregenz. I never did find out what my driver was carrying in his truck, and that suited me. The less we knew about each other the better for both. He didn't say anything the whole trip. Two hours later in the faint light of a cloudy sky we passed through Munich. I could see bomb damage from air raids. Whole blocks of buildings were vacant lots with debris covered in snow. Another hour and a half and we were out of the Alpine foothills and crossed the medieval Stone Bridge over the Danube into Regensburg. Not a significant military target, Regensburg had escaped damage, the Altstadt and Gothic Dom surviving untouched reminders of a different world. A couple of policemen were talking on a street corner. Some Friday morning shoppers were bundled up and hurrying in the cold. I was dropped off in a side street. I handed the driver some Reichsmarks and he drove away. My choice was either walk to Pilsen or hop a freight.

I looked for railroad tracks. They would lead to a station and marshaling yards where I could hide in a boxcar or gondola or among the freight on a flatcar. I had to be careful. The Nazis were desperately drafting males of almost any age and condition and I wasn't in uniform. They were hanging deserters and draft evaders from streetlights and I would easily qualify for a rope as a fugitive correspondent and likely spy. What were the chances of an empty train heading east? A loaded train meant soldiers with anti-aircraft and machine guns against air attacks and partisans. But Pilsen was a hundred miles away in western Bohemia, on the other side of the Bavarian Forest, and I could postpone hiking through all that scenery.

In twenty minutes I found tracks and another thirty the marshaling yards. A military train on a siding was eastbound. Crouching among nearby piles of track ties smelling of creosote, I timed the sentries. After dark I climbed into a gondola and hid between packing crates under a tarpaulin. I was hungry and ate one of two extra slices of rye given me at the Bodensee. The salt in the rye made me thirsty. A while later I heard somebody, maybe an army supply clerk checking bills of lading on the cars, talking to a sentry. "If anything hits this one, it will go up like fireworks." I ate the other slice of rye. I dozed and hours later looked out from under the tarpaulin. The eastern horizon was getting lighter, a lampshade gradually lifted off a light bulb. Soon the train left with a nudge that passed down the line of cars. After traveling the first half hour at moderate speed, it slowed noticeably. I had boarded before the locomotive arrived but there would be an armored flatcar in front with soldiers looking for loosened rails or signs of planted explosives. In case the train was headed elsewhere or derailed, I decided to get off after ninety miles. It would be a rough guess but I would take a chance. I had no food and it was cold. That chance came an hour later when I heard shouts and the train came to a stop. Boots and voices rushed past and I peeked out and saw a bank close by covered with trees and thick brush. I waited, slipped out and dropped down onto the tracks, between the gondola and the boxcar behind. All the shouting and cursing was up front. There would be guards at the rear but I was close to the middle, the bank was ten feet away, the undergrowth two feet beyond. I dove across and buried myself in the snow and crawled between the bushes. No cries of alarm and no gunfire. I had to get further away before those up front returned. I scuttled up the bank, blindly felt a trunk under the snow and got behind it. I reached several more trunks before sliding up in back of one and seeing I had crawled thirty yards through snow up the bank and hill beyond.

I didn't hang around to congratulate myself. The returning soldiers would see my marks in the snow and unless they thought an animal made them might come after me. I had to get to Pilsen before dark. I had guessed better than I thought. I could see a Gothic tower before I got there and was told afterwards it was part of St. Bartholomew's Cathedral. Staying out of the way of the police, I found the address of my contact, Jan Drabek. He lived on the third floor of an apartment building in a working-class neighborhood. Nobody answered my knock. Why should anybody have answered? I wasn't expected, it was Saturday and people had things to do. I was hungry and tired, not the best condition for rational thought. A white-haired woman with a cane came out of the apartment next door and gave me a long look before saying something in Czech. I didn't speak Czech, I answered in French. She didn't understand so I tried English. No good. German? *Ja*. Was I German? *Nein. Gut.* They would be back late in the afternoon. Would I like to rest in her suite? I would. She had running water, a welcome change from munching on snow. I drank slowly. No sense in intestinal discomfort. I sat down on a couch and she brought me a plate of cookies. I could have eaten the plate and the hand that held it. She looked poor. I took two. I offered to pay but she wouldn't hear of it. These are tough times, please take something. She did. I should sleep. I did. I dreamed Loulou wasn't happy. Something about dogs. The dogs wore helmets with SS runes. She frowned. Good soldiers, good killers. Dogs or men? Men are dogs, aren't they? Obedience training. Commands. Enjoy hunting your own species. What are medals for, anyway? Same as uniforms and parades. It's all a pat on the head. Be proud. You can tell your own. The bark is the same. It's you and you and you and you. Nobody else. Why should there be?

It was after dark when I woke up. I felt chilly but that's expected after an impromptu sleep. But the air was chilly. My host was knitting in a rocking chair across from me, a small lamp for a light.

"They have returned. You were sleeping soundly, so I did not try to wake you."

"Thank you for everything."

She nodded and kept knitting. I shut the apartment door softly behind me, as if in gratitude. Next door opened quickly to my knock. A skinny man with lots of frizzy hair stared at me. I told him in English who sent me. He motioned me inside with a jerk of his head and shut the door. The apartment had three rooms, like the other, but the furniture was modern and there were bookshelves. A woman was cooking at a stove. We stood near the door. He squinted at me.

"What do you want?"

"I have to get to East Prussia. I need your help as far as Prague and Breslau."

"It makes no sense."

"It makes sense to me."

"There is heavy fighting. You will probably get killed."

"You may be right."

The woman at the stove turned to us.

"He has a reason, Jan. Have something to eat, sir. You must be hungry. I can offer you only potatoes fried in pork fat but food is hard to find now."

"I appreciate anything you can give me. I should be the one apologizing, for eating your food."

Afterwards we sat at the kitchen table and talked, drinking ersatz something. Drabek was full of hatred.

"We will take our revenge. We will make them pay. No Germans on our land ever again. And they can take the Jews with them."

His wife sighed.

"Six years. I cannot believe it will finally end."

Drabek spread his hands on the table.

"Since last November the attacks on partisans have been worse. Anybody suspected of helping the resistance is hanged in public. The bodies are left hanging for two days. The SS throws petrol on people and sets fire to them. I have seen their corpses. Burnt like roasted meat. No face any more. Nothing but charred twisted lumps. In villages pregnant women are beaten to death. Swollen blackened smashed faces. I saw a belly that had been ripped open, a dead fetus hanging on its umbilical cord. Germans."

He spit on his plate. We sat in silence. His wife got up and took the plates to the sink and washed them. He said we would talk the next day about getting to Breslau. It was getting late. I spent the night on the couch.

I woke up the next morning at dawn. They had gone out. Drabek's wife, whose name was Anna, returned two hours later and said he was fixing things so I could leave that evening. Another cup of ersatz at the kitchen table. More fried potatoes, which embarrassed her, but they were tasty and I told her so. She was tall, with a narrow face. Living on short rations had given her an emaciated look, exaggerating her natural thinness. Like her husband, she was bitter.

"We are living in a protectorate. But who will protect us from our protectors?"

"The first victims are always words. No blood, no loss of income, so most people ignore it. Anything can mean anything. Until meaning itself becomes meaningless. That leaves belief. People have an endless need to believe. A secret police, some hired hacks, a few slogans and you can run a country."

"We are socialists. Are there many in America?"

"Mostly transplants. Like communists, they shrivel on American soil."

"What are you?"

"An idealist who sees reality. Anybody who lets me say what I think gets my vote."

"We are not hard-liners. Except for hating Germans."

Drabek didn't return until four.

"When did you get off that train?"

"Between ten and eleven yesterday morning."

"That was the one. It was blown up further down the line, after it left Pilsen. Explosives were planted alongside the tracks. The soldiers saw nothing. An armored car, the locomotive and many other cars were derailed and some of the soldiers killed."

He drank his ersatz, staring at me across the kitchen table.

"I have somebody who will take you to Prague tonight. Breslau will be difficult. Many Germans are leaving Poland and going there. There may be somebody in Prague who will help you. Or you will have to go yourself."

Anna gave me a piece of bread for the journey. At six there was a light knock on the door. Drabek opened it and whispered. I said goodbye to Anna. Drabek nodded and I slipped out into the hallway, peering into the cold darkness. After a few seconds I could make out a short burly shape and a hand that gestured for me to follow. Down dark stairs following that shape and out into a blackout. Street after street, alleyways, maybe a cat lurking in the shadows. Everything sounds louder, you hear your own breath, your boots scraping against icy cobblestones.

Where were the police? I had not been stopped so far on my secret travels in the Reich. For my own purposes I had become part of the resistance. Resisting tyranny is a matter of survival. Darkness is your friend. Keep moving. Keep quiet. Slow when you have to be and quick when you can. Luck is with those who know the difference. Somebody will help you. Somebody will betray you. Most will ignore you. If you are stopped, papers are everything. Forged are as good as real. Most officials don't know the difference. Innocence is calm, guilt nervous. Be indignant but be careful. Too much challenges, too little is weak. Danger has a face. Officials look for it. If you have that face, don't stop no matter what.

Half an hour in the cold led to a warehouse. The man unlocked and slid open a large door and wheeled out a motorcycle with a sidecar. He shut and locked the door, started the motorcycle and said a couple of words in Czech that obviously meant get in. We set off slowly, the engine exhaust popping fervently. Moving raised the chill factor. I was wearing the scarf Sophie had knitted for me. I pulled it higher to cover my face. I wondered what she was doing back in New Hampshire. Probably typing her book by a log fire in the comfort of a quiet room, writing about institutionalized murder and not fearing a knock on the door. A tap on her door would mean her mother bringing her a cup of tea. We hadn't exchanged many cables in three and a half years. She was relieved I escaped to Switzerland and thanked me for the T4 material. Her book was taking longer to finish than she expected and she was discouraged by the lack of response from publishers. After the United States entered the war not many Americans were going to be interested in the secret euthanasia of Germans. In her last cable, in June, she said the book was almost finished and she was putting aside efforts to publish it. She would be joining American forces in Europe as a war correspondent. She didn't know when but hoped it would be before the war was over. Her time at home must have seemed dull. She had always wanted to be where the action was. Sophie back, part of the chase. I grinned as I kept my head down in the wind.

When I looked up a blacked-out Pilsen had become a dark road into the night, the sky swept by stringy clouds, flung uncoilings of a banshee's hair. The ride through the freezing air lasted an hour and a half. Hills and forest in a black outline like a paper cutout against a broken sky. Gaps were meadows or farmland, with an occasional glimpse of a house. As we neared the outskirts of Prague the number and size of buildings increased. In the murky blackout of a conquered city the driver stopped on a backstreet, left the engine running and whispered an address to me. I couldn't understand him, took out a pencil and notebook and told him to write it down. He wrote quickly, breaking the point but kept writing and thrust pencil and notebook back at me. I got out, stiff and cold, and he lurched away in a smell of exhaust. The buzzing of the engine faded into the darkness and I was alone and without a flashlight.

I looked at the address, scrawled with a blunt pencil. It would have been hard to read in good light. Prague was too big for me to wander around looking for a location written indecipherably in Czech. I would have to find somebody to read it for me. I would have to be quick, it was getting colder, the night ahead of me, but I would be more at risk asking for directions in daylight. I squinted at my watch. It was past eight. I walked the streets, looking for a blue pilot light, thinking that like Berlin it would mean a hotel or restaurant. I didn't see any but after several blocks I saw a thread of light at one edge of the blinds of a restaurant window. I knocked on the glass panel in the door and the door opened a crack. In English I said I needed help. A woman answered.

"Closed. We are cleaning."

"I need to get to this address tonight."

I showed her the notebook page with the address on it. The door opened wider, the woman put her head and a hand out and squinted at the page, moving her forefinger under the writing. She invited me in. It was dim inside the small room, a single bulb behind a short counter. A scrawny man stood behind the counter, his sleeves rolled up. Several tables had been pushed into a corner. The woman shut the door. A slim brunette with her hair tied in a bun, she was holding a straw broom worn down to a stump.

"I know the street. I finish here, then I take you. Hungry? You want something?"

"A piece of bread if you have it."

She pointed to a chair.

The chairs had been pushed beside the tables. I sat down and she brought me a day-old crusty roll that I demolished.

Twenty minutes later she was finished, said something to the man behind the counter and we left. Obviously used to the blackout, she walked quickly back the way I had come. Within minutes she pointed to a narrow shape across the street from where we stood. Third floor, she told me. Number ten. I thanked her and she disappeared in seconds. I walked across the street.

The door to the building was on the left side. There was a lock but it was worn and I forced the door open. Inside I waited until my eyes grew accustomed to the darkness. The vestibule was tiny. I could see a narrow wooden stairway alongside the left wall. As I climbed the threadbare runner the stairs gave a series of ascending creaks. The third was the top floor, number ten at the end of the hallway. I felt my way along, peering at numbers. I knocked. The door shook on its hinges. I waited, it opened and a man stood in front of me in an SS uniform. I had been trapped. A call had been made. I cursed myself for a goddam fool. I began turning to head for the stairs. He grinned, his bulky shape outlined by a light inside the apartment. He wasn't holding a gun.

"*Komm herein.*"

I looked again. He hadn't shaved in a couple of days. He smelled of beer. The uniform had food stains on it. No insignia to show he was SD or a Gestapo agent, and the SS wouldn't be waiting in a run-down apartment building for members of the resistance or enemy agents or wandering foreign correspondents like me to pop in on a cold night. He waved me inside and left me standing in the doorway. I shook my head and followed him.

The apartment was a jumble of suitcases, cardboard boxes and wooden crates. On a desk with a cowl lamp there were rubber stamps and inkpads and a magnifying glass and documents in various stages of preparation. There were bottles of ink, pens and pencils in beer steins, passport photos, a pair of scissors and a bottle of glue. On the floor nearby were empty beer bottles. Beside them was an electric hotplate with a saucepan on it.

The man came over to me.

"I am Heinz Lutz. I work for the Czech resistance forging papers. I was a printer and engraver. I can see you are English so I will speak your language."

I introduced myself and he looked around at the stacked luggage, boxes and crates as if seeing them for the first time.

"Sit down somewhere. I have one chair that I need. There is little room here. But I manage."

He sat in a wooden armchair beside the desk and I sat on a crate. He rubbed his forehead before passing a hand through his tangled gray hair and scratching his scalp. He had the face of a medieval burgher, square with strong features. It was a very German face, stolid, self-sufficient. A grin creased the vertical lines at the sides of his mouth.

"You are wondering about my uniform. I could see that when I opened the door you were surprised. I forgot I was wearing it. Somebody left it here. It is good quality, warm for the winter. There is a small hole in the jacket. A knife, I think. No bloodstain. Washed, maybe. I must be more careful."

He pursed his lips.

"Where are you going?"

"Breslau, and through Poland to East Prussia."

"I can get you to Breslau. It is full of soldiers. Also Germans getting away from the Russians. I can give you papers. Passports, travel permits, entry and exit visas. East Prussia is hard. You must contact the Polish resistance to get through Poland."

"How would I do that?"

"Not easy. The resistance is many groups, right wing and left wing. If you meet the right, the Russians are your enemy. Meet the left, they are your friends. But they all hate the Germans. Go where there are no Russians or Germans. There you will find Poles. Poles will like you. You are English."

"American."

"They will like you too. I am a German. You are surprised to find that I work for the Czech resistance? The only way I can be a true German is to be against the Nazis. Do you see that? Many Germans would not agree. To them our government must be obeyed, no matter who it is. No, I am not a dog to obey any master who whistles to him."

"I know other Germans who are anti-Nazi."

"Is that why you want to go to East Prussia?"

"No."

"Are you working for the American government?"

"Strictly on my own."

"Your business. But you are either crazy or a fool."

"There could be another possibility."

He thought for a moment and gave up.

"I have a bottle of beer for you. I will find you something."

He looked around and picked up a stein with pencils in it and probably dust, bits of graphite and eraser crumbs. I said we didn't need to stand on ceremony, I would drink from the bottle. He poked around among the bottles on the floor, found a full one, opened it and brought it over to me. I thanked him and took a swig. It was good German lager. He opened another bottle and drank from the neck in long swallows. After he drained the bottle he remembered to offer me some bread and cheese. The cheese was old, the bread stale. They would go well, he said, with a second bottle. So I had another and so did he and he became mellow.

"It is not easy being a German. You always stand to attention. You must be neat and clean and orderly. If you cannot do a thing you are not a good German. We dislike being inferior. We must be the best. Some of us are. The rest always try. The British stick their noses up in the air, the French sneer, the Spanish take a siesta, the Italians pinch women, the Russians get drunk. What do we Germans do? We march."

He slid his bottle in among the others on the floor.

"People leave things here. They say they will pick them up but forget or disappear. So I have all this. You will need a suitcase to look like a traveler. Search in them all. Put any clothes you want to into it. Your papers will say you are a Swedish businessman making your way to Königsberg for passage home. A second set will say Swiss businessman bound for Zurich. Use what you need. Swedish first, the other if you come back."

"I don't speak Swedish."

"Nobody does. Give me your passport, I will begin work. Tomorrow morning everything will be ready and you can take the train to Breslau. You can sleep tonight on those boxes."

I got up and handed him my passport. He put on a visor, picked up a magnifying glass and set to work. I didn't see a camera or dark room but there was a door to another room. I looked at the boxes. The top flaps of some were concave. Others had slept on them. I arranged some of them and tried to make myself comfortable. I fell asleep, a cardboard corner sticking into my collarbone.

When I woke up I could see light at the edges of the window drapes. Holding a bottle of beer at a precarious angle, Lutz was asleep in the armchair. I became aware of a box corner poking me and got up. I picked out a suitcase that looked as if it had belonged to a businessman. It was empty and I put my jacket and boots into it and covered them with shirts from the other suitcases. I found a suit and shoes that were my size. The only overcoat was tight under the armpits and too small on me and I would have to wear it unbuttoned. Lutz woke up and handed me two passports with entry visas, travel permits to East Prussia and back and exit visas to Sweden and Switzerland. I put the Swedish passport in my inside suit jacket pocket and hid everything else, including my American passport, in the suitcase. He said my clothes were good but I should behave more like a businessman.

"How does a businessman behave?"

"As if he has cheated somebody and is happy or is miserable because he has been cheated. Either one will do."

I peeked between the drapes and the window frame at the first light of dawn. I was anxious to be off the streets before daylight. Lutz gave me directions to the railroad station and I left. The stairway was still dark as I made my way downstairs. I opened the door to the street and glanced around. No cars or people. I stepped out and hurried along that block of narrow apartment buildings in the dry cold under a white overcast sky. I was near the corner when a black sedan raced by and stopped in front of the building I had left. Four men got out and disappeared inside. They wore SS field-gray uniforms but were SD or more likely Gestapo. I crouched in the doorway and waited, shivering in the cold. Within five minutes two of the men emerged, dragging Heinz Lutz by his hair and ears across the sidewalk and pushing and kicking him into the car. He was in his underwear and his face was bleeding from a gash in his right cheek, which was hanging by a shred of skin. The other men came out, one holding a smashed beer bottle dripping blood from a jagged edge. He dropped it into the gutter. The other man was carrying one of the cardboard boxes I had slept on, its flaps open and filled to the edges with Lutz's equipment. Over his shoulder was the SS uniform that had startled me last night. The car roared away from the curb. In seconds the street was empty and silent. A curtain across the way closed. Everything was the same except for the smeared trail of blood across the sidewalk and the smashed bottle in the gutter.

On my way to the station I saw Prague Castle above me and crossed the

Charles Bridge, with its three roofed medieval towers in the pale light. Near the station a black sedan pulled over to the curb and two uniformed Gestapo agents got out demanding to see my papers, one snapping his fingers. Keeping my hand steady, I reached inside my jacket for the documents. The fingersnapper went through them quickly and thrust them back at me and asked where I was going and I said the railroad station. They turned away abruptly, got into the car and drove away. The station was crowded, people speaking Czech and German and jostling each other in boarding the train. The Feldpolizei were on the platform and asked to see my papers. The officer I handed them to looked at them and then me for a few long seconds before handing them back. Where did I live in Sweden? Stockholm, I said, my fingers squeezing my passport. I was there on holiday many years ago, he said. I had a good time. I grinned. They left and I boarded, pushing and shoving and not getting a seat but glad to be off the platform and lost among the anonymous. An hour later the train pulled out and the station slipped away. I remembered Heinz Lutz.

A trip that would have taken four and a half hours before the war took twelve hours. We left at eight in the morning and arrived in Breslau after eight that evening. The train had crawled through the frigid snowbound landscape, soldiers in the armored car in front eyeing the tracks for explosives and loosened rails. We stopped repeatedly for track inspection. As the Russians were getting closer the resistance was increasing its attacks on trains, tracks and stations. The coaches were cold, passengers huddled in silent frustration and fear. A few had brought food and munched on bread or makeshift sandwiches. As the journey went on, stomach growling increased.

Because of the blackout the station was in darkness when we arrived. Hundreds of people were pushing into and stumbling over each other, platform pillars and baggage. The air was full of cries, groans, yells and curses. The restaurant was packed. The only food I could get were bread rolls and a cup of ersatz coffee. After standing for hours in the train I had to find a seat somewhere. Finally somebody vacated a chair and I grabbed it before others standing could react. I ate, warmed by the ersatz coffee, and it made the rolls more chewable. I dozed for a couple of hours, trying to get comfortable in that tight overcoat. When I woke up the restaurant wasn't as full, those remaining planning to spend the night there. I left and found a clerk in the ticket office and asked about trains going east and he said there weren't any. An unscheduled freight or troop train headed east might be put together at any time but neither would take a passenger. I went back to the restaurant and found a chair. I slept through the night.

I was awake at dawn and went out to look at the city and found a fortress full of troops, military vehicles and refugees. Ethnic Germans were arriving from Lodz, in occupied Poland, where they had been settled since 1939 in the planned colonization of the East. Now they were getting out as fast as they could. The talk in the streets and among refugees was about the Russians. Who could stop the Red Army? Some believed miracle weapons would, others put their faith in the Führer and the rest had the truth written on their faces. I asked about East Prussia. No one knew what was happening there. A man said he heard there would be a Russian offensive. A safe bet, but when? I went back to the station to find a train.

Out in the yard a train was being put together. I walked along the tracks to get a closer look but a guard stopped me. I told him I wanted to see the officer in charge of the train. Not possible. Why? Busy. Where is he? In that office. He pointed to a nearby shack for hostlers and brakemen. Would you tell him I would like to see him? He considered. All right. He walked over to the shack, went in and emerged minutes later with an officer. The officer waved me over to him. An army captain who had been assigned to put a train together, he looked harried. I showed him my passport and told him my travel plans and could see what he thought. A *Dummkopf.*

"This train goes to Lodz, the last one. From Lodz there are nothing but Russians and Poles until you get to Königsberg. Königsberg is under threat of attack now. You have a better chance if you go west to Germany and then north."

I told him the truth in a roundabout way, which sometimes works.

"I have to see a woman before I go home."

"You will never see her. I am under orders. None of us will get to Lodz. But we leave in under two hours."

I thanked him and returned to the station restaurant for rolls and ersatz coffee and managed to get a piece of cheese as well. Forty-five minutes later I was in the yard and saw the train was preparing to pull out. I had to hurry. I shoved open an unlocked boxcar door, tossed in my suitcase and climbed aboard. The boxcar was empty except for broken slats from packing crates. Why would a train of empty boxcars be headed for Lodz? To disassemble and bring back factory equipment, if it got there.

The boxcar was cold and I was preparing to close the door when I saw I had a companion, a large rat. Neither of us was happy at having to share with the other. I slid open the other door and picked up the biggest slat I could find. I approached him and he ran past to get to the other end and I whirled, swung and knocked him out into the snow alongside the tracks. At least he wouldn't be killed on the way to Lodz.

Before closing the doors I checked my watch. It was half past nine. I sat in a corner and figured things. If I remembered right, it was 140 miles from Breslau to Lodz, but distance close to a front is different. The tracks had to be checked and cleared. Time is different too. It takes a second to blast a body into eternity. It was Tuesday January 9, the sixth day of my journey. The longest part was ahead. Between Lodz and Altenburg were 200 miles and nothing traveling in that direction. I had extra rolls and a piece of cheese in my overcoat pocket, enough for two days. With the snow, water wouldn't be a problem. Why bother with Lodz? There wouldn't be anybody there except the military. Lodz was doomed. The Germans would evacuate factory equipment and if they had time destroy everything else. I would change into my leather jacket and boots and head into the countryside. Try to find the Polish resistance. I didn't want to think about whether Loulou would still be alive. I believed she was. That's all I needed. I sat back against the wooden wall of the boxcar and dozed listening to the rhythm of the wheels clicking over the rail joints.

Gunfire, yelling and the sound of splintering wood woke me. The train was being strafed by Soviet fighters. A piece of flying wood hit me in the shoulder. I winced. There were ragged holes in the sides of the boxcar. The roof had partly collapsed. There were no anti-aircraft batteries to return fire.

The train was being shot to pieces. A louder noise among the others. The locomotive had exploded. I flattened myself against the floor in a corner of the boxcar. Five minutes later everything was silent. After waiting, I got up and slid open a door. I jumped down and walked along the tracks. The boxcars were windy skeletons. The locomotive hissed as it burned. Bodies lay beside the tracks. One was headless. Others had been scalded or burnt. Shreds of uniform. A dented helmet. The soldiers had been hiding in the tender. I saw the captain. He was right. None of them got to Lodz.

I looked east along the tracks and could see on the horizon a blur that was Lodz. Smoke from the burning locomotive would draw attention. German troops might show up and soon. I went back to the boxcar and opened the suitcase. I had packed a pair of woolen pants along with shirts back in Prague. I put them on and the leather jacket, the boots, my scarf and gloves and felt warmer. I decided to leave the suitcase behind, and the overcoat, suit, tie, handkerchief, shoes and extra shirts. All my documents I put inside the cotton shirt I was wearing. Thad had given me a small compass. The woodsman and fisherman's friend, he said. My watch said half past noon. I set off due north.

The snow wasn't deep and I made good progress, crossing a couple of east-west roads. To the east on one road I could see a long column of refugees heading my way. I hid in nearby woods and watched as they passed in wagons and carts, some pulled by horses and others by men and women. I had seen refugees in France, their shocked and scared faces. These looked tired and defeated, the ghosts of Lebensraum, the playthings of Nazi fantasy. It was a long way to Breslau and there were partisans and Soviet fighters. They moved by in silence, the horses' steamy breath vanishing into the cold air.

I headed north again. It was three o'clock, the light was fading. It would be a cold night to spend outdoors and I began looking for shelter. I saw no farms. I didn't know what kind of reception I would get. Which peasants could be trusted? I saw bushes and small trees in the stretches of snow ahead of me but no forest. As twilight came on I decided to fix a place for myself. With my gloved hands I dug beneath the snow on a hillside. Within minutes I made a burrow for myself. I crawled inside and ate one of the rolls and half of the cheese. I closed the burrow entrance with snow and drew myself up into a ball. My body heat warmed the snow and I felt comfortable. At least I wouldn't freeze during the night. I was tired and fell asleep right away. I woke up in complete darkness and felt cold and cramped. I shifted around and poked a gloved finger through the snow at the entrance. Colder air rushed in through the tiny porthole. I could glimpse a sky with strands of high thin cloud and streaks of blue night between. I filled the hole and fell asleep. When I woke again the night was fading, slipping into dawn, and my dark blanket became tinted with the early light.

During the second day I saw no farms or forest. I had two rolls and a small piece of cheese left. I didn't think about the war now. I was cold and hungry and time was dwindling away. I ate part of a roll in the morning to keep going. That night in another snow burrow I finished the roll and the remaining cheese. I was feeling weaker, was covering less ground and faced the third day with my last roll. As I fell asleep I thought of Loulou. I knew she would be there, but for how long? I wouldn't think about that.

I munched on snow the next morning and ate half of the remaining roll. After hours of crossing snow-covered fields in the early afternoon I saw a farmhouse. As I got near I saw the weathered gray siding, holes in the roof, the opening where a window had been and a doorway with no door. It was a place to starve to death. But it wasn't a hole in the snow. I would stay the night and move on the next morning. There could be other farmhouses nearby, maybe not abandoned. I would walk no more, save my energy and find a place to sleep inside away from the stinging night air. The one-room house was empty except for a cupboard minus its shelves and nailed to a wall. The wood was rotten and split easily and I managed to pry the cupboard loose. Between it and the wall was a cozy space for me to lie down. Tired from the effort and from walking, I took a couple of bites of the roll and lay down as the evening came on.

I dreamed of a butterfly with wings of flame fluttering close to my eyes. I waved it away but it hovered nearby. It had a voice whispering hisses. The butterfly spoke Polish. At least it wouldn't have swastikas for markings. It would be friendly. What was it trying to say? I opened my eyes, saw a kerosene lantern and dark shapes looking down at me. More whispers, louder now. I heard "English."

"No, American."

One of the voices spoke to me.

"Pie-lot?"

"Correspondent. I work for newspapers."

I got to my feet slowly, muscles stiff. There were three of them. One had a rifle. The man with the lantern was thin and bony, with knuckles like walnut halves. The third was stocky, with a beard. The man holding the lantern gestured with his hand towards the doorway. Raising the lantern glass, which squeaked against the metal frame, he blew out the flame. I followed them into the frozen night. After being asleep I shivered, feeling the cold. After I had walked for a while I stopped shivering.

We walked for half an hour across the snow, the sky overcast with thin cloud. In single file we entered a pine forest. I brought up the rear, watching the moving shape in front of me on the path as we went deeper into the dense darkness. We bent low for hanging boughs or used a hand to push them away. In a clearing I saw a dark mound, which turned out to be a hut. Other huts were behind it. The men led me to one that was in the middle and larger than the others and we all went inside. A candle burned in a saucer on a rough-hewn wooden table and a man and woman sat on a mat beside it. The man was thin and wiry, with intense dark eyes. He wore an officer's cap and tunic and suit pants. The woman was round-faced and sturdily built, her hair cut short. She wore men's clothes, a soldier's jacket, a checked woolen shirt and denim pants. The man with the lantern spoke to the one at the table, who nodded, and the three men who brought me left. The officer stood up, came over and spoke to me in English.

"I am Milosz and this is Ula."

He nodded at the woman, who smiled. I told them I was hungry and would appreciate something to eat. Ula left the hut and returned a couple of minutes later with an earthenware bowl filled with a thick creamy soup. She handed me the bowl and one of the biggest spoons I've ever seen. I ate the soup too quickly to linger over what it was. The heat from it warmed me. I thanked Ula and she shook her head.

"No trouble."

Milosz scratched the stubble on his chin.

"They said you are not a pilot but they could not understand what you said you were."

"I work in Switzerland as a correspondent for an American news agency."

"Why are you here?"

"I want to get to East Prussia."

"You must have a good reason. You are lucky they saw your tracks in the snow. We are out at night. Our patrols search the area. We are not safe in daylight from the Germans or Russians."

"That bad, is it?"

"I was in Warsaw. The Soviet army was close. Their radio told us to begin the uprising. We had rifles and machine guns. The Germans had artillery and tanks. We fought street by street, in shelled buildings. Many died. Women and children. We fought until we had nothing left and had to surrender. Some escaped, like us. A few thousand. The Soviet army never came. We were betrayed. They were kilometers away and did nothing. British and American planes dropped supplies for us. The Germans got most of them. The Soviets would not let the planes land at their forward air bases to refuel. Many planes ran out of fuel and crashed. Polish troops in the Soviet forces tried to relieve us but could not do it. Stalin finally ordered the Soviet air force to drop fifty pistols and two machine guns. Yes, and you know why? He hoped we would commit suicide with them.

"Stalin wanted the Germans to do his dirty work for him. The Home Army is Polish, owes nothing to the Reds. NKVD is after us now. We have to become Reds or go to Siberia. If you are an officer you will be shot, anyway. They massacred us in Katyn. The Germans found the bodies."

He put out his hands, palms up.

"I have no hate for the Russian people. They are Slavs. It is Stalin doing this. And his Communist Party comrades. They have killed many Russians and Ukrainians."

We agreed to talk about my situation in the morning. I slept in the hut that night on pine branches, luxury after sleeping standing in coach aisles, on a restaurant chair and under a blanket of snow. The next morning somebody banged on the door and shouted that their radio was picking up reports of a new Soviet offensive. Ula and Milosz rushed out. When they returned he said the offensive was all along the front, including East Prussia. I figured the objective there would be Königsberg. Altenburg might escape for a few more days. It was Friday January 12, the ninth day of my journey.

According to my host, I was more than 200 kilometers from East Prussia. That was about 125 miles. I believed the Germans would fight harder in the north. They would be defending the first part of Germany to be invaded. The fall of Königsberg would be a blow to morale. It would be turned into a fortress, like Breslau. A port, it could be supplied and reinforced by sea as well as land. The Soviet armies would probably make better progress in Poland. The Germans would fight hard, making strategic retreats. In the coming weeks there would be a fluid front in the south and center and a gradual siege around Königsberg. I would try to slip between opposing armies.

Milosz offered to send somebody north with me to make contact with another resistance group. My guide would be Marek, the man with the rifle last night. He spoke no English but he knew the area to the north. I had more soup before setting out at dawn that morning after thanking Ula for the soup and the heavy chunk of dark rye she handed me.

"No problem."

The sky was overcast and the forest was almost as dark as at night. I looked back after a few yards and couldn't see the huts. I followed Marek, who saw a trail where I saw nothing but moss-covered rocks, clumps of fern and pine needles strewn over snaking bulges of tree roots. When you travel with somebody who knows where he's going you cover more ground. And you don't get worn down mentally trying to figure out where you are. He didn't need a compass. We crossed snow-covered grassland, frozen streams and gently sloping hills. I saw a farmhouse occasionally and once what looked like a small village but he kept going.

After a couple of hours we came to a road, the snow chewed up by tank tracks. They looked recent. Marek pulled me back by the sleeve and pointed to the east. I could see traffic half a mile away coming towards us, probably retreating Germans. We ran to a depression in the snow and hid there. The roar of tanks and the grinding whine of truck engines grew, and of clanking tread and bouncing axles and springs. If somebody happened to look our way and see us? Marek's rifle wouldn't have been of much use against panzers. And he was in the resistance. I wouldn't even have had time to get out my passports. We would be shot at the side of the road. I caught a sooty whiff of diesel exhaust. Diesels in German tanks? When the sounds began to recede I peeked. In the column of trucks and half-tracks pulling artillery were a Tiger II and three Panthers, the guns of the Panthers turned to face the oncoming Russians. Marek's face broke into a grin. The Germans were on the run.

We crossed the road and went north. More Germans would be on the way west and we didn't want to interrupt their travel plans. More miles across the snow. At times the wind picked up, cutting through my jacket. The sky became darker. More snow was coming. By late afternoon I was getting tired. We hadn't stopped to rest or eat. My guide knew our destination. I should have guessed somebody who knew the countryside wouldn't be walking blindly into nowhere. We went through woods to a farmhouse far away from any road. The farmer was pinch-faced, raised pigs and chickens in a nearby barn. A sow was lying on her side on some straw in a corner of the one-room house. I wondered about the domestic arrangements. He wasn't happy to see us but wouldn't want to make enemies in the resistance. Marek's head bobbed up and down as they talked and finally the farmer held up one finger. I would be gone by tomorrow. I figured the resistance would be stopping by and giving me directions. After Marek left the farmer came over and rubbed his thumb and forefinger together. I shook my head. I wasn't going to pay for a night's rest in hog hollow. He frowned. I wasn't going to get anything to eat from him but I had Ula's bread. During the night I woke up to grunting and squealing but the blessing of fatigue overtook me.

Before dawn I awoke again. Somebody was speaking in a low voice to the farmer. I couldn't hear his answers. I opened my eyes. On an unvarnished homemade wooden table a candle was burning. Two men were standing near the farmer. They were in uniform and rifles were slung on shoulder straps across their backs. I sat up on the straw I had used for a bed. They turned and looked at me, their faces unshaven and tired. One came over.

"You come with Milosz's man?"

"Yes."

"Where you go?"

"North to East Prussia."

"You want we help?"

I nodded.

"Come."

I got up and shook the straw off my jacket and pants. The farmer began to complain and the resistance fighters laughed.

"He wants money for wife," the one who spoke to me said.

Outside it was snowing lightly. The eastern horizon was a gray cape fading against the dawn. Three hours later I was in another resistance camp in another forest. The camp was empty. One of the men told me the others had set out to attack a German supply train. Their leader was Wojciech Glodowski. He was a major in the Polish army. How far was East Prussia? The man guessed 160 kilometers, a bit less than 100 miles. Many Russians, many Germans there. Many here, I said. I asked if they could spare some food and one brought me a piece of dark rye. Did the resistance use the same baker? They pointed to a hut and I went inside, ate the rye and rested.

Major Glodowski returned four hours later. He and many of his men were in uniform, the rest with an army cap or jacket. One man had been wounded in the foot and was being helped by two others, each with an arm under his shoulder. The hut I was in was used as a makeshift emergency ward. One of the soldiers was a medical student. The wounded man was brought in and treated and laid out on a cot. The student doctor spoke to him. From his tone of voice and gestures it was plain the wound wasn't serious. Major Glodowski entered the hut. He was a rawboned man with sharp features. After speaking with the patient, he glanced in my direction and I knew he had been told. He gestured with his hand for me to follow him and in two steps was through the doorway of the hut.

I emerged in time to see him enter a nearby hut. I went in and he was already seated on a cot. The only chair was a campstool. He pointed at it and I sat down. There wasn't much else in the hut except a belly stove, a small trunk and a folding table with papers on it. A man with a lot to think about, he wasn't in a good mood. He couldn't speak English so we spoke German. I briefed him and he scowled.

"The Home Army as a force will be no more. The NKVD is after us. The communists claim to be the only partisans. My men may survive. I am an officer. My only chance will be to escape. Poland is being torn apart by Russians and Germans and you want to go to East Prussia. Do you think I have the time to consider such trifles?"

"I need directions. Maybe some advice. If you could spare some food I would be grateful. I have money."

"Keep your money. Poles are not bloodsucking Jews."

I stood up. He waved his hand and I sat down.

"I have relatives who are Masuren Poles. I lived in Ostpreußen when I was a young boy and learned to speak German. They attempted to make us second-class Germans or get rid of us. We dirty Poles were never good enough to be Germans."

His frown disappeared. He allowed himself a grin.

"I will say this. One thought gives me pleasure these days. Do you know who kills more Germans than anybody else? Hitler."

He leaned back, hands on his knees.

"We have an operation tomorrow. Near Ostpreußen. Come with us. Afterwards I will send two of my men to take you there."

"You mind my asking what kind of operation?"

"You will find out. Get something to eat. And some sleep. We leave early."

The emergency ward hut was also the mess. More rye and a bowl of stew. It was warming. I slept on a cot. The wounded man snored but that didn't keep me awake. A hand shook me awake before dawn. More stew. I never found what was in it but you had to be hungry to get it down. It tasted of lard and old rutabagas. They were resistance fighters, not cooks.

The partisans assembled outside Major Glodowski's hut. There were fourteen, including him. Not everyone in the camp was going. There were at least seven left behind. The major and some of the others carried submachine guns. The rest had rifles with shoulder straps slung across their backs. Most of the group carried grenades or explosives. Two had a canteen of something, maybe water. They took no food. I figured the objective was within a few hours' walk. They planned to be back for dinner. There was no discussion. Everyone knew where and what. There was an informal order about the band. Glodowski's eyes told you discipline would be quick and severe. A couple of questions in Polish and we set off. The major led the way through the forest.

We walked in single file. I was second from last. The man behind me was the rear guard. Nobody spoke as we made our way through the darkness. The only sounds were our boots snapping twigs and squishing the soggy earth of the forest floor. There was little snow and mostly on branches. Occasionally somebody brushed against a bough and a clump of snow would fall in an icy spray. Where the light was better, at the edge of the forest in the predawn glow, the clumps of falling snow were comets with powdery trails.

At the edge of the forest Glodowski stopped. We had walked several miles. The open country was one broad sweep of snow, dotted randomly with barns and farmhouses. On the horizon sat a dark shape. We made for that. Low clouds covered the sky, so dawn was going to be dim. An hour later and closer the dark shape was more distinct. The objective was a rail junction. I could see telegraph poles and railroad tracks leading to a station, and close by was a small village, hardly more than a hamlet. Near the station were spur lines and sidings. A freight was on a siding. A passenger train had stopped temporarily on the main line. On the near side of the tracks stood a grove of pine less than a hundred and fifty yards from the station. The major signaled with a wave of his hand for us to lie down and we began crawling towards the grove. There would be guards in the station and maybe on the train. The trains were on the other side of the station. The tracks on the near side were empty.

When we reached the grove Glodowski gave orders. The men began to crawl. They fanned out around the station. The major remembered me.

"Stay here."

"I want to come with you."

He shrugged.

"All right. Keep your head down."

Half crouching, half crawling, he made his way towards the station. I followed like a spasmodic crab. The clouds were steel blue, the air raw. I was shivering with the cold. I didn't see guards around the station. They were probably inside keeping warm. A freezing winter dawn was the perfect time for a surprise attack. Through the near side window of the station I could see a silhouette move like a shadow. I heard steam escaping from the locomotive of the passenger train. If I had had a gun there would have been no time to think. That might have been better in those last few moments before violent death between strangers. In this fragment of war every movement and sound became monumental. The shape moved past the window again, this time seeming faster. The locomotive wheezed wisps of steam.

The major and his men reached the tracks. There was no cover between the tracks and the station. The men flattened themselves against the snow. A couple of yards behind them I did the same. Seconds later the major led his men in a running crouch across the tracks towards the station. Bursts from his submachine gun hammered the near side window to pieces. Grenades were hurled through the smashed window, dull explosions shook the air, muffling and silencing shouts and cries in German and Polish. The other windows vanished in volleys of fire, grenades following. The door was riddled, flung open and a final blast of fire directed inside. In a crouch some of the partisans raced towards the passenger train.

Guards and station employees were killed immediately. On the passenger train the engineer and fireman shot back with pistols and were killed. It turned out to be a train full of wounded soldiers. I returned to the station. The door was off its hinges. Dead bodies lay among mangled track switches and telegraph equipment and scattered heaps of ledgers, signal and code books and railroad manuals. The only sounds were the hissing of the locomotive and Glodowski's voice giving orders. I went outside and heard rifle shots coming from the coaches. I went over to the major.

"Those men are wounded."

"Stay out of this. You know nothing about it."

He jabbed at his left sleeve with a forefinger and walked away.

Regular German army units wore an eagle insignia on the right breast of their tunic. SS wore it on the left sleeve. There were three coaches. In the first some of the wounded were SS. The ones that couldn't move were killed where they lay. The rest were helped or carried outside, lined up against the pockmarked wall of the station and shot by a firing squad. They were on crutches and had bandaged heads or arms. One couldn't see and had to be put against the wall. Not a word was said. It was done in complete silence. Both sides knew the rules. No quarter given and none asked. Five were killed at the wall and three in the coaches. The rest of the wounded, from the regular army, were left alone. They would wait for rescue, if it came. If it didn't, they would die from their wounds, dehydration or starvation. The executions were quicker.

I climbed aboard the first coach and saw the SS dead and four DRKs, German Red Cross nurses, and a doctor. The doctor, who wore a white gown, was speaking with them in the aisle. The nurses were in the standard blue-and-white pinstriped uniform with white collar, white bib apron and cap. There was a red cross on the cap and another on an enameled pin at the collar. They were discussing what to do about the dead in the coach and outside. The senior nurse was for burying all of them locally after the partisans departed. The doctor said that it was too much work with the ground frozen and the wounded wouldn't be able to help. And they would be in danger of attack by the villagers. It would be better to stay on the train and wait for German troops passing that way. They would bury the bodies or get the villagers to do it. He looked at me, wondering what I was doing there. He spoke to me in Polish and then tried a few words of Russian. I answered in German, telling him I was an American. He asked why I was in Poland.

"I must get to East Prussia."

That confused them. But my accent told them I was American. I asked where they were from. The senior nurse said a soldiers' home near the Czech border. In the last few months it had become a makeshift hospital and finally a dressing station for increasing numbers of wounded as the Red Army got closer. Early yesterday they had received orders to pack up and leave immediately. Some of the staff and the more lightly wounded left in trucks. The remainder of the staff and the critically wounded were put on the train. Everything had gone well until the train stopped for water and fuel and the engineer went to check with the yardmaster about the line ahead. The nurse was stout and bluff but she couldn't hide her concern. It was for the other nurses and for the soldiers.

"Are they going to kill us?"

"No. You will be left here to die."

The doctor sounded implacably optimistic.

"Our troops will be coming through on another train or will be passing on the road that goes through the village. At least one will know how to drive the locomotive. The partisans have done their worst. They will leave before our soldiers arrive."

The doctor didn't believe a word of it. It was propaganda for the nurses and soldiers. The senior nurse suspected. I disabused the doctor.

"The tracks will be blown up. No more trains will be coming through in either direction. There may possibly be road transport but unless it passes nearby, the soldiers may not see you. Even an army retreating in good order will only stop when forced to fight a rearguard action. If the soldiers did stop and considered driving the train, they would have to fix the track. They would have neither the time nor the tools to fix it nor replacement parts. Expecting any help at this point would be deluding yourselves. Your options are damned few."

"Our army is retreating in a disciplined fashion. German soldiers would not leave their wounded at the mercy of Russians."

"Not willingly, no. But they may be under orders to keep going, have no choice. Have you seen retreating columns? I have. Both civilian and military look straight ahead. One thing is on their minds. The same as yours."

He wanted to say I was wrong but he knew I wasn't. He went to the next coach. Three of the nurses left as well. The youngest nurse looked at the partisans putting explosives inside the flanges of track in the junction. Of the remaining nurses, two were middle-aged, the other younger. I went through the coaches and looked at the soldiers. Seats had been removed so the wounded could be laid on blankets or mattresses in rows of three on either side of the aisle. The aisle was a boot-width wide. I counted seventy-nine soldiers, plus the three dead, who lay in the first coach covered with sheets. It was cold but the smells of urine and feces, suppurating wounds, putrefaction and discarded pus and blood-soaked dressings made the frigid air stink. Some of the men were unconscious and some moaned in restless sleep or semiconsciousness. The worst cases were drugged. In the third coach I made way in the aisle for the senior nurse. She was heading for the vestibule at the far end, where the doctor was standing. As she passed I spoke to her.

"Why did they wait so long before issuing the order for evacuation?"

She growled at me.

"Why do they always wait so long? They still pretend we are winning. They live on lies. How can you expect anything from such people?"

I got off the coach and went to look at the locomotive and tender. There were small dents on the side of the cab and tender from bullets. I climbed into the cab. The bodies of the engineer and fireman, still holding pistols, were lying on the floor. It was warm in the cab but the heat wasn't doing anybody any good. I returned to the third coach. All of the nurses were in or nearby the last vestibule talking with the doctor. He was smoking. They were discussing their situation. The senior nurse saw me and waved to me to join them. They had decided and she was staring out of the depths of their defeat.

"We have concluded it is hopeless. We have little water or food and enough drugs and medicines for at most a few days. I have talked with the other nurses. One will stay with me in these final hours but the others are uncertain. Would you be able to help them? Would it be possible for them to go with you? You know the partisans."

"I know the major."

I was introduced to everyone. The senior nurse's name was Agathe, the other middle-aged nurse was Irmgarde and the two younger ones were Erika and Renate. The doctor nodded slightly and introduced himself as Richard Erxleben. He offered me a cigarette. I declined. The younger nurses were the ones who were thinking about leaving. They felt guilty. Agathe persuaded them they were not needed and would be throwing their lives away.

"We can do what is necessary. You will not be required. It will help us to think of you. That it was not all hopeless."

Glodowski's men set explosives on the main and spur lines and blew up the tracks. They cut the telegraph wires and blew up several poles. From the first burst of gunfire to blowing up the poles took them less than an hour. One of the partisans had been wounded in the neck. He had been lucky. The bullet had missed his jugular vein, leaving a deep crease like a burn mark. One of the others wrapped a strip of cloth around it. The group prepared to leave. I got two of them to carry the dead SS off the train. They put them with the others at the station wall. Glodowski came over to me, still angry about my protest. His thin lips were thinner and drawn back.

"What do you know about my country? What we have suffered? I should leave you to go on alone. You deserve no help."

"What purpose did killing wounded soldiers serve? Why is revenge part of your military objective? You could have left them to die like the others. At least that way you would not be part of the barbarity of this war."

I thought for a moment he was going to shoot me. He managed to control his temper.

"Every man here has lost relatives. Some their fathers, mothers, wives and children. Many have no family. You want principles in war? Tell the Germans first."

"I expect nothing from Nazis. I expect better from Poles."

He took a deep breath, the nervous excitement of the attack having worn off.

"It is easy to be better if you have not suffered as we have. Or are facing what we are."

"I admit I know little about your country. I travel here as a stranger. This is an unusual time. We argue in a language not yours or mine but that of our enemy."

"You are the first American I have met. Are they all like you?"

"I assume that is a rhetorical question."

"If I understand you, I say yes. We should leave. Germans may come. There may be informers in the village. Not every Pole is a patriot."

"I need a favor. Another one. The nurses on that train know their situation is hopeless. Two will stay with the wounded. The other two would like to leave. I told them I would ask if you would take them. If you say no, I will take them with me."

His head bobbed up and down for a few moments as he stared at me. He arched his back, looked up at the sky and he was all right.

"Take them with you? What chance would they have? I will take them. Tell them to get ready."

The nurses got off the train, hugged and kissed and said goodbye. The two leaving were given letters from the other nurses and the soldiers to take with them in a leather pouch. The doctor stood in the vestibule looking down at them and smoking. I led them across the tracks, coats over their uniforms. I took a final look at the hissing locomotive and the coaches of wounded soldiers. I thought of the dead inside the station, the fallen wires and the tangle of twisted track. I thought of the dead slumped on the concrete platform in front of the station. People would come sooner or later, from the village or somewhere else. They would bury the dead and maybe save some of the wounded or shoot them. They would move the train, unhitch the locomotive and clean the blood and pus and piss and shit off the floors. The platform would be washed of blood and the station rebuilt. Telegraph and telephone service would be restored and new track laid. It didn't matter who did this except that it be done. That was what civilized people did. They cleaned up the past, its stink and blood, removing all reminders there would be a next time, and even worse. After a while, maybe a long time, there would be nobody to remember what happened that day near a Polish village. Trains would pass through and people use the station as if nothing had happened. Elsewhere there were bronze and marble memorials to our big mistakes, where politicians stand and bow their heads in homage to the buried past. All this is usual. But I knew the day was coming when there would be nobody to clean up the mess. On that day there would be nobody to remember, or why.

Glodowski called his men together. They glanced at the nurses but didn't say anything, knowing the major had accepted them. They looked at me, figuring I had something to do with it. We crossed the tracks, heading for the fields. An hour later we were back in the forest and Glodowski called a halt. He picked two men to take me to East Prussia, the two who brought me to camp. From a nearby cache of weapons, ammunition and food we were given a loaf of rye and a small package of lard. The rest set off into the forest, slipping between the trees, the caps of the nurses like a pair of white birds. Within a minute they had disappeared. It was eight o'clock.

We came out of the forest and crossed the white fields in a light snowfall. The only sound was our breathing. We kept going until late morning before stopping. We were on a hill with a good view of the surrounding countryside, which was mostly flat. We squatted and they ate rye smeared with lard and I ate rye without. Good, they said, nodding. I got enough in the stew, I said. Their names were Wladislaw and Wiktor and both understood some English and Wiktor spoke a few words. How far inside East Prussia would I be when I left them? Maybe two kilometers, he reckoned. Less than two miles, which left twenty-two more to Altenburg. I better take some lard with me, I said. They grinned. It had stopped snowing and the sky was clearing, the high cloud stretching and thinning and coming apart in a gusty wind. Minutes later Soviet Yak fighters flew low over us heading west. We heard gunfire and explosions not far away. We stood up and could see smoke and tiny flames in the distance as the planes like angry wasps dived at a string of vehicles. Five minutes and the attack was over, leaving a burning smoking slash in the snow. We decided to have a closer look. Fifteen minutes later I could feel the heat from the burning metal. Armored cars, trucks, half-tracks and artillery were in flame or blown apart. Bodies were scattered around, dyeing the snow red. The survivors were beyond help. Their moans and cries were silenced by Wladislaw with a bullet in the back of the head. We had to leave before another retreating German convoy or pursuing Russian units arrived. As I looked around I had noticed among several destroyed motorcycles one that seemed to be undamaged. It was what I needed.

I called them and we went over and looked at it. It was a side-valve BMW R75 with a sidecar. It was in a ditch at the side of the road, front tire half-buried in the snow. The driver and soldiers he carried had scattered when the planes began their strafing run. Their bodies were lying within a few yards of the motorcycle. We pulled it back onto the road. Wiktor examined the tires and wheels and checked the levers and gearshift and shaft drive.

"Is all good."

I grinned.

"We'll take it. Can you drive?"

"Not this one. I try."

Within minutes he had it figured: left-hand timing lever and clutch, right-hand throttle and brake lever, and a right-side shift knob shifted by hand like a car. Right heel for the brake. Shifting was close throttle, change gears and back to throttle. Wiktor pushed the ignition switch on the headlight, pulled back the timing lever and pushed the starter crank down with his foot. The engine caught, he pushed the timing lever forward and gunned the throttle. He jumped on and drove around in circles, changing gears. He ran over arms and legs in the road as the wind picked up, bringing the smells of oily smoke, burning metal and scorched flesh.

It was Wladislaw's turn and then they wanted me to try. I wasn't as good with the gears as they were. We found a half-empty jerry can and topped up the bike. I got into the sidecar, Wiktor drove and Wladislaw sat behind him. We followed the road for several miles, watching for signs of German rearguard detachments. I said we should leave the road and drive across country. The Germans wouldn't be pleased if they caught us with a captured BMW. Wladislaw pounded the sidecar with his fist. He said something in Polish that probably meant go faster. Wiktor laughed into the wind battering us, the bike careening like a toboggan along the icy road.

"They shoot us anyway."

They enjoyed driving a German machine as they watched Germans retreating. There was a cheerful fatalism about them, distilled in deep hatred. Wiktor could have driven around those dismembered arms and legs. Nazi atrocities in Poland had been genocidal. And that was only part of it. Glodowski had mentioned the Home Army being targeted by the NKVD. What future did they have?

Wiktor eventually left the road. We pushed the motorcycle up hills and dragged it through snowdrifts. We made up for that on flat stretches. I thought about not having to walk all those miles traveled since getting the bike. Between walking four hours and riding almost three we had to be forty miles closer to Altenburg. That left sixty miles. I took over the driving at three o'clock and kept up a steady pace for two hours. No hills or snow banks on my run. Wladislaw unscrewed the top of his canteen and he and Wiktor began sharing swigs of something that made them a lot merrier than water would. I turned down a swig. I had to concentrate in the gathering dusk. In the complete darkness at five o'clock even the headlight wasn't much help on the bumpy terrain. We were near a forest and decided to stop for the night. I hoped my stint had taken off another ten miles.

Using their knives, they cut pine branches to make a shelter. We ate slices of rye. I passed up lard again. Nobody said anything. We were tired and it was cold. We slept through the evening, not waking until an hour before dawn. There was a rumbling to the east and stuttering bursts of light along the dark horizon, like a sunrise having trouble getting started. Soviet artillery was opening up.

The motorcycle started on the second try and after a few coughs settled into a steady rhythm. Wladislaw drove. I slept in the sidecar to the frenzied threshing of the engine. I must have been very tired. Wiktor had to pound on my shoulder to wake me.

"East Prussia."

I looked around. All I could see was the same white countryside I'd been looking at for days.

"Are you sure?"

"When boy I came with mother, see grandmother. Insterburg."

Mina had told me Insterburg was a garrison town, von Pommer's regiment had been quartered there, and it wasn't far from Altenburg.

"Is Insterburg near a big estate?"

He thought for a while before pointing west.

"Five kilometers. Mother asked way to Insterburg. They said. You are good now?"

"I know the way."

More swigs from Wladislaw's canteen, against the cold they said, waving goodbye as the motorcycle was absorbed into the white distance.

The extra miles they drove me meant I had three to go. It was Monday January 15. Twelve days to Altenburg. I looked at my watch. It was quarter to twelve. I might be in time for lunch. No need for the chunk of rye in my jacket pocket. But I would leave it there. She might be on short rations. Not for a moment had I believed she had gone or something happened to her. It was not a rational feeling. But it was as strong as anything I ever felt. I suddenly remembered I hadn't washed or shaved since Breslau. There would be soap there and a razor I could use. How much time would I have? The Soviet armies were on their way. What in the hell was I doing daydreaming in the middle of a snow-covered pasture?

# Masuren

Hurrying for an hour across that white landscape, the odd snowflake drifting on a cold wind with rumors of distant guns. Wagon, cart and horseshoe tracks and footprints were all that remained of a vanished population. Along the driveway to the house wheel ruts in the hard-packed snow. My boots slipscrunched on the snow, caking it like white sand. One of the entrance doors was ajar, swung open to my touch. My steps echoed on the marble floor of the entrance hall. I went to the dining hall. She was seated at her accustomed place at the table. It was empty except for a silver fork, knife and spoon and a dinner plate with the Altenburg family crest in Prussian blue in front of her. Next to the spoon was a Luger with walnut grip panels. It was Count Wilhelm's service pistol. Mina had used it at the woodcutter's hut. When I walked in, Loulou was staring at the plate. She raised her eyes, looked blankly at me. Should I have been turned away at the servants' entrance?

*"Es ist alles hoffnungslos.* Why are you here?"

"I have not come eleven hundred miles to be target practice for three million Russians or on the final extermination list of the Gestapo."

"You are so American."

"Would you prefer some existentialist nosepicker who would debate the moral niceties with you as he probed your choices with nicotine-stained fingers?"

"Vulgar."

"Sir Galahad on a white charger I am not, only a guy who will lend a helping hand if you need it."

"*Es ist zu spät.* Too late for everything."

"All right. You win. Play countess with a bunch of ghosts until Russian gang rapists show up in truckloads. Give my regards to the Kremlin."

I walked away, swearing under my breath. I went back into the entrance hall. That damn pile of hats and gloves and boots was still there. The nonchalance of privilege. Let somebody else clean up. You can always find a sucker. I remembered what Julia said. Artists don't apologize. Somebody will do it for them. Aristocrats too, apparently. But Julia was a great talent. She gave the world pleasure. What had these antiques ever given anybody? It was all an illusion, institutionalized extortion of money and labor for the legitimacy of a myth. Get the law and the church on your side and you're set. So who was to blame? It was a system. You were born into it. Mina died for it. To her it had meant tradition and what she called duty. To me it meant nothing. I had the excuse of circumstance, courtesy of Sophie, and now it was time to look into a mirror and see myself for the fool I was.

Chair legs squeaked against the parquet of the dining hall. Why hang around? I stepped outside and saw the trail my boots had made in the snow, the blurred edges where they had slipped. Heading down the driveway, I heard her.

"Did I ask you to leave?"

I stopped and turned.

"Do I need your permission?"

"You must be hungry."

"I have a piece of bread."

"We have not said goodbye."

"Goodbye."

"One word? After your journey?"

"I came to help you. You refused my help."

"I am not well. I did not recognize you at first."

"Do you know that many Americans who speak bad German?"

"I have to explain so you will understand. Come inside, it is not as cold, and we will talk."

She was standing in the doorway in a thin blouse and skirt, her arms hugging her shoulders. I decided I would play it out to the end. What else did I have to do? She turned and stepped back into the entrance hall as I reached the doorway. She spoke offhandedly as I followed her.

"We should have a fire."

"No time. The Russians are coming."

"So you said. Not this minute, though."

"Why do I meet women who insist on contradicting me?"

"You should think about that."

"No time for a fire. I plan on saving myself at least."

Back in the dining hall she sat at the table and pointed to a chair across from her and I sat down. At least I was off my feet.

"What have you to fear from the Russians? You are American."

"My Russian amounts to a handful of words. I would be shot before I used up the lot of them."

"You exaggerate. I am the one in danger, as you so bluntly pointed out." She nodded in the direction of the Luger.

"I have a pistol. I have never fired one, though."

"You should have time for one good shot. I suggest you put the end of the barrel against your temple. Keep your hand steady. Pull the trigger gently."

She didn't say anything. She was staring at the Luger. She was thinking about Mina. And maybe about Count Wilhelm. The whole Prussian military tradition. It was her heritage. A good part of it. How much did it mean to her? I would let her decide. One thing I did know. If she had to she would use the pistol, on herself or on those who threatened her. Did she want that? She had to work things out for herself. She looked around the hall, glancing quickly at the shields with the Altenburg coat of arms, then her eyes rested on her mother's chair and then Mina's. It wasn't tradition, finally. It was those she loved who were holding onto her, and she had to turn her back on them to get out of there. It was the most important moment in her life, so I waited, trying to forget the minutes passing by like empty trains.

She looked at me. She didn't say anything, so I did.

"Anything else before I go?"

"You came a long way. I appreciate your trouble. You may not think so, but I do. Would you answer a question? If I stay, would you be angry?"

"I was angry earlier but not any more. I think I understand how you feel. I came for you. If you want to stay, I have to respect your decision. I can walk away if you want that."

She wasn't listening to me. She had something to explain, to herself as well as to me.

"My life was determined for me before I was born. I was brought up with a set of strict beliefs. All Junkers are. It is like an old dance with many couples facing each other in two lines, the men on one side, the women on the other. Everybody is in costume. Each pair must move as part of a precise pattern for the dance to be a success. You must rely on others to think exactly like you. To an outsider it looks stiff, quaintly decorous. To us it is proper, and because of that, comforting. I am a good dancer, better than Mina, as I told you. From minuet to waltz, tango and foxtrot. I say that not to boast but tell you dancing has been my way of expressing myself. Her way was sports, guns, war and rebellion. All I need is a place to dance. Everything is gone. You came to rescue a prisoner locked away many years ago. The prison is empty now except for me. I have become my jailer. No one has done this to me. I am responsible. I have determined what my fate should be."

I was ready to leave but not without a last try. I switched to English, she kept speaking German. A strange situation. But it was.

"You want an outsider's opinion?"

"Please."

"You're not your sister. You're a healer, not a soldier. She had the same conquest mania infecting Prussians since the Teutonic Knights came back from the Crusades. She fought the battles, you bandaged the dolls."

"Who told you?"

"Klaus."

"So long ago."

"In your last letter you mentioned my first dinner at Altenburg, reminding me what you said about feeling like a stranger in your own land. You don't ask someone to remember unless there's a reason. I knew the reason. You had to find out if the one in the summer house who got away would help you to break free. As much as you wanted it to happen, you couldn't let yourself believe it would. But it did. I'm here."

She pushed her empty plate away and stood up and walked around the end of the table. I got up. She came to tell me a secret but I had a hunch what it was. I knew her well enough for that. Her face was gaunt but her eyes flared softly like the first blue of a summer dawn.

"Thank you for coming. I always wanted to be like Mina. But I resented feeling that way. Mina did what she wanted. She was punished for that sometimes. But she was always fierce and proud. And what was I? Good little Louisa, who always did what she was told. Louisa the obedient child, girl, woman, daughter, fiancée. I want to get out of here."

"Wear your mother's wedding ring. It's the only way I can get you past the Russians. That and maybe my passport. Bring your passport in case we meet Germans. We can't take much. We need the smallest amount of food with the most fat. Wear your oldest clothes. You've got dress warm and look drab."

"Butter and chocolate would be best. We have been hoarding chocolate for years."

"Where is your uncle's book?"

"Upstairs in the library."

"We'll take it. Do you have a sled?"

"One we used as children. I think it must be in the stables."

"We'll put what we can on it. We'll take the pistol and extra ammunition and a flashlight. You get the book, ammunition and flashlight while I get the sled. We've got room for a canvas. Which do you want?"

She didn't hesitate.

"The one at the lake. It is with the others in the stables, in the last stall."

I found the sled in the tack room and went to the last stall. Large, narrow crates were stacked and leaning against a wall. There were several canvases in each, mannerist hack work by an expert borrower of other artists' ideas. Mina's were together. The other three were better than the junk I had seen, but the one of her rising from the lake outclassed everything. Loulou was right. Mina raised him for a moment to a different level. On a canvas of thirty by fifty inches she emerged from the lake into the blue sky of a spring morning. Water slipped from her like a sheath, sliding in rings off her ankles as she stepped out. Glossy as pink and white porcelain, sleek hair darkened to golden waves and tight dripping curls, she floated on the flowing air, eyes flaring in the sun. The paint glistened, slick as dew. This was Mina as she always wanted to be, goddess of the world she loved.

I removed the canvas from its frame, rolled it up and wrapped a saddle blanket around it, tucking it into the ends of the cylinder. Loulou was waiting in the dining hall and I was hungry.

"Anything to eat?"

"Lotte made pots of stewed pickled beef with cabbage for me before she left."

"Let's gather everything in the entrance hall before we eat. I'll wash, and shave too if you'll get me a razor."

An hour later we were at the door, bundles of food and clothing strapped to the sled, our voices sounding hollow in the empty hall. She paused to look at the grand staircase.

"Goodbye to seven hundred years and all the counts and countesses."

"You're the countess now."

"The last," she said and we left.

It had stopped snowing, shredded cloud and a counterfeit coin against a faded sky. We headed southwest into the forests and lakes of Masuren, a leather strap from the sled wound around my gloved hand. I looked at Loulou occasionally to see how she was faring. She had tied her hair back with a rubber band. She was dressed in woolen pants, baggy sweater, padded leather jacket, boots and had tied a cotton handkerchief around her head. She took shallow breaths, as glad as I was there wasn't a strong wind to inject the freezing air into our bones. Taking the lead, she chose side roads to avoid encountering anybody. The countryside was an undulating silent whiteness, empty farmhouses in the distance and no sign of people. Two hours of this and Loulou said she was lost because of the snow. Ten minutes later the road curved around a hill and joined a main road. Too late we saw railroad tracks and a line of boxcars. Before we could leave a shout stopped us. From the boxcars two Soviet soldiers with rifles walked towards us in their round pot helmets, tobacco brown uniforms and calf-length boots. I unwound and dropped the leather strap and raised my arms and shouted loudly.

"*Amerikanskaya. Amerikanskaya.*"

The soldiers came over slowly, their rifles pointing at us.

"*Amerikanskaya?*"

"*Da. Amerikanskaya. Tovarishch.*"

One swung his rifle in Loulou's direction.

"Frau."

I picked up her hand and pulled off her glove to show the ring and pointed my index finger at my chest.

"See? She is my wife. I want to see your *komandir. Vash ofitser. Vash komandir.*"

The other soldier pointed to a hut further up the tracks. We followed him there. He knocked on the door, opened it after receiving a disgruntled answer and went inside. When he came out he nodded at us to go inside. I pulled the sled beside the door and we went in and he closed it behind us. The wooden hut was one room with a table on which sat a radiotelephone and a kerosene lantern among bundles of paper. There were maps, orders and proclamations tacked onto the walls. Seated behind the table was an officer who told us in good English that he was Colonel Maxim Voronov and invited us to sit down. Loulou slumped into a chair, closed her eyes and fell asleep and I handed my American passport to the colonel and sat down in the remaining chair. I mentioned his English. He said he had studied at the State Institute of Foreign Languages in Moscow. He said we were in luck because he was there that afternoon to clear up a problem.

Colonel Voronov was bulky, his deep-set eyes the color of wet cement. His hair was combed back smoothly from his forehead and temples. He looked at my passport. He didn't ask to see any of the other documents I mentioned. He pushed it back across the table. After picking up an amber-colored cigarette holder and fitting a long cigarette into it, he lit the cigarette with a nickel-plated lighter and smoked. He was used to speaking when ready.

"Why are you here?"

"I came for my wife."

He waved his hand.

"She is not your wife. I am married. Many years. I know what a wife looks like, how she behaves. The truth, please."

"I'm a correspondent working in Switzerland. She and I wrote to each other for three years. In her last letter she told me about her desperate situation and I came to get her. I'd visited her family home before, in 1940 and '41."

"Where is her family?"

"All dead."

"And what kind of help do you want from me?"

"To avoid being shot out of hand by your soldiers I asked to see their commanding officer. German women stand a good chance of being raped and murdered here. That's why she's posing as my wife. We're going west. We're trying to reach the American lines."

"If you reach the German lines you are the one who will be in danger."

"I'll take that chance."

"To save one woman. Do you know how many are dead in my country?"

"If you can help me, good. If not, we'll be on our way."

"You think I can help protect this woman? I can see behind her clothes and silence. She is an aristocrat. An automatic enemy of the people. I am speaking the party line. I do not believe it but that is between us. Outside of this hut I must have her executed without trial. Let me tell you something. Political commissars oversee the behavior of all ranks. If I did more than issue general proclamations on good behavior, I would be stripped of my rank, tried as a formality and given a prison sentence. If I were found protecting an aristocrat, I would be shot along with her. If she were raped and murdered, I could do nothing. These soldiers are uneducated peasants, naturally stupid, and the worst of them are animals that will rape and kill at any opportunity. They are too stupid to guess your secret. In Russia as in Germany the worst rule and the rest are either mindless robots or must keep their mouths shut. You have my silence. That is the most I can give you."

He smoked for a while, looking up at the open rafters.

"We treat our tankmen well, and our artillery personnel and supply units. Do you know that many are married and their wives are soldiers? But from the beginning Soviet generals have squandered the rifle divisions, thrown them into battles like buckets of water onto a fire. Discipline has been brutally enforced. Millions have been lost. We have been reduced to scavenging the furthest peasant villages and taking anybody and everybody and using Mongolians and Uzbeks and the like for replacements. Their officers treat them like shit. Our tank armies and best shock troops move on, these move in. Should what happens be surprising? They are the rapists. German, Polish, Russian, Ukrainian women are not safe from them.

"Should it surprise me that our best behaved soldiers are the most politically committed? They would no more rape a German woman than a Russian one. One thing I do not understand. Our women soldiers show no sympathy. I have heard they laugh as they watch the rapes."

His mind changed tack.

"The big war is here. In the west you are annoying the German. We are smashing him. He fears us and surrenders to you."

I picked up my passport.

"The war is being won by Russian blood and American industry."

His reply confined itself to a noncommittal shake of his head about the American part. After removing the butt from the holder, he put in another cigarette, lit it and smoked, the blue strands rising to join the haze in the rafters. Loulou opened her eyes and looked startled. She glanced around before focusing on Colonel Voronov's burning cigarette. He tapped the holder with his forefinger and a limp cylinder of ash fell onto the table. Loulou blinked. The colonel studied her for a few moments before turning to me.

"You should leave before a commissar comes. Go to the southwest. You have a chance to avoid Soviet troops there now. Next time you will not be so lucky."

The late afternoon light was fading. We crossed the open road and walked over fields to the southwest. We needed to find a wooded area for protection during the night. After an hour I saw a forest on the other side of a lake covered in snow except for a small patch of ice in the center. We walked around the lake and 150 yards into the forest I saw a clearing with a canopy of branches. Loulou leaned against the trunk of a pine and I went over to her. Her face was drawn.

"I am not strong. I have not been eating."

"Have some chocolate."

I opened a bundle on the sled, unwrapped a chunk of chocolate, broke off a piece and handed it to her. She nibbled at the edges and began to perk up. Using a knife I found in the tack room I cut branches. I began building a shelter. She watched me after moving over to sit on the sled.

"That looks good."

"I learned this from partisans."

I finished quickly. Rough but roomy. She was finishing the chocolate. I sat next to her on the sled.

"Our best hope is to find the resistance. They'll help us get to the west or down to Switzerland."

"I will try. I am not well. It has been too much. When you came that was another shock."

"Your reaction was a shock to me."

"How could I expect you to come all that way? I could not believe it was you. I almost resented you. I had willed myself to die. Writing those last letters was my only link to sanity. In the days afterwards I became resigned to my end. I must not be a disappointment after all that has happened."

Random flakes fluttered down like fluff between the branches as she remembered. After a long time I broke the silence.

"We'll have to bundle up together to stay warm at night. I've never taken advantage of a woman."

She turned to face me.

"Saying that was unnecessary. You are a Sir Galahad."

"It helps that you're a countess."

"I am a countess with no home."

"You're a damsel in distress."

"*Ach, ich verstehe.*"

Her sadness had gone. I took no credit. The chocolate worked. Usually does.

We ate butter and chocolate for dinner. Revolting unless you're freezing. It was dark by then and we got into the shelter. The more rest the better and we had many miles to cover in the next few days. She was asleep before I settled in, and I followed her in minutes.

Somebody was forcing a mask onto my face. It had red-hot nails. They were being driven into my skin, fastening the mask into place. I heard screams.

"Mina, Mina, Mina, Mina."

I woke up feeling Loulou's hand clutching my face, her fingernails digging into it. I pried her fingers off and pulled her hand away. She was writhing, kicking out and knocking the branches around. I held her and said she was all right and she calmed down and looked at me.

"What happened?"

"You had a nightmare. You were calling out your sister's name."

"I have it every night. I should have told you."

"You'd better wear gloves when you sleep or you'll be leading around a blind correspondent."

"Did I scratch you?"

"No damage. Speaking of which, I'll put the branches back."

"That was the best sleep I have had in weeks. I feel better."

"I'm glad somebody does."

"Sorry. I promise to wear gloves."

I was up at dawn. Loulou was still sleeping. I exited the shelter quietly and walked to the lake. The light snow during the night had stopped and the clouds were clearing, the anemic eastern sky tinting to a frosty orange. I could hear faraway artillery to the east, like somebody knocking on the earth to get in. The lake was smaller than I remembered, more of a pond. The snow covering most of it looked like shaving cream. I didn't see any signs of fighting or troops nearby. I doubled back and cut around the shelter to avoid disturbing Loulou. Leaving a trail of broken branches I entered the dense forest. It was a perfect hiding place but only if you had a steady food supply. I hadn't seen any farms on our way there yesterday. Not many were likely to be in operation in a battle zone. And we were in Masuren, in the Soviet theater of operations. The Americans and British would never get there. The Soviet armies would be getting closer and soon we would be cut off, living on pine needles after we ran out of food. I went back to the clearing and saw her sitting on the sled, arms around her shoulders.

"Where did you go?"

"Reconnoitering."

"You could have told me."

"I didn't want to wake you."

"Your face. Are my fingernails that long?"

"Long enough. It'll heal. We'll eat and head west through the forest. We're safe in here."

She used the knife to cut our butter and chocolate and we ate in silence. Afterwards I threw the shelter branches among the trees and tried to make the clearing look undisturbed and we set off. I used the compass. We went due west. The forest became denser, until we could see only a couple of yards ahead. That's when he appeared, a tall narrow shape among the low-slung branches. We stopped and I began to reach for the pistol packed with our things on the sled. Loulou put her hand out to stop me and hailed him.

*"Ich bin Deutsche. Wir sind Freunde."*

"Thanks for *ich*."

"Did I lie? I did say *wir*."

He came towards us slowly, pushing branches aside. When he got close we could see he was scrawny and his face wrinkled. He wore a peaked cap, ankle boots and jacket and pants of greenish brown. The last and poorest of Wehrmacht uniforms, half rayon and half recycled wool, it was given to military units like the Volkssturm, the national militia. He carried no weapons. Loulou questioned him in her understated Junker manner, authoritative but not condescending. His name was Otto Dieterle, he was ninety-two. He had been conscripted into the Volkssturm, deserted with others and escaped into the forest. They had a camp nearby. There were twenty-five there now. Others had found it and stayed. He was the oldest in the camp. The youngest was twelve. He was relieving himself when he heard us and came to investigate. He thought we were deserters or refugees.

Loulou told him we were married and on the run and meant no harm. He led us to the camp, in a hollow surrounded by bluffs and screened by dense growth, the sort of place you stumble on, you don't find. The inhabitants were living in shelters made of pine boughs, crate slats and rags. There were twelve shelters in a loose cluster. I didn't smell smoke or cooked food. It looked sudden and temporary, not as substantial as the camps of the Polish partisans. Our voices brought out the entire camp, from boys to middle-aged and older men. One of the middle-aged men was wearing a Volkssturm armband, black with red and white stripes and between two eagle insignias, "Deutscher Volkssturm Wehrmacht." The one silver pip pinned to the collar of his tunic meant he was a Gruppenführer, a squad leader, equivalent to a corporal in the regular army. He was holding a rifle, the only one in the group carrying a weapon. It wasn't the standard service rifle, the K98k, but one of the Volkssturmgewehr models, inferior rifles produced near the end for the militia. They all stared at Loulou. She told them she was my wife and a nurse. Her aristocratic accent got their notice, I got curious glances as the American-looking husband and being a nurse guaranteed her their attention. Two of the younger guys immediately said they had problems they wanted her to treat. Her face stiffened, the no-nonsense nurse, in case they were making fun of her. She told them she would treat their ailments as soon as possible.

Broad-faced and stocky, the man with the rifle seemed their leader. He introduced himself as Alfred Beisser. He told us they had grenades and Panzerfausts as well as rifles. Loulou asked him why he was wearing the Volkssturm armband. He took it off and put it into his pocket.

"If you were spies the armband would make you think about whether we really could be deserters. That would give me time to shoot you."

"How did you know we were not spies?"

"Somebody like you would not be a spy roaming the woods."

Beisser looked at me.

"You are an American?"

"Is it that obvious?"

"I have seen American films. You look like the actors."

"How long have you been here?"

"Five days. We were sent from Königsberg to fight Russians. We stole a truck, drove here and hid the truck. Some know these woods. Others came."

"Why did you desert?"

"The war is lost. We are not soldiers and would be killed for nothing."

"What kind of treatment do you expect from the Russians?"

"We are workers and farmers, not Nazis."

He looked at Loulou.

"Not Junkers."

Loulou raised her eyebrows.

"So you find it convenient to be a communist now."

"I am a worker. My class must save Germany."

"Poor Germany if she depends on you and your kind."

He fingered his rifle. Glancing at the sled, I tried to figure how long it would take to get the pistol. I decided I could tackle him quicker. He sneered at her.

"Your kind has led Germany to ruin. Workers and farmers have been slaves too long. It is our turn to be the masters. Not tools of the capitalists."

"How dare you speak for all Germans? Your masters have been trained in Moscow. Their masters speak Russian. You are German by permission."

"What kind of German are you? You married an American."

Loulou opened her mouth to answer but thought better of it. Turning to me, Beisser pressed home what he thought was an advantage.

"You must be rich."

"You are speaking to a member of the working press. A reporter."

"You serve your capitalist masters."

"I do my best to get the truth to the American people."

"Capitalist slaves."

"No American believes that."

"They are fools."

"Try telling them."

"Their minds are poisoned by lies."

Speaking low in English, I glanced at Loulou.

"How did the Gestapo miss this guy?"

Beisser lifted the muzzle of his rifle until it was pointed directly at my chest.

"You are not welcome here."

Dieterle had been standing by and listening. He broke in.

"You are not the leader. No one is."

"Keep quiet, old man."

"She is a nurse. She can stay."

"They must go."

"We will vote."

"There is no need to vote."

"You have no right to turn anybody away. I took Nazi orders for twelve years. I will not take communist orders. Either say they can stay or we vote."

Beisser walked away after giving Loulou and me a long look. Dieterle spoke to Loulou.

"You look tired. Please, you rest in my shelter until your husband has built one for you."

They went to his shelter, at the edge of the cluster. I took the knife out of a bundle on the sled. One of the bystanders offered the loan of his hatchet. In twenty minutes I had made a sturdy shelter and put our stuff inside. I brought Loulou and she fell asleep. Dieterle appeared at the entrance. He wanted to talk. I explained that the strain of the last few weeks and lack of food was giving Loulou nightmares and I had to stay with her. I invited him in and we sat on blankets and I gave him a piece of chocolate. It was mid morning and below freezing and so I had covered the entrance with branches, leaving a small opening for light. In the semidarkness we spoke low so as not to disturb Loulou. Her breathing was even. Dieterle was worried about Beisser. From the beginning he wanted them to seek out the Soviet army. He said the Russians would not harm boys and old men. They were hesitating, he was angry and fought with Loulou and me. What did I think about meeting the Russians?

"Not yet. They will be looking for revenge and not too fussy about who and you might be the first Germans they see."

"Beisser is a communist."

"The approved ones from Moscow will be brought in later on. A German is a German to them now. Wait a bit and see what happens. The Soviet offensive is only five days old."

"Where are you and your wife going?"

"West to the Americans. You should think about that."

"Ostpreußen is our home."

"The war changes everything. Get out while you can."

He wanted to talk about the difference between him and Beisser.

"I was a carpenter in Königsberg. My wife died six years ago. She was much younger but she was sick for many years. I have no children or relatives. I am used to living alone. A man like me enjoys what he has or is miserable. I think I will not have a better life, so it is up to me. Do I want to live? I say yes and that is all there is to it. Even when I was a boy I was happy with little. I never wanted to be rich, not that I would be as a carpenter. I could have been a cabinetmaker but I like working outside. I did not want to smell the glue and stain and varnish and sawdust of a workroom. I am not an artisan. To me a tree is beautiful and a cabinet or a table or chair is something to use and not to spend much time over. They should be well made and last and nothing more. Though I think the grain of finished oak is more beautiful than any painting I have seen. Give me a saw, hammer and nails and good timber and I will build you a place. Even now I can climb ladders and work on roofs. There is no building now. Only bombs falling. Perhaps some day. I am dreaming. What is wrong with that? I will never build another house but perhaps a cottage. I know that. But the dream is in me and that is all I ask.

"I know this Beisser. He does not build. He pulls things down. He does not think of Germans but communists. What is a communist? Beisser will explain to you for hours but it ends up the same thing. He says you must think of classes. What is a class? I have never seen one. Rich people are your enemy, he said. All of them? I said. Yes, they must be destroyed. You are talking about them the same way the Nazis talk about Jews, I said. And Poles and Russians and socialists and communists. They are wrong, I am right, he said. How do I know that? I said. I will give you books that explain everything, he said. You read them and you will see I am right. How do I know the books are right? I said. Listen, old man, if you are too stupid to understand, it is your fault. He calls me 'old man' whenever he argues with me. I could call him short or pockmarked but no, I am not like him.

"There are five other men here and Beisser has had an easier time with them. They never argue with him. What they believe, who knows? But the boys have no experience and so he works on them. They were in the Hitlerjugend and are working class and he tells them that they were tools of the capitalist class. He says everything is falling apart because what they were told by the Nazis was a lie. The boys are afraid and want so bad to believe in something. They have heard me arguing with him. They have asked me what I think about what he says. Think for yourselves, I said, instead of believing somebody who is starving, living in a shelter in the forest and says he knows all about the world. Beisser heard. Mind your own business, old man, or I will fix you. You waste your time threatening me, I said. They asked me what I thought and I told them. What a good example of your perfect society. A man cannot say what he thinks. Not when he tells lies, old man. I tell lies because I disagree with you? I am only a carpenter. But if I tried to build a house the way you argue, it would never be more than a couple of posts in the ground. Look to the East, he said. There is a mighty house that has stood for many years. It is not a house, I said. It is a prison. And you want to build one here.

"He does not talk to me any more. I must keep watch all the time. He meant what he said. He would like to get rid of me so he can twist the minds of the rest."

I was lying beside Loulou later and her movements woke me from a nap. She sounded relieved.

"I did not have a nightmare. It must be the camp."

"It's me being here."

"Why not the camp? I was with you last night and had a nightmare."

"That was the first night. You're used to having me around now. I'm not taking credit personally. It's somebody being with you."

"Have it your way."

"I'm not having it my way, I'm saying you were alone too long under too much strain. Maybe a dog would have kept you from having nightmares."

"You are my dog."

"Not bloody likely, as the British say."

"What happened to Sir Galahad?"

"He's around."

Loulou cut the chocolate and butter for our dinner and we talked about our plans. I was for moving on quickly to avoid being trapped in the forest by the Soviet armies. She wanted to stay three or four more days, sure she would feel better. I said her health was more important than anything else.

"We still have plenty of food."

"Do they have any?"

"They must have something. I gave Dieterle a piece of chocolate. He didn't say anything about their food supply. The farms we've seen have been abandoned. They could be relying on game. Boar, rabbits. But I haven't smelled cooked meat."

We agreed that anyone needing food would be given some. The next morning Dieterle brought a small sack to our shelter. He told us that on their escape to the forest they had seen a farm. It had been abandoned but they looked in the barn and found sacks of oats. They had been living on them since. He brought a sack for us. For pots they used German helmets they had taken off crosses in a cemetery near the forest. "No one was using them," he said, shrugging. He offered us the use of his helmet. Loulou said we would use a cup she had packed together with our stuff. She gave him some butter, saying his oats would taste better and he thanked her and left. Loulou unpacked the cup. I filled it with snow outside and she added oats and made cold porridge and held out the cup to me. I told her to eat first but she said no. We argued but she wouldn't change her mind, even when I said she was weak and might pick up germs from me. Stubborn woman. I finished, added more snow and handed her the cup, said it was small and she frowned.

"Better than something taken from a cemetery."

"You're not using butter. What about those lavish-loving aristocratic taste buds of yours?"

"A Junker learns to save."

The oats helped Loulou and in the next couple of days she became stronger. She treated patients but without antiseptics and surgical dressings there wasn't much she could do beyond cleaning infections and tying strips of rag around cuts and sores. Everybody felt better after her visits, except for Beisser, who was jealous of her popularity among the younger inhabitants of the camp. He was out for converts and she stood in his way. That changed on our fourth day there. I asked Loulou if she felt well enough to leave and she said early the following week would be better. Around noon we heard shouting and everybody came out of the shelters. Beisser had shot a boar and was asking for help to bring it into camp. There was no shortage of volunteers and he chose four, all boys. An hour later they returned, the boar hanging upside down, feet strapped to a trimmed pine bough. Beisser skinned and gutted the boar with the hatchet I used to build a shelter. He fetched a jerry can of petrol he had taken from the truck before hiding it and the boys cut and chopped pine branches and piled them. He poured petrol over the branches and lit them with a rag ignited by a cigarette lighter. The boar was impaled on the trimmed pine bough and hung over the fire between two forked branches embedded in the ground. The spit was turned as the meat roasted. Everybody was invited to the feast later except Loulou, Dieterle and me. Loulou said she wouldn't have gone because the boar had an "Oh God, what am I doing here" look in his eyes. She put a sliver of butter on her oats at dinner. That night we heard the festivities outside, feebly lit by smoldering pine branches. Dieterle came and Loulou offered him a piece of chocolate and had some herself. I breathed in the smell of cooked pork on the freezing air. That was the one time I didn't smell pine branches as I fell asleep.

The next morning Loulou had most of the camp as patients. The boar had been undercooked and everybody had eaten too much. Vomiting and diarrhea were widespread. There wasn't much Loulou could do except recommend oats and rest. She was tired and fell asleep eating dinner. Most of her patients were beyond recovery. She said the boar probably hadn't been properly cleaned and fecal bacteria on the underdone meat were in their gut, as well as parasites from the boar. Already weakened by semistarvation, most died within days. From twenty-seven the camp dwindled to eight. Because they had eaten first, taking fully cooked meat from the outside, Beisser and his volunteers survived. To get rid of the stink and the threat of infection Dieterle and I carried the bodies into the forest, along with the boar bones. We covered the corpses with branches because we had no shovels to dig graves.

Loulou was too tired from nursing the sick and the dying for us to leave as planned. There were more bags of oats available now. Dieterle collected them from the empty shelters and they were distributed among the survivors. Beisser was quick to collect any available weapons for his group and all we had were Loulou's pistol and Dieterle's Volkssturm Panzerfaust. Only she and I knew about the pistol. Beisser and his group stayed by themselves. They believed their survival showed they were superior to the rest. I knew Beisser would force us out when he thought the moment was right. As we were going anyway, I didn't care beyond making sure Loulou was well enough to travel. I warned Dieterle about Beisser and said he should come with us. He shook his head.

"I will stay here."

"How will you survive?"

"I have oats and there is snow for my water. The Russians will never come this far into the forest."

A few days later Loulou was feeling stronger. We decided to leave the next day, Saturday January 27. For the first time in the camp we heard the low rumble of artillery. Returning from hunting, an excited Beisser said the Russians were getting closer. He strutted over to our shelter and watched us as we packed.

"You better hope you can keep away from the Russians, you and your Junker. If you were as smart as you think, you would leave now."

"Tomorrow is good enough. Unless someone informs on us."

"Who would tell them? They will know friends from enemies."

He sauntered away whistling the Internationale. Loulou frowned.

"I still cannot believe he is stupid enough to think he will be welcomed."

That night we slept in three-hour shifts. I suspected Beisser of wanting to turn Loulou in as proof of his communist sympathies. I took the first shift and woke her at midnight. She shook me awake at two.

I sat up. Whispering in the dark like rustling leaves. I had the pistol ready. Five against two. But we had the darkness on our side once they lost the advantage of surprise. I whispered to Loulou to flatten herself against the bedding. I crept to the shelter entrance and pushed aside a pine bough. Against the blue darkness of the clear sky black shapes moved in a semicircle towards the shelter. I figured they would surprise us, kill me and take Loulou prisoner. If I was wrong, they were going to shoot us both with rifles or toss in grenades. Either way there was no choice. I shot five times, once at each shape. Two went down. Moans and cries and the rest scattered. A couple of wild shots smashed through the branches of the roof. A grenade exploded but too far away to cause any damage. I waited in the silence that followed.

"Hold your fire, it is Otto."

I peered out and saw him holding a torch, a petrol-soaked rag on a stick. The shadow of the flame wavered like a black flag over three shapes sprawled in the snow. I asked Loulou if she was all right. She said yes and I stood up and went outside, still holding the pistol. The shapes in the snow were dead. I had killed two and the third had blown himself up with the grenade, waiting too long after he pulled the pin. His hand was blown off and part of his head was missing. They were teenaged boys. Their blood made dark blots in the snow. I looked at Dieterle.

"I had to do it. There was no other way."

He shrugged.

"It is the war."

Loulou came out and looked. I turned to her and neither of us said anything.

Dieterle spent the rest of the night in our shelter. We each took a turn keeping watch. At the edge of the camp the next morning we found another body, another boy. Loulou examined him and said there were no wounds, he was weak from diarrhea and died from hypothermia during the night. He was the twelve-year-old Dieterle had told us about, the youngest inhabitant of the camp. Beisser was probably trying to find the Russians. There had been more artillery fire early in the morning.

We left that day. We couldn't convince Dieterle to come with us.

*"Dies ist meine Heimat."*

The last I saw of him was his tall frame standing at the edge of the camp, hand raised in farewell.

I had put a couple of sacks of oats on the sled. With our remaining butter and chocolate, we had enough food for a long time. Loulou was stronger now, though she still rested at every opportunity. The weather continued cold, with occasional flurries of powdery snow. We avoided roads, heading away from the sound of the guns and looking for forest. Loulou said we were still in Masuren. Soviet fighters and fighter-bombers flew over every day. For several days we made our way across the vast white landscape, two tiny figures headed west. We didn't talk about our journey except for practical things. How much to eat, keeping dry, keeping warm, avoiding fatigue. We had no idea where the front lines were, east or west. We had to keep guessing where the Russians would be and were hoping the British and Americans had crossed the Rhine.

Two days after leaving the camp we found one place the Russians had been. We saw a line of carts and wagons along a road about a mile away. It wasn't moving and there didn't seem to be anybody around. I decided to have a closer look and left Loulou in a wooded area. A hundred yards away I smelled the oversweet stench of rotting flesh. Bodies lay on both sides of the road. The men and boys had been bludgeoned faceless and shot and the women and girls, naked below the waist, slaughtered like hogs. Fleeing East Prussia they had been overtaken and killed, the women and girls raped so brutally some had bled between their legs. One girl couldn't have been more than ten. Breasts had been sliced off and private parts hacked to pieces, eyes had been gouged out and faces beaten to red mush. There were infants in diapers, their heads smashed in by rifle butts. Some had been skewered with a bayonet and tossed into the snow beyond the road.

The massacre had likely taken place less than twenty-four hours earlier, late the night before or very early in the morning. I was about to leave when I saw a hand move. A mutilated woman, still alive, had lifted her palm a few inches. I went over and knelt beside her. Her mouth pulverized by a rifle butt, she couldn't speak. Her blood-caked eyebrows raised, she stared at me. I knew she wanted me to shoot her. I had the pistol with me but I couldn't do it. I held onto her hand. I don't know how long I held it but nothing could have taken me away from her. We were bound together as I watched her die, her eyes slowly seeing nothing.

When I got back, Loulou was sitting on the sled.

"What was it?"

"Refugees. They were massacred last night or this morning."

"You were a long time."

"I held the hand of a woman. She was dying."

"Could I have helped?"

"No one could. Let's stay here tonight. We'll move deeper in. It'll be safer when we're closer to the German lines."

"For me perhaps. Not for you."

"I forgot to tell you that I'm a Swiss businessman. I should have a look at my papers, see who I am."

She began to say something and slumped over onto the snow. I picked her up and put her on the sled and she opened her eyes.

"What happened?"

"You passed out."

"I feel ill."

"Can you walk?"

"No."

"We'll stay here. I'll make a shelter."

We were at the edge of the wooded area but it was getting dark and there was no sign of anybody nearby. We would be up early. I had taken the hatchet when we left. Dieterle said he had an axe, didn't need the hatchet. I didn't believe him but he insisted I take it. In fifteen minutes the shelter was finished and I carried Loulou inside and laid her on branches. She was out. I made myself some oats and ate them as I watched the sky darken. Afterwards I lay down beside her and considered our options. Her breathing was uneven. If she became sick we were done for. More walking would drain what energy she had. The countryside was full of refugees and most would get to Germany. Massacres were inevitable but would be committed against those in the rear. By my reckoning we were close to or in Poland and headed in the direction of Silesia. The unlucky refugees were those in East Prussia. I decided we should take a chance on the main roads. We would meet up with a column of refugees and I would try to get Loulou a ride on a wagon. I had money and food to offer as payment. Or I could pay somebody to carry our supplies, put her on the sled and pull her. Less dignified, but dignity was dead weight now.

The next morning Loulou was still sleeping. I let her sleep while I went further into the woods. The fighting was getting closer. Traveling through forest we could stop more and with less risk of being seen until we joined a column of refugees. The extra rest would help her. I left a trail of broken branches as I moved deeper among the trees. Fifteen minutes and I could see the pines had thinned, replaced by brush, with open countryside beyond. The forest turned out to be a patch of woods, of no use to us. The sky had darkened and isolated flakes began drifting down. Their fall seemed accidental, as if somebody was shaking a feather pillow with a tear in it. I headed back, looking for the last broken branch but before I could find it the feathers had become a white curtain. It slanted down across the trees, piling more snow on their boughs. The green needles and gray trunks faded to outlines of themselves, identical blurred shapes. I took out my compass. I had come almost due west, so I headed east. In the blizzard I walked into those vague shapes, invisible bare twigs like wires scratching my face. One jabbed the corner of my right eye. After the sting the eye teared and I rubbed it so I could see better. I thought of yelling so Loulou would hear me, answer and I could fix on her location. But the silence of the snow seemed to absorb all sounds as it absorbed color. I could hardly see my boots. I stepped on what I thought was a root but was a decayed trunk lying over a depression filled with dead branches and rotting humus. I fell in up to my shoulders and was wedged into a tight weave of tangled branches. If they're not rotten, dead branches can be stiff and sinewy. I reached up and took hold of the trunk to pull myself out but it was rotten. Handfuls of bark and wood came loose like wads of wet paper. The jagged split ends of branches stabbed into my jacket.

The snow was falling faster. I didn't want Loulou to wake up and think I was lost in the snow, maybe injured. She might try to find me, and with her limited strength that would be fatal. I should have checked the sky earlier.

But there was no use cursing myself for being a fool. I had to get out of that tangle of debris. There was a bare pine bough three feet above my head. I figured if I could grab hold of it I could pull myself out. I lunged for the bough and missed. I tried several more times, each time the branches holding me giving way before pinioning me again. The eighth time I managed to grab the bough and tried to pull but the end was thin and dry and broke off. My only chance was to break free from the branches. The coldness of the earth around me was seeping into my clothes. To find out where the branches were, I squeezed my hands down through the openings. The biggest branches were around my waist and knees, the ones higher up thinner, with more give.

The first of the higher branches I bent snapped easily. The rest twisted like leather. I pulled them apart strand by strand, and in twenty minutes my shoulders and chest were free. I had taken off my gloves to work on the branches. My fingers were sore and getting numb. I rubbed them until the feeling came back. The lower branches were as thick as arms. I couldn't break them. I knew if I could get one foot free I could use it to pry the branches away from the other one. First I had to deal with the ones around my waist. The solution came to me. Squeeze down between them and use my arms to free my feet. With my arms straining I pushed myself down. The worst part was getting my head through. Visions of Puritan stocks came to me. Once below and hunched over in that cramped darkness I felt around and pushed the lowest branches far enough apart to free one foot, then the other. Finally I could squeeze upward and out into the snowstorm.

That was when I first heard it. Not like a sound at first but the impression of one, dull and metallic among the whirling cascade of snow around me. I yelled, "I'm coming, I'm coming." Everywhere was the same whiteness, the same tree repeated endlessly. I listened more intently. The almost inaudible sound repeated itself at intervals of ten seconds. The falling snow and snow-laden trees muffled it. It had to be coming from the east. I looked at my compass and headed in that direction, treading carefully and ignoring the random scratches and pokes from twigs. Slowly the sound became more definite and I could tell it was metal on metal.

I almost walked into the shelter before I saw it. A white hump now, the pine branches were completely covered in snow. Her back to me, Loulou was slumped over on the sled. She was holding a large spoon and banging it against a runner.

"I'm sorry," I said.

She turned and glanced up at me, her eyes with a look I couldn't read.

"I should've checked the sky and seen the snow coming. I fell into a hole and had one hell of a time getting out. I heard you banging. I used it and the compass to get back here. Did you hear my shouts?"

"No." Her voice sounded tired.

"Thanks for the direction finder."

"There was nothing else to do. I could not think of you dead."

"I couldn't think of you alone."

We looked at each other.

"I need some chocolate," she said.

"You must be freezing. Let's get inside the igloo."

I managed to get her to eat some oats as well as the chocolate. She agreed with me about joining a column of refugees.

"I am slowing you down."

"You wore yourself out taking care of the sick in the camp. It's been three days since we left, so we have to be out of Masuren."

"Before I lost consciousness I was going to say we probably are in Poland."

"We could leave as soon as the blizzard lets up, unless you need more time."

"No. Give me another piece of chocolate and let me rest until we can go."

"I don't want you passing out again. If you feel weak, we'll stop."

By early afternoon the snow had stopped falling and we set off on the road where the massacre happened, entering it to the west. That day we saw no one and nothing but things thrown away by passing refugees. Tables, cuckoo clocks, rocking chairs, trunks, dolls, pots, pans, crockery, anything to lighten a cart or wagon. We found what looked like a main road crossing the one we were on, but the light was fading and we stopped for the night. We saw an abandoned farm and spent that night in a barn. The family had probably fled in the last couple of days. A pitchfork was sticking into a pile of hay and a lantern hung from a post nail. Dieterle had found Beisser's lighter and given it to me, saying he had one of his own. I lit the lantern. Loulou dropped down onto the pile of hay. I made her eat some oats before she fell asleep. Mice rustled around in the empty stalls. An owl unfurling in silent swoop picked off a mouse and carried it up into the loft. The mouse disappeared, its tail a strand of spaghetti sliding between the owl's beak. I put out the flame in the lantern and lay beside Loulou and fell asleep as wind slipped like blades of ice through cracks in the siding.

I was awake before dawn. Loulou slept until first light and we ate and left. On the main road another trail of detritus lay like discarded fate. We saw no refugees but another farm. Loulou was worn out and I held her as we stepped towards the barn door. Thirty yards from it I saw footprints in the snow. They had been made by a man's boots. I couldn't tell how recent they were. It was getting dark, there was no forest for shelter and we were too tired to traipse around the countryside searching for something else. One man, probably on the run like us, but if he was armed and we walked in he might shoot before I could say anything. I lowered her onto the sled and took out the pistol. I went to the side of the door and pushed it open with my foot.

"Please come in, you must be tired."

English upper class accent, but I had to be sure about him.

"How do I know this isn't a trick and you don't have a gun?"

"It isn't and I don't. How do I know you don't have one?"

"I do."

"Then you hold all the cards, Yank."

"How do I—? To hell with it. I'm bringing a woman in. She's exhausted."

"Do you need any help?"

"No."

After telling Loulou about the man in the barn I walked her in and she slumped onto a pile of hay under the loft. I got blankets from the sled and made her comfortable and she promptly fell asleep. From the loft the Englishman had been watching us, his legs dangling over the edge. Figuring we would need it, I had taken the lantern from the other barn. I lit it and hung it from a nail on a post. The Englishman climbed down a ladder and came over. He was a little above average height and had a ginger beard and was wearing the uniform of a captain in the British army. Leaning slightly, he glanced at Loulou, who was in a deep sleep.

"Is the lady ill?"

"She's been through a lot."

"Doesn't look the usual. Bit delicate for sleeping in barns."

"It wasn't an option."

"Point taken. I'm Captain Alex Greville, captured in Holland, escaped from a camp and am trying to get west to join up with the British Second Army."

"Jim Brian. I work for a news agency when I'm not rescuing women."

"She seems worth it, I should say. Couldn't believe it when I heard your voice. An American. In the wilds of—. Where are we?"

"Probably Poland."

"You don't know either. How did you end up out here?"

"Courtesy of the lady."

"At least you've got a sidearm. Would you have any food?"

"We have butter, chocolate and oats, with a side order of snow. Tonight only, the oats will be hot."

"Sounds delicious. I haven't eaten in two days."

He found a bucket and filled it with snow and I put in oats and made a fire with hay outside. I gave him a piece of chocolate. Loulou woke and ate a cupful of oats. I introduced her to the captain. She fell asleep almost immediately. Afterwards he and I talked. He spoke about being a prisoner.

"Can't say we were badly treated, but one never gets used to guard dogs and sentries with machine guns in towers. Would they shoot prisoners when it came to the end? There were stories of bomber crews shot by Germans who captured them. About Polish and Russian POWs. Were they planning to surrender to the British or Americans? Wouldn't do to treat us badly. But one never knew. One's duty was to rejoin the unit. A prisoner is a beaten dog. Escaping was the ticket. Kept one's mind off the rest."

He bit into the chocolate and chewed for a while, staring into the dark as he remembered.

"Time is all a prisoner has. Time to ponder over the perimeter wire and the dogs. The choice is, cut the wire or tunnel under it. Tunneling is better, longer before discovery and the dogs come after you. There were ten of us. Months of digging and hiding all those piles of dirt. Planned it for New Year's. Even Jerry celebrates. It was bloody cold. We crawled, single file and out. Into the woods, adrenalin pumping. Barking and shots, we had been seen or smelled, and we scattered. Don't know who got away. I wake up hearing those dogs. Broken into farmhouses, slept in the woods since. My first barn. Escapee's tour of Germany."

He finished the chocolate.

"Where are you off to?"

"West, same as you. We're going to join a column of refugees."

"That lets me out. Uniform. Can't speak German. Stick out like a sore thumb. Be back behind the wire or up against a wall. In mufti I'd be shot as a spy. There was one bloke we heard about. Flyer who pretended he was wearing the uniform of the Romanian navy, spoke garbled Latin. Got as far as Rostock before they picked him up. If I sported a naval uniform I could say I was in the Swedish navy. Get to a port, a Swedish freighter and home to old Stockholm."

"You might luck out, with so many on the move. Could you use some oats?"

I took a sack of oats off the sled and handed it to him. He thanked me and climbed into the loft to sleep, taking the sack with him.

"Make a good pillow."

A hand shook me awake during the night. Loulou whispered into my ear. "Somebody is moving outside."

The same as the night before, I had put out the flame in the lantern, saving kerosene and giving us the added protection of darkness. I crawled over to the sled and got the pistol. I crawled back to Loulou and we waited. The door creaked as it was pushed open slightly and the oval of a flashlight beam slid over the pine floor. Whispers infiltrated the dark. A pale eye, the oval floated along walls and bent around posts. As it rose into the rafters it became narrower and longer. It rested on the ladder and became a foot climbing each rung in silent steps to the opening in the loft. It faded into the blackness up there. Loulou whispered.

"Wait. They may be refugees."

A ball of something flung from the loft landed close to us. Explosions of rifle fire as muzzle flashes lit up the darkness. I fired several rounds at the door. A rush of footsteps faded into the night. I waited for a few minutes. I got the flashlight from the sled and went to the door. Footprints led away into the night. I went to the ladder.

"Greville?" No answer.

"Greville? Are you all right?"

I climbed to the loft. He was sprawled against a pile of hay, almost vertical, with his arms outstretched. A rifle bullet had punched a hole through his right eye socket. The force of the bullet had made him stagger backward and fall onto the hay. The bag of oats I had given him was nearby and open. He tried to warn us with a ball of oats he likely moistened with spit. He was unarmed and I had the pistol. A shot in a million killed him instantly. I didn't check to see if he was carrying any identification. If I was searched by the Gestapo or Feldpolizei, anything linking me with an escaped POW would have been fatal. I would contact the British army and write his family. I climbed down and told Loulou.

"Poor man. And I fell asleep in front of him."

"The ground is too hard for me to bury him. You were right. They were a couple of refugees looking for a place to stay for the night. Not part of a large group. I saw two sets of footprints. I didn't hit anybody or they wouldn't have gotten away so fast. I think they had a hunting rifle. When I returned fire they probably thought we were soldiers. Desperate deserters. Aren't they always, though?"

"What do you mean?"

"It was an aside, a pointless remark. I'm good at making them."

"I shall remember that."

As we got to the road the next morning a column of refugees and soldiers was passing, strung out to the horizon. The soldiers were retreating in good order but with the harried look of the defeated. We joined a line of farm wagons and I tried to find a family who would let Loulou ride with them but all said there wasn't room. Finally a man with a pipe sticking out from under his bushy white mustache motioned for her to come up and sit beside him. I helped Loulou climb up and saw a little girl sitting among the bundles in the back. Would it be all right if I gave her chocolate? The man said yes, I handed her some and she grinned shyly. I climbed down again and pulled the sled alongside the wagon.

The human stream trickled under a flat white sky towards a horizon that seemed forever beyond the reach of sore feet and creaking axles. It was flight but it was orderly, Teutonic to a point. Anxious faces fixed west betrayed desperation with glances at the Soviet sky, ears cocked for the grumbling belly of artillery encroaching. That German sense of confidence, buttressed by twelve years of propaganda, had begun to erode. Rumors had become stories had become fact. The Nazi myth hadn't worked out. Everything was happening in reverse.

It went on through the night more slowly, with the inevitable accidents caused by drivers falling asleep in the complete darkness. Loulou slept among the bundles on the wagon. I became a sleepwalker, pulling the sled and stumbling into perdition. At least the planes didn't come at night. In the morning she sat beside the driver. An attack by fighters and fighter-bombers and bodies scrambled off carts and wagons into ditches and fields, soldiers scattering, flattening themselves against the frozen ground. Face down in the snow, I fell asleep. Loulou's shouts woke me and I looked up and saw her leaning back towards me from the wagon as it moved along the road. Other wagons had been hit, some mere piles of wood strewn around dead horses. Dead and dying bodies torn apart by strafing littered the snow, splutterings of blood crimson blots on white, avant-garde art from a nightmare. Headless children had been flung like discarded dolls. I had slept through it all.

A second and third day and we were out of Poland and in Silesia. Ethnic Germans from further east mingled with Silesians, all heading west. Military traffic added to the congestion. Trucks full of soldiers, motorcycles, armored cars, half-tracks pulling artillery. Periodically a staff car would honk its way along the column, forcing pedestrians and vehicles to make room for it to pass.

On the fourth day a staff car was forced to stop because an accident in front of us had blocked the road. A wagon had lost a wheel and fallen over onto its rear axle, spilling boxes and crates. An adjutant got out of the car and went to see to the cleanup. Drumming his fingers on the dashboard, a major glanced around. He focused on Loulou. He got out, went over and called up to her. She stared for a few seconds before recognizing who he was. Her drained face flushed pink and she leaned over the side of the wagon. She smiled, they began talking and she climbed down with his help. They spoke for a while before she glanced in my direction. The adjutant returned and the major looked at his watch. Loulou came over and took the painting of Mina off the sled. She spoke in a tone I hadn't heard since Altenburg. The Junker imperative.

"He is Hugo von Hohenstein. A friend of Mina's and mine. So many memories. He says he will get me to Hesse. My mother's family is there."

"As long as you're safe."

She put out her hand. We shook hands, her grip firm.

"Thank you for everything. I owe you so much."

"There doesn't have to be a price."

She let go of my hand.

"Allow me to say things my way."

"Say them any way you want. That's what it's all about."

"What do you mean? I was—."

"It doesn't matter."

"I had better go. Hugo is waiting."

She smiled. It was formal.

"Good luck."

"Same to you."

I heard a car door slam and the car drive away. I gave the rest of the chocolate to the little girl in the wagon. The man said there was room for the sled and me. I sat beside him. He pointed at the road ahead and looked at me.

"Junker?"

I nodded and he spit over the side of the wagon.

That night I dozed as I sat on the wagon. I was being interrogated by the

Gestapo. "Who was she?" a voice asked. "A piece of history," I said.

The next day I had a look at my Swiss passport. I was Herr Georg Zeiss of Zurich, a watch salesman. Stamped in the passport were an entry visa, a travel permit allowing me to stay in the Reich until the end of March and an exit visa. I thought about Lutz, who had done a superb job of forging the documents. All that skill used to subvert the worst instincts of his own people, which finally found him out and killed him. To many Germans he betrayed his own. Even the decent ones would find that hard to forgive. They would justify their own safe obedience by denying him his right to fight it. That night I left the wagon to burn my Swedish passport. My American one was next to my skin.

With Loulou gone my situation wasn't as critical. The choice was easy. The British and Americans were too far away for me to meet up with them. Soviet armies were advancing through Poland, closing in on Czechoslovakia and threatening the rest of eastern Europe. A return to Switzerland through what remained of the Reich was my best option. I would cross the border into Brandenburg or Saxony and head south. Simple enough, but in the early months of 1945 the Third Reich was a cornered rat. Anyone suspected of treason was shot or hanged. A few months earlier or later and that final lashing out of the dying animal would have been premature or over. It was the worst possible time but millions were on the move. To be ignored was a blessing.

As we headed west the numbers of refugees swelled and they brought news of disasters. Königsberg had been cut off. The last train left on January 20, full of children who ultimately froze to death. The only escape was across the frozen Vistula Lagoon to Danzig and Gdingen and evacuation by ship. Soviet planes were strafing, breaking up the ice, and wagons were falling through, horses and people drowning in the freezing water. Elsewhere, frozen babies in diapers were being left at the side of the road by frantic refugees. As the news spread the desperation increased. We waited for hours to cross a bridge as the mass of retreating soldiers and civilians pushed forward onto the narrow span. Nobody stopped, day or night, those behind overtaking those ahead if they slackened a bit. Where to go? Pomerania and Silesia were doomed. Breslau was in danger of being surrounded and cut off. Dresden looked safer and many were heading there, including us. Others would go further west to escape from the Soviet army.

I stayed with Emil and Martha, the man and the girl, for three days. He told me she was the daughter of a cousin in a neighboring village. After hiding her in a closet, her parents had been killed by the Russians. She was discovered wandering the streets by retreating German soldiers. She told them she had relatives in his village and they brought her to him. He and the girl had left with the soldiers and joined the column of refugees. Where was I going? I told him I was Swiss and would be going south after resting a night in Dresden. I gave him the remaining butter. I gave the sled to Martha.

We arrived in Dresden on February 13. The city was crowded with refugees, some staying at the homes of local residents, some in the air raid shelter in the Hauptbahnhof, the main railroad station. Others were in camps around the city. The shelter was packed and no one around the Altmarkt could help us with accommodation, so we went to a camp. The camp huts looked like army barracks. We found room in one already occupied by a family of ethnic Germans from Poland. There was a stove and I had a hot meal. Cooked oats. It was early evening and we were tired. Martha and Emil shared a bed. I laid some blankets on the floor. A warm room after a month, an unbelievable luxury, and I planned to sleep until late morning. A siren woke me. I sat up in the dark and heard a woman's voice.

"Forget it. They go off every night."

The siren stopped and I lay down. Minutes later the explosions began, like a drumroll on a bass drum. I got up and went outside, felt the ground shake as flashes of high explosive and incendiary bombs lit the city center like a nighttime fireworks display. My reporter's instinct drew me towards the destruction. A couple of blocks and the heat singed my hair. The city center was a furnace of red flame and black smoke and sparks and hot wind whirling through the streets. Phosphorus from the incendiaries was setting hundreds of fires that were combining into larger and larger ones, sucking up more and more oxygen and creating gale-force winds. Human torches were running up and down the streets, women with their clothes and hair on fire, carrying babies and screaming. Some were blown into burning buildings and others crushed by falling walls. People suffocated, fainting and dropping in the streets and were burnt to cinders. Wagons and carts with refugees were burning, people and horses shrieking. Arms and legs were lying everywhere, bits of clothing and charred flesh blew past. Through the roaring wind came shouts for children, for families. Burnt bodies were piling up in heaps. The heat seared my skin, my lungs burned with superheated air. I ran gasping through the streets, stumbling over the dead and dying. All I could think of was not turning into flame.

I kept running until the heat was bearable, then fell onto a patch of grass and fought to catch my breath. I must have passed out. When I regained consciousness I looked up. I was in a small park, the snow melted by the heat. The trees, unlike those closer to the firestorm, had not been incinerated or uprooted and blown away. I got up, glancing around. I had run further than I thought and was in a suburb. The howling a couple of miles away was reduced to a dull roar and the air breathable. It smelled of wood embers and brick dust, scorched flesh and burnt fat. Bits of ash floated by like black butterflies.

Three hours later there was another raid, calculated it seemed, to catch the rescue teams at work. I walked some of the way back towards the firestorm and saw rescue workers and soldiers lying dead among their ropes, shovels and lamps. I went back to the camp to see if Martha and Emil were safe. I had heard bombs exploding in that direction during the second raid. The camp had been hit. Piles of debris littered the site. The few survivors wandered around stunned, most injured. I asked about Martha and Emil and got blank stares. I tried to figure out where the hut we had been staying in was and I poked among the smoldering wood. I picked up a piece of twisted partially melted metal. It looked like the runner of a sled. It was still hot.

I left Dresden that morning. There was another raid that day and another the day after. The night raids had been by the RAF and the last two, during the noon hour, were made by the USAAF. Back at planning ops were the brains behind these attacks. They had names for what this was: carpet, area or saturation bombing. Sound clinical, like operation, mission and target. Cool language suggesting a clear and moral purpose. Neither they nor the aircrews saw the roasted flesh, blackened bones, shrunken corpses, people hiding in basements rendered into puddles of fat, or heard the screaming infants. It was done according to the first law of human conduct: the innocent pay for the guilty. An undefended city full of baroque architecture, of wounded soldiers, prisoners of war and refugees would be an easy target to impress on the Soviets the possible dangers of getting too close to western Europe, and to tie in a bit of not so incidental revenge for Coventry and London. Why would such brains spend any time thinking about human suffering? Wars are fought by the numbers. I had cheered the RAF when they bombed Berlin. Now, with the war almost over and bombing unnecessary, I felt disgust.

I left Dresden at dawn. Parts of the city center were still burning. In the early light it was a smoking ruin littered with piles of corpses. In one street I had to clear a path through a tangle of nothing but arms and legs to cross to the other side. Smoke drifted through the city. The relief and rescue workers were overwhelmed. Stunned survivors were finding shelter wherever they could. There was no point in my staying any longer. I still had my compass, papers and money. And I had found the summer house book among the debris of the hut. Loulou had put it into a steel box. The box had been blackened and was warm when I found it but the manuscript wasn't damaged. I tore off the covers, rolled up the manuscript and put it inside my jacket. I hadn't eaten since last evening and had no food. At a farm on the outskirts I bought a small sack of oats and drank well water and shaved with the straight razor Loulou had given me. She said it had belonged to her father. A Solingen blade.

Four days and twice as many rides on makeshift trains on short trips and lots of waiting in stations and some walking and I was in Munich. While I was waiting on the platform for a train to get me to Basel or close to the border two Gestapo agents approached. They asked to see my papers. I knew from the way they glanced instead of looked at them they were picking up people at random for questioning. I was arrested and driven to the Wittelsbacher Palais, Gestapo headquarters and prison in Munich. With red brick towers and pointed window arches, this copy of nineteenth-century English Gothic looked straight out of a low-budget horror film. The Palais had suffered bomb damage. Despite fallen walls and rubble suspects were being brought in to the undamaged sections, interrogated and some put in the prison in the palace park. I had been through it before, the long table, interrogators on one side, victim on the other. Rapid-fire questions, intimidation, threats. As before, the agents at the station were former policemen and my interrogators were university graduates in pressed suits and clean shirts. One took the lead, pasty, thin-lipped, with a mechanical delivery.

"What are you doing in Munich?"

"Returning to Switzerland."

"What is your business here?"

"I represent a watch firm."

"You are a liar. Where is your catalog? Where are your order forms? Do you have a letter from your company?"

"I lost my briefcase in the firestorm in Dresden, with all my forms and letters and orders."

"Your accent is American. You look American."

"My father worked in the United States when I was a kid. I went to school there."

"You are not Swiss. Name one Swiss businessman I would recognize."

"Gustav Gottschalk."

"Another lie."

"I know his daughter, Frieda, too. She works for the Red Cross. I have her phone number in Zurich. Her personal number."

I gave him one of those innuendo-charged looks men will give each other when talking about women. He shifted around in his chair.

"We will speak about that later. Why are you wearing those clothes?"

"Mine were full of smoke, my shoes filthy. I bartered them for food."

"We will interrogate you further. You will be held in a cell until we contact the company you said you worked for."

I had given them the name of a major watchmaker. He was bluffing. The Gestapo wouldn't contact a Swiss firm. I counter-bluffed.

"I demand to see the Swiss consul."

"You are in no position to demand anything. If you are not lying you have nothing to fear."

He was so punctilious, so much the Nazi official, he couldn't see the obvious, that no foreign salesman would have ventured into the Third Reich in 1945 unless it was unavoidable, and selling Swiss watches wouldn't be worth the risk.

"Frieda knows I planned to pass through Munich. She expects me in Zurich by Tuesday. If I fail to arrive, she will contact the Swiss consul. Save yourself trouble, let me call her and you can listen in."

As if he wouldn't. He went for it. I gave him the number and he contacted the operator. I waited and could hear the phone ring at the other end, somewhere mythically free, beyond the reach of the interrogators in that room. One, two, three, four rings, each one rippling out to the ends of a silent universe, and finally the impossible click and Frieda's voice. He handed me the receiver and picked up another one. I let my American accent fracture my German, enough for her but not him to catch on.

"*Allo*, Frieda, this is Georg Zeiss, Loulou's friend. I am being detained in Munich. It seems I have much too much of an American accent actually to be Swiss. All I want is to sell my watches. Would you please tell the gentleman I am who I say?"

She caught on right away and demanded to speak to the authorities. Combining indignation and good humor tinged with a Swiss-style noblesse oblige, she vouched for me.

When I hung up my interrogator was smiling, convinced I was the genuine article. We stood up and he shook my hand.

"Germany and Switzerland have always been friends."

"*Der Führer* called Switzerland 'a pimple on the face of Europe.'"

"He was obviously joking."

"There was a plan to invade my country."

"A vicious rumor spread by the British."

"We were prepared to hold out in the mountains to the last man to preserve our heritage."

He was looking uncomfortable, clearly a painful subject to a man who had spent the war behind the lines persecuting his own people with the help of some of those people, informers of all classes and both sexes, including professors. How's that for equal-opportunity oppression?

He got an underling to give me a lift to the station. First-class treatment for a first-class liar, the only ones worth believing. His kind had been manipulated for twelve years by lies. Nothing like a conditioned reflex to show the system still works in its final throes.

In the last months of the Third Reich many wandered the countryside, passing through cities. Bombed out of their homes or refugees from the east, they strained the system. The authorities were overwhelmed looking after and keeping track of them. The Nazis had turned traditional German efficiency into a fanatical officiousness as a way of keeping a close eye on people. Personal identity, job, travel, authority to do anything or be anywhere, a change of residence, playing a sport, had to be documented. Every document had to be stamped and signed, some more than once. Every stamp and signature had to be correct. Standing in a coach aisle on the way to Basel, I looked at the people around me. I wondered how many were carrying forged papers. The forgeries probably weren't as good as mine. No matter how efficient a system is it can be beaten. Its very size and complexity become a handicap and a way of defeating it. But chance can lend a hand and I had Frieda Gottschalk. I phoned her from the station in Basel.

"When you said all you wanted was to sell your watches, I almost laughed."

"Nothing like an intelligent woman."

"I wish more men felt that way. What were you doing in Germany?"

"Escaping."

"I heard about Mina from Loulou. After that she stopped writing."

"She's on her way to Hesse."

"You must tell me everything. I'll be in Berne next week."

"Dinner's on me. With champagne."

I took a train the next day to Berne and on Tuesday morning was at the office. Dillard and Barbara were civil. It was the end of her stint as a correspondent. Back to the fondue. I had plenty of stuff on German refugees and the Dresden bombings. But I knew Thad knew Americans wouldn't go for it. Americans were still fighting Germans. So I suggested feature stories on my escape and how the Third Reich was disintegrating. Thad's arms strained, pulling back on an imaginary fishing rod. Get on it right away, he said.

Frieda called on Friday and I took her out to dinner. I omitted a lot of what happened and downplayed everything, thinking the less I said the better because she would probably hear from Loulou. As she listened she traced the rim of her champagne glass with her finger. She livened up at the mention of Hugo von Hohenstein.

"Imagine Loulou meeting Hugo like that? He's half Junker, half Austrian. Mother was quite the society beauty in Imperial Vienna before 1914. He cut a dashing figure between the wars. He owned sailboats, racing cars, an airplane. His mother was wealthy and well connected and his father had a small estate. Why she converted and married him, nobody knows. After her son was born she went back to Vienna. Took him with her and reconverted to Catholicism. Later on Hugo would go back to see his father and attend parties and balls. He was one of the most eligible bachelors in Europe. All the high society girls had a crush on him. He's one of those people who, when they walk into a room, all heads turn to look. Were you introduced?"

"No. Wasn't the best of circumstances."

"I suppose not. It would have been embarrassing for a Wehrmacht officer to be introduced to an American. Would have been Hugo's duty to arrest you, strictly speaking. Loulou probably passed you off as one of her tenant farmers. Did she know about your Swiss identity?"

"I told her."

"Strange. Still, he probably would have recognized your accent. And you don't look or sound in the least Swiss. Not everybody is as stupid as that Gestapo officer I spoke with. But being old school and all that, Hugo would have accepted the Swiss business. Doubt anything a woman of Loulou's standing said? Impugn her honor? The very idea. That reminds me of something. It seems so fantastic now I don't believe it happened."

"Maybe it didn't."

"I'm too Swiss to be delusional."

"Except about money. One of the more practical delusions."

"I'm glad you added that. Care to hear?"

"I feel I'm going to, anyway. How do you know all this stuff?"

"The higher up, the smaller Europe is."

"Even for the democratic Swiss?"

"Money has its privileges. Aristocrats need it, like anybody else."

"And that gives you an in."

"That's putting it crudely."

"I'm a crude American."

"Don't be so smug. Do you know how many wealthy American girls have married European titles?"

"A blot on the American Constitution and the Bill of Rights."

"You amaze me. Whoever cared about them?"

"Fools like me. We try not to see the world for what it is and keep getting hit over the head by those who do."

"Serves you right. Keep an eye on your money."

"What money? Are you getting drunk?"

"Don't ask, pour. Terrible about poor Mina."

"The Queen of Prussia."

"She was a dear friend. For an idealist, you are a cynical bastard."

"I can never decide whether to be a cynical idealist or an idealistic cynic."

"Decide on your own time. I want to remember my friend and you should be ashamed of yourself for speaking so callously."

"Those aren't my words. They're the butler's. Apparently she thought that way about herself when she was a girl. You're itching to tell me something, aren't you?"

"Are you willing to listen now that I've chastised you?"

"We'll drown our sorrows together, clichés aside."

"I was thinking about the parties and balls I attended over the years at Altenburg. The ballroom is impressive. You must have seen it. Then again, on our slight acquaintance I'm guessing you haven't."

"Balls and ballrooms have never interested me."

"It's on the upper floor and to the right side of the main staircase as you walk up, on the opposite side from the study and library. Quite a grand room. Very eighteenth century, with a gallery for the musicians and walls covered in stucco swags and bas-reliefs. Period chairs against the walls and a wonderful floor for dancing. Do you dance?"

"Not if I can help it."

"If you were a dancer you would have appreciated that floor. I've encountered one other like it and it's in Vienna. There are stories about balls held there before my time. Guest lists included crowned heads and the very highest level of the aristocracy. My first ball was in the mid Thirties and things had changed. The crowned heads were gone and the aristocrats were in trouble financially and so people like poor me were allowed in. That's my little joke. Mina and Loulou were wonderful to me over the years and I tried to reciprocate their hospitality. A ball was an experience. My last and most memorable—memorable for the right or the wrong reasons, depending on how you look at it—was a costume ball in 1938. It turned out to be the last ball held there. The war starting not long after was part of the reason. But there was another. The theme was eighteenth-century, with a passing nod at the Ancien Régime. And now I'm finally getting to my point. Hugo was there. I had heard about him but had never met him. I was dressed as—you probably will have guessed—Marie Antoinette. Mina came as Madame de Pompadour and Loulou surprised everyone by coming as a shepherdess, complete with a crook with a bow. Her fiancé, Gerd, was under the impression he was Frederick the Great, and Hugo came as Mozart. Genius was charmed by the shepherdess. They danced, without the crook if you're worried about that, and pardon my cliché, but they did make a lovely couple. Loulou has wings on her feet when she dances and a tilt to her head and a look in her eyes that would render any man helpless. You have a strange look. Am I boring you? Tell me. I shall stop."

"No."

"For the sake of appearances Hugo danced once with one of the debutantes, Lise von Tiefenthaler, and once with a Hohenzollern princess, north or south branch, I forget which. Back to Loulou each time. Nobody could tempt him away from her. From a bachelor of Hugo's standing, it was quite a tribute. And where was Gerd but at the refreshments table getting drunk. At one point his three-cornered hat and his wig fell off and he stood there swaying, looking like the village idiot. Loulou ignored him.

"I had noticed an undercurrent of something between them that night. Not that I was looking for it. But one can't help notice when chills come off an engaged couple. I don't mean the usual lovers' tiff but something with ice all over it. They hardly exchanged a word. They didn't look at each other. Loulou had kept postponing their marriage. A tiny scandal to people with nothing better on their minds. I thought she was throwing herself away on him, but you know these arranged marriages. The Countess picked him. They had known each other since they were children but that doesn't always work.

"Hugo saw nothing, I'm guessing. He was simply captivated by Loulou. And she was radiant that night. He went to get her a glass of punch and there was Gerd, without his hat and wig and teetering and glowering at him. I was in the middle of a conversation with my dancing partner, a rather persistent Prussian dressed as a famous general and who I seem to remember loved horses—don't they all?—and I had to offer some comment to keep him from thinking he had been holding a mannequin. Turn your back for a second and you miss out. They had words. Don't you love the sound of that? So out of date and gentlemanly. I rid myself of my Prussian. I got close enough in time to see and hear. They were standing a foot apart, Hugo suave and debonair as ever and Gerd red-faced and, knowing the other's reputation, obviously jealous.

"'She is my fiancée.'

"'This is a ball. I see no fence around her.'

"'You dance only with her.'

"'I danced with others. She is the best dancer here.'

"'I am not blind.'

"'You must be to imagine that my intentions are not honorable.'

"'I know what you Viennese mean by honorable.'

"'I bear a Junker name with a lineage as good as yours, if not better.'

"'Your mother is a Viennese.'

"'Careful. I will not take insults from you.'

"'You insult me by parading my fiancée around as if she belonged to you.'

"'She is not a piece of property. If she chooses to dance with me, that is our affair. I will not apologize. And if I may speak for the lady, neither should she.'

"'Fine words, you Viennese cream puff.'

"'I thought Junkers could hold their liquor. You have lost more than your wig.'

"Some of the onlookers laughed at this and Gerd became angrier. He was shouting now and had the attention of the whole assembly. The music stopped and Loulou came over. She didn't look upset. She had inherited with Mina a sangfroid that is so effortless it seems spiritual. There was something going on between her and Gerd and it had nothing to do with Hugo. She spoke offhandedly.

"'Behave yourself, Gerd.'

"'You behave yourself.'

"'I do. And always have.'

"I knew she had no use for him, would never marry him. Gerd was one of those men I find intolerable, which is to say he was incredibly stupid. He could never understand her. Without wig and hat he stood there red-faced, reminding me of a sulking schoolboy dressed for a pageant and trying to remember his lines. He knew he had made a fool out of himself. For a man like him there was one way out. The blockhead even forgot what century he was living in.

"'I demand satisfaction.'

"Hugo laughed.

"'Pistols at fifty paces?'

"'Swords.'

"Always with that touch of class, Hugo didn't say a word, bowed his head, accepting the challenge.

"'Ridiculous,' Loulou said, and the Countess, sitting with mothers, chaperones and other old friends, heard what was going on and sent word she forbade dueling. Mina took off her huge wig and stepped in, saying that they could duel with foils with buttons on the end. They kept them in the weapons hall, as well as sabers, épées, rapiers, medieval broadswords and even an old pirate cutlass. Each fencer would have a piece of cloth pinned to his chest and whoever hit the target first would win—touché. She shouldn't have mentioned the inventory but it was her pride in the Altenburg tradition of arms. Gerd insisted on sabers. As a cavalry officer he would have been trained in the use of a saber. I had heard that Hugo had a commission in the army, which of course meant that he would be at a disadvantage. He had accepted Mina's idea but didn't want to look cowardly now. He said he had been challenged and had the right to pick the weapons and chose épées. I found out soon afterwards that among his many accomplishments he was a fencer. Gerd accepted his choice.

"Mina tried to reassert control by declaring that whoever drew first blood would be the winner, no matter how slight the wound. They were not to fight to inflict a serious injury. Both accepted. She said the duel would be held on the back lawn. Can you picture the scene? Aristocrats, except for yours truly, dressed in eighteenth-century costumes and gathering on a torchlit lawn to watch two of their own fight a duel over a woman. It was very warm that summer night, even at ten o'clock. What an excuse to go out for a breath of air.

"Everybody was there except the Countess, a couple of her friends and Loulou, who had ignored Gerd and said something I didn't hear to Hugo. Mina went to get the swords. The weapons hall is next to the ballroom. I see I have your interest."

"I wondered where the halberds and suits of armor were keeping. Convenient location for questions of honor arising on the dance floor. Stepping on a lady's foot. Cutting in on a quadrille."

"Did Mina or Loulou not show you the weapons hall?"

"With a war going on, it might be considered beside the point to show off obsolete weaponry."

"Mina showed me the first time I visited, in 1936. The hall is full of things. I'm not one for weapons. She told me the names of everything. There were crossed swords. Some had elaborately worked hilts and were in ornate scabbards. All kinds of muskets. Matchlocks, flintlocks, wheel lock pistols, a blunderbuss. Percussion rifles. Helmets, breastplates, lances. Banners, pennons, flags. There were bloodstains on one, a battle flag. She told me she'd fired every gun in the room. The blacksmith made the balls. The gamekeeper had taught her to shoot. She was an excellent fencer too. I fenced with her and she quickly got the better of me. Gerd or Hugo wouldn't have stood a chance with her. As she was showing me everything she spoke about her father as if she knew him well. I thought that was strange because she was a small child when he died. I think weapons were her contact with him. And when you think about it, much of the family tradition is founded on arms. I got the impression she was living in the past. Many of her type do."

"Type?"

"Well, Junkers are stuck in another age, don't you think? Look at the Countess. Those dinners. I hope I'm not sounding ungrateful but their relatives were the most hidebound people I ever met. When they heard I was Swiss they looked as if they were waiting for me to yodel. Or lend them money. I think a Junker can only talk to another Junker. Now where was I?

"On her way back she explained to her mother what had happened and the Countess simply nodded. I think her prohibition was a matter of form and she wished she could watch. The only one in distress was Loulou, mostly because of the position Hugo had been put in. Mina carried out the weapons, handed each an épée, had them cross swords and broke the swords, swinging up a huge broadsword with both hands. Velvet coats off, in shirts with lace cuffs and collars, knee breeches, white stockings and shoes with buckles, the duelists were cautious at first. Hugo seemed to be looking to inflict a slight wound and end the matter. But Gerd, quite sober now, waved his sword in wide nervous arcs, preparing for the one thrust that would do in Hugo. He would feint, seemingly off balance to entice Hugo into an overeager counter-thrust, but that didn't work. Gerd became eager, lunging recklessly, trying to force Hugo back. Suddenly it happened before you realized you were seeing it. Hugo retreated to avoid a lunge, parried the blade and darted the point of his own over Gerd's and into his shoulder. He winced and blood began seeping from the tear in his shirt. But he kept lunging at Hugo and Mina shouted 'Hold.' He wouldn't and she swung the broadsword and knocked the épée out of Gerd's hand. He swore, turned and walked round the side of the house.

"Soon afterwards I could hear the sound of Gerd's car driving away. Many of the guests left. The ones who were visiting gathered in the dining hall for coffee. Hugo took his leave, saying goodbye to the Countess and Mina and to Loulou, who had come down from the ballroom. She had been told the outcome of the duel by now. She was the last to speak with him. They were off in a corner. I could see she was blushing a little, from the general excitement or for another reason, I couldn't and wouldn't guess. He left and the Countess said, 'There is a man who reminds me of the old days.' Later I heard Loulou and Gerd patched things up but I still felt she wouldn't marry him. Hugo was the man she missed out on. There were only dinner parties after that night. The ballroom was never used again, closing a chapter in the history of Altenburg."

She sipped her champagne and glanced around the restaurant before continuing a little too casually.

"Quite a romantic story in a way. As I mentioned to you over the phone, the last I heard from Loulou was her letter telling me of Mina's death. I brought two letters to your office. I assume one was about Mina and the other about something else. Something that would make you go to Altenburg, or am I assuming too much?"

"The trip was on my own initiative. Americans like to help Europeans."

"That settles that, I guess. You can't blame me for being curious. Despite your reticence, it must have been dangerous. You were a guest there, like me, and I suppose the place does cast its spell on us plebeians, even those who don't like dancing."

"Let that be our last cliché."

She drained her glass.

"It would be mine, wouldn't it?"

I leaned forward and she pushed me back with a forefinger in my chest.

"My intentions could be honorable."

"Oh, I hope not. I'm tired of honorable intentions. They leave you standing at the altar. The other kind can be fun sometimes."

"Thad's a decent man."

"He's married to his fish. Even looks like one."

"Not quite on your social and financial level?"

"You might be, if—."

"That's a big if."

"There's a price for everything."

"I've never thought of it as a price."

"What?"

"What you're thinking of."

"What am I thinking of?"

"How the hell would I know? That's how many bottles?"

"Too many. You must let me pay."

"I won't be a kept man."

"Strictly a financial transaction."

"That's what whores say."

She slapped me gently with the back of her hand.

"I will spend my father's money any way I like. Besides, some of it's mine."

"I'm a fully paid off member of the working press, so don't press your luck."

"This is the second time you've gotten drunk in my company."

"You're a scheming woman."

"I'm at the age when a woman thinks every move better be the right one."

"So the panties don't come down unless—."

"You're there to hand them to me in the morning."

"That's graphic. Sends chills up your spine."

"Are you that much of a bachelor?"

"Afraid so. What about those dishonorable intentions we were discussing?"

"Too late in the day."

"You're brutal."

"I'm rich."

"Are you sure that's ethical?"

"Would you tell a beautiful woman not to use her beauty?"

"So what about romance?"

"I can't afford it. Unless—."

"We're back to that again."

That's the last thing I remember until I felt something prodding at my shoulder. I opened my eyes, looked around and saw a waiter trying to hide a smirk.

"The lady departed half an hour ago, sir. She left this for you."

He handed me a folded slip of notepaper on Frieda's personal stationery, a watermarked cream linen bond with an embossed letterhead. Her stiff close-packed handwriting was like a regiment of Prussian guards marching into battle.

I have an appointment in Zurich tomorrow. I thought I should leave before I could not be held accountable for my actions. You were saying something about champagne not being your drink. You ordered bourbon. You fell into a stupor immediately afterward, probably a good thing for your liver. I didn't desert the ship. You were floating somewhere else."

You have my number.

Frieda

I spent the last ten weeks of the war cabling feature stories on my escape, editing out whatever might have been construed as overt sympathy for Germans. I wrote of the flight of a lone American correspondent and brought in the plight of the refugees to convey the extent of their misery. I left out everything and everyone else. It was easier describing the crumbling of the Nazi state. I had wanted to cover the military campaign firsthand but stayed put out of loyalty to Thad. Dillard was a mediocre writer. Barbara had tried but failed to help him improve his style. At Thad's suggestion I rewrote Dillard's dispatches. I owed Thad that much after taking off for Altenburg. He never did ask me why I went, though he did hint about me staying in Berne. "I guess you're sick and tired of Germans for a while."

# Paris 1945

In May head office wanted to reopen the Paris bureau. Harry Dunn had gone back to the States in 1941, was working in Boston. He recommended me as his replacement. New York cabled the offer and I accepted. By the end of June I had found a suite of rooms, an improvement on our cramped former location, bought equipment and hired the staff. Paris was still recovering from the occupation. There were shortages, inflated prices and a black market but eggs, cheese, butter and vegetables were coming in more regularly from Normandy. By May the U.S. Army had broken up extensive black market operations run by AWOL GIs. Organized gangs had sold, among other things, petrol and American cigarettes.

In July Julia phoned.

"Hi, I'm in Paris. I need your help."

"What about your flyer?"

"He was killed two weeks after I talked to you. We never met again. I'm under arrest. They think I was a Nazi."

"You weren't. Your mother was."

"You'll never guess what she went and did. Got engaged to an overgrumpyführer."

"A what?"

"I don't know, some big SS guy. He's using her because she's American, to get to the States. I told her but she won't listen. She's hardheaded."

"Family trait. You really stuck the knife in last time."

"I didn't mean to."

"You know your career is dead. You'll have to stay here and get what you can."

"I know."

She started sniffling. I waited. You always waited for Julia. At least I did. A small voice came over the line.

"Will you help me?"

"Remember your pistol?"

"That gun?"

"It saved me."

The sniffling stopped.

"You owe me."

"I'd have helped anyway, seeing as you said, we know each other so well. Who arrested you?"

"The American Army. They wanted me to perform for the soldiers. Then they found out I'd appeared with Mengelberg. And played in Germany."

"Let me see what I can find out. Give me your number and I'll get back to you."

"I'm worried."

"Don't get wrinkles for nothing. Political priorities will change. Nazis are going to become an endangered species. It'll be open season on commies soon."

"I'm on my own most of the time. My mother is with him."

"One will dump the other. You'll get her back."

"You think so?"

"The safest bet in Christendom."

"That doesn't sound right."

"Wasn't meant to. That's the point."

"I don't get it."

"You don't have to. It's not compulsory."

I phoned the Judge Advocate Department of the U.S. Army in Paris and at first no one wanted to talk. I pestered them for a couple of days. Finally I got the military attorney who was handling her case. It didn't hurt that he had read my stories about escaping from the Nazis. I went to see him and told him everything I knew. A secretary took it down and typed it and I signed. The attorney said the case was a way of putting distance between the army and Julia after asking her to perform for the soldiers. My statement would help ease the way towards dropping the charges. I phoned Julia and she was happy. Then Mrs. Fusco grabbed the receiver.

"It's you again, is it? You've got a lot of gall bothering my daughter after all the trouble you've caused. Don't you dare show your face around here. I'll get the army after you."

"Which army?" I wanted to say. I had to laugh and she hung up on me hard enough to make my ears ring.

The publicity about Julia's arrest and her alleged pro-Nazi sympathies virtually ended her career as a soloist. In the United States no symphony orchestra would engage her. She gave recitals in London and New York but even Mrs. Fusco couldn't strong-arm the cool audiences. Apparently her technique was still there but she hadn't lived up to her promise. The prodigy had faded from great to good. She gave a few concerts in Germany, wasn't invited back, and taught in music schools in Switzerland. With her mother in tow, or should it be the other way around, she slipped into obscurity.

At the end of July Sophie dropped in at the office. She had been following in the wake of the American forces, cabling dispatches and broadcasting war news. She was wearing her correspondent's uniform, side cap, tunic, pants, shirt and tie. On a round patch halfway between shoulder and elbow was "U.S. WAR CORRESPONDENT" and "CORRESPONDENT" stitched above the left breast pocket of the tunic. I casually mentioned the war in Europe ended months ago. Sophie told me she hated to give up the uniform. I saw the ring. She noticed.

"You heard, didn't you? Peter and I got married a year ago."

I shook my head.

"At least you're inhaling good American smoke now."

That put a frown on her face but not for long.

"Mutual is letting me go. A lot of women broadcasters are getting the axe now that more men are available. Peter's moved on to *Collier's*. *Liberty* wanted him too, after the *Tribune* wouldn't agree to a pay raise and let him go. But he has standards. Could you happen to use a couple of ace correspondents? Our esteemed news agency has given my old Berlin job to Beckmann. I suppose I'll be their roving European correspondent."

"I wouldn't count on that."

"Why not?" Her perky confidence evaporated, her face sagged.

"Never give a reporter a story that he can check. I talked with Beckmann about his stint in Berlin with you. A phone call and a couple of cables straightened things out. He didn't try to get your job. He wouldn't be your driver, legman and courier and write your dispatches while you were honing your technique as a broadcaster. You were smarter with me, took your time. I ended up doing everything you wanted. The final step would have been getting me to write your dispatches. He wouldn't be persuaded about any of it, so you got rid of him. The Propaganda Ministry received an anonymous tip that he was filing dispatches under another name in Stockholm and Berne. They gave him the boot. He told me the alias. It was one of yours, the same one on the story the Gestapo planted in the office to set you up. They got it right the second time. Maybe *Liberty* can use you."

She pulled at the shoulder strap of her purse and stood up.

"I'm a damn good reporter."

"I didn't say you weren't."

"All those years in Berlin and I didn't get a thank you. Gave them exclusives. Scooped everybody else. I beat everyone on the Pact in '39. Head office sat on it. If I were a guy they would've sent it out. When the story finally broke and everybody had it, they went with my dispatch. And even then a lot of papers took the AP feed. Sticking my neck out with the Gestapo and Goebbels, and for what? You get Paris. I get stiffed."

I stood up and leaned towards her.

"If it'll help, take a swing at me."

"You're not a bad guy but you don't deserve Paris."

"You've got no kick coming with me. I stayed in Berlin. And whatever happened to New Hampshire? Was that to make sure I'd pick up and send the stuff on T4?"

"You're full of smart remarks. Mr. See-it-all-as-a-joke. Try being a woman in this business. If you're good, they're jealous. Foul up, they say told you so."

I stepped around the desk and stood in front of her.

"I did everything Beckmann wouldn't. Maybe he should have compromised. But you don't betray a colleague. He didn't deserve that. He spent a week in a cell. They wanted his sources. They were your sources. You had everybody fooled."

Her face twisted into a grin.

"I don't know what got me more. His laziness or his pawing me every chance he got. Soap rationing never bothered him. Head office wouldn't have listened. Sex-starved spinster's imagination. I meant what I said about New Hampshire. But I was never first with you. Driving through the Tiergarten that night after the Christmas program I pretended to sleep because I had tears in my eyes. I was happy being with you and miserable because you had someone. You're the kind of guy who won't stay with a woman who picks him. You have to pick the woman. I wanted you to pick me. You never did. You couldn't expect me to wait around and be a consolation prize."

"Goodbye, Miss Henser."

"Goodbye, Mr. Jim."

After she left I stared out of the window for a long time at the passing traffic.

Late in the summer Jack Harrison came by the office. He was on his way to Berlin to reopen the INS office. We went to a café in Montparnasse. I told him about Sophie. He stopped drinking in mid-swig, gagged and put down his wineglass.

"That so? She certainly had me fooled. Imagine doing that to Bill? I guess you didn't miss out after all."

"She kept expenditures down so head office would think no one could replace her. She needed extracurricular help after taking on the broadcasts and with all that stuff on T4."

"Peter will pick up after her now. What happened out there in East Prussia? Nobody except that dummy Joe would believe your story about soil erosion. Ever meet the Junker dolls?"

"One's dead and the other's probably in Hesse with her mother's people."
"Anything personal in it?"
"Let it go. What happened to you guys after Pearl Harbor?"
"On December 15 embassy staff and correspondents were interned in a hotel away from Berlin. In May '42, a Swede ship, the *Drottningholm*, picked us up in Lisbon and took us across. On her return voyage she brought back our German counterparts. Warring nations will cooperate, especially to help their diplomats, and we got in on that. Never made the headlines, natch. Like that flight corridor from Switzerland across Vichy, Spain and Portugal. Planes on both sides left the traffic alone. You hear about American soldiers raping French women, including prostitutes? Our guys? Our guys. Head office wouldn't touch it. I'm an old newshound. Came back last July. We don't die, we turn into newsprint.

"I'm going back for the show. The shit will be flying thick and fast. Nazis will be as rare as hen's teeth. The guards will be saying no women and kids in the camp while they were on duty. Must have been somewhere else. SS brass will be saying they were obeying orders. They're not sorry for what they've done. They're mad they didn't get it right. The rockets and jet fighters arrived too late. Not enough U-boats when Britain could've been starved. Didn't develop the A-bomb. If cancer grows in a national soul, Germany is one big tumor."

"Germans are no different from anybody else, Jack. They were trapped in an historical vise of Prussian militarism and centuries of ingrained obedience, and Nazi censorship and propaganda kept the truth from them. They had their first real taste of democracy with Weimar. That was doomed by Social Democrats yearning for a return of the monarchy and by the fanatics on either side of them. It's not hard to explain the SA, SS and Gestapo. The worst can be found anywhere. Give a certain kind a job with a uniform and tell him he's special and the rest of us are turds and you'll get a sadistic killer. It's as simple as that."

"So there's nothing wrong with Germans? You could have fooled me. I saw their hysterical faces at rallies trying to catch a glimpse of the Führer, cheering his crude boasts and threats and his playing the injured victim. They weren't all SA with bulging necks and pig faces wearing party uniforms. Plenty of regular folks were there too, swallowing his lies about poor poor Germans. And don't tell me they didn't love his cheap victories or ever shed a tear for the Czechs or Poles or Norwegians or Russians. They're the one people in Europe capable of doing what they did. They know it too. The military tribunals and courts will hang a few of the biggest Nazis and their killer dogs. The rest of those who are caught will go free to become respectable citizens in a new German democratic state, American style. I've heard the Catholic Church has already begun helping SS escape to Spain and South America. Don't be surprised when Americans and Russians recruit SD and Gestapo to spy on each other. The world stinks, fella."

"You're blaming Germans for everything but being human. And they're that, if nothing else. Ostracizing them is the same as the Nazis separating Jews from the rest of society. We're all in this. We go down, we go down together. In the ghoulish green half-light of Nazi dogma there's a truth about the human psyche. Musician sycophants, professor informers, amoral scientists, doctor sadists and soldier mass murderers are normal in a country governed by those with the stunted minds of vicious schoolboys. The most dangerous thing on the planet is the human brain. It will justify anything. It thrives on self-interest and self-deception. It's rarest quality is humility and it's the least valued despite the lip service paid to it. The bravest act in any society is to tell the truth, not the phony truths of politics and philosophy but the joys and laments of the heart. They're the hardest to tell because they strip away the rituals, dogma and uniforms. The fanatics hate them for exposing the universal naked soul. They would rather kill us all."

"Got everything figured, huh? Have anything to do with the Junker dolls?"

"I'll pretend I didn't hear that."

"I'm kidding, fella. I wouldn't want to tangle with you. You're too Irish. A good friend. A bad enemy."

I filled our glasses, emptying the bottle. Jack reached for his wallet.

"I'm buying the next bottle."

"Forget it. I'm a bureau chief now."

"How you fixed for blades?"

"I've been setting up an office for the last two months. Give me time."

"This is Paris, fella. If you can't get it here, you're dead."

"How is the expert doing?"

"Not so good lately."

"Maybe you need somebody steady."

"Married life isn't for me. I tried it twice. I didn't like the hours. My philosophy is, if you can't meet the right woman, get a lot of the wrong ones."

"Has it worked out?"

"Lots of faces and places. They all blur together. No alibis. No alimony."

I ordered another bottle. The waiter brought along with it a quart of bourbon and two whiskey glasses. He said that an American officer left the bourbon at the café a year ago. He hadn't returned.

"The statute of limitations has run out," I said, taking the bottle and offering Jack a drink. He gestured with the back of his hand.

"The bourbon is all yours. I'm generous to women and free with booze. That reminds me. In London in 1919 on the way home from the front I met a good-time broad. Known far and wide. Quite an ass on her. She was called the 'London derrière.' Ah, the pleasure of repartee."

"I think you mean something else. Sure you won't have a shot?"

"I'm devoted to the grape. Nothing like a good glass of red. I had to drink their frog snot in Berlin to keep the Heinies happy. And that icicle piss. You earned your hangover there. Missed the Chianti after the Alpenhaus closed. And the spaghetti."

"I thought of something. What's a blemish here or there when she's got beauty to spare?"

"What's that about?"

"Blemish refers to her character."

"So you'd forgive a broad anything if she's a doll."

"To a point."

"What point?"

"That's the point."

"That corn liquor is going to your head. You're a sucker for women."

"If you're looking for a category to put me in, include me with those who will make a mistake if that's all they're allowed."

"Can't talk a guy out of the women he picks. I should know. The next bottle is on me. And don't give me bullshit about being a bureau chief."

"Know what's sad, Jack? When the final history of the human race is ready to be written, there will be no one to write it. There won't be anybody to read it, either. Unless a rocket ship gets here from somewhere. Will they be able to read English? We're gone without a trace. I think the mosquitos will miss us. And lice and germs. The animals we eat and those we shoot will hold a party. There'll be a memorial service for all the species we made extinct. The carnivores won't show up. They'll be hiding in the bushes waiting to pick off stragglers afterwards. We were too efficient, hungry, greedy, overpopulated. What's the right word? That's the problem, isn't it? Picking the right word. A lie is as straight as a die. The truth is uncouth. Not to be heard in decent company. There are ways to tell it, that's all. It comes down to your truth or mine.

"What did you say, Jack? You can have the last word. All the last words. After I'm heard at being absurd. Where did you go? What are you doing on the floor?

"Know what I always wanted to be? Little bit unique. Exempt from the synonymous anonymous. That asking too much? To be better at something. Better than better. So there's no one better. Most people are sand in somebody's shoe.

"Monsieur is all right. He's resting. He's been in worse places. He's listening to me. I'm making a point. Don't worry, he'll get up. Let him rest for a while. Should be sitting in his chair? I know you have rules. You've got one other customer, waiting for customers. She's not concerned about him. Let me tell you something. He doesn't like people bothering him. He starts swinging. It's a reflex. I'll get him up. I know how.

"Where was I? The job will find the man. Don't assume the leader is strong because the people are weak. The rest is PR, which is BS, which is wholly writ or broadmassed by fee-at for the great unwashable. Here's your lead: His Worshipped opened the twenty-first session of the blah-blah today, which conferred emergency powers on His Worshipped for ever and ever because of

the omnipresent danger and then voted itself out of business with big pensions and perks.

"While we're embalming ourselves, let there be a wake for dead words. Whilom, a Saxon village idiot. Quondam, a contraceptive device. Quotidian, a Roman emperor. Jakes, synonymous with quakes. Repast, synonym for review. Parsimonious, synonym for sanctimonious clergy. Sanctimonious, holy chant, also chance. Purslane, medieval, finder's keepers. Vellum, Old English, hesitation. Piscatorial, a university urinal. Nonce, Elizabethan slang, nonsense. Furze, illiterate. Do I have to spell it out?

"Bring a mop and pail. He's puked on the floor. I've turned him over so he won't swallow his vomit. Wipe his face with a cloth while I'm phoning for a taxi. And don't let him gag. I'll get you to your hotel, Jack. You in pain? I'd better call an ambulance. I think he's had a heart attack. Hold on, Jack."

I rode in the ambulance to the hospital. By then Jack had lapsed into a coma. He never came out of it. He died early in the morning. I phoned Ted McCracken, bureau chief of INS in Paris. He cabled Jack's relatives in Michigan. He said Jack had pains in his chest and down his left arm when he talked with him in a bar a few days before. He wouldn't see a doctor. "Those sawbones are only going to tell me what I already know. It's my carcass. I'll do what I want with it." I never went back to the café for the bourbon. I left it as a memorial. To a lot of things.

In September one of the secretaries came into my office and said someone wanted to see me. Loulou walked in wearing a tailored suit. It wasn't new and probably had belonged to a relative. One of her jacket buttons didn't match. Somebody had made alterations or she had done them herself at the last minute for the trip. I thought of the first time I saw her, when she entered the dining hall at Altenburg. I didn't put aside the cable I was reading or stand up. There's always been something contrary about me. She wasn't going to see my best manner. She had been living in Hesse. Her mother's relatives were solvent, having hidden family money and jewels during the war, and land and buildings on their estate hadn't suffered any damage. She was undecided about what she would do. Perhaps work as a journalist. I listened, nodding occasionally. After a while she got around to us.

"You were abrupt with me when we parted."

"I can take a hint."

"Hint?"

"Owe you so much. Remember? You owe me nothing. Glad to be of service."

"English is not my first language. Perhaps I used the wrong words."

"There's only one way to say that kind of thing and you said it."

"Are you saying I wanted to give you the brush-off?"

"You're learning American fast."

"I was going to say something and you stopped me. You dismissed me."

"There's a linguistic gulf. Let's leave it at that."

"You are determined to see it your way."

"I don't see any other."

"Don't you?"

She stared at me, that Junker imperative again, and I put down the cable as if I was going to, anyway.

"I have not come to thank you. I have done that already. I lost my mother and sister and was desperate when you came for me. I was miserable about my lost past when you stayed with us the second time. I went to the summer house because talking with you healed me. Talking with you has always been pleasant. I hope that word does not offend you. I was planning to visit you more but you went to Switzerland. I left with Hugo because I was ill. I did not want to be a burden. What good would it have done had I died in the snow? I can accept what must happen but not things that don't. I am an Altenburg, always. I don't need American aid. *Mein Englisch ist klar?*"

"Perfectly, Louisa."

"I prefer Louisa to Loulou. You never called me by either until now."

"I needed permission. You never gave it. We never crossed the *Sie/du* line. In English they're verbs. First comes see, then do. I told you, I don't take advantage. Especially of you."

She raised her eyebrows, her lips parted slightly. I had to grin.

"You look like a kitten that's had a sip of cream."

"I would be happy with milk."

"Cream for a countess."

Traffic sounds and cool autumn air came in through the open window. The evening sun was slipping below the horizon and tinting it a rosy peach. Off to the side the ghost of a moon was rising. Paris had become itself again, streetlights and headlights strung out like strands of pearls along the boulevards. She turned to look. In the outer office a correspondent was talking with a secretary. Another secretary stopped typing to answer a phone. The news business is one long story. You tell it as best you can. You can become part of that story, as I had, and meet a woman who knew what would always belong to us. Every look and word had told us from the beginning. The journey from Altenburg began when we met.

Louisa looked at me.

"I would like to see Paris."

"You want a tour?"

"*Ja.*"

"It may never end."

She smiled.

"That is the best kind."